THE HOOK

THE HOOK

Tim O'Mara

This first world edition published 2019
in Great Britain and 2020 in the USA by
SEVERN HOUSE PUBLISHERS LTD of
Eardley House, 4 Uxbridge Street, London W8 7SY.
Trade paperback edition first published
in Great Britain and the USA 2020 by
SEVERN HOUSE PUBLISHERS LTD.

British Library Cataloguing in Publication Data
A CIP catalogue record for this title is available from the British Library.

ISBN-13: 978-0-7278-8918-8 (cased)
ISBN-13: 978-1-78029-669-2 (trade paper)
ISBN-13: 978-1-4483-0367-0 (e-book)

All Severn House titles are printed on acid-free paper.

Severn House Publishers support the Forest Stewardship Council™ [FSC™],
the leading international forest certification organisation.
All our titles that are printed on FSC certified paper carry the FSC logo.

MIX
Paper from
responsible sources
FSC
www.fsc.org   FSC® C013056

Typeset by Palimpsest Book Production Ltd.,
Falkirk, Stirlingshire, Scotland.
Printed and bound in Great Britain by
TJ International, Padstow, Cornwall.

To my non-law enforcement siblings:
Jack, Ann, and Erin – and their families.
Mom says you now have to read my books.

ACKNOWLEDGMENTS

Sunday, August 4, 2019

This page looked a lot different yesterday. To all those who were mentioned, please know that I love you and appreciate your support in my personal, teaching, and writing lives.

Yesterday, a gunman in Dayton, Ohio, killed nine of his fellow Americans using what law enforcement has described as an 'assault-style weapon' along with a high-capacity magazine capable of holding one hundred rounds. As I write this, his motive is unknown. What is known is that the carnage would have been much worse were it not for the quick and brave response of Dayton police.

Hours earlier yesterday, a gunman in El Paso, Texas, shot and killed twenty-two people – fourteen of whom were his fellow Americans – with an AK-47 assault-style rifle. Law enforcement agents, both local and federal, are calling this an act of 'domestic terrorism' based on a manifesto the shooter posted online regarding immigrants and praising the White Supremacist from Christchurch, New Zealand, who killed fifty-one worshippers at mosques earlier this year. Again, more carnage was avoided due to the courage and professionalism of El Paso's police.

It is my profound hope that my country's politicians – my fellow Americans – can agree upon more sensible gun laws to protect our citizens. Today I walked into a sporting goods store and was told I could walk out with a rifle – possibly assault-style – after passing a five-minute 'background check.' No one needs a gun that quickly.

It is also my hope that my fellows citizens of Earth can begin to see past the hateful rhetoric of a small few – some in great positions of power – and realize that we're all in this together no matter what our color, country of origin, gender identity, or religion.

So today, the day after one of the worst days of gun violence in American history, I choose to acknowledge the brave men and women of law enforcement, those who preach love instead of hate, and those who are unafraid to call out hateful and violent rhetoric, especially when it may be uncomfortable to do so.

ONE

Detective James Royce of Brooklyn North, NYPD, looked down at Maurice Joseph's lifeless body lying in two inches of freshly fallen snow with an arrow sticking out of his back. 'You, Mr Donne,' he said, still looking at the dead man in front of us, 'are turning into Williamsburg's own Jessica Fuckin' Fletcher.'

'What's that supposed to mean?' I asked.

He turned his glance to me. 'Come on. *Murder, She Wrote.* Jessica Fletcher?'

'I get the reference, Detective. My mom used to watch it every Sunday night. The one hour a week she wouldn't answer the phone. I don't know what it has to do—'

'Being with you is like visiting Cabot Cove, Maine.' He shook his head. 'Dead bodies just seem to pop up everywhere you go.'

I rubbed my weary eyes. 'Royce, I know it seems that—'

'No, no. Really, Mr Donne.' He held up his right hand like a traffic cop. 'I've known you . . . what, now . . . five, six years?'

'Give or take, yeah.'

'And in that time, you've been around more dead bodies than an intern at the city morgue.' He scratched at his salt-and-pepper goatee. I noticed his closely cropped Afro was also getting white. Deep down, I knew I was the reason behind some of that gray hair. 'I mean, no offense, but if my daughter attended school here, I'd transfer her the hell out. I'd be afraid something would happen to her.'

I knew he was trying to be funny – in that gallows humor sort of way that so many cops think they have – but I was not in the mood. A guy I worked with had just been murdered on the roof of my school as he was checking out his hydroponic vegetable garden and his pigeons. The fact he'd been killed by an arrow – as in *bow-and-arrow* – added to the surreal feeling coursing through my body. I did a slow eyes-wide-open three-sixty and took a few deep breaths.

'What are you doing?' asked Royce, tapping his notebook against his thigh.

'I'm trying to calm myself down. You think I get used to seeing dead bodies?'

'No,' he said. 'I'd worry about *that*.' He scratched his chin again. 'I also know you're not just calming yourself down. Most people do that with their eyes closed. You're doing something completely different.'

'Really? What else am I doing, Detective?'

He grinned and touched my shoulder with his index finger a few times. 'You're scoping out the crime scene, *Mister* Donne.' The grin turned into a few short chuckles. 'I truly don't think you can help yourself.'

'I don't know what you're talking about.' I took a step back from him. 'And lose the laughter, OK?'

'Sorry,' he said. 'But I believe I just watched you case the crime scene. At least this part of it.'

I shook my head. 'Listen, you got my statement, can't I just—'

'Whatta ya know, Donne? What did that little' – he pointed his index finger toward the sky and spun it around – 'observational pirouette you just did tell you?'

He wasn't going to give up. Partly because he liked annoying me, partly because we both knew he was right. I could not help myself.

I took in some air. 'First,' I said, 'this was not a random incident. Nobody waits around for someone to show up on the roof of a school building for target practice.'

'Agreed,' Royce said.

'Out of the four buildings around the school,' I began, 'there're three rooftops the shooter could have used. Kind of risky using a rooftop; lots of exposure.' Three of the four buildings around us were five-storys high, a good ten feet higher than my school. I looked down at the arrow sticking out of MoJo's back. 'I'm not sure about the windows because it would be hard for the killer to be able to get into an apartment. That's also risky, possibly noisy and too traceable. Based on the angle of the entry of the arrow, I think we can assume this was not an accident.'

'OK,' Royce said. 'What else?'

'Whoever did this knew MoJo would be up here at this time. Again, you don't wait around on a roof in early April snow flurries hoping your intended target shows up before someone notices you on the roof of a housing project with a bow and arrow.' I thought of the other option. 'Same goes for a window. You're not going to use your own place, so you only have a small . . . window of time to get the job done. The shooter knew MoJo'd be up here at this time. Means he scoped out the area for a while. Once the deed is done, you'd wanna get gone as soon as possible.'

'Good.' Royce nodded. 'That reminds me,' he said. 'I know you told the responding officers, but tell me how *you* happened to be up on the school roof at four-thirty on a Thursday afternoon. Isn't there a beer with your name on it somewhere?'

'I was finishing up some paperwork,' I said. 'I got a text from MoJo to meet—'

'A text from who?'

'MoJo.' I gestured with my head down at Maurice. 'He liked to be called MoJo. It was a mix of his first and last names.'

Royce nodded. 'So he texted you . . . why?'

'I don't know. He asked if I was still in the building. When I said I was, he asked me to meet him on the roof. I told him I'd be up in fifteen, twenty minutes, and . . .'

Royce and I looked around the roof: crime scene techs, a couple of uniforms, and my principal, Ron Thomas, pacing and looking as if he were about to have a stroke. Ron was perfectly happy having me speak with the cops. He didn't like talking to them, but I used to be one of them. A perfect match.

'And he was up here . . .'

'Checking on his garden,' I said. 'He was concerned about the snow and his hydroponics system. He was going to cover the plants for the weekend. There might be more snow coming tonight.'

'What about the pigeons?'

'They're pigeons. I'm not sure if he was going to cover them, but I think they'll survive a nuclear blast. With the cockroaches.'

'I mean, why have them up here at all?'

'It was one of his hobbies,' I said. 'He made a deal with Mr Thomas and the head custodian. He'd teach the kids about organic gardening, if he could keep a coop of pigeons on the roof.'

'So, Mr Maurice worked here?'

'Mr Joseph,' I corrected. 'He didn't actually work here. He was doing community service three days a week. Monday, Wednesday and Friday.'

Royce's face went quizzical. 'Community service? For what?'

'MoJo was a repeat drug offender. An addict. This' – I waved my hand at the garden and pigeon coop – 'was part of his outpatient program. You ever hear of Newer Leaves, Detective?'

'They let him work around kids?'

'Yeah,' I said, not hiding my disgust with his attitude. 'MoJo was an addict, Detective. Not a Catholic priest. He was a non-violent offender. Like most addicts. He was no more of a danger to the kids than I am.'

I could tell he wanted to bring up the Jessica Fletcher thing again, but he thought better of it.

'Not all addicts are non-violent, Mr Donne,' Royce felt the need to add. 'Just ask all the victims of purse-snatching and smash-and-grabs.'

'Well, MoJo was,' I said. 'He and his wife both had decent jobs. He didn't have to scrounge for drug money.'

'Sounds like he—' Royce began, but I interrupted.

'He lost his job because of the addiction. He and his wife Lisa are expecting. She's planning on working as long as she can.'

'What kinda work did he do?'

'IT, mostly,' I said. 'He specialized in building firewalls, protecting companies from getting their systems hacked, stuff like that. He was making a small income from that.' I paused. 'You remember my friend, Edgar Martinez? From The LineUp.'

Royce smiled. 'You don't forget a guy like Edgar.'

'True. Edgar hooked him up with me. They've known – knew – each other for a few years; they met online, then in-person, then started a small company doing security. Virtual and actual.'

That's when it hit me I'd have to break the news to Edgar. Edgar didn't take the news of an unexpected Yankee trade well; God knew how he'd handle this. He didn't have many friends outside of me, my girlfriend Allison, and MoJo. We were working on that. My phone buzzed. Allison.

'Excuse me, Detective,' I said to Royce.

'We're not done, Donne,' he said and smiled at the way that sounded.

'I should take this.' I took a few steps away. 'Hey, Allie.'

'What's wrong, Raymond?' she asked. That was one of the problems with living with a reporter: you couldn't put much past one. Especially one as good as Allison.

I lowered my voice. 'You remember Maurice Joseph?'

Three-second pause, then, 'MoJo? Sure. What about him?'

I cleared my voice and swallowed. 'He's dead. Someone shot him.'

Silence from her end for about five seconds before, 'Oh my God, Ray. What happened?'

I gave her the thirty-second version – and had to repeat the part about the arrow – and she told me she was on her way. I almost asked if she were coming as my caring girlfriend or a curious journalist. I didn't ask that question because I had learned not to ask that question. And I'd learned it the hard way. Royce wasn't so far off about dead bodies and me, and this would not be the first time that Allison's job and my connections to recently deceased people collided.

Knowing there was nothing else to say, I said, 'I'll see you when you get here.'

She broke off our conversation without saying goodbye. Like they do on TV shows all the time.

I turned back to Royce. He was writing something in his notebook, and without looking at me, said, 'That your girlfriend?' Before I could ask how he knew who I was talking to, he added, 'I'm a detective, Mr Donne. With real training. I do hope you told her to stay away from the active crime scene.'

I waited for him to laugh. When he didn't, I said, 'You can tell her when she gets here, Detective. That's a conversation I don't have with her. Anymore.'

He pointed the eraser of his pencil at me. 'At least you're learning. Why is she interested anyway? I heard she got shit-canned with all the other less-senior journalists at her paper. Did she land another gig?'

'She did.' Allison had been let go in the latest wave of cutbacks. More victims of the Internet. 'She and some friends started a website, kind of a citywide all-five-boroughs thing. She mostly covers the crime beat.'

'And this pays her rent?'

I could have told him I was paying her rent, but decided not to. 'They've got a few advertisers and subscribers,' I said. 'And a rich friend from college who's giving them a year to show viability.'

'Viability?'

'That's how the investment class refers to making a profit. It's kinda like Facebook meets *America's Most Wanted* meets the off-beat news cycle. They make money on subscribers, some ads – business and personal.'

'Now you're dating yourself, Mr Donne. People don't read personal ads anymore. They swipe left or right. Either way,' he added, 'paper, electronic, smoke signals, no reporters will be allowed up here to the crime scene. The school is city property. If a photo of the victim with an arrow in his back shows up online or in print, I'll know whose shoes to bust.'

'You think I'd take advantage of my access to the crime scene just to make my girlfriend's job easier?'

Detective Royce smirked. 'No,' he said. 'That'd never happen. Not up here in Cabot Cove.'

TWO

Ten minutes later, Allison got out of a taxi right in front of my school. She was wearing her light blue winter jacket I'd bought for her this past Christmas. She had this thing about wearing winter clothes until the second week of April. It was one of her few superstitions. She was born during a rare Midwestern April blizzard and here we were now in early April snow flurries. Which reminded me that I'd have to go birthday shopping in the next few days. I stepped over, we kissed hello, and she went right into journalist mode: holding her phone in one hand and a reporter's notebook in the other. The phone, I knew from experience, was in Record mode.

'Tell me everything you know,' she said.

'I knew the guy, Allie,' I reminded her. 'Take it down a notch, OK?'

She took a breath and kissed me again. 'I'm sorry,' she said. 'It's just that we've been under pressure from Anthony to break as many stories as we can before the traditional press.' Anthony was the money guy behind the blog/website. She paused. 'I am sorry. My first question should have been, how are you doing?'

She was learning, too. 'I'm OK. I was in my office finishing up some paperwork and MoJo called me. He asked if . . .'

A few minutes later I was through with my story. This was the second time I'd told it to Allison, but now it was official because it was recorded. 'A real honest-to-God fucking arrow?'

'Yep.'

'The cops're still up there?' she asked.

'Yeah. And Royce told me to tell you no reporters are allowed up there. So no photos on this one, Allie.'

She laughed, reached into her bag, and pulled out a cube the size of a small Chinese food take-out box. She opened it and took out what at first looked to me like a children's toy. As she unfolded it, I realized what it was.

'When'd you get that?'

When it was completely unfolded she said, 'Just this week, actually. This is my second time using it.'

'Royce is not gonna like that.'

'Too bad for him. The city may own the school. They don't own the air rights.'

Her 'toy' was a video drone. It came with a remote control and was available to the public through those cool tech catalogues you get in the mail three times a week around the holidays. She turned it on with the control box and the drone flew up to the roof of the building. Allison handed me her phone. 'Hold this,' she said.

'Isn't there a rule about using these around schools?' I asked.

She ignored that and had already switched the phone to the drone app. We both watched as the camera/drone rose about twenty feet above the school: a good sixty feet in the air. She maneuvered it until it was over the crime scene and then took about a dozen photos. After a minute, she switched it to video mode. The picture was amazing. We saw the roof, MoJo's pigeon coop, and his body. At one point we saw Royce looking up as if he'd just spotted a UFO.

'Can you get a close-up of how unhappy he is?' I asked.

She ignored that and a minute later used the controls to bring her high-tech crime scene trespasser back home to her. We used her phone to review the images the drone had taken. *Unbelievable*, I thought. As much as I missed being a cop sometimes, I could not imagine being one nowadays when everything I did could be captured for the whole World Wide Web to see.

'Why do you bother leaving the apartment?' I asked. 'You could do your job from home these days.'

'But then I wouldn't get to interview insightful people like yourself, Ray.' She folded her drone back into a cube, put it in her bag, and slipped her notebook into her back pocket. She raised her phone to me. 'I have to file this. What're your plans?'

'The LineUp. I have to break the news to Edgar about MoJo and
that's gonna take a few beers. Maybe more.'

'Mind if I tag along? I can write and upload this from anywhere.
And before you say no, I promise not to ask Edgar anything about
Maurice.'

'OK.'

'But if he offers . . .'

'Don't push it, Allie.'

'Too soon to question the detective?'

'Way too soon.'

I turned to start the ten-minute walk to The LineUp. Allison took
my hand and slipped her other one – the one holding her phone
and newly acquired crime scene footage – into her pocket.

By the time we got to the bar, Edgar was already in his regular
seat. In front of him were his laptop, a half-finished pint of Bass
Ale and a small can of tomato juice. The look on his face was hard
to read – it always was – but I had the feeling that I was late in
breaking the news to him about his friend's death. Allison and I
walked over to him and before sitting down, I said, 'You OK,
Edgar?'

Without taking his eyes off his beer, he said, 'No. But you already
know that, Ray.' Again, eyes still on the pint glass, he added, 'Hi,
Allison.'

'Hi, Edgar.' She gently placed her hand on his shoulder. Besides
me, Allison was one of the few people who could touch Edgar
without his recoiling. It had taken her a few years to earn that level
of trust. 'I am so sorry about your friend.'

'Thanks,' he said. 'I guess. Isn't that what people say? *Thanks?*'
He touched his glass. 'I never understood that. Someone you're
close to dies, someone else says sorry, and you say thanks. For
what? And why say sorry? It's not like it's your fault. People say
dumb things when other people die.'

'I guess you're right, Edgar,' I said. 'It's just what we do.'

'It's stupid.'

'I agree. Can we sit with you, or do you want to be left alone?'

'You can sit with me, Ray,' he said. 'You, too, Allison. I just
don't know if I'm gonna talk all that much.'

I pulled out the stool next to him. 'That's up to you, man. Talk
as little or as much as you like.' Those were words I'd never said

to Edgar during our entire friendship. On most occasions, you could not shut him up.

'I'm gonna go in the back room and grab a table for a bit, Edgar,' she said. 'I've got a little more work to do before calling it a day.'

'OK,' he said.

'You want a drink?' I asked her.

'When I'm done. Don't wanna be one of those reporters who drink on the job. It's so cliché.'

Allison gave me another quick kiss and went to one of the new back tables Mrs McVernon had put in, hoping for a bigger lunch crowd. I slid in next to Edgar, and Mikey came over with a pint of Brooklyn Pilsner for me. I pulled out my credit card and signaled by circling my index finger that everything was on me. He nodded and went off to take care of a trio of young women who'd come in right behind Allison and me.

'How'd you find out?' I asked Edgar after taking a sip.

'Police scanner. They didn't use his name, but they mentioned the address of the school and a quick description of the vic.' He caught himself. 'Of the murder victim. It wasn't hard to figure out from there.'

'That sucks, man. I got here as soon as I could. I wanted to be able to tell you.'

'Why?'

'Because I'm your friend,' I said. 'Bad news is better when it comes from a friend, don'tcha think?'

'Maybe in your world. Doesn't matter to me how I hear it. Bad news is bad news. There's no good way to tell me what happened to MoJo.'

Edgar's never been officially diagnosed, but it was my professional opinion – as a special education teacher and as one of his only friends – that, if tested, Edgar would show up somewhere on 'The Spectrum.' He had all the hallmarks of Asperger's; most prevalent of these were a high intelligence and a severe lack of social skills. That being said, he's had my back for some years now, and he's been a real help when it comes to my needing tech assistance. He's become one of my accidental best friends.

'You're right,' I agreed.

'Who caught the case?' he wanted to know. Edgar knew the names of Brooklyn North's detectives as well as he knew players on the Yankees and Mets.

'Royce.'

'Good,' Edgar said. 'He's thorough and you've worked with him before.'

'He is good and thorough, but I won't be *working* with him, Edgar. I gave him my statement, told him what I knew about MoJo, and that's it.'

Edgar poured some tomato juice into his Bass. 'That's never it with you, Raymond. Even I know that.'

I ignored that. 'He is, however,' I said, 'going to have some questions for you.'

'About what?'

'About your relationship with MoJo. Your company, what you've been working on. Finances. Stuff like that.'

The way Edgar adjusted himself on his barstool, I could tell that wasn't sitting well with him. Literally. He was very private about his technological abilities now that he used them for a living. While working with NYC Transit it was just a hobby, and he wouldn't shut up about the new toys he'd bought and what he could do with them. Now, it was akin to lawyer/client confidentiality. Now that he had real *clients*, Edgar was pretty tightlipped about what he was involved in.

'Can you be with me when he asks me the questions?'

'That's not standard procedure. But I'll see what I can do. Royce is a pretty reasonable guy.' I paused. 'For a cop.'

That brought a brief smile to Edgar's face. 'When is he going to interview me?'

'I have no idea. You want me to call him and see if I can arrange a time?'

'Yeah. Thanks.'

'No problem.' I pulled out my phone and wondered how many employees of the New York City Department of Education had an NYPD detective's number programmed into their cell phones. I bet Jessica Fletcher didn't.

I called Royce and it went straight to voicemail. I said he could call me anytime. Like he needed my permission for that. I turned back to Edgar. 'Another beer?'

He finished the one in front of him. 'Thanks. And thanks for calling Royce.'

I signaled to Mikey to bring another two. When he brought them over, I asked him to see if Allison was good. 'I already asked,'

Mikey said. 'She told me she was working and she'd come to the bar when she was done.'

'Sounds like Allie.'

'She like that at home?'

I took a sip of pilsner. 'Why don't you go ask her.'

Truth was, when Allison was working a story, Mardi Gras could be going on and I'd have trouble getting her away from her screen. Now that she was working the website, her focus was doubled; if she didn't get the story out fast, if it didn't scoop the other sites and TV and radio, that didn't increase subscribers or advertisers. She hated the way the journalism business was these days, but considered herself lucky to have a job. And a domestic partner with health insurance.

I looked to the back of the bar and saw her face lit up by the glare from her laptop. Based on the notes I'd seen her take down at the scene – and the images from the drone – I figured she'd be another fifteen to thirty minutes filing the story and editing and uploading the video. By then, we'd both be ready for dinner and, I hoped, a quiet night at home. After today's events, I needed one.

'You guys gonna eat here?' Edgar asked. Like he was reading my mind.

'We could do that. Wanna eat with us?'

'Not if it's like a date or something. I don't wanna be a third wheel, Ray.'

'We live together, Edgar,' I reminded him. 'We can have a "date" whenever we want. Tonight, we'll eat with you.'

He poured a little more tomato juice into his Bass. 'Thanks. I know I don't usually ask, but I think I need the company right now.'

'You got it.' I made a line with my index finger up and down the side of my frosty pint glass. 'You mind me asking when's the last time you spoke with MoJo? You guys working on anything right now?'

He thought about that. 'You sound like Detective Royce. That's the kinda thing he's gonna ask, right?'

I smiled. 'You caught me, Edgar. I just thought I'd sneak in a little prep for your talk with him. Make it a little easier, y'know?'

He nodded. 'Yeah. Thanks.'

I waited for him to answer. 'So . . .'

'Oh. Yeah. We were doing a job over in Sunnyside. A convenience store right on the other side of the Greenpoint Bridge. They're having more problems than usual with inventory going missing and the owner wants to know if it's local kids or his new workers helping themselves to the five-finger employee discount.'

'So . . .'

'So MoJo and I are putting in some hidden cameras to go along with the ones the public sees. Kinda like security on top of security. Have to work nights during the few hours when the place is closed so the employees don't know about it.'

It didn't occur to Edgar that he was speaking of Maurice in the present tense. That was going to take a while for him. Edgar was the kind of person who lived mostly in the present. His few excursions into the past and future mostly involved who the Yankees should pick up or get rid of and whatever new technology was coming down the pipeline. I could probably count on one hand the number of times we had had an in-depth conversation about the past outside of criminal matters and baseball.

My phone buzzed. I looked down to see Royce's number. 'Hey.'

'You still at The LineUp?'

I was about to ask him how he knew where I was, but decided against it. 'I was just about to order dinner.'

'Edgar with you?'

'Shouldn't you know that, Detective?'

I could imagine the look on Royce's face. 'Get me a turkey cheeseburger with onion rings. I'll be there in ten. Your boy in the mood to talk?'

Although I'd never admit it to his face, I liked that Royce had the insight to ask that question. It's one of the things that made him a good cop. I looked at Edgar and whispered, 'It's Royce. You ready to talk?'

Edgar whispered back, 'Here?'

I nodded, and Edgar nodded back. I went back to Royce. 'If you do the interview here, I think so, yeah. See ya in ten minutes.'

He broke the connection without saying goodbye. 'Royce'll be here in ten minutes. Looks like he's willing to talk to you over dinner. Less formal than a station interview. You sure you're cool with that?'

Edgar nodded. 'Allison gonna join us?'

'If she's done submitting – uploading – her story, yeah.' I took another sip. 'And we'll know that when she tells us.'

As if on cue, Allison came up behind us and put her arms around both of our shoulders. 'Workday's over,' she said. 'Who wants to buy me a beer and some wings? Winner gets to sit next to me.'

We made room for her to sit between the two of us and I said, 'You got that filed pretty quick. You're getting good at this online journalist thing.'

'Now that *good* equates to *quick*. I used to only have to worry about getting it ready for the morning paper. But,' she added, taking her seat at the bar, 'I scooped everyone else by a few hours. That's the benefit of being my own editor and field producer. I got quotes, art and video no one else has.'

'Is it online now?' Edgar asked.

'Click away, Edgar. And if you don't mind, I'd like to talk to you when I do my follow-up piece.'

'After I speak with Detective Royce, OK?'

'Of course.' She got up and pointed at my near-empty glass. 'Get me one of those, some wings, and I gotta pee.' She pointed at Edgar's laptop. 'Now, you read.'

MAN FOUND MURDERED ON
ROOFTOP OF BROOKLYN SCHOOL

A Williamsburg, Brooklyn, school aide was found shot to death this afternoon on top of the building in which he worked. The body of the school aide, 35, was discovered by a teacher shortly after 4:30. The police are withholding the identity of the victim until his family have been notified. In a somewhat bizarre twist, the murder weapon was an arrow. Police are unsure of where the arrow shot originated but are canvassing the neighboring residences and rooftops in search of clues and witnesses.

According to a co-worker – who wished to remain anonymous – the victim was working at the school as part of his community service requirement. The co-worker stated that the victim was recently released from a residential rehabilitation center for drug use and was popular with both teachers and students.

'He got along with everyone,' the co-worker said. 'He liked the kids and they seemed fascinated by his knowledge of hydroponics. Most of our kids have never tasted an organic tomato before, let alone one that was grown on top of a school. That's why he was up on the roof to begin with. He was covering up his plants because of the snow and cold.'

The victim also kept pigeons on the school rooftop, a hobby apparently unrelated to his official school duties.

CLICK HERE FOR VIDEO AND PHOTOS OF CRIME SCENE

Edgar clicked and for the second time in as many hours, I saw the video and pictures Allison had taken of the crime scene. With the little editing she had done, it looked slickly produced. We went back to reading the article.

'It's a damn shame,' said the co-worker. 'He was really starting to get his life back together. He was part-owner of a security company and told me he was thinking about working toward a teaching license. He was a good guy. It's a real loss what happened here.'

The case is being investigated by NYPD Det. James Royce of Brooklyn North, who was unavailable for comment as of this posting. Detective Royce is expected to comment on today's events soon.

An online search could not determine the last time a New York City resident was killed by an arrow. A Long Island man was shot and killed by an arrow during a neighborhood dispute in 2006. Also, a woman in the Bronx was shot in the stomach in 2009 in an incident the police officially ruled an accidental shooting.

Allison Rogers for *NYC Here and Now*

It took Edgar about a minute before he spoke. I waited as he processed what he'd just seen and read. I wondered what the chances were that Royce had seen Allison's post, and if he had, how he felt about starring in her video.

'How long has she had the video drone?' Edgar asked.

I was not surprised his first response was about the drone. 'It's pretty new. Today was the first I saw it.'

'Those things are amazing. Some of the higher-end ones – like the one I just bought – shoot at 4K with a one-eighty tilt gimbal. It's got a three-axis image stabilizer and two-point-eight lossless zoom. Operates over a distance of more than two miles.'

When Edgar had difficulty dealing with emotions, he always found comfort in his technology.

'But,' he finished, 'hers is good for what she needs.' Edgar, a single man with no kids and a good pension, didn't understand why everyone could not afford top-of-the-line technology.

'What'd ya think of the story?' I asked.

He shrugged. 'Good, I guess. Got all the facts out and no fake drama.'

'You think you can give her a quote or two for the follow-up piece? Be good for her readers to see how MoJo was getting his life back together and becoming a productive part of society. Most people don't understand the importance of rehab and how it affects society as a whole. You saw it firsthand.'

Edgar held his breath and put both hands on his pint glass. After maybe a ten-count, he said, 'Yeah, but I'm not gonna speak on video. Just for print.'

'I'm sure that'll work.'

'What will work?' Allison asked as she came back to the bar.

'I'll talk to you about MoJo,' Edgar said, 'but not on video.'

She touched his shoulder. 'Thank you, Edgar.'

Mikey came by and gave Edgar and me fresh beers and Allison her first. 'You guys eating with us?' he asked.

'Absolutely,' I said. We gave him our orders and I included the turkey burger and rings for Detective Royce just as he came through the door. When he saw me, he headed our way and gave us something that might have been a wave. 'And another pilsner,' I said. 'Long day, Detective?' I pulled out a stool.

'I'm gonna stand,' he said, waving off the seat. 'Back and shoulders have been acting up again lately. Too much damn sitting in this job sometimes.' He looked at Allison. 'How about you, Lois Lane? Long day?'

'So long it hasn't ended yet, Detective.' Allison pulled out her reporter's notebook and pen and placed them both on the bar. 'Ever vigilant and all that.'

He smiled and grabbed the pint glass Mikey had just slid in front of him. He took a sip and turned to Edgar. 'Sorry about your loss, Mr Martinez. I understand you and Mr Joseph were close.'

Edgar nodded. 'Yeah. He was my friend and we worked together so I guess you could say we were close.'

Royce took out his notebook. 'Would you mind grabbing a table with me so I can ask you a few questions?'

Edgar got a little flustered by that. 'Can Ray come with us?'

'That's not normally how we do this.'

'You also don't normally interview people at bars,' Edgar said. *Look at him,* I thought. *Sticking up for himself.* 'I'm a bit nervous about being asked questions.'

I knew exactly what was going through Royce's mind: Do this by the book and it'll take hours to get through it. Do it here and now with me next to Edgar and he's eating dinner in ten minutes and heading home soon.

'Why don't the three of us go get a table?' he said.

THREE

'About two years ago at the Hudson Valley Technology Expo,' Edgar answered. 'We were both checking out this German company's video enhancement software. You know that stuff on TV – *CSI* and all that – is all horse hockey. You blow up a blurred video image in real life and all you get is a bigger blurred image. Now with this software – that is not on the market yet – you get enhanced—'

'I get the point, Mr Martinez,' said Royce. 'And where was Mr Joseph residing at that time?'

'In Queens. Sunnyside, 47th and Bliss on the 7 train. Before his stay in rehab.'

'Was he married then?'

Edgar looked at me and then back at Royce. 'Why are you asking me all these questions? Can't you look all this up? Ask his wife, Lisa?'

'Yes,' Royce said and took a sip of beer. 'But we're waiting until tomorrow to interview her and, as I'm sure you know, there are some questions you can't get the answer to on a computer.'

Royce might as well have told Edgar that the Earth was a cube. Edgar got almost all his answers from the Internet. This interpersonal stuff was still new to him.

'What Detective Royce is saying, Edgar,' I said, 'is that it's always best to back up your second-hand sources with primary sources.'

Royce looked at me and smiled. 'Thank you, Mr Donne.' The smile wasn't real; it was Royce's way of telling me to shut up.

Edgar went on. 'He met Lisa at Newer Leaves after we met. She was a counselor – she still is – and they started dating. They got married right after he was released from the residential program. They have a rule about clients and counselors dating. I was asked to wear a tuxedo and be in the wedding party.'

'And you two have remained friendly?'

I wasn't sure why he was doing this with Edgar, but Royce was using the old interrogation technique of repeating a question using different words. *Old habits?*

'We started a business together, so, yeah, we stayed friendly.'

'No problems with the business?'

Edgar squirmed. 'What kind of problems?'

'Financial, personal. Client disputes.'

'No, no, no. Nothing like that. We get along just great. He does most of the dealing with the clients and I do most of the office and field tech work.' He paused. 'I'm not as good with people as MoJo is. He's always been . . .'

And there it was: the point where Edgar realized he was still talking about MoJo in the present tense. Royce gave Edgar time for that to sink in. Edgar stared at his beer as if there were an answer or two to be found in the amber liquid. I knew that wouldn't last long; he and I both knew many regulars of The LineUp who'd been down that path.

After a few deep breaths, Edgar picked an onion ring off his plate and held it with all five fingertips of his right hand, almost like he was showing a rookie pitcher how to throw a knuckleball. He took the ring, dipped it in a mixture of ketchup and Tabasco and shoved it into his mouth. As he chewed, Nancy, the server, came over to the table and I signaled for three more beers.

Royce said, 'Not for me. Just some more water, please.'

I'd forgotten he had at least an hour drive back home to Long Island. Like most city cops, Royce commuted to work from the outer suburbs: Long Island, Jersey, or Westchester. A lot of teachers did the same thing. Firefighters, nurses, EMTs. There were so many people needed and willing to help the residents of New York City. Not as many wanting – or able to afford – to live in the five boroughs.

They didn't know what they were missing. Having grown up on Long Island, I had taken a vow never to return as a resident. If I died without ever owning another car, that'd be fine with me.

'He . . . was . . . good with people,' Edgar continued. He looked at me. 'He was a lot like you, Ray. People liked to talk to him. He sponsored a few guys in his support group.'

'Did he talk about his support group a lot?' Royce asked.

'No. He took the anonymous part real seriously. It was through Newer Leaves. They met a few times a week at a church in Greenpoint.' Edgar mentioned the church. It was a few blocks from school. Greenpoint and Williamsburg were next-door neighbors; if they'd been twins, they would have been conjoined, hard to tell where one started and the other ended. I was of the belief that McCarren Park was the borderline. 'He went at least once a week.'

Royce finished his beer as Nancy put down two beers and Royce's water. 'Did he ever mention anything about relapsing? Falling off the wagon?'

'Not to me,' Edgar said. 'Why?'

Royce got uncharacteristically silent as he took the last bites of his turkey burger.

'Detective?' I said when I realized he was ignoring Edgar's question.

Royce swallowed and took a long sip of water. Barely above a whisper, he said, 'We found something in his room.'

'His what?' I said, knowing for a fact MoJo didn't have a 'room' at the school. He had what little space could be cleared out of a book closet. We were able to find him an old desk, a chair, and a filing cabinet that looked like it had been last used when Eleanor Roosevelt visited the school shortly after it opened in the late nineteen-forties. And, MoJo being MoJo, he had found a way to get hooked into the school's WiFi.

'We found a hole in the wall behind some books,' Royce explained. 'About forty copies of *The Great Gatsby*. There was a toolbox inside. It contained a couple of cell phones – we're checking them out now – some computer cables, and . . .'

It was a rare occurrence when Detective Royce was at a loss for words. Edgar picked up on it after about ten seconds.

'And what, Detective Royce?' Edgar asked.

'A shoot-up kit.'

'What?' I asked. Not because I didn't hear him, but because I did.

Royce spoke a little louder. 'A shoot-up kit. It's a—'

'I know what a shoot-up kit is, Detective. Are you saying MoJo was using at school? Did you find any drugs in the kit?'

'No. Just the instruments: a few needles, a spoon, a lighter, and a rubber tie-off.'

'He was not using,' Edgar said too loudly. 'I would've known if he was using. We worked together. He was still going through the program. He was sponsoring people.' He looked at me. 'I woulda known if he was using. Right, Ray?'

Like I don't answer enough tough questions at work. 'I think so, Edgar. But it's hard to tell with . . .' I struggled to find a better word, but MoJo himself would have said there was no better way to say it. 'It's hard to tell with addicts.' I turned to Royce. 'I never saw any of the signs. I'm not an expert, but I've seen enough junkies on the street to know a little more than your average person.'

'He wasn't a junkie, Ray,' Edgar said.

'You're right, Edgar. Bad choice of words,' said the man who took another sip of his fourth beer of the evening. 'I meant addicts.'

Royce directed his next question at me. 'And you met with his case worker?'

'It was one of the conditions of his working at the school. She came by once every week or so to check up on him, and he had to call every day he worked from the school's landline to prove he was there.' I thought about how close we were – freak April snow-storm not withstanding – to the end of the school year. 'He had less than three months to finish up. Then he was pretty much free to work full-time with Edgar at the security company. I don't see him blowing that – or his family – by bringing drug paraphernalia into the school.'

'Like you said,' Royce said. 'You never know with addicts.'

I was about to say something about that when Royce's phone went off. He looked at the number, stood up and said, 'I gotta take this.' He walked away.

'I don't like calling MoJo an addict, Ray,' Edgar said.

'I hear ya, Edgar, but it's a fact of life. There's no such thing as a former addict or former alcoholic. They're in recovery or they're inactive, but they're always looking over their shoulders for the dragon.'

'The dragon?'

'A lot of active users call it that. "Chasing the dragon." When you're fighting the addiction, sometimes you realize the dragon's chasing you.'

'And you know this because . . .'

'It's not just people on the street, Edgar. I know a lot of cops who've had problems with drugs.' I took another sip. 'A lot of them will tell you it's the job, nobody understands them, the pressure at home. But I think most of them come to the job with problems. They may not be active, but the potential is there. The job becomes a pretty good scapegoat.'

'You boys done with your interview?' Allison had come over to the booth. I slid over to make room for her.

'Not sure,' I said. I motioned with my head toward the detective. 'Royce got a call and went for a stroll.'

'How are you doing, Edgar?' she asked.

He nodded. 'Better now that I ate. Thanks.'

Allison took out her notebook, opened to a blank page, and put it on the table between herself and Edgar. 'Feel like telling me a little about Maurice? Something I can use to flesh him out a bit, make him sound less like a victim and more like a person?'

Without missing a beat, Edgar said, 'He knew more about audio and video surveillance than anyone I ever met.'

Allison's face could do nothing to hide her surprise at that comment. 'More than you?' Even if it were true, I couldn't see Edgar admitting to it.

Edgar thought about that. 'It was probably close, but he was teaching me a lot of stuff over the past year.'

'What kind of stuff?'

Edgar got quiet again. 'Is this for your story?'

'It's on the record unless you tell me otherwise,' she said and lowered her voice. Royce was still about twenty feet away and on the phone, so he couldn't hear us. 'Was Maurice into stuff you don't wanna tell the detective? Any illegal activities?'

Edgar slowly moved his head back and forth. 'No, no, no. Not MoJo. Since he's been out of rehab, he was keeping clean. For his wife and his kid.'

'Then just tell me the stuff he was working on.' She tapped her pencil twice. 'And don't get too technical. Our readers want a good story, not a tutorial, but the technical stuff could help flesh him out a bit. Make him more than just a murder victim. Keep it simple, though.'

That would be tough for Edgar. Things he considered common knowledge would be above most people's heads. It was hard for the best of us to talk about things that we took for granted. One of the problems with the educational system in this country – if you ask me – is most subjects were taught by people who were always good in those areas. Math majors taught math, English majors taught ELA, and so on. They had problems understanding when others didn't grasp something right away. Just because you know more than most people about a subject, doesn't make you a good teacher. And Edgar was not so good at dumbing things down.

Allison read the look on his face. 'Just speak to me like I'm an intelligent person who knows nothing about what you're talking about.'

'Like the time we talked about baseball?' he asked. 'And you wanted to know how ERAs were calculated and slugging percentage?'

'And that in-fielder's flying thing.'

For the first time since we'd arrived, Edgar laughed. 'The in-field fly rule.'

'That's it. Just speak to me like that.'

Before he got started, Royce came back. 'They've notified Mr Joseph's wife,' he said to all of us. Then to Allison, he said, 'You can use his name in your next report.'

Allison nodded. 'Edgar was just about to talk about MoJo's knowledge of surveillance equipment. Are you done with your interview, Detective?'

'For now, yeah. I'll talk with Mr Joseph's wife tomorrow.'

'Can you give me a quote for my update?' Allison held up her phone to record.

Royce took a few seconds to think. He let out a deep breath. 'One particular challenge we're gonna face in this investigation – almost unique for us here in the city – is you can't run ballistics on an arrow. There's no shell casing to be found, and so far none of the neighbors have told us anything of real value. We'll go back and knock on some more doors tomorrow.' He reached out and finished his water. 'That good?'

'Great,' Allison said. 'For now. Thanks.'

He offered his hand to Edgar, who took it reluctantly. 'Thanks,' Royce said. 'I may have some more questions after we speak with Mrs Joseph. You want to exchange cards?' They did and then Royce reached into his wallet and pulled out a couple of bills.

'It's OK, Detective,' I said. 'We got this.'

'Not while I'm on duty and still wanna keep my job, you don't. Can't take a free cup of coffee these days. Had to sit through a three-hour training session to re-learn that. And, apparently, I'm still not allowed to have sexual relations with witnesses or suspects.' He put down a twenty and a five. 'I'm sure we'll be in touch soon.' I guessed that was his way of saying goodbye, because he turned around and left the bar.

'Guy's a real stickler for the rules, huh?' Edgar asked.

'Not so much that he's above conducting an interview here,' I said.

Edgar nodded. 'Guess you're right.' He turned to Allison. 'You ready for me to tell you about the business?'

'Whenever you're ready,' she said.

'MoJo was real up-to-date on all the German and Russian technology,' Edgar began. 'The Russkies still make a lot of the best stuff. He had recorders – audio – that could pick up clear audio from thirty-two feet away, worked on a timer, and could record on one battery charge for eighty-five hours. That's over three-point-five days. We're talking top-of-the-line.'

I did my best to suppress a smile; Edgar loved talking in decimals. Most people would have said three-and-a-half days. Edgar was not most people.

'We just bought some cell phone recorders. Voice-activated, up to six days' storage, twenty-hour battery.'

'Who's the market for those?' Allison asked. 'No names, of course, but what was your typical client for something like that?'

'Bosses who don't trust their employees, jealous and suspicious spouses, parents who want to know who and what their kids are texting and talking to.'

'Jesus,' she said.

'We even showed folks how to use an iPhone recovery stick. They're a big seller. You can find where Junior or Hubby was going on their phone. Porn detection software's a big seller.' Edgar took another sip. 'Most people think they're going on the web, no one knows what they're doing. Horse hockey. You can't go online without leaving a trace. Privacy is an illusion.' He paused, maybe considering that for the company's motto. 'I remember in high school we read *1984* and everyone, including the teacher, was talking about how scary it all was. I was the only one who thought it was pretty cool. And Orwell didn't even imagine half the stuff we can do now.'

'And this is what you do?' Allison said. 'Spy tech?'

Edgar looked a little hurt by that oversimplified description. I thought that was going to shut him up. I was wrong. 'We do a lot of security work, Allison. Businesses come to us to make sure they know what their employees are doing. You know how much manpower is wasted by workers going online, drivers lying about where they've been, merchandise going missing?'

'I guess I don't.'

'Maybe you should do a story about that. I bet your readers have no idea, either. You could really help people out with a story on that.'

'I'm going to think on that, Edgar. It's a good idea.'

'Darn straight it is.'

For the next fifteen minutes, Edgar schooled Allison on the ins and outs of the security business, how technology could help more at airports, the seaports, and keeping track of undocumented immigrants. He used the term 'untapped potential' as much as any school counselor I'd ever worked with. I'd heard it all before so most of my attention was tuned to the TV above the bar, which was recapping last night's early season baseball game and previewing tonight's. The next thing I knew, Allison was tapping my arm.

'You wanna stay for the game or go home?'

I looked at Edgar and got the strong feeling he still wanted – needed – company. I could do that and said so to Allison.

She slid out of the booth. 'Well, don't be up too late boys. It *is* a school night and you both have to be bright-eyed and bushy-tailed in the morning.'

Edgar and I gave polite and simultaneous smiles. Allison leaned over and kissed me. 'Be quiet if you get in late. One of us does take their sleep seriously.'

'Will do,' I said. 'I love you.'

'Back at ya, tough guy.' Then she kissed Edgar on the cheek. 'Be good.'

'Or at least don't get caught,' he said. As we both watched Allison leave, he said to me, 'That's nice, Ray. That's real nice.'

'I couldn't agree more, Edgar.' I finished my beer and said, 'Let's grab a couple of stools and watch the game.'

FOUR

The school bell – picture a giant-sized annoying alarm clock signaling the beginning of the Friday school day – had gone off thirty minutes ago. I had cleared the playground, monitored the door for latecomers, and made sure the hallways were empty and everyone was pretty much where they were supposed to be. By nine o'clock I had returned three emails, made two phone calls and finished my second cup of coffee. Now I was standing inside the closet that had served as MoJo's 'room.'

Just as Royce had explained yesterday, three-dozen or so copies of *The Great Gatsby* had been moved off the shelves, revealing a small hole in the wall where MoJo apparently kept his secret stash. The hole was empty. Anything of relevance, I assumed, had been removed by the police.

Except for a few catalogs offering hydroponics equipment, a copy of this month's *Purebred Pigeon Magazine* – who knew? – an opened ream of copier paper, a stapler, and some assorted desk supplies strewn across an old wooden table, it was almost as if Maurice Joseph had never been there.

There was a light tapping on the door. Elaine Stiles, our school counselor, was standing in the doorway.

'Hey, Ray,' she said, 'I'm really sorry about Maurice.'

'Pretty shitty for everyone. How much do the kids know?'

'Just what they heard on the street and their phones. Ron wants to have an assembly last period so we can explain to the kids what happened. We also need to offer any grief counseling that we can.' She looked at her watch. 'I'm expecting some grief counselors from the DOE any minute.'

That's standard procedure when a school loses a staff member or student so suddenly and violently. Grief counselors were also available for catastrophes that took place outside the school, such as 9/11 or other traumatic events the kids would need help processing. Just two days ago we had had a hard lockdown drill. The kind of thing we were mandated to practice in the event of an active-shooter situation. Makes you appreciate a good old-fashioned fire drill.

'I can give you a list of kids he was close to,' I offered.

'That'd be good.' She touched my arm. 'How are you doing?'

'That's a good question, Elaine.' I told her about Royce comparing me to Jessica Fletcher. 'I'm starting to wonder if he has a point.'

'He does not have a point, Ray.'

'He kinda does, Elaine. Some people collect stamps or coins. I seem to collect crime scenes. I'm starting to feel that maybe I somehow invite violence into my life.'

'You do not.' She stepped over to hug me. 'What you do is you put yourself out there for people in crisis. You help them make sense out of what's going on. And as much as I think you'd like to, you can't save everyone.'

'I'm not trying to save anyone,' I said, returning the hug. 'If I were, I'd be doing a pretty crappy job of it.'

'Crappy job of what?'

Elaine and I broke the hug. Ron Thomas was just outside the doorway. Like most times, he had his sleeves rolled up, ready for action.

'Ray's upset about Maurice, Ron. I was just . . .'

'I could see what you were . . . just. Anyway.' He looked at Elaine while he adjusted his tie. It must have been weird for Ron to understand two of his teachers were truly fond of each other. Poor guy. It must have been so much easier on him when he was teaching Phys Ed. 'There're two . . . "grief counselors" waiting in the office for you. Why wasn't I told they were coming?'

Elaine explained their presence, and also that as principal, Ron should have been expecting them. He had no snarky boss answer for that.

'Well, please go down and do what you need to do to prepare for the assembly, Ms Stiles. I'll make an announcement after the final lunch that last period will be canceled and we will meet in the auditorium for a full-school assembly.'

'Yes, Ron,' she said. To me, 'Talk later, Ray?'

'Let's see how the day goes, but yeah, I'd like that.'

As she walked away, Ron said to me, 'I guess you've seen the papers today?'

'No, Ron. I haven't had time to read the papers this morning.' I said this knowing full well that Ron subscribed to all three local papers and made sure to read them every morning. He also, a few years back, had the bright idea of installing a large-screen HD

television in his office. He told me once that he wanted to 'keep up
to date on current events.' He was especially interested in those
current events that involved rich white guys hitting a small ball
great distances.

'Well, we're in all three of them and all over the local news. I
told you that inviting a convicted drug abuser to the school could
backfire on us.' He let out a sigh. 'A goddamned arrow? Really?'

Fucking Ron. If it were up to him, he'd be principal of a talented
and gifted middle school somewhere in mythical Suburbia. Such
was his lot that each day he had to get up, drive an hour to
Williamsburg, Brooklyn, and run a school with needy kids who
were darker-skinned than he was. And now, one of his staff was
murdered on his rooftop and the media were on it like holy on the
Pope. Life was like that sometimes.

'We took a chance on a good guy, Ron.'

'*I* took the chance, Ray. Based on *your* recommendation. If I'd
had any idea how this would play out—'

I raised my hand. 'Hey, Ron. Give it a rest, will ya? There's no
way any of us had any idea what was going to happen. MoJo was
worth the chance and *we* took it.'

'MoJo,' he repeated, not trying at all to hide his sarcasm. 'Just
the name should've tipped me off.' He brushed something invisible
off his shirtsleeve. 'What are the police saying?'

Again, like I had a secret pipeline. 'Just what you heard on the
news or read in the papers, Ron. Allie told me that this kind of
killing – by arrow – is extremely rare, so the press is going to be
on it for a while. It's a story.'

'Fucking reporters.' I watched his face as he remembered what
my girlfriend does for a living. 'No offense.'

'Don't worry about it.' I stepped out of the closet and made sure
the door was locked when I closed it. 'I'm going to swing through
the halls. Unless there was something else you wanted to talk about?'

He gave that some thought and said, 'No, not now. Just keep
your walkie on.'

'It's never off, Ron,' I said and walked away from my boss.

It was pushing one o'clock and I had just completed eighth-grade
lunch duty. Imagine two hundred and fifty hormone-filled middle-
school students all lining up for lunch in a crowded, noisy room;
sitting with some amount of decorum while eating this lunch; lining

up again to get rid of what they had not eaten – in many cases most of the government-subsidized food; and then sitting back down and waiting for the bell to signal lunch was now over and it was time to go to the next class. As one of three adults in the room, and the one with the whistle and walkie-talkie, it was my duty to make sure that this fifty-minute part of the day came off with no fights – food, fists, or otherwise – and that the students left the lunchroom looking pretty much as they had when they walked in. This was one of those subjects they did not cover during my master's program. But a good friend who runs a summer camp once told me, 'Maintain order in the dining area and you maintain order throughout the whole facility.' I took lunch duty very seriously.

Just as the last diner was leaving the lunchroom, my cell phone rang. It was Edgar. 'Hey, man. What's up?'

'I just got a call from a guy who said he was a client,' Edgar said.

'OK.'

'A client of Maurice Joseph.'

I let that sink in. 'Someone you didn't know about?'

'Never heard of him, Ray. Said he was working strictly with MoJo.'

'And I guess you didn't exactly know what to say to that?'

'No, but he said that he needed to drop by.'

'Did he?'

'Did he what?'

'Drop by.'

'No. I was able to convince him that I was too busy and told him he'd have to wait until later.'

'Did you schedule an appointment with him?'

'Yeah. Today at four.'

'Good. So what did you want to talk to me about?'

I could hear his deep breath. 'Are you free today at four?'

Oh, boy. 'Because you don't want to meet with him alone?'

'Right.'

I went through my mental schedule. If I left right after school and put off some paperwork, I could make that happen. Edgar lived not far from school. 'Yeah, I can do that. Where are you meeting him, Edgar? Your apartment?'

'No, Ray. I'm not going to meet him at my apartment. That would make us – me – look like an amateur.'

'So . . .'

'I told him we could meet at The LineUp.'

'Because meeting at a bar would make you look more professional?'

'I told him that I was busy all day with clients and would be having an early dinner at The LineUp and I could squeeze a meeting with him in then.'

I considered that. 'That's pretty good, Edgar. Smart thinking.'

'I saw it on an old episode of *Rockford Files*. I figured if it worked for Jim Rockford, it could work for me.'

I watched those reruns, too, and seemed to remember Jim Rockford getting beat up a lot. I didn't mention that.

'So what do you want me to do at this meeting?'

'I'm gonna spend the next few hours going through all of MoJo's stuff and see if I can find out who this guy is. All I got is his name. David Henderson. I don't want him to realize that I had no idea MoJo had a client I didn't know about.' He paused. 'I guess I need you for support.'

'You got me, Edgar. It may cost you a beer or two.'

'Thanks, Ray. I'll see you at four.' Before hanging up, he quickly added, 'And I told him you were a partner of mine.'

Then he hung up, apparently impatient to figure out why his real partner was doing business with a client he had no idea about.

The rest of the day went by without incident. Just the kind of buzz going through the building you'd expect on a warm Friday afternoon in April – a day after it had snowed. The assembly did not go the way Ron Thomas had planned. That is until Elaine Stiles took the microphone. If Ron had any clue the students had more respect for her than him, his immense ego protected him from that knowledge. She made sure the students knew counseling was available after school and into the next week for anyone in need. She introduced the grief counselors who'd said that they, too, would be around after school and back on Monday. That was pretty much it.

It was just your normal assembly program a school conducts after one of the adults in the building is murdered by an arrow on the roof of the building.

I called Allison and left a message that I'd be at The LineUp helping out Edgar and for her to give me a call about dinner. I got to The LineUp a little before four and found Edgar in a booth in the back. He had his laptop, a manila folder, his cell phone, and a pint glass of water.

And, for the first time I could remember, maybe since the funeral service for Mr McVernon, the owner of the bar in which we sat, Edgar was wearing a jacket and tie.

I took in the look. 'Dressed to impress, I see.'

'I'm nervous, Ray,' he said. 'I don't know what to expect and I don't know what Mr Henderson's expecting, so . . .' He took a sip of water. 'Do I look too . . . dorky?'

'You look fine, Edgar. First time you've ever made me feel underdressed. I'm glad Allie's not here to see this. She'd make me go shopping.'

Edgar looked at his watch. 'Henderson's gonna be here any minute.'

I slid into the booth across from him. 'What do you want me to do?'

'I'm glad you asked.' He cleared his throat. 'I'm going to try and do most of the talking – more listening, I hope – but you know how sometimes I can't find the right words? How I get mixed up with people?'

'I've noticed that,' I said. 'From time to time.'

'If you see me stumbling or something, please jump in until I get my thoughts together. You're good at that.'

I looked at the stuff in front of him. 'Have you been able to figure out who this Henderson guy is and what MoJo was doing for him?'

He shook his head. 'Not a clue, Ray. And I've been looking since we spoke. There's a lot of David Hendersons out there. I'm guessing MoJo had the info stored somewhere else. Somewhere I wouldn't find it. Probably at home or school.'

I could tell the thought of that – more than any other at the moment aside from MoJo's murder – was what was bothering Edgar. He took the partnership seriously and would never hide anything from MoJo. He wasn't capable of that type of thinking.

'Mr Martinez?'

We looked up and saw a large man in a blue suit standing above us. He had brown hair that was going gray and he was large enough – and in good enough shape – to have played football not so long ago. My second thought was that he carried himself like a cop. I pegged him for about fifty, give or take. Edgar and I stood and shook his hand. He slid into the booth next to Edgar. 'I'm David Henderson. Thank you for seeing me so soon.' He looked at me. 'I know this is a horrible time for you both.'

'It is,' Edgar said. 'Mr Henderson.'

'Please,' Henderson said. 'Call me David. Maurice did.'

'Sure,' Edgar said. 'David.'

Henderson lowered his voice. 'First of all,' he began, 'let me apologize for keeping you in the dark.'

'I don't understand,' Edgar said. And, of course, that was true.

'It was my idea,' Henderson said, 'for Maurice not to tell you what he was working on with me. I'm very . . .' he struggled for the right word, 'uncomfortable with the situation and I'm hoping you'll understand when I explain.'

Edgar nodded. 'OK.'

'I employed Maurice because I knew him through a friend who attends the Newer Leaves meetings. I knew he would keep things quiet and confidential. The fewer people who know about this the better. And that included you, I'm afraid. And again' – he put his hand on his chest – 'that's on me. Maurice was not comfortable with the arrangement.'

This time I nodded along with Edgar. 'Go on,' Edgar said.

'My son is missing,' Henderson said. He rubbed his eyes. 'Stepson, to be exact. From my second marriage. Keeping it as quiet as possible was my wife's idea. This is quite a sensitive subject.'

Edgar took that in. 'Because . . .'

'We've had a hard time with Brian,' he said. 'My stepson. He didn't take his mother and father's divorce well, his grades went down terribly, and he's disappeared a few times only to show up a week or so later with no explanation of where he'd been.'

Edgar was quiet for a while. When he didn't speak for ten seconds, I broke my vow of silence. 'What did the police say?'

Henderson looked down at the table. 'We didn't want the police involved. Brian's also had a history of drug use and we were afraid if we got the police involved it would only make the situation worse.'

I waited again for Edgar. Nothing.

'How long has Brian been missing this time?' I asked.

'Eight days.'

'So. You just assumed Brian would come home on his own, knowing that he may have been involved with drugs.'

From the look on his face, I could tell Henderson – David – didn't like that question. Maybe he thought I was judging his step-parenting abilities. I didn't give a shit. This may have been MoJo's client, and Edgar's business, but something about this guy was rubbing me the wrong way – aside from the feeling that he was not telling us the complete story. Maybe if he talked long enough, he would. I just severely doubted that.

'Brian,' Henderson said, 'always kept in touch with us when he . . . went away. He called every day, or every other day, and let us know he was OK.' He paused. 'He made it clear that if we called the police or tried to find him, we never would. And then pretty soon after that, he would just come home.'

I reached over and took a sip from Edgar's water. He looked at me and I gave him a look back; he needed to be in on this conversation. It took him a while to figure that out. But when he did, he asked exactly the question I was thinking of.

'What makes this time different?' Edgar said, and I subtly nodded my approval.

Henderson took that question in. I watched his face as he did so. Again, I couldn't shake the cop feeling this guy was giving off. I also believed the next thing out of his mouth was not going to be the complete truth, but that could've been an occupational hazard. When you work with kids in crisis and education bureaucrats, you expect lies and half-truths. I often expected it when someone's lips were moving.

'He hasn't called us this time,' Henderson said. 'He left his phone at home, which he's done before, but he's always found a way to call us. Never a landline, though. I guess he knew they could be traced. He told us he was borrowing other people's phones or using those pre-paid ones.'

'Burners,' Edgar said. 'Hard to trace.'

'That's what Maurice suggested.'

'What do you do, Mr Henderson?' I asked, hoping to catch him off-guard.

'I manage a hedge fund,' he said. 'Money is no problem if that's—'

'No,' I said. 'It's just that your stepson is missing, you don't get the police involved, and you don't hire a private investigator. But, you do hire a security expert with little to no investigative experience.'

'I knew Maurice from my friend who goes to the Newer Leaves

meetings. I trusted him. He said he would deal with the police if need be, but we would talk about hiring a private investigator before that. Maurice promised to do what he could to keep my family's name out of this. He was the closest person I knew to law enforcement without being law enforcement. My wife was not even comfortable with that.'

The cop smell coming off this guy was getting stronger. David Henderson was as much a hedge fund manager as I was a peach farmer. I told myself to ask for a card before the meeting was over, but a business card was the easiest thing to fake. I could get one in two hours that claimed I played second base for the Seattle Mariners.

'Was MoJo able to tell you anything useful?' I asked.

'No. I wanted to meet with you,' he looked at Edgar, 'to see if maybe he had told you anything, given you any information on what he had found before he . . . you know . . . was murdered.'

Edgar shook his head. 'No,' he said. 'I just found out about . . . this when you called. If Maurice told you he wouldn't say anything to me, he meant it.'

Again, I couldn't help myself. 'You have no reason to believe,' I said, 'that what happened to MoJo had anything to do with what he was doing for you, do you?'

'I don't see how, but not knowing what he found out, I can't say.' He thought about that some more. 'No, absolutely not. I don't see it having any connection. Brian's a sixteen-year-old kid who's missing. How does that connect to someone being murdered?'

Following a question with a question. It reminded me too much of the kids I worked with now, and the cops and perps I worked with years ago.

'It probably doesn't,' I said.

Edgar said, 'Where do you live, David?'

'Midtown.' He gave us an embarrassed grin. 'We're in one of those newer buildings on the west side of Manhattan. You ever hear of MiMa?'

I nodded. 'MiMa' was a name the real estate people came up with for Midtown Manhattan in the hopes of rivaling SoHo, NoHo, Tribeca: a fake name that sounded desperately fancy. MiMa never took off. I think because it sounded too much like what an Italian kid called his grandmother. I had some friends in that neighborhood and the rule they went by was if you owned your apartment in that area, you called it Clinton or Midtown West. If you rented, you were living in Hell's Kitchen.

'We still have our place up in the Catskills, but we spend most of our time down here in the city.'

'Do you have any other children?' Edgar asked.

'Just Brian. Believe me, he's more than enough.'

'You've obviously reached out to all of Brian's friends?' I asked.

'The ones we know about, yes.'

'And when was the last time you were up at your house in . . .'

'Palenville,' David said. 'Not far from Hunter Mountain. We all like to ski. We checked the house two days after Brian left. No sign of him being there. We have a neighbor up there looking in on the place every day. Nothing.'

We sat in silence, all of us in our own thoughts. I had more to say but reminded myself this was Edgar's meeting and I wasn't going to take over. That's what I told myself until the silence got to be too much.

'Well, David,' I said, 'our advice is that it's time to go to the police. Eight days is a long time and the longer it gets, the more likely something bad's going to happen.'

Henderson looked at Edgar. 'You don't think you can take over where your partner left off?'

Edgar took a breath. 'That's . . . I don't know where Maurice left off because I didn't know what was going on. Raymond's right. You should really call the police. Or a private investigator who does missing persons. They're good at this. I do high-tech security, jobs like that.'

Henderson picked up a napkin, rolled it into a ball, and then worked it with his fingers as he mulled over our advice. 'You're probably right,' he finally said. 'I'm going to have to run that past Maureen. My wife.'

'Yeah,' I said. 'You should do that.'

He got up. 'Do I owe you anything for your time, Mr Martinez?'

Edgar shook his head. 'No.'

'I do believe I owe Mr Joseph for his. How would I go about . . .?'

Edgar pulled a card out and handed it to Henderson. 'You can send a check to our office. I'll make sure it gets to his wife.'

'I appreciate that.' He shook our hands. 'Thank you both for your time.'

I got up. 'How'd you get here? Drive?'

'Yes.'

'I'll walk you to your car.'

'There's no need for that, Raymond. I'm familiar with this neighborhood.'

'I need the air, Dave.' If he could lie, so could I. 'I'll be right back, Edgar. Why don't you get us a couple of beers? It's almost five.'

'OK, Ray.'

When we got outside, Henderson said, 'Really, Raymond. You don't need to—'

'Yeah, I do,' I said. 'Besides, you forgot to give us your card.'

He made that look people make when they forget the obvious and pulled his wallet from his jacket. He handed me a card. Sure enough, it stated for anyone who wished to know that David Henderson was a hedge fund manager for DH Consultants.

'You an American League fan?' I asked.

'I like the sound of "DH." Are you a fan of baseball, Raymond?'

'You could say that, Dave. I'm not a fan of being lied to, though.'

He stopped walking. 'I don't think I follow you.'

'I think you do,' I said. 'I had you pegged for a cop before you sat down.'

He laughed. 'I assure you, Raymond. I am not a cop. Just a money guy. If I were a cop, why would I need help finding my son?'

'Stepson,' I reminded him. 'I don't know, David. But if you're such a money guy, I'd think you could buy the best private investigator you could who would eagerly take your money to look for Brian while keeping his mouth shut.'

He started walking again. I followed. 'You're a suspicious man, Raymond. I guess that serves you well in your business.'

I was about to ask him why that was when I realized he still believed Edgar and I were partners in a security firm. 'It helps,' I said. 'So, ex-military maybe?'

We got to his car and he pulled out his keys. 'You got me there,' he said. 'Ten years in the National Guard. Mostly weekend warrior stuff. I got out when my business took off. No time to play Saturday Soldier, you know?'

'I guess not.' I stuck out my hand. 'Good luck. Do take our advice and contact the police no matter what Maura says.'

He gave me a puzzled look. 'Maureen, Raymond. My wife's

name is Maureen.' He knew what I was doing, which made me think again that he was something other than he said he was.

'Oh, right. Sorry.'

'Goodbye, Raymond.'

'Goodbye, David. Get home safe.'

'Always do.'

Back inside The LineUp, Edgar was at the bar with two pint glasses and a can of tomato juice in front of him. He was busy on his laptop when I slid onto the stool next to him. 'Hey,' I said, handing him the business card. 'I think you should run another check on David Henderson.'

He looked at me as if I'd just told him Halle Berry was hot. He turned his laptop so I could see the screen and said, 'David Alan Henderson. DH Consultants. This is his website. Two addresses: one on West Forty Second in the city, one in Palenville, New York. Married to Maureen Henderson, one stepson named Brian Sean Henderson, taking his stepfather's last name. Former National Guard member, he has a permit to carry in New York State and a valid New York State driver's license.'

'So,' I said. 'He appears to be who he says he is.'

'*Appears?* You are one suspicious hombre, Ray.'

'Yeah,' I said and took a sip of pilsner. 'I just heard that from someone.'

FIVE

Allison came by the bar just after six. She took a stool next to mine, ordered a white wine, kissed my cheek hello, and wiggled her fingers at Edgar. I'd known Allison long enough to know the white wine order was a sure sign she had to work tonight and stay clearheaded.

'What's breaking?' I asked.

'Not breaking, really,' she said. 'A guy I was waiting to hear from finally reached out to me today. He said he could meet me tonight and he's not sure how the rest of his week is going to play out. I'm looking at this as a possible series for the website, so I gotta jump when he says so for the moment.'

'Cool. You gonna eat with us?'

'No. Just a quick glass of wine and I'm out of here.' She took a sip.

'What's so important about this guy?'

Silence. There was a line I had clearly missed, even as I was stepping over it.

'Remember those talks we've had about how sometimes you know something that I want to know but how you can't tell me because I'm a reporter?'

I grabbed my beer. 'Yeah.'

'This is one of those times *I can't tell you something* because I'm a reporter.'

I took a sip. 'So this is what that feels like.'

'This is what that feels like, tough guy.'

Edgar looked at Allison's drink of choice. 'Working tonight?'

A long sip of pinot this time. 'Yeah. Hate to drink and run, but this is how we get subscribers, and subscribers is how we get advertisers, and advertisers is how I get paid.'

'Shouldn't that be "are" how?' I asked.

'Could be, Ray.' She looked at her watch and took a finishing gulp of her wine. 'I'll check in with Strunk and White when I get the chance and get back to you.'

She slid off her stool as I said, 'Speaking of getting back . . .'

'I have no idea. I'll call or text when I'm done.'

'And you're sure you're gonna be—'

'I will be as safe as I would be if I didn't know you, Ray.' She kissed me again, this time on the lips, gave Edgar a quick shoulder squeeze and was out the door like she'd never been there.

She was right, but it still got to me. Allison Rogers was a reporter long before I had met her, and she always handled herself like a pro. She was never one to put herself in unnecessary danger. Now that we were living together, though, I found myself worrying more about her. Sure, it had to do with how my feelings for her had grown, but not knowing when the woman I loved and slept with was going to be home kept me up until she was. In my entire adult life, I had never had someone at home to worry about. This was a new feeling for me.

At least I admit it.

'So, Ray,' Edgar said. 'What was it about Henderson that got your spider senses tingling?'

'I didn't believe his story. And something about him smells like a cop.'

'He told you about his time with the National Guard?'

'Yeah, that could be it. But it's also the whole not wanting to get the cops involved or hiring a real private investigator. And it's not sitting well with me that someone in the Newer Leaves program would just give up MoJo's name like that.'

'Maybe the guy asked MoJo and MoJo said OK.'

'Maybe. I'm probably still jittery over finding the body.' I told him what Royce had said about Jessica Fletcher and me.

He gave me an awkward smile. 'That is kinda funny, Ray.'

'Not to me.'

He was about to say something when his phone buzzed. He looked at the screen. 'Lisa. Maurice's wife.'

'Talk to her. I gotta hit the head.' On my way to the men's room I heard him say, 'Hey, Lisa.' Even from here, I could tell he was nervous.

When I got back, our food had arrived. Edgar was politely waiting for me before eating. 'Lisa wants me to go by the house tomorrow.'

'OK.'

'Can you come with me?'

I thought about that. 'I wasn't invited. Maybe she just wants to talk with you.'

'She said she had some stuff MoJo left in an envelope for me. Stuff to do with the business. I can do that, but I'm not . . . I'm not used to talking with people who just lost a husband, you know? What do I do after she gives me the envelope?'

'In my experience,' I said as I shook some hot sauce onto my onion rings, 'you just listen. Whatever she has to give you can wait if you think about it. Sounds to me like she wants you more for company than anything else.'

'That's what I can't do, Ray.' He took off his glasses and rubbed his eyes. 'You know me better than anyone. I'm not good at . . . people.'

I ate a few rings and took a bite of my burger. 'OK. Text her back and see if it's OK if I come along. If she sounds doubtful, you're on your own.'

He picked up his phone. 'Thanks.'

As he was texting Lisa, Mikey came up with two fresh beers. Since we were just a little more than halfway through the ones in front of us, I suspected Mikey had something on his mind. I wasn't wrong.

'Any chance you can take my Tuesday night shift, Ray?' he asked. 'I gotta date with a girl I've been working on for weeks. The one who comes in here twice a week for lunch? She works over on the avenue.'

'Sorry, man. I've given all my April shifts to Maggie. She needs them more than I do. Summer courses. Why don't you ask her? If she can't, I'll take the shift.'

'Good idea. It took me three asks to get this date.'

'You like this one, huh?'

'First one I've met in a long time got her own place, a real job, and no kids.'

Mikey was third-generation Greenpoint Polish. Between his day job working UPS, a bachelor's in business, and the three nights a week he worked at The LineUp, he was considered quite the catch among the local ladies, especially those with Polish Catholic daughters pushing twenty-five, still unmarried and without kids.

'I'll get back to ya, Ray. Gonna call her now.' He pulled out his cell, pointed at the fresh beers and said, 'Those are with me, man.'

'Thanks.'

'Lisa said she'd love to see you,' Edgar said. 'Tomorrow morning work?'

'Yeah, I guess.' One plus about being a dean instead of a classroom teacher was I didn't have hours and hours of papers to grade over the weekend. 'You want me to meet you there or can you pick me up?'

'I'll come get ya, Ray. That way we can walk in together. Thanks.'

'You got it.'

We finished our meals just as the Yankee game started. Something was still gnawing at me and that something was David Henderson. I didn't want to bug Edgar with it again – it was just the kind of thing he'd obsess over – so I told him I was going to step outside and check in with Allison about something. She beat me to it.

'You missing me already?' I asked.

'You sitting down?' she asked.

'No, I'm outside the bar. I was just going to call you to follow up on that guy I met with Edgar earlier. Why should I be sitting down?'

'Is Edgar with you?'

'He's inside, Allie. Why? What's going on?'

'I just got a call from my guy over at the medical examiner's office.'

'OK.'

'He told me that they found fifty bags of heroin on MoJo when he came in yesterday. Sixty bags, Ray.'

Whoa. 'Where did they—'

'They don't take up much room. All he needed was a pair of pants. He had the bags in his pockets.'

'How do they know it was heroin?'

'They run field tests right away when they suspect drugs.' Allison let me process that info. 'He was either active again or selling. If he'd been caught with that much on him, he'd have been charged with possession with intent to distribute.' She paused. 'You said you saw no signs that he was using again?'

'None. But like I said to Edgar, it's tough to spot with some people.' I took a breath. 'But I'm not buying it, Allie.'

A few seconds pause. 'Not buying it or can't buy it, Ray?'

Shit. 'Did they run a blood test on him?'

'That's going to take a little longer to get the results. Probably tomorrow, maybe Sunday. Sorry to be the one to tell you this, Ray. You gonna tell Edgar?'

'Not until the blood test comes back, at least.' From the noise in the background, I figured Allison was at a restaurant of some kind. I heard dishes and silverware clanging and lots of voices. 'Your guy show up yet?'

'No. I got here early to make sure I didn't miss him.'

'Thanks for calling,' I said and almost forgot why I wanted to call her. 'Can you check with your sources and see if the name David Henderson rings a bell. I think he's some kind of cop.'

'That the guy you met with Edgar?'

'Yeah.'

'Why don't you have Edgar . . . Oh, because he'll use his search engines and go down the rabbit hole?'

'Something like that.'

'And asking your uncle is out of the question,' she said. 'OK, I'll see what I can dig up, if anything.'

'You're still going to be home late?' I asked.

'Yeah. Sorry. I'll see ya at home.'

'You still not going to tell me who you're meeting with?'

'Not now, Ray. But I promise you'll find out soon enough.'

With that, she ended the call. I went back inside, where Edgar was still watching the game. He had his laptop open, looking at stats. 'How's Allison?'

'Busy.' He didn't need to know what we had spoken about. All that could wait. Right now was time for baseball and beer.

SIX

Mojo and his wife lived on the second floor of a two-story house not too far from school. This was one of those rare blocks in Williamsburg facing little to no risk of ever becoming hip. This street was filled with old-world Italian families who'd lived here for years. The women had parties where they made their own pasta sauce in their garages; a few of the homes had grape vines growing over their fences for winemaking; no house was more than three storys tall, and that's the way the folks on the block had liked it for the past hundred or so years.

Edgar, who was wearing his ever-present brown leather laptop bag over his shoulder, explained to me that the house MoJo had lived in had an apartment in the basement, a floor-through apartment on the first floor with backyard access – the 'Garden Apartment' in Brooklyn real estate circles – and two double bedrooms on the second. One of those was now a single-occupant residence, as MoJo's wife was now MoJo's widow.

And Lisa Joseph was a very pregnant widow. She was a beautiful African-American woman whose face reminded me of that TV actress who played a Washington, D.C., lawyer or journalist who apparently slept with the President of the United States when not practicing law or journalism. I'd seen the subway and bus ads, not the show.

'Come in,' she said, and Edgar and I squeezed past her belly into the apartment. 'It's not very clean, but . . .' Her voice trailed off as she shut the door.

I followed Edgar through the small kitchen into the living room. He took his bag off and sat down on the couch without being asked. I guessed he had been here before. I remained standing until Lisa said, 'Please, Raymond. Sit.' I did. 'Thank you both for coming. It was nice of you to send flowers, Edgar.'

She gestured to the bouquet that sat on the coffee table. For the second time in two days, I felt outclassed by Edgar. First the suit yesterday, now flowers.

'Can I get you anything?' Lisa asked. 'Iced tea, water?'

'No, thank you,' Edgar and I said at the same time. Edgar added, 'You're welcome for the flowers.' He ran his hands gently over the bag on his lap.

'How are you doing, Lisa?' I asked, because that's what people ask after other people lose a loved one.

She gave that some thought as she slid down into a big chair in the corner of the room. 'I don't know, Ray.' She placed her right hand on her stomach and gently tapped it. 'This little guy's been kicking up a storm and I hadn't been sleeping much anyway, so . . .' She took a deep breath. 'I got my sister and my mama coming up tonight. It took them a while to get coverage for the kids down there. Good to have cousins.'

'South Carolina,' Edgar told me. 'Are they still driving up?' he asked Lisa.

'They started out before sunrise. My sis just called me from Virginia. They won't get here much before midnight.'

'You shoulda let me fly them up, Lisa. MoJo would have insisted.'

'Edgar, you don't know my mama. She won't accept anything that comes close to smelling like a handout. Now my sister . . . she'da come first class if she could have. Bad enough she's gonna have to sleep on the fold-out in the baby's room.'

I smiled, thinking back to the time I'd flown with my mother out to California for a cousin's wedding and we got bumped up to first class. There were more buttons on the TV in front of her seat than she knew what to do with. But, as always, when it came to my mother, the food made up for it.

'I never thought to ask,' I said. 'What are the funeral arrangements?'

'There are none,' Lisa said. 'Not really. MoJo and I spoke about stuff like this. Neither one of us is . . . was religious. The whole church service and viewing and funeral mass, we just didn't want that.'

'But your mother and sister are coming up?'

'There will be a small memorial Monday night, down by the river and then at a bar afterwards. Maurice and I liked it down there. My mother and sister are not happy I'm not doing the whole "He's-With-God-Now" thing. But they're still coming, so . . .'

'Is there anything we can help you with before they get here?' I asked. 'You need anything moved or cleaned or anything? Any food shopping?'

Lisa shook her head. 'Thanks, but I'll clean a bit later. I can't be sitting around all day. I have some groceries being delivered in a few hours. And look around, Ray. We don't have too much in terms of furniture that needs to be moved. Except for the baby's room.' She drifted off for a few seconds. 'Everything else around here is done in MoJo's style; he always said he wanted to be able to move out in less than six hours, if needed.'

I knew that was her polite way of saying that ex-drug users like MoJo aren't used to having too much stuff as they were often forced to move because they didn't have enough money to make the rent. MoJo once told me that the six months he'd been in this apartment with Lisa was the longest he'd lived in one place since he turned twenty, almost ten years ago.

Edgar leaned forward. 'You said you had some stuff for me?'

'Oh, yeah. I meant to bring that in here.' She patted her belly again. 'Would you mind, Edgar? I put it all in an envelope with your name on it. I wasn't sure if any of it was important. It's in our bedroom on Maurice's desk by his laptop.'

Edgar stood. 'I got it.' Then he paused. 'OK to go in there?'

'Yes, Edgar,' Lisa said. 'It's OK.'

He looked uncomfortable. 'It's just that . . . you know . . . it's your bedroom . . .'

'Thank you, Edgar. But it's fine.'

He went to the door to our right and opened it. After waiting five seconds, he entered and Lisa and I exchanged slightly amused looks. 'He can be very respectful at times,' I explained. 'Sometimes overly so.'

She nodded. 'So I've noticed. We've had him over a few times. He's been really . . . I don't know . . . cute about the baby coming. He's acting like he's going to be an uncle, you know. It's kinda sweet. Now with . . .' She started to tear up. I was surprised it had taken this long. 'I don't know what I'm gonna do, Raymond.' Her hand made circles around her stomach. 'This was all we wanted,

Maurice and me.' She took a couple of breaths and then the tearing up turned into full-blown weeping.

I had spotted a box of tissues in the kitchen on the way in and went there now. When I came back into the living room, Edgar was standing by the bedroom door holding a large manila envelope with his name on it. I gave some tissues to Lisa as Edgar said, 'What happened?'

'I'll explain later, Edgar,' I said.

'Did I do something? Should I have not gone into the bedroom?'

'Nobody did anything, Edgar. We'll talk about it later.'

'I'm just tired is all, Edgar,' Lisa said. 'What I really need to do is try and take a nap before I tidy this place up and the food comes.' She adjusted the pillow behind her; she was going to take a nap right where she was. 'You mind seeing yourselves out? I'm finally comfortable in the longest damn time and I don't wanna move.'

'You sure you don't need us to do anything?'

'Thanks, Ray, but I'm good.' She shut her eyes. 'I just gotta sleep.'

'OK,' Edgar said. 'Bye. And thanks for the envelope.'

'You have Edgar's number, right?' I asked.

She mumbled something that sounded positive.

'Then call if you need anything.'

Another mumble and I motioned with my head for Edgar to start heading toward the door. He put the envelope in his bag. I followed him and made sure the door was locked. Neither one of us said a word until we were half a block from the apartment.

'I don't know if it gets tougher than that,' I said. 'Maybe losing a child, but . . .'

'MoJo had it all coming together,' Edgar said. 'All he could talk about was the baby and finishing up his community service so he could work full time at the company. He was even gonna do weekends until . . .' He stopped walking. 'Ah, Jeez. It's just me now, Ray. I'm not sure what I'm gonna do. I only started the company because I had MoJo. What am I going to do now?'

This was another characteristic of Edgar: when faced with anything along the lines of tragedy, he resorted to something that resembled selfishness. He often found the best way to deal with the world when it was raining shit was to withdraw into himself. Not that his concerns about the business were unfounded, more that he was basically not equipped to deal with mourning too long for his friend. I've learned at times like these, to keep him as much in the present as I could.

'Right now?' I said. 'Let's go do some lunch. You choose.'

Knowing what he'd choose, there was no surprise when he said, 'The LineUp.'

'Good idea,' I said. 'Feels like it's been hours since we've been there.'

Another good idea was we decided to walk. Since the weather was starting to act more like April, it allowed us to clear our heads, and the exercise made me feel I had earned the beer that had just been placed in front of me. I raised my glass to Edgar. 'Here's to life.' Edgar's pint remained on the bar. Being half-Irish, he should have known that was bad luck. 'I think MoJo would like the idea that we were toasting his new baby.'

Edgar gave me a brief smile, lifted his pint of Bass, and tapped it against mine. After the quickest of sips, he went back to perusing the items he had taken out of the envelope. From what I could tell, there was nothing too exciting in there: some paper clips, a cell phone, a couple of pens, some USB cords, and what I assumed were the receipts for these items. Most of the office supplies, Edgar explained, were being kept at his apartment until he and MoJo had procured a loan from the bank that would allow them to rent a real brick-and-mortar office where they could have clients come by. Nothing too big: just enough space to have meetings and maybe sell some of the less expensive security equipment.

Edgar picked up the cell phone and ran his fingers over it like it was the most fascinating thing he'd seen in months. He opened the case, observed it a little more and said, 'Jeez, Louise.'

'You didn't know he bought another phone?'

'First of all, any purchase over fifty dollars has to be approved by both of us. This goes for about four hundred online. Second of all,' he said as he continued to study the phone, 'it's not about this being a "cell phone."'

I looked again. Unless one of us was losing it, he was holding a cell phone and I told him as much.

He handed it to me. 'Here. Check it out.' His tone had taken on that teacher quality he had picked up from me over the years. 'What do you observe, Raymond?' He was laying it on thick now.

The first thing that came to mind was it was heavier than I had thought it would be. I said so and he nodded. I ran my fingers over it; there was nothing different there. I touched the screen and the number pad showed up. 'What's the code?'

He gave it to me and I entered it into the keypad. The normal stuff showed up and after about twenty seconds, I said, 'It's a phone.'

He took it back. 'Of course *that*'s a phone, Ray. That's how I knew the code. It's one of ours. It's not about the phone.'

I was confused. 'Then what is it about, Edgar?'

He smiled – for real this time – and slipped the phone out if its case and handed me back the case. I took a closer look and then I saw what he was going on about.

'This,' I said, 'looks like a camera case.'

He practically snapped it out of my hand before I realized I had just broken one of Edgar's sacred rules: *Never refer to any of his technological devices with anything but respect.*

'What you are referring to, Raymond,' he was close to snapping at me, 'is a cell phone case recorder that has the ability to record at a 1080p resolution, is motion-activated, and has a battery life of up to three hours. It also has a built-in memory of sixteen gigabytes.'

I stood corrected. It was not a camera case. 'And you use it for . . .?'

I got the 'Duh' face. 'We would be using it for recording people close-up without them knowing it, but we hadn't bought one yet and none of our clients have asked us to do that kind of surveillance.' A light bulb went off over his head and he grabbed the receipts off the bar and quickly found the one he was looking for. 'But here it says MoJo did buy one.' He gave the receipt a closer look. 'Eight days ago.'

'Without telling you, I assume?'

'Without telling me, which is a clear violation of our purchasing agreement. Now I have to ask – now I have to figure out why he did that.'

We gave that some thought. I sipped and came up with an idea after a few moments but waited to see what Edgar was thinking. After another half-minute, I finally picked up a USB cable. 'Can we hook this up and see if there's anything on there?'

Edgar nodded. 'That's good, Ray.' He removed his laptop from his bag, turned it and the case recorder on, and connected the recorder to the computer using one of the USB cords. He pressed a bunch of buttons and in less than a minute a picture popped up on the screen. It was a still shot of a man who looked slightly familiar to me. In the same way a guy you saw on a commercial many times five years ago looks familiar. He was sitting behind a desk, wearing a white shirt with a blue tie. His hair was very gray, and my guess was he had many years – and quite a few pounds – on me. He reminded me of a mix between Santa Claus and Ernest Hemingway. Edgar pressed Play. The man was in the middle of speaking.

'*That's the way we see it, too, Mr Joseph,*' the gray man said. '*And if we can bring it within our budget, I can sell it to my guys as a necessity.*'

'*I don't see that being a problem, sir.*' The camera stayed focused on Gray Man but that was clearly MoJo speaking. Edgar's face showed real confusion. '*I'll just run it by my people,*' MoJo continued, '*and make sure they see things the way we do. I mean, if we don't look out for each other . . .*'

'*No one else will,*' Gray Man said. '*I had a feeling we were simpatico on this.*'

Edgar clicked on Pause. '"My people"?' he said. '*I'm* his people. At least I thought I was his people.'

I touched Edgar on the elbow. 'MoJo's probably just trying to make your company seem bigger than it is. He's selling your services.' I looked at the screen. 'Do you recognize that guy he's talking to?'

'Nope,' Edgar said, and then after thinking about it for a bit, added, 'Kinda, almost. Like maybe if his hair wasn't so gray and the beard, you know?'

'Yeah, I do.'

Edgar clicked on Play.

'*Very much so,*' MoJo said. '*So, just to review, we're looking at security for the front drive, about a dozen motion-detection cameras, four motion-detection flood lights for outside the office, security for your phones and laptops, and a fully accessible GPS system for all your vehicles.*'

Gray Man rubbed his beard. '*That's gonna be the tricky part, Mr Joseph. Mosta those vehicles are privately owned. I don't want my guys knowing I'm keeping track of them, if you know what I mean. That's why I'm going outside with this job. We usually take care of it ourselves, understand?*'

'*Exactly, sir,*' MoJo said. '*The GPS wouldn't be doing its job if the folks you're tracking knew about it. That's why you hire us.*' MoJo was good at this.

Gray Man stood up. He was bigger than I had first imagined. His white shirt was fighting with his belly and was a few cheeseburgers away from losing. He offered his hand out to MoJo, who we still could not see.

'*Pleasure doing business with ya, Mr Joseph. I'll hear from you in a few days?*'

The camera now moved and all we could see was darkness. MoJo must have put the recorder in his pocket. The sound was a little muffled now, but MoJo clearly said, '*As soon as I run the numbers by the guys at the office, sir. But from what we've discussed so far, this project is extremely doable.*'

Gray Man laughed. '*Good to hear, son. That's good to hear.*' A brief pause, then, '*You know we're gonna have to take you out the same way we took you in?*'

MoJo's turn to laugh. '*If I didn't, I wouldn't be much of a security consultant.*'

Gray Man laughed one more time, MoJo joined in, and then the sound and picture disappeared. Edgar pressed another button bringing the video back to the beginning.

I watched as Edgar continued staring at Gray Man. This was now more info he had to process. I didn't know how much he could handle at one time. Between seeing MoJo's pregnant widow, getting an unexpected envelope filled with business stuff he didn't know about, and then watching the video of MoJo doing security business with another guy Edgar had never seen before, I was expecting a mental shutdown. The best thing for me to do was to stay shut and be patient. Good thing there was a beer in front of me, and a pre-game show on the television.

'You boys playing with your toys again?'

I turned and got a full kiss on the mouth from Allison. I was going to ask how she knew where I was, but I was smarter than that. She gave Edgar a kiss on the back of his head. Deep in thought, he barely noticed. Allison took a look at Gray Man's picture on the laptop and said, 'Why the hell are you watching him?'

When neither of us responded, she pointed at the screen. 'That's Duke Lansing,' she said. I gave her a blank stare. Edgar remained silent. 'If you didn't know that, why are you watching his show?'

'Show?' I asked.

Allison put her hands on my shoulders. 'What am I missing here, Ray?'

'Less than I am. Who's Duke Lansing and why does he . . .?' Now it came to me.

'The White Supremacist guy?' Edgar said.

'The one and only.' Allison squeezed between us. 'And it's White *Nationalist*. And calling it a show is being kind. He has a channel on social media. He spews his racist shit in the guise of American Values and people who probably still use rotary phones call the show to speak with him. I'm actually thinking of doing a series on what's left of his movement.' As Mikey came by she ordered a white wine. Working tonight? Then she repeated, 'Why the hell are you watching this?'

As I explained, it came to me why I had had trouble placing Lansing's face. Five years ago he had darker hair, fifty fewer pounds on him, was beardless and running for a seat on the New York City Council. Some right-wing group had paid for a lot of TV spots that played during the local news and Yankees games. His main point seemed to be that *certain* people were ruining our city, our state and our country, and those *certain* people didn't look like us.

'Edgar,' Allison said, 'you were working for him and didn't know who he was?'

'I wasn't working for him.' Pause. 'MoJo was.'

Allison and I both got silent again. After a while, we both said, 'Shit.'

Edgar, eyes still on the screen, agreed. 'Yeah,' he said. 'Crapola.'

SEVEN

We all had fresh drinks in front of us and were sharing plates of chicken wings, calamari, and onion rings. Looks like I picked the wrong day to start on that diet. Allison dipped a ring in a mixture of hot sauce and ketchup and brought us up to date.

'After he lost the city council race,' she said, 'Lansing and his family went underground. Some say literally.'

'Meaning . . .?' I said.

'They owned land upstate. Dozens of acres by some accounts. He's reportedly got some rebuilt bomb shelters on the property and the rumor was that he lived in them after the election, fearing for his family's life.'

'With all the shit that came out of his mouth,' I said, 'I don't blame him.'

'I tried to get an interview with him after he lost. I was still the new girl at the paper and thought it would be a big scoop, get my name out there, so I went up to what he called his estate. Big house, no one home. I walked around for a few hours hoping to find someone to talk to.'

'Did you?'

'A couple of guys dressed in camouflage from head to toe, carrying automatic weapons, who asked me to leave.'

'Asked?'

She laughed, but not like I had said something funny. 'After I assured them I was not a member of the Jewish-run liberal media, only a real estate agent looking for the owner.'

'Quick thinking,' Edgar said.

'Standard line for reporters. Especially those of us who work for the Jewish-run liberal media.' She took a sip of wine. 'There have been three times I've been afraid for my life. That was one of them.'

I knew about one of those times – Allison had been run over by a Jeep while running in high school – and made a mental note to find out about the other. 'So, did they ever resurface?' I asked. 'The Lansings?'

'Not that I know of. The house and property were sold. They have that web channel and a podcast but that could be coming from anywhere in the world.'

'Or beyond,' Edgar added. 'With the right equipment, you can hide the physical location of your server and your phone.' He thought about that. 'It really sucks that some people use this technology to spread hate instead of to bring people together. Then they hide behind the same technology because they're cowards.'

I put my hand on Edgar's shoulder. 'That was well said.'

'I don't get people sometimes, Ray.' He touched his pint glass but made no effort to lift it. 'And what was MoJo doing with him? He woulda known I wouldn't work with someone like Lansing.'

'Maybe that's why he didn't tell you,' Allison said.

'No, no. There's more to it than that. There has to be.'

I knew there didn't have to be; Edgar wanted there to be. That was another tough thing about being Edgar. Like Kennedy said, some people see the world the way it should be and ask, 'Why not?' JFK never had to deal with the Internet.

'You said so yourself, Edgar. With the baby coming, MoJo was looking forward to earning more money. Maybe this was something he felt he had to do and didn't want to tell you because he knew you'd say no.'

'No!' Edgar said loud enough to get the attention of everyone at the bar. 'MoJo would not do that. It's not the way we set things up. We agreed to discuss any purchases over fifty dollars and not to take on any clients without the other partner knowing about it.' He took a few breaths to make up for the ones lost during that little outburst. 'That's what we agreed on. Any change in the rules had to be discussed.'

'We know that, Edgar,' Allison said just above a whisper. 'But having a child on the way changes the rules sometimes. It's possible that – with his past history of instability and now finally getting himself clean – MoJo wanted this Lansing job so much that he changed the rules without telling you, knowing you'd say no and he'd miss out on all this money for his family.'

The three of us went silent again and the rest of the bar patrons went back to whatever they'd been doing before Edgar's outburst. After a few more sips of beer and eating the rest of the appetizers, I couldn't hold it in anymore. There was – as my mother would say – an elephant in the room that no one was addressing.

'How,' I finally said, 'did MoJo get in touch with Duke Lansing?' Edgar and Allison turned their gazes to me. 'If this guy and his family were laying so low that no one knew where they were, how did they get in touch with each other? Did MoJo find Lansing? Or was it the other way around? These are two guys from completely different worlds. Lansing would never do business with MoJo if he knew MoJo's pregnant wife was black. That was one of his big things,' I continued. 'The mixing of the races. The extinction of the white male by means of miscegenation. He stoked up a lot of fear and anger during that campaign by basically saying, "They're stealing our men. They're mating with our women." I don't think any candidate for any office anywhere got more use out of the word "mongrel." This was not a business relationship that should have happened.' I paused. 'So how did it?'

This question just brought about more silence. Mikey, who'd just come on shift, must have picked up that the silence was tension-filled, so without saying a word he brought us another round of drinks and cleared our plates away. I gave him a Thank You smile just before Edgar spoke again.

'Well, I wouldn't know, would I? He didn't tell me shit.'

In all the years I've known him, that may have been only the third time I'd heard a curse word cross Edgar's lips. This was eating him up.

'Is there anything else in the bag, Edgar?' Allison asked. 'Something that maybe connects MoJo to Lansing?'

Edgar went through the receipts again, this time much slower. Nothing there. He opened the box of paper clips and found nothing unusual. He picked up the two pens and rolled them around with his fingers. He put one down, but seemed extra interested in the one he was still holding. He looked back at the receipts and shook his head.

'What's up?' I asked.

'Spy pen,' he said. 'Another thing I didn't know he had, and it's not listed on the receipts like the camera case recorder is.'

'A spy pen,' Allison said. 'Is that what it sounds like?'

'Yep.' Edgar placed the pen in his shirt pocket and rotated it so the clip was facing us. 'I just click this and it records. You can even write with it.'

'Sounds like something out of James Bond,' I said.

He took it out. With great care, he unscrewed the pen so it was now in two parts. He removed something and held it up for Allison and me to check out. 'A micro SD card,' he explained. 'You get about an hour on one charge of the pen and thirty-two gigs of memory with the card. A lot of corporate guys and gals use them to record meetings. This is the kinda stuff we were going to sell when we opened our office. We have a few at my place. I don't know why MoJo has his own.'

I looked at the card. 'Can you put that in your computer and see what's on it?'

Without a word, he slipped the card into the side of his laptop, pressed a few buttons again and up came a picture on the screen. This picture was not as clear as the other one, but we could easily make out a man of about thirty with glasses and a dark beard. The guy was wearing a white sweatshirt and jeans. Edgar pressed Play and the man started talking.

'. . . *to see you again, Maurice. How's Lisa?*'

'*Getting bigger every day,*' MoJo said. '*June fifth. We're glad she doesn't have to carry over the summer.*'

'*Thank God for small blessings,*' the man said. '*You've seen the guys I guess?*'

'*Most of them,*' MoJo said. '*Everybody's looking good.*'

'*You're a good role model, Maurice. It's nice you were able to take the time and come up. They need to see how well you're doing as much as you want to see them.*'

'*Working works, right?*' MoJo said.

The man laughed. '*Don'tcha love a rule that fits on a bumper sticker?*'

'*Yeah. Even I can remember them.*'

The picture froze and the three of us looked at each other. Edgar said, 'I guess the battery ran out. Maybe he didn't know he was recording.'

'Any idea who that was?' I asked.

He shook his head. 'Nope.' Then he leaned into the screen and studied it for a while. 'There's a logo on the sweatshirt,' he said. 'Looks like a house and a bunch of trees. No idea.'

I got closer to the screen and saw what Edgar saw, except I had seen that logo before. It took about ten seconds to remember where.

'That's the residential facility MoJo was at. *Newer Leaves.*'

'You've been there?' Allison asked.

'No. It was on the letterhead of their stationery when they sent me the paperwork to sponsor MoJo at the school. Corny name, but good program.'

'Did he say anything about going up there, Edgar?'

'Not to me. But there's no reason he would tell me, I guess. I mean if he's keeping the other secrets from me, then I guess there's—'

I held up my hand. 'Part of the program required MoJo to go back up to Newer Leaves on a regular basis. It was like part check-in and part showing the other residents what you were up to. Like the guy said, he was a good role model. MoJo also kept a journal while at the school. I think he took it upstate whenever he visited.'

We all took final sips from our glasses and Mikey was right with us as he placed fresh ones in front of us. 'You guys watching anything good?'

Edgar quickly shut the screen down. 'No, Mikey. Nothing.'

'Fine, man.' Mikey picked up a bar rag. 'Just asking.' He walked away.

'So what do we do with this stuff, Raymond?' Edgar asked.

I gave that some thought. 'You gotta let Detective Royce see the video with Duke Lansing. Too big to be a coincidence that MoJo has a meeting with that guy and then ends up dead.'

Edgar closed his eyes. 'You think Lansing had something to do with MoJo's—'

'I don't think anything yet, Edgar. That's going to be up to Royce to decide.'

Edgar got quiet for about thirty seconds. 'Can you call Royce?'

'Don't you think that's something you should do? MoJo was your partner and this is a business thing.'

I believed every word I had said. I also believed the more I got involved with Royce, the more pissed off he'd be. I didn't need that; this investigation didn't need that.

'Besides, you just had a good talk with him. You guys exchanged cards and said you'd be in touch if anything came up.' I touched his shoulder. 'This is something that came up, Edgar.'

Again, he got quiet. I decided that if he asked me one more time, I'd agree to do it. Reluctantly. He asked one more time. *Shit.*

'OK,' I said. 'But this is the kind of stuff we've been talking about, Edgar. I can't keep holding your hand. You have a business now. I'll help out when I can, but it's your circus, your monkeys.'

'Thanks, Ray.'

I looked at my watch and decided, 'I'll call him in the morning. There's no rush and it's a Saturday. The last thing he needs right now is to hear from me.'

Edgar picked up the pen and examined it more closely. 'The stuff I have at home is much better than this. This looks like it's from a couple of years ago.'

'Maybe MoJo was just using it as a pen,' Allison suggested.

'I guess. Why would he secretly be taping up at the recovery house? You really think he didn't know it was recording?'

'Like you said, it's an old pen and a recent recording. He's talking about Lisa being pregnant. My uncle always tells his cops, "When you hear hooves, think horses, not zebras."' When I realized Edgar didn't get that, I added, 'The obvious answer is usually the right one. He was using the spy pen as a pen and it must've had a little juice left in it.'

Then again, if I believed it was too big a coincidence for MoJo to be secretly recording Duke Lansing around the time of his death, what made the other recording more than mere coincidence?

And then I was reminded of something else my Uncle Ray always says: *Ray, you think too damned much.*

EIGHT

I found out on Sunday morning – along with everybody else who subscribed to and read *New York Here and Now* – who Allison had been meeting with on Friday night. I was sitting on the futon in our living room, drinking coffee, eating a buttered bagel, and reading her website on my laptop.

WHITE NATIONALIST TO AMERICAN RUNAWAY
A YOUNG MAN'S JOURNEY OUT OF NYC WHITE SUPREMACY
First in a series by Allison Rogers

Harlan S. stands just a little over 5 feet 6 inches and weighs maybe 140 pounds wearing the skin he was born in, but he is the owner of 'one hell of a right hand.' He knows this because even at the tender young age of sixteen, he has used it to get himself into and out of trouble any number of times.

'Lost count after a dozen or so fights,' he tells me at a New York City area diner. 'I don't mean to say I'm proud of that.' He pauses to sip from his diet cola. 'Not anymore, I mean.'

If you didn't know any better, just by looking at Harlan – not his real name – you'd think he was a tourist from the American Heartland. He's got the blond hair and blue eyes of a Missouri farm boy and the muscles to go with them. If his haircut were any shorter, you'd think he was heading off to boot camp. Or maybe posing for a White Nationalist poster.

Which he has.

'I was born into it,' he explains. 'Just like babies are born

Catholic or Jewish or Muslim. I didn't have a choice. My whole family was White Nationalist, so I was White Nationalist.'

But Harlan was not born in the Midwest or Appalachia or someplace where tourists have difficulty getting a cell phone signal. He was born right here in New York City. It doesn't matter which borough; Harlan is a born-and-bred native New Yorker.

He is one of us. Now he wants out of what he was born into.

'I've done some terrible things,' he tells me, his blue eyes getting shiny. 'Ever since I can remember, it's been Race, Family, Country. In that order. So if I did something bad to "protect" any of those three things, it wasn't considered bad. I was praised and celebrated. Like a Little Leaguer hitting a home run. Some of the stuff I've done's been . . .'

As he trails off, I can't help but think, here's a kid who should be enjoying tenth grade, playing sports, chasing girls. Instead, he's afraid of things the rest of us take for granted: Where's my next meal coming from? Where do I sleep tonight?

And, worst of all: What if my family finds me?

Harlan S. is from the (Home) School of Hard Knocks.

'I never met a black kid until I ran away,' he says. 'Not in the sense that most people mean. I mean I saw them on the other side of police barricades. I was close enough to throw rocks at them, let the air out of their daddy's and mammy's tires. But *met* met? Nope. Same goes for Hispanics, Jews, Muslims, Chinese. I didn't know anyone except white Christians.'

The African-American server comes over to our table and asks if there's anything else we'd like.

'No, ma'am,' Harlan says. As she walks away, he whispers, 'See that? That woulda been impossible for me three months ago.'

We plan to start talking about those three months – and a lot of what led up to them – in our next meeting. Right now, Harlan has to get back to the shelter where he's been staying – hiding, truth be told. A place, he told me, his family will never think to look for him.

'It's like the United Nations in there. And they got a curfew,' he explains. 'For everybody.'

I put some money down on the table and we exit the diner. Harlan takes a deep breath as if the air a few blocks from the Brooklyn/Queens Expressway were refreshing. He shoves his hands into the pockets of his jeans in an Aw-Shucks kind of way.

'I'll call you,' he says to me. That's the way it has to be for now. Harlan has no phone of his own and there's no other way to reach him. He's not even sure where he'll sleep tomorrow night.

Harlan S. lives in the now. He has to; it's all he has left.

'Wow,' I said when I was done. 'That is really good stuff, Allie.' I paused to take a sip of my coffee. 'I mean like Jimmy Breslin/ Pete Hamill good.' Part of me knew I was kissing her ass a bit, comparing her to two of the best investigative reporters to ever write for New York City papers, but I meant it. I skimmed through it again. 'I see why you were so surprised the other night when you saw Duke Lansing on Edgar's computer. You think Harlan is connected to Lansing?'

'Harlan's never come right out and said so. I'll push around the edges of it the next time we speak. I'll obviously find a way to work it into the series. But I don't want to scare Harlan off by asking more than he's ready to tell me. He's just a kid. A scared kid.'

I gave that some thought. 'You know I usually don't believe in coincidences.'

'It's not as coincidental as you think, Ray.' She paused. 'The other night when I saw that video with MoJo and Lansing, I wasn't as surprised as I let on.'

'What does that mean?'

She looked like a kid who'd just been caught lying. She tapped the computer screen. 'MoJo put me in touch with Harlan. Now that part of the story is weird.'

'I've got nothing but time,' I said, trying to hide the fact that I was unhappy that she'd kept this from me. I took a final bite of my bagel and another sip of coffee. 'Tell me.'

'You remember that part of the video MoJo took with Lansing when Lansing said something along the lines of MoJo was going to have to leave the same way he came in?'

'You spoke with MoJo about what he was doing?'

'I did. And he made me promise not to tell anyone. Especially you and Edgar. He did not want you two involved.' She waited for me to say something. When I didn't she continued. 'The part about how MoJo should come and go?'

'I wasn't sure what that meant.'

'MoJo told me it was like something out of a bad spy film. He was instructed to drive upstate to a service station and wait for one of Lansing's people to pick him up.'

'OK.'

'When MoJo got picked up – each time at a different service station – they blindfolded him so he couldn't see where they were going. And where they were going was Lansing's secret compound.'

'That does sound like a bad movie.' It also sounded like something Allison was going to have to tell Detective Royce. Holding back stuff from me was one thing; not telling the detective-in-charge was quite another.

'Anyway,' Allison continued. 'MoJo had been there a few times because he was doing business with Lansing. He told MoJo that his group, The New White Man, had been receiving lots of threats lately. Texts and emails to their website mostly, some from other ultra-right-wing groups. You'd think there'd be enough hate and fear to go around, right? Lansing really did feel the need to upgrade his security.'

'Why MoJo though? How did Lansing know about him?'

'MoJo didn't tell me that. He said it was better off I didn't know.'

'Any idea why he was so secretive?' I said, and then realized the obvious.

'He was playing it safe. For both of us. This is a White Nationalist, remember.'

'And how did he run into this guy in your piece? Harlan?'

'That's even weirder. Long story short, Harlan somehow hid himself in the trunk of the car that shuttled MoJo back and forth between the service station and the compound. The kid's pretty slick. He was able to get into and out of the trunk without being seen. Like if Houdini were in the KKK.'

I let out some air that sounded like a laugh. It wasn't. 'And this kid just calls you up when he feels like talking?'

'Friday was the first time he called. MoJo told me he'd given Harlan my info, but that was it. MoJo knew Harlan had a story to tell. No promises, no guarantee that he'd call. We're supposed to meet again later this week. That's not a sure thing either.'

'You think he's gonna be OK out there by himself?'

'Harlan was raised pretty much to be a survivalist, Ray. That's a big skill when you're a White Nationalist. I'm not sure whether he's staying in the city or whatever, but between the shelters and Dumpster diving, I hate to say it, but he's going to be fine.'

The thought of any kid having to live like that in this city put a burn in my gut. The richest city in the world and we've got a sub-demographic who live off other people's garbage. I know the movies make it seem romantic sometimes, but it's anything but. I've heard that New York City throws away almost forty percent of the food it has, enough to feed some small countries.

'I know it's not in your piece,' I said, 'but do you think he knows anything about MoJo's murder? Did he say anything?'

'If he does, he's playing it real close to the vest,' she said. 'I've thought about that, though. But he's been in hiding for over a week and concentrating mostly on staying underground and alive. Again, I'll try to work the conversation around to it.'

My mind started working the way certain people keep complaining that my mind works. 'There might be a chance that someone from Lansing's group made the connection between MoJo and Harlan and came looking this way.'

Allison thought about that. 'That makes some kind of sense, but then why kill MoJo? If he's the link to Harlan, they just got rid of him.'

She had a point there. 'I'm still not comfortable believing that MoJo was willing to work for someone like Duke Lansing. We weren't best friends, but I knew him pretty well; MoJo didn't strike me as the kind of guy to do something just for the money. Even with a kid on the way.'

'You have any other ideas that might explain what we saw on the recording?'

'No, I don't.' And now the tough part. 'Royce needs to know about this, you know that, right?' She already knew I was planning to call Royce about MoJo's recording of Lansing.

'Know about what part of this, Ray? I'm not going to risk scaring Harlan away. He's frightened enough right now. The last thing he needs is the cops on his ass.'

'I know that. But you agree Royce needs to know MoJo was involved with Duke Lansing. I think that includes your boy Harlan.'

'Then he's going to want to talk with Harlan. I'm not sure about that.'

'It's not your decision, Allie.'

'I'm not saying it is, but is sure as hell isn't yours,' she said. 'It's not even Royce's. You read the piece, Ray. This kid is all over the place. He may be a survivalist, but he's frightened. If he doesn't want to be found, trust me, he's not going to be found.'

Goddamn it. 'So I have to call Royce and tell him about MoJo and Lansing while *not* telling him about this kid Harlan who may be connected to MoJo's murder?'

Allison leaned back on the futon and closed her eyes. 'That's what I need you to do, Ray. Think you can control yourself?'

I stood up. 'Don't do that, Allie. We've had this talk before. I have information Royce needs. You have information Royce needs. The information is almost certainly connected. If it helps Royce find out who killed MoJo, I think he should know about it.'

'And,' she said, eyes still closed, 'if it ends up scaring Harlan away – or worse – what then? You willing to make that call? Literally?'

I'm not proud of the next word out of my mouth, but if I had held it in I think I might have imploded. *'Fuck!'*

That got her to open her eyes. 'Real mature, Ray. Is that how you teach your students to handle conflict? Pick the first four-letter word that comes to mind and scream it loud enough for the neighbors to hear?'

Like I said, I wasn't proud of myself. I took a few deep breaths and picked my phone off the coffee table and walked to the kitchen.

'Where are you going?' Allison asked.

'To the balcony,' I answered in the calmest tone I could muster. 'I need to call Detective Royce.'

'Be careful what you say, Ray.'

I looked at her and pointed my index finger at her. 'Don't,' I said. Again, I'm not real proud of that. My conflict resolution training said to never point your finger in anger. I headed out to the balcony and pressed the number for Royce.

'You have got to be kidding me, Mr Donne,' he said. 'I'm just getting out of my car and heading into church.'

'I wouldn't have called if it weren't important.'

'No,' he said. 'You wouldn't have called if you didn't *think* it was important. I've learned there's a big difference when it comes to you.'

I breathed. Deeply. I decided to come right out with it. Just like I teach the students to at school.

'Maurice Joseph was somehow involved with Duke Lansing.'

That was met with ten seconds of silence. Then, 'You are talking about *the* Duke Lansing, I assume?'

'Is there another one?'

A few more beats passed. 'And would you please explain what you mean by "somehow involved"?'

I told him about the recording we had found on MoJo's phone. I did not mention MoJo putting Allison in touch with Harlan. Yet.

'So,' Royce said, 'if I'm hearing you right, Mr Joseph was doing some work for Duke Lansing and Lansing had no idea that Mr Joseph was recording him.'

'You heard me correctly, Detective.'

'And you found this out when?'

'Yesterday,' I said.

'After I interviewed Edgar Martinez who also didn't know about this until yesterday even though they were partners?'

'You know what I know.'

'That's not a comforting thought, Mr Donne.' I heard a car door shut. Maybe slam was more like it. 'Where is this recording now?'

'I have it with me. It was making Edgar uncomfortable, so he gave it to me. We want you to have it.'

'How nice of you both.' I could hear him thinking. 'OK, let me explain what is going to happen. You're at home with the recording?'

'Yes.'

'You are to stay there with the recording, Mr Donne. You got that?'

'Got it.'

'I will be going to church with my family, then a quick brunch and I will be at your place by two o'clock. I assume you're still at the same address?'

'I am.'

'Good.' He waited a bit before saying, 'Do you pray, Mr Donne?'

'No, Detective. I do not.'

Just before hanging up, he said, 'You might wanna start.'

NINE

I slipped my phone into my pocket, leaned on the edge of the balcony, and took in the city skyline in the late morning sun. It was promising to be another nice spring day. Like the man said, days like this made me think people who didn't live in New York City were just kidding themselves. Maybe Allison and I could walk over to the Williamsburg flea market after Royce came. That's if we were still speaking. Allison and I, that is.

'What did Royce say?'

Allison was holding a coffee cup and had one foot on the balcony and the other inside, almost as if my answer would be the determining factor in whether she joined me outside.

'He's coming by around two to pick up the Lansing recording. He also suggested I might want to try praying.'

'Right after the Pope develops a taste for Brooklyn Pilsner,' she said with a smile. Then she got serious. 'Did you mention Harlan?'

'You know I didn't, Allie. I wouldn't do that until we spoke more about it.'

'Then let's do that.'

I looked at the woman I loved. I looked up at the clear blue Brooklyn sky. 'How about we table that for now? Let me give the stuff to Royce and take my licks. You and I can enjoy today and talk about Harlan later.'

'And you'll be able to enjoy the day without settling the Harlan thing?'

'Why wouldn't I?'

'Because when something is running laps in the gray area of your brain,' she said, 'you tend to get real distracted. Some of my girlfriends might say morose.'

I looked at her and waited for a smile. None came. 'Good thing you're not one of your girlfriends, huh?'

'Good thing.' She stepped out onto the balcony. 'We make for weird bedfellows, Raymond. None of my other friends have this . . . issue with their partners.'

'Issue?' I repeated. 'Is that what this is? An issue?'

'None are in relationships where they have to tiptoe around when they're talking about their jobs. None of them are with . . . someone like you.'

Another deep breath. 'And what am I like?'

'You know the answer to that, Ray. You may be a schoolteacher now, but you're still a cop inside,' she said. 'You always want to do the right thing – what you think is the right thing – and have trouble hearing the other side.' She came two steps closer and touched my elbow. 'Remember how my parents reacted when they heard I was . . . with a school teacher?'

'They were thrilled you had a partner with a steady job and health insurance.'

'They don't see this side of the relationship.' She did that thing where she went back and forth with her index finger: me, her, me, her. 'They don't realize that you do police work for a hobby.'

'*You* know, though,' I said. 'You know that I can't ignore stuff that comes my way if I can do something about it. And it's not like I seek this shit out, Allie.'

'I did and I know,' she admitted. 'I didn't know it was going to be this frequent. I met you when Frankie Rivas' father was killed and Frankie and his sister went missing. Then there was Dougie Lee getting murdered. After we started dating it was Ricky Torres, and I almost lost you in that shooting.' She paused to sniffle. 'Then you find Marty Stover after he got killed at his own party. Now this.' She came close and hugged me. 'It's not that I don't appreciate your help with my career, Raymond.' She let out a small giggle. 'But I think I'm beginning to feel like the spouse of a cop. I never know what's going to happen when you leave for work.'

Holding onto the hug, I said, 'This coming from the journalist who trespassed onto a White Nationalist's property five years ago and is currently starting a series of clandestine interviews with a runaway who – according to him – is in danger of being killed by the people he ran away from.'

I could feel her smiling on my chest. 'We do make an interesting couple, don't we,' she said.

'"Interesting" is an interesting word for the kind of couple we make, Allison.'

'Good thing we found each other, huh?'

'More than a good thing,' I said, squeezing her tighter.

We stayed like that for maybe another minute: two people hugging each other in silence as the world of Brooklyn did whatever it does on beautiful Sunday mornings. The silence was broken when Allison said, 'So, you won't tell Royce about Harlan?'

'Shut up,' I said.

'OK.'

Almost to the second when one-fifty-nine turned into two o'clock, my phone went off. It was Royce. 'Hey,' I said.

'I'm downstairs. Buzz me up.'

'Why didn't you just—' He'd already hung up. When I opened my door to let him in, I finished my question. 'Why didn't you just buzz up, Detective.'

'I was afraid,' he said as he stepped into my apartment, 'that my annoyed tone wouldn't translate so well through the intercom.'

As he passed me, I told him he had nothing to worry about there.

'The recording?' he said.

I stepped over to the coffee table just as Allison was stepping out of the bedroom. She had changed from her breakfast clothes into a more Sunday-morning-going-for-a-stroll outfit: shorts, a Word bookstore T-shirt, and sneakers.

'Good mor–good afternoon, Detective Royce,' she said. 'Like some coffee?'

'I just ate, Ms Rogers. But thanks.' He turned to check out the impressive view from our kitchen. 'Nice piece on your website,' he said. 'You were kind enough to get my good side.'

'Wow,' Allison said. 'I didn't know you read my work.'

'I don't,' he said as he turned back to us. 'My daughter has this weird hobby of googling my name once a week. This one was quite the surprise. You open yourself up to charges of interfering with an ongoing investigation with stunts like that, Ms Rogers.'

'Not until they pass some laws concerning new technology and air space. As far as I know, I broke no laws by shooting that video, Detective.'

A sound came out of his mouth that was halfway between anger and exasperation. One of the words rhymed with truck.

'Here's the recording,' I said, holding out the phone case. Royce gave it a weird look until I explained what it was.

'Fucking technology.' The word came out clearly when he wanted

it to. He held up the case. 'Who else knows about this, Mr Donne?'
He said it to me, but looked straight at Allison.

'Just Edgar, Allison, and I,' I said. 'And now you.'

'I'm not going to see or hear about it – *or from it* – on any online
news sites?'

Allison spoke before I could. 'No, Detective. You won't.'

'Because,' he said, 'that *would be* real close to breaking a law,
Ms Rogers. Publicly releasing evidence in an ongoing investigation
is up to the police, not the press. The First Amendment protects
you only so far. Even on the web.'

'I understand that.'

'Good.' Back to me. 'Just so I have this clear, Mr Donne. As far
as you know' – he held up the recording – 'this went from Mr
Joseph, to his wife, to Mr Martinez, to you, and then to me.'

'As far as I know, yes.' He was rightly concerned about the chain
of evidence if the recording were ever entered into evidence in a
court of law. 'Ms Rogers did see it as well, but she was never in
possession of it.'

'And I know the answer to this already, but I need to ask. Are
you aware of any other copies of this evidence, Mr Donne?'

'No. I am not.'

'Good.' Royce looked around my apartment. 'The place looks
better than the last time I was here.'

'The last time you were here,' I said for Allison's benefit, 'the
place had just been broken into.'

'There is that. But there's also what my wife would call a . . .
woman's touch to the place now. It suits you, Mr Donne. It's the
kind of look that says the guy who lives here knows how and when
to mind his own business.'

'Royce,' I said, 'do I need to remind you that I did not go looking
for this recording?'

'You don't need to, no,' he said. 'It is good to hear it, though.'

He headed toward the door. I said, 'Any developments on the
case?'

He held up the phone case recorder. 'One,' he said. 'But I'm not
at liberty to discuss it at this point. With friends, family, or the press.'
He kept walking. 'I'll see myself out, Mr Donne. You two have a
great day now.'

After the door closed, I said to Allison, 'That was relatively
painless.'

'Maybe he prayed on it while at church.'

'Possibly,' I said. 'Let me get dressed and we'll hit the flea market. Then maybe Teddy's for an early dinner after?'

'Sounds like a plan.'

TEN

Allison and I got back to the apartment just in time to see the last of the orange sky sinking behind the skyline. The day, the weekend, was almost over and when I reflected on the past dozen hours – Sunday brunch, hanging out on the deck in seventy-degree weather, giving evidence in a murder case to the detective-in-charge, going to the flea market by the East River, dinner and beers at a favorite Williamsburg hangout with the woman I loved – I found myself feeling lucky. It's a weird feeling for me, as I don't believe in luck. I believe in things happening because we make choices.

Allison went into the bedroom to change. I grabbed a beer from the fridge and went back out on the balcony to catch that early evening breeze. My cell phone rang. Rachel.

'Little sister,' I said.

'Ray,' she said. 'Murcer and I just got back from upstate and heard the news. Are you OK?' Murcer was my brother-in-law. We also used to be cops together. That's how he met my sister. He was now a detective.

'Not exactly OK, Rache, but I'm fine. MoJo was a good guy. I spent some time with his wife yesterday. She's the one you should be concerned about.'

'I know. Do the cops know what happened?'

'Just what you've read in the papers. Did you see Allie's story online?'

'Yeah, of course. We didn't have Internet upstate – more like we were avoiding it – but as soon as we got home, I checked my email and went online.'

My sister Rachel and her husband did this twice a year: they'd take a four-day weekend away from the city and away from phones and computers. With her job as head of marketing for a greeting card company and his as a detective in Manhattan, they deserved a few days off the grid a couple of times a year.

'Murcer called some friends in Brooklyn North,' Rachel said. 'Did you know that MoJo was using again?'

'They don't know that for sure, Rachel. They found heroin on him. The results from the toxicology report aren't back yet.'

She was quiet for a few moments and then said, 'Yeah, they are, Ray. I'm sorry. I thought you knew. Murcer told me they did a rush job and MoJo tested positive.'

Shit. 'For heroin?'

'Worse,' she said. 'Fentanyl.'

Holy shit. Fentanyl was fifty to a hundred times stronger than heroin. What the hell was MoJo thinking?

'That's not possible, Rachel. When MoJo was using, it was heroin. He wouldn't be stupid enough to go near fentanyl.'

More silence. Then, 'Listen to yourself, Ray. Just because you knew the guy doesn't mean he's above making bad moves. You know as well as I do the number of people in rehab who slip.'

She was right. But fentanyl? No way. Not unless he didn't know it was fentanyl. Not only was fentanyl stronger than heroin, it was also cheaper. A lot of dealers were not above mixing heroin with the cheaper stuff and selling it for what the buyer thought was pure H. If that were the case here, MoJo would not have known what he was doing. He never stood a chance.

Goddamn it!

'Does his wife know yet?'

'Murcer doesn't think so. His guy at the nine-oh said they were going to speak with her again tomorrow. That guy you know. Ross?'

'Royce,' I said. 'We've been talking a lot lately.' I brought her up to date with all I knew. I left out the part about the recording with Duke Lansing. 'This is going to wreck that woman, Rachel. She's seven months pregnant and her mother and sister just drove up from South Carolina. The wake is tomorrow night.'

'Sounds like a potential shit storm, Ray.'

'Yeah.' I tried to think of something else to say but came up empty.

Rachel picked up on that. 'I gotta go unpack, Ray. I'm exhausted. You must be, too. Call me when you need to.'

'Thanks, Rache.'

We said goodbye and hung up. I closed my eyes, took a deep

breath, and reminded myself how much I loved living in Williamsburg, Brooklyn, New York City.

'Sounded like that was your sister.'

Allison came out of the bedroom wearing her University of Missouri football jersey and a pair of shorts. She had told me a while ago that my voice took on a certain tone whenever I was talking on the phone with Rachel.

'Yeah.' I then told her why she had called. Allison was as shocked as I was.

'They're sure about that? Fentanyl?'

'That's what Murcer's guy told him. I just can't wrap my mind around it.'

She closed the distance between us and took me into a hug. 'Wrap your arms around me, Ray.'

Since that was the nicest offer I had received in a long time, I did. A few minutes later, I got another pretty good offer, which I also accepted. Not too long after that, Allison and I fell asleep in each other's arms.

Somewhere over the next few hours, Sunday evening turned into Monday morning and a new week had arrived.

ELEVEN

My Monday morning duties discharged, I decided to risk it and stick my head in Principal Ron Thomas's office. At first I thought he had the radio on, but it turned out to be his TV: a replay of some golf tournament. He was on the phone, but saw me in his doorway, waved me in, and said a cheerful goodbye to the person he was talking to. Say what you want about my boss, he has very nice phone manners.

'That,' he said, gesturing with his chin to the phone, 'was the head of the biology department at CUNY. They heard what happened here on Thursday and about our hydroponics project.' I noticed how he referred to MoJo's murder as 'what happened here' and accented the word *our*. 'They're offering to send some grad students over to take over MoJo's – Maurice's – hydroponic farm and his pigeon coop. There might even be some grant money in it for us.'

'That's a good piece of news,' I said. The City University of New York was known for its commitment to science and had some impressive faculty. If you don't believe me, check out their ads on the subway.

'Yes, it is, Raymond. And apparently we have your girlfriend to thank for it.'

I gave him a quizzical look. 'How's that?'

'I was just informed that Allison's website is a big hit with CUNY students who don't seem to trust the print media as much as our generation.' He rubbed his fingers together as if talking about money. 'They don't like getting ink on their fingers, I guess.'

'She'll be happy to hear that, Ron.'

'And it seems the mainstream media have gone on to other matters. I had only one call to my cell this weekend. I'd love to find out how they got my number.' He stood up and stretched. 'And there were only three messages on the machine when I came in this morning. It was the same old, same old – reporters looking for new developments. Let them call the fucking cops. I am done and ready to move on.'

His comment would have been more impressive if it hadn't been accompanied by the sound of The Golf Channel coming from his TV. 'How nice for you,' I said.

He gave me a look. 'You know, Raymond. I wonder sometimes if you realize how sarcastic you can come across.'

'I'll work on that, Ron.'

'You should. You're close with Elaine Stiles. She's a good counselor. Maybe she can help you with that.' His voice got a little more serious. 'You know, if you ever want to become an assistant principal, you are going to have to learn to talk to people more diplomatically.'

Apparently a skill you need to become an assistant principal but can ditch once you became principal.

'Duly noted, Ron.' My walkie-talkie went off – School Safety telling me I was needed upstairs in Room 321. I looked at Ron. 'Gotta go be a dean now, Ron. Let me know how that CUNY thing works out.' I headed off to Room 321.

An hour later, I had finished up a meeting with the father of a student who was just returning from a five-day suspension for sexually harassing a seventh-grade girl, both in-person and through text messages. Dad seemed annoyed with me, as the meeting was going to make him two hours late to work at the auto body shop.

I told him I fully understood his frustration, and yes, I could have scheduled the meeting for the first thing in the day, but the beginning of my day was always unpredictable and I wanted to make sure we had each other's full attention to deal with this very serious matter.

Dad said, 'I don't see what the big deal is anyway. Jaquan was just telling the girl how pretty she was and that he wanted to go out with her. I used to do the same thing.'

'Did you,' I asked, taking out my hard copy of Jaquan's text messages, 'tell the girls you liked that they were "hot bitches" and you'd like to – and I'm quoting your son now – "Hit that shit"?'

Dad got quiet. Finally, he said, 'We didn't have cell phones back in my day.'

And that was the kind of answer that led me to believe this would not be the last time Jaquan ended up in my office. I shook the man's hand and told him I hoped he had a good day at work.

The rest of the day was fairly uneventful. Two kids had to be removed from one of the social studies classes because they had the disrespect to fall asleep and started snoring while their teacher was playing the TV series *Roots* as part of his lesson on the causes of the Civil War. This was the same teacher who often played videos while teaching. Once he came to my office to see if I had replacement batteries for his remote control. He seemed annoyed I didn't provide the same services as Best Buy.

I stopped a fight before it started in the lunchroom when I noticed a young lady – with the help of her friends – removing her earrings, and a second young lady – also with the help of her friends – pulling her long hair back into a tight bun; they were planning on fighting over a boy they both liked. It turned out the boy was clueless about either girl's affection, but after a brief talk with me, seemed flattered by the attention.

I took a few phone calls from the district office. One was regarding an eighth-grader who was about to be transferred to our school after a weapons possession suspension at a school a few blocks away. I suggested they call my principal and was informed that Ron had transferred them to me. Another call informed me of an eight-week conflict-resolution workshop, starting the following week, that they'd like me to recruit five of my teachers to attend after school for per-session pay, about fifty bucks an hour. With summer less than three months away, I didn't think I'd have a problem finding half a dozen teachers who needed a little more cash.

I decided to spend most of the rest of the afternoon out of my office and 'on patrol.' I was still a bit edgy over the whole MoJo thing, and with the latest revelation about what they had found in his system, I felt the need to be mobile. It is, as they say, hard to hit a moving target.

As I was walking down the steps of the building after the kids had been dismissed, I recognized a familiar face standing by the gate. Familiar, and yet completely out of context. I'm not sure I'd ever seen him out of the pizza shop he owned, which served as a front for some of his more lucrative enterprises. He was dressed in a dark sweatshirt, jeans, and a pair of sneakers that looked brand new.

'Tio,' I said. 'You getting your hands dirty these days, delivering pizzas?'

He gave me that smile I haven't been able to figure out as long as I've known him; it was somewhere between finding me amusing and finding me thinking I was amusing. But, hell, he was coming to see me. Usually it was the other way around.

'That's good, Teacherman,' he said. He reached out, gave me a three-part handshake and a quick bro hug. He looked around at the nearly empty front of the school. 'I take it you got a minute or two?'

'For you? I can make it five.'

'You remember Gator?' Right to the point – that's Tio.

'Gator?' My baseball mind immediately flashed back to Ron Guidry, the Yankees pitcher from the seventies. Being a flamethrower from Louisiana, he quickly earned the nickname 'Gator' from the New York sportswriters. I had no idea who Tio was talking about. I shook my head.

'Gabriel,' Tio said. 'Ocasio. Lives across the street.' Tio turned and pointed to the housing unit across the avenue. 'Fifth floor, corner apartment on the northwest side.'

'Can you be a bit more specific?' I said, remembering Gabriel now. They called him Gator because of his massive over-bite and a propensity for big grins.

And again, I got that smile from Tio. 'He wants to talk to you.'

'Really. I haven't seen him in years. I wasn't even sure he was still living across the street. I heard he'd moved.'

'He did. Then he . . . moved back a month ago. Which means,' he paused for dramatic effect, 'he was living here on Thursday.'

He looked at me like I should understand what he was talking about. I didn't and told him so.

'Thursday,' he repeated. 'The day your co-worker was shot by the arrow.'

'OK. What does that have to do with—?'

'Gator has some four-one-one, might be helpful to the detective checking into the murder. Your amigo Royce.'

'First,' I said, 'Royce is not my amigo. Second, if Gator has something to tell the cops, why doesn't he go to . . . oh.'

'Yeah,' Tio said. 'Oh.' He took out a cigarette and stuck it in his mouth. It would remain unlit. Even with all the dangerous shit he got himself involved with, Tio was too smart to add smoking to that list. 'Gator didn't exactly move away, Teacherman. He was a guest of the state for eighteen months.'

'Shit,' I said. 'For what?'

'Possession with intent. He pleaded and got back from up top a month ago.'

'So he's back home living with his mom?'

'He was.'

'Meaning . . .'

'He got picked up again two days ago.'

That would've been Saturday. 'For?'

'Possession with intent.'

'Ah, Jesus, Tio.' I squeezed the space between my eyes. 'Gabe was never the sharpest pencil in the box, but that's asshat behavior even for him.' I looked across the street. 'What does he wanna talk to me about? I taught him math when he was in eighth grade. We weren't particularly close.'

'He says he's got somethin' to trade and he wants you to be the middleman between him and the cops.'

'Why me?'

'Says he trusts you. And before you ask, yeah, it also helps that your uncle is Chief of Dees. He figures he helps the cops out and they may be more likely to help him out, especially if your name is attached to a piece of paper.'

'Did he say what he has to trade?'

'Wouldn't tell me and I didn't ask.' He rubbed his thumb, forefinger and middle finger together. 'Information is coin 'round here, Teach, you know that. For all Gator knows if he tells me I may steal that info and use it for my own good.'

I looked him in the eyes. 'But you wouldn't do that.'

'Don't be so sure. Never know when you might need a Get-outta-jail-free card.' Then he added, 'But you feel me, I wouldn't do that. Probably.'

So Gabriel 'Gator' Ocasio wanted to talk to me about some info he had regarding MoJo's murder. This was not exactly what Royce had in mind when he told me to stay away from the case.

'Where's Gator now?'

'Revisiting the Island.'

'Riker's,' I said. 'Has he been to a judge yet?'

'Next week, that's why he wants to see you right away.'

'Define "right away," Tio.'

He turned around again and pointed to a car across the street. Behind the wheel was a young woman who appeared to be texting.

'Who's that?'

'Jessica,' he said. 'She runs a literature workshop at Riker's. And other things. You should hear her go on about the thirty years of research on how reading and writing increase empathy and that kinda shit.'

'Let me guess.' I looked at my watch; it was pushing four. 'She's on her way to Riker's now?'

'See why I come to you, Teacherman? You ain't as slow as some people say.'

I took a few breaths. The fact I was even considering this was not the brightest thing I could have been doing. Besides, I had to attend the memorial service for MoJo tonight. 'How's she gonna get me on the Island?'

Tio smiled. This time for real. 'She'll explain that on the way, Teach.'

TWELVE

I t turned out that Jess was twenty-three, had the right side of her head shaved, leaving the rest of her blond hair flowing down her back. With her funky haircut and striking blue eyes, she could have passed for a Swedish rock star. Instead, she was getting her master's in social work from Columbia and doing her thesis on the impact of writing on incarcerated youth. To that end, she took a weekly trip to Riker's Island and worked with eighteen- to twenty-one-year-olds while they waited for a court date, sentencing, or the trip 'up top,' to one of New York State's prisons – literally *Up the River.*

We were crossing the new and improved Kosciuszko Bridge, which connects Brooklyn to Queens, when Jess told me how she knew Tio.

'I worked with some of his . . . kids,' she explained, 'at a couple of youth facilities in Queens. He'd come by and visit, make sure they had money in their accounts, envelopes with stamps on them to write home, and books to read. He seems particularly fond of Charles Dickens, R.L. Stine, and Junot Diaz. He's keenly aware that these kids need to read about characters who are not white. He brings those books, as well.'

'Interesting guy, Tio,' I said. 'You could probably do your thesis on him.'

'Don't think it didn't cross my mind,' she said. 'He doesn't like talking about himself too much, though.'

'There is that. So, how am I going to get onto the Island? Don't I need an ID or something?'

'I'll get you a gate pass. Anybody asks, you're with me to see if you wanna get involved with the program. Who knows,' she added, 'maybe you will be.'

'Stranger things have happened.'

'I know,' she said. 'Tio's told me a bit about you.'

'Anything good?'

'He said you have a certain knack for getting yourself involved with kids in crisis. He thinks you were probably a good cop who never got it out of his system.'

'I know a few people who'd agree with him,' I said. 'Including an NYPD detective and my uncle.' I left out Allison.

'Raymond Donne. Chief of Detectives at One Police Plaza.'

'That would be him.'

'I appreciate you doing this, Ray. I know you're putting not only your name out there, but also your uncle's.'

'Funny what kids remember,' I said. 'I'm not sure how much Gator – Gabriel – took away from my math class, but he sure remembered who my uncle was.'

'Kids who live in situations like Gator's retain what they need

to. It's a survival skill. Let's be honest: knowing how to find the
missing angle of a pentagon is not going to do much for a kid who
thinks like him.'

Oh, man, I thought. I lean to the left myself, but Jess was really
tilting here.

'Part of my job,' I said, 'is to teach kids like Gator to think
differently. Algebra is a means to an end. It teaches problem-solving.
You got some info here, some info there, and you gotta put them
together to find the unknown.'

Jess smiled. 'Kind of like police work.'

'I could say that it's also kinda like social work.'

'I think you just did.' She took the exit toward LaGuardia Airport,
which also led to Riker's. We passed the old Bulova Building, where
they used to make watches. 'But a young man like Gator is going
to remember that your uncle is a bigwig cop before he remembers
math formulas and how to diagram a sentence. Think about it, we
wouldn't be having this conversation if he didn't have the retention
skills that allowed him to recall that information. There's a lot of
research out there that says our ancestors who had better recall
ability also had a better chance of survival. Where's the best place
to hunt? Where was there danger the last time my boys and I went
hunting?'

'Whose uncle could help me get out from under a possession
with intent charge?'

I got a full-out laugh from her on that one.

'Tio told me about your cynicism,' she said. 'I guess that's one
of *your* survival skills. Along with the sense of humor.'

I was close to blushing. 'Thanks.'

'I didn't say I liked it, Ray.'

Touché. I looked over hoping for a smile. She must have been
hiding it.

Half an hour later we were walking down the longest hallway I'd
ever seen; it was at least the length of two football fields. I'd already
signed in, gone through a metal detector, and given up my driver's
license in exchange for a pass. We had left our cell phones in the
car to avoid having to lock them up. Every corrections officer we
passed during our walk down the hallway had nodded, said hello,
told us to have a nice day, and then gone back to looking serious.
Jess was carrying a transparent book bag filled with journals,

composition paper, pens, magazines, and paperback books. She wasn't allowed to bring in hardcover books because they could be used as weapons. As for why they allowed her to bring in pens and give them to the young men for journaling, who knew?

We stopped in front of a metal door, and Jess pounded on the window and held her pass up to the video camera. I did the same. We got buzzed in, got buzzed in a second door, and then a third.

The unit we entered looked like an out-of-issue army barracks. All the windows had bars on them and the floor looked like it had seen its best days during World War II. There were three rows of ten metal cots, about half of them in use, in the big part of the room. Off to the side were another half-dozen. It smelled like the boys' locker room back at school. Times five. The young men on the cots either ignored us or glanced at us with disinterest. Some were playing cards, some were watching the card-playing, and some were sleeping. I saw more than a few lumps under gray blankets. They were all dressed in the same drab khaki shirts and pants. It looked like a dress rehearsal for the all-minority teenage version of *Cool Hand Luke.*

I did a quick head count and it came to about twenty young men, seventeen of whom were black or Hispanic. On the surface, that didn't make sense, because about eighty-five percent of the crimes committed in a city like New York were not committed by non-whites. But when it came to posting cash bail – being able to pay your way out of a stay in prison until you saw a judge – not having three thousand dollars could land you in Riker's. And you could put a color on that. Most of these inmates – no matter what they were picked up for – were currently in Riker's because they were unable to come up with the bail money. They were incarcerated for being poor. I knew the city and the state were working on this, I just hoped the solution was quick enough to keep these young men from forgetting what life was like on the outside.

A few of the young men were in the day room watching a TV that was encased behind a plastic barrier. The TV was tuned to one of those shows that does paternity tests to prove whether you were the Baby Daddy. Why people went on these shows was beyond me. We headed over that way, and two of the young men stood up when we entered and said, 'Hey, Miz Jessica.' Then they looked at me. The taller of the two said, 'Who that?'

Before Jess could answer, I said, 'Raymond.' Remembering not to give out my last name. 'I'm working with Miz Jessica today. I hear you guys like to write.' Normally, I would have reached out for a fist bump, but I didn't think that would go over right now.

The shorter one said, 'Sometimes.' He paused. 'For Miz Jessica.' He eyed me, waiting for my reaction. I'd seen that look many times before; it was the look of a young man who'd spent too much time on the streets clocking other males, playing an eyeball variation of chicken, waiting to see who'd blink first.

Before it turned into a staring contest, I said, 'I'll just watch and learn then. If that's OK with you guys.' Just like on the streets, I knew I had to show respect; this was their hood. I was just a visitor.

They both thought about my offer and looked at each other for a bit. After a pair of shrugs, the taller one said, 'A'ight.' They left the room.

'They're going to get last week's work,' Jess explained. She reached into her bag and started arranging books and journals on the only clean table in the room. 'This always attracts a few more of them,' she said. 'They love their journals and urban fiction. I need to remember to bring some automobile and tattoo magazines next week. I only have the music ones today.'

Sure enough, as soon as the books and journals and magazines hit the metal table, a slew of young men came into the room like it was Christmas morning. Jess knew most of them and reminded them what reading materials they had asked for the week before. The magazines went quickly. All seemed to be equally popular.

'Is Gabriel around?' I asked Jessica.

'He's out there on one of the bunks,' she said, paying more attention to laying out the books than to me. 'Go ahead. I got this.'

I went back into the bigger room and looked out over the rows of cots and the young men spread around the room. I hadn't seen Gabriel for a few years and wasn't sure I'd recognize him. Turns out, I didn't have to. A tall guy of about twenty got up and started walking toward me. As soon as he got about ten feet away, he smiled. *The teeth.*

Gator.

He reached out his hand. 'Yo, Mr D. Thanks for coming.'

'Hey, Gator. I hear you been busy.'

He looked down at his feet and kicked at an imaginary object. 'Fucked up,' he said. 'I was holding for a friend. And before you say anything, that's the truth. Gave me a book bag, said he'd be right back and before I knew it, five-oh was pulling up on me.'

'Bad break.'

'I'm thinkin' maybe I made a bad decision.'

Ya think? 'What happened to your friend?'

'Nothin'. More like an associate, my moms would say. I don't know what I was thinking.' Before I could answer, he said, 'I know I wasn't the best student, Mr D, but even I know not to carry that much weight just after I got home.'

He was right, but I wasn't here to help him revisit past mistakes.

'Tio said you have some info you want me to give the detective investigating the murder of MoJo.' He gave me a blank look. 'The guy on the roof of my school.'

Gator's face turned real serious. He looked around the big room. 'Let me grab a journal and a book, Mr D. I don't want the COs or the guys to think we're not working.'

'You wanna talk in the day room?' I asked. 'Or on your cot?'

He scanned the room again and his eyes stopped on an empty cot away from the other young men. He gestured with his head. 'Meet me over there. It's the closest to private we gonna get around here.'

I did as I was told and Gator joined me in less than two minutes. He'd picked a red journal and a book by an author whose name I did not recognize. The book had a light-skinned black woman in light-blue underwear on its cover. *Urban fiction, indeed.*

He opened up the journal and started writing. As he did, he said, 'You know where I live, right?'

'Yes.'

'Right across from the school. Corner apartment.'

'OK . . .'

'Last week, a coupla days before the . . . whatta ya callit . . . arrow shooting, I heard some noises from the place above ours. It's been empty for a few months, and every once in a while, some a the local crackheads sneak into the building and go up there to smoke.' He wrote some more; it was basically the same stuff he was telling me. Proving one of my educational theories by the way: If you can speak, you can write. 'I went up to chase them away and some white guy came bustin' out the door, knockin' me on my ass.'

'Did you get a good look at him?'

'Nah, it happened with a quickness. That's a fact. He was wearing a hoodie, a pair of jeans and wraparound sunglasses. Kinda looked like that Unabomber guy.'

I stayed silent for a while, processing the information. I wasn't sure what this had to do with . . . It took me a minute before it hit me. Maybe Gator wasn't the brightest kid in the math class, but he may have been onto something more important.

'This empty apartment,' I said. 'Does it have a view of the school roof?'

I got the famous Gator grin. 'Now you feelin' me, Mr D.'

This was definitely worth telling Detective Royce about and risking his anger – again – for not following his instructions to mind my own business. I told Gator as much.

'You think you can put in a good word for me with the five-oh?' He paused. 'Especially your uncle?'

'I can do that. But I can't make any promises.'

'I feel ya. Just say some good stuff 'bout me to the right people. I shouldn't be here, Mr D. I got some things need doin' on the outside.'

'I hope that doesn't include getting in your friend's face. The one who asked you to hold the bag?'

'That's my bizness,' Gator said. 'Gotta do what I gotta do. Know what I'm sayin'?'

'I hear ya, Gator.' I looked around. 'I just don't wanna see you back in here if we're able to get you out again. You're too smart to be in a place like this, especially when you know exactly why you're here.'

Gator shrugged. He was going to do what he was going to do. Nothing I said was going to change that. That wasn't just the rules of the street or jail; it also came with being twenty years old.

As I sat there pondering Gator's options, I heard the planes taking off and landing at LaGuardia airport, literally less than a half-mile away. It reminded me of the Johnny Cash song where the guy's in jail for shooting a man in Reno just to watch him die. Whenever he hears that lonesome whistle of the passing trains, he imagines who's on those trains and where they're going with those big cigars hanging out of their mouths.

Is that what goes through the minds of these young men stuck in here for an indefinite period of time? Planes taking off and landing. Where they from? Where they going? Take me with you, anywhere but here. *Blow my blues away.*

'I got a girl, y'know,' Gator said, bringing me back to the now.

'Congrats. Is she from the school?'

'From high school. She finished up and now she's pushing me to get my GED.'

'Sounds like a good influence.'

'She's also pregnant,' he said. 'Told me she wants both the kid's parents to have high school diplomas. That's another reason I wanna get outta here and not come back.'

I stood up. 'I'll do what I can do, Gator. I'll even help when you do get out, if you want. I know a guy runs a GED-prep program. He owes me a favor.'

'That'd be cool, Mr D. First, I gotta get outta here, though.'

'I hear ya. One step at a time. When's your girlfriend due?'

'End of September. Be good to have my GED and a job by then. Can't afford to even do a city bullet.' A city bullet was eight months, six with good behavior.

'Then,' I said, sticking out my hand, 'let's make that happen.'

'I remember you used to say that in math class.'

'See? Some things you learn in school do come in handy in real life.'

We said our goodbyes and I promised him I'd see what I could do. He looked like most minority kids do when a white guy promised something. But, again, he had come to me. Through Tio.

I went back into the day room to see what Jess was up to. She had the two young men I'd met earlier reading aloud from a copy of a poem one of them had written since her last visit. It was the 'Where I'm From' poem we used in school to prompt kids to write. I remembered the first time I'd taught that to my self-contained class of twelve kids. I read them one I had done:

I am from green lawns you could not run across
I am from Bayer aspirin and Clorox bleach
I am from crucifixes on every floor and church every Sunday
I am from Fish Sticks Friday and Meatloaf Mondays

I don't remember the rest, but you get the idea. It's a great way to get kids who 'don't write poetry' to write poetry. I liked this program Jess was running; I'd have to look at my schedule and see if I could get more involved. For now, I just observed.

* * *

'Did you get what you needed from Gabriel?' she asked. 'Gator?' We were exiting the building and were safely out of earshot of anyone who'd care. The Manhattan skyline was a few miles away to the west, the sun setting behind the tall buildings most of the young men we'd just been with may never even get close to. I was always amazed at the number of kids from the other four boroughs who never went into Manhattan.

'Now I just have to figure out the best way to present what I know to the detective in charge of the case.'

'Can't you just tell him? This information helps his investigation, right?'

'It's not that simple,' I said. 'Detective Royce and I have a bit of a history and sometimes he thinks I help too much.' I slid into the passenger seat. 'He's right.'

'Is what Gator told you enough to help him out?'

'Sounds like it could be, yeah. Again, I have to give that information to Royce in just the right way. If our past is any indication, he'll be pissed at me for getting involved and then use the info anyway.'

'Are you going to ask your uncle to help?'

'I could, but he feels like Royce does, and the less I involve him, the better.'

Jess started the car and backed out of the parking spot. 'I wish I could say I understand, Ray. But I don't.'

'Yeah,' I said. 'It's kind of a boy thing. A boy/cop thing.'

Jess dropped me off at my place about fifteen minutes later.

We said our goodbyes and she told me to think about getting more involved with her Riker's program. She held my gaze a bit longer than I would have expected, and I told her I would. Think more about it.

Before I went upstairs, I called Royce from the street. He didn't sound surprised to hear from me. I told him what I had learned from Gabriel Ocasio.

Royce said, 'And he reached out to you because . . .'

'No offense, but he has reason not to trust the police, Detective,' I said. 'He feels he may have been set up on that possession charge.'

'Which one?'

I was not going to play that game. 'The most recent one. Also, he figured if he came to me, I might be able to get my uncle to get him home quicker.'

'Now why would he think that?'

'So you'll head over to the apartment above Gator's?'

'No,' he said. 'I'll just ignore the tip and continue to feel my way around blindly. Yes, I'll head over to the apartment. My wife's been complaining that I've been having dinner with my family too much lately.'

I love cop sarcasm. 'Thanks, Royce.'

'Actually, I was getting to the point where I was running out of avenues of investigation. This could get me back on track.'

'So, me following up on this without telling you—'

'Was still unadvisable. But in this case, I can see your reasoning.'

Figuring that this was as close to a thanks as I was going to get, I said goodbye to the detective and said I'd see him soon.

'I do not doubt that, Mr Donne.'

Allison was upstairs putting away the dishes from dinner. Something smelled good and garlicky in the kitchen and I told her so.

'There's leftover pasta in the fridge,' she said. 'How was jail?'

I laughed and grabbed a Brooklyn Pilsner from the fridge. 'Good. That Jessica really seems to have her shit together.'

Allison gave me a quizzical look. 'Really?'

'Yeah. She's not only doing her thesis on how journaling and other forms of writing affect incarcerated youth, she's walking the walk.'

'You sound impressed.'

'I am,' I said. Just to clarify, I added, 'With her work.'

'What did you think I meant, Ray?'

I reached out, grabbed Allison by the waist and gave her a long kiss on the lips. 'I don't know what you meant by that question.'

'You ever notice that when I ask you a question that makes you the slightest bit . . . I don't know . . . uncomfortable, you give me a kiss?'

'I did not notice that,' I said. 'And what makes you think your question made me the slightest bit uncomfortable?'

She paused to look me in the eyes. 'Never mind.'

'OK.' I told her about the info I got from Gator. 'And you,' I added, 'are not to print anything until Royce acts upon that information and gives the OK.'

'I don't need Royce's approval to print anything. As long as I didn't break the law to get information, I can run with it.'

'That's not what I meant, Allie, and you know it. Right now, I'm treating Gator as a CI. We both need to respect that.'

Allison shook her head. 'I can see why you keep getting under Royce's skin. You do not have confidential informants, Ray. You're a dean at a middle school.'

Oh, good. This argument again. And so soon after the last one.

'I know that, Allie. I'm just saying Gator needs to be treated with the same respect cops give their informants. The last thing he needs is this blowing back on him.'

'And you.'

'And me. And by extension, you.'

'We discussed this. I don't need your protection, Ray.'

No. Just my health insurance. Fuck.

'Maybe your new friend Jessica should worry, but I'm OK, Mr Donne.'

I hated it when she called me that and she knew it. Two more ill-conceived sentences and this was going to be a full-blown argument. I was too tired and not in the mood for one of those. Not that I ever was.

'I'm glad to hear that, Allie.' I took a long sip of beer as she turned around to the sink. The wall behind the sink was mostly windows and gave us a postcard view of the Manhattan skyline. I stared at it sometimes when frustrated. Like now.

Allison finished up in the sink, walked past me into the living room. 'Don't forget the pasta in the fridge.'

'Thanks. Can you help me with something first?'

'Depends.' She sat down on the futon and picked up the remote like she was threatening to turn the TV on and me off.

'I need your opinion on something.'

She thought about that, put the remote on her lap and said, 'Hit me, tough guy.'

Tough guy. We were on the way to good again. 'Do you think it's kinda odd that someone who's just been released after eighteen months for possession with intent gets picked up less than a week later for the same offense in the same location?'

'Depends on who it is,' she said. 'I assume you're talking about Gator?'

'Yeah. Again, not the brightest crayon in the box, but not the dullest, either.'

She brushed the remote along her thigh. 'What're you thinking?'

I sat down next to her and put my beer on the coffee table. 'It's a relatively small offense. It was a smaller weight than last time. It'll keep him on the Island for at least a few weeks, but I'm wondering if Gator got set up.'

'By his friend?'

'Acquaintance,' I said, and gave her the Reader's Digest version of Gator's story.

'You're right,' she said. 'Pretty small-time set-up.'

'Unless someone wanted Gator out of the hood for a while.'

'Someone like . . .?'

I grabbed my beer and shook my head. 'That is the question.'

THIRTEEN

The small memorial service for MoJo was already in full swing by the time Allison and I arrived a little before nine. It was being held in this small old-timer bar on a corner in Greenpoint. Outside the window, you could see both the small park where MoJo's kid would be playing someday and the Catholic church he would not be attending. This was not a bar I went to often, but I remembered watching the snow fall here one Friday some winters ago before I met Allison and wasn't in the mood for The LineUp.

She and I joined Edgar, who was nursing his usual under one of the two TV sets above the bar. I grabbed Allison and myself a couple of pints and we settled in next to our friend. I realized I'd have to start the conversation.

'How ya doing, Edgar?'

He straightened his glasses. 'OK. I don't know why they call these things memorials. Like it's supposed to help me remember MoJo? I'll never forget MoJo, Ray. I can be at The LineUp doing this.'

'This is just a way – another way – to show support for Lisa. It may not make a lot of sense, but there are a lot of people here who haven't seen her or MoJo for a long time and this helps them process what happened.'

I glanced over my shoulder and saw Lisa Joseph with two women

I assumed were her mother and sister. They were in the corner
greeting folks who were coming by to pay their respects. Lisa looked
like she had gotten some rest since I'd seen her on Saturday. Her
mother and sister seemed to be doing most of the talking, though,
as if protecting Lisa from too much attention and expenditure of
energy.

'Have you said hello to Lisa yet?' Allison asked Edgar.

He nodded. 'Then it got real busy around her so I grabbed a seat
over here.' He turned to me. 'How long do I have to stay, Ray?'

I took a sip of beer. 'There're no rules, Edgar. I think as long as
you've spoken to Lisa and maybe met her mom and sister, you're
good. Just drink your beer and relax. You've fulfilled your responsibility. Now we're just like movie extras. The more people around
her right now, the more positive energy.'

'Speaking of which,' Allison said, 'let's take advantage of the
lull and head over and express our condolences.' She gave Edgar a
tap on his upper arm. 'I don't like these things either. The sooner
we can do our duty, the better.' She grabbed my hand. 'Let's say
hello, Ray.'

I had just seen Lisa so there wasn't much for me to say to her,
but she introduced me to her mother and sister, who both thanked
me for helping Maurice and being there for Lisa. I introduced
Allison, who'd only met Lisa once, and she seemed pretty much at
ease for someone who didn't like stuff like this. Like me she had
grown up Catholic and had spent a lot of time visiting dead relatives
in funeral homes with the guest of honor on display. I appreciated
not having MoJo's body around. Other relatives came by, so we
excused ourselves and went back to Edgar.

And that's when we ran into two guys in suits who looked out
of place. It turned out they were Eddie Price and Denny McLain,
who told us they were from Newer Leaves. We all shook hands.

'Nice of you both to come down all this way,' I said.

Eddie Price said, 'Maurice was kind of special to us, Mr Donne.
It's a tough loss for the program. For all of us.'

Price looked familiar to me but I couldn't figure out why. Before
it could come to me, McLain said, 'Maurice was doing good work
for us down here at our support group meetings. He was a living
example of continuing the work of the program after your two
years.'

'I'd like to hear more about that, Mr McLain,' Allison said and then explained she was a reporter. 'I could see a piece on the post-program aspect being of interest to our readers and maybe even others in need.'

'I'll have to think on that, Ms Rogers,' Eddie said, but I could tell by his voice that the possibility made him uncomfortable. 'We take the confidentiality of our clients quite seriously, you understand.'

'Completely,' Allison said. 'No names, just stories. Hopeful and helpful.'

'I like that,' McLain said. 'Hopeful and helpful,' he repeated as if it would become their new slogan. 'We'll get back to you.' When he saw Allison's confusion, he explained that he was the lawyer for Newer Leaves. 'Everybody needs a lawyer these days.' To prove his point, he pulled out a card and handed it to Allison.

She looked at it. 'Thanks.' To me, she said, 'I'm going back to Edgar.'

'Sure,' I said. 'I'll be right over, then we'll go.'

'You've been here awhile, Mr Donne?' McLain asked.

'Just a beer's worth, I guess, and long enough to give my regards to Lisa's family. You guys drive down, I guess?'

'Our . . . associate drove us down,' Price said. 'He's looking for a place to park, but I don't expect him to come in. He's awkward in these situations.'

'Memorials?'

'Social,' McLain said. 'He's one of our more . . . fragile former clients. But he does great work upstate on the property.'

'That's good.' I shook their hands again and said, 'I'm going to finish my beer and head out. Nice seeing you both.'

'Same here,' they said in unison.

Allison and Edgar were putting the finishing touches on their drinks so I did the same. 'You both look ready to go home,' I said.

'I gotta head off to work,' Edgar said. 'That store over the bridge I was telling you about. It closes soon and I gotta work on the surveillance system.'

The three of us headed out. Just as we hit the street, I saw a guy getting out of his car across from the bar. I recognized him right away, but didn't want Edgar to see him. I steered him and Allison the other way as the guy leaned against his car.

'Edgar,' I said, 'can you drive Allie home?'

'Why? What are you doing?'

'Yeah, Ray?' Allison said. 'What are you doing?'

'I want to talk to Lisa and her family again,' I lied. 'Make sure they appreciate what MoJo was doing at the school. How much the kids liked him. Shouldn't take long but I might wanna stay for another beer. Catch the end of the Yankees game.'

They gave me questioning looks but chose not to push it. It's nice to have people in your life who know you so well. I kissed Allison. 'I'll be home soon.'

She hugged me and whispered in my ear, 'With an explanation?'

'Absolutely,' I said and thanked Edgar for taking her home.

As they walked away, the guy I had recognized crossed the street and said, 'I thought that was you. I was hoping we'd run into each other again.'

'Mr Henderson,' I said, sticking out my hand, willing to pretend for the moment that running into each other was not on purpose. 'David. Why's that?'

He shook my hand, harder than the last time we had met. 'I believe we have a conversation to finish.' He punctuated that sentence by opening his wallet and showing me a badge. I couldn't see much in the low light of the street. That would soon change.

'The FBI? And there I was insulting you by thinking you were just a cop.'

Henderson smiled at me. We were sitting at another bar, just a few blocks away from where MoJo's memorial was being held. This one was on the Avenue, situated just right for people getting off the bus and not wanting to go straight home.

'Two things I was told about you, Mr Donne,' he said. 'You're quicker than most people think and not as funny as you think.'

I took a sip of the beer he had insisted on buying me. It was the least I could do. It's not every day the federal government springs for drinks. 'I'm going to say fuck you to the first,' I said. 'And too bad to the second.'

He pointed at me. 'There might have been a third thing. Something about you and authority figures.'

Enough bullshit. 'What were you doing with MoJo, David?'

'First,' he said, 'just so I know for the future. What led you to believe that I was not exactly who I said I was?'

I laughed. 'You just give off a vibe. Kinda like a cat person at a dog park.'

'But not quite an unaccompanied bachelor at a playground?'

'Not that creepy. No. You and MoJo?'

I was drinking a Six Point Crisp and he was having a Bud Light – the beer of choice when you're buying on the federal credit card.

'Understand,' he began, 'I can only tell you so much. I really shouldn't be telling you anything at all, but since I started this and—'

'And lied to us in the process,' I interrupted. 'Don't forget that part.'

'Yeah,' he said. 'There is that.' He paused and said, 'I was using Maurice Joseph as a CI in an ongoing investigation.'

I experienced my normal reaction when someone comes out with surprising information: I got silent and processed it. An FBI agent had just told me that he was using my friend and colleague as a confidential informant. I hoped he was not going to try and make me believe that his investigation had nothing to do with MoJo's murder.

As if reading my mind, he said, 'I know. The reasonable conclusion is that his involvement with me led to his death. But I gotta tell you, Raymond, I don't see how. We had just started, and we had the situation under control.'

We'd get back to that, I thought. 'Does your investigation have anything to do with Duke Lansing?' I asked.

It's a good thing David Henderson did not play poker for a living. He didn't even try to hide the look on his face. 'How the fuck did you know that?' he asked in one of the loudest whispers I'd ever heard. He looked around to see if anyone had heard him. Satisfied that no one had, he continued. More controlled this time. 'What the hell did he tell you about Duke Lansing?'

'MoJo,' I said, 'didn't *tell* me anything, David. His wife found a recording device in his office that she thought belonged to her husband and Edgar. When she found it, she called Edgar and we looked at it.'

'*We?*'

I decided to keep Allison out of it. 'Edgar and I. Edgar knew nothing about it and, in fact, was quite upset that MoJo was doing something without telling him.'

'So you saw the recording?'

'Yes.'

'Where is it now?' he wanted to know.

'With the detective in charge of the case. James Royce, Brooklyn North.'

He looked as if I'd just told him I'd secretly put arsenic in his Bud Light. I thought he might throw up at the bar. Instead, he said, 'Fuck, fuck, fuck.' He drained what was left of his Bud and called the bartender over. 'Let me get a double of your best bourbon,' he requested. He looked at me. 'You good?'

I told him I could use another, but no whiskey for me on a school night.

His bourbon came. I could smell its smoky goodness from where I was sitting. I made a mental note to have one on Friday night. He drank half of it in one sip. He tightened up his face and stayed silent for a few moments. When the bourbon started doing its job, he spoke again.

'You're telling me,' he said, 'that evidence from an ongoing federal investigation is now in possession of the New York Police Department?'

'They *are* investigating the murder.' I didn't have a lot of experience working with the feds when I was a cop, but what little I did have taught me they sometimes lost sight of the little picture while laser-focused on what they were trying to accomplish: *The Big Picture*. 'The recording was in the belongings of the victim. When Edgar and I realized what it was, we had no choice but to give it to Royce.' I took a sip of my fresh beer. 'Part of an active murder investigation.'

'Goddamn it,' he said. 'Did Maurice tell you anything about what he was doing for me, Mr Donne?'

Didn't I just answer that? 'I knew nothing about it until you just told me. And you didn't tell me much. All we knew was that he had a recording in his possession of one of the more popular White Nationalists. If you told MoJo he was working for you confidentially, he would have taken that very seriously. Edgar told you that.'

'I expect so.'

I lowered my voice to an almost conspiratorial volume. 'What did you have on Maurice, by the way? He came to my school highly recommended from one of the best rehabilitation centers in this part of the country.'

'You know I can't tell you that, Mr Donne. That's also confidential.'

And convenient for you. I thought back to what Allison's friend at the ME's office had told her. 'Was MoJo clean?'

'When he started working for me – us – he was,' he said. 'Beyond that, I can't comment. Let's just say he agreed to work with us, based on what was best for him.'

'So now that he's dead, what happens to your investigation?'

Here's where he was supposed to say something along the lines of that's where Edgar and I came in. He came back to Williamsburg for one reason: he still needed help in his investigation. He did not disappoint.

'How well do you know Mr Martinez?'

'Pretty well,' I said. 'Why?'

'Is he equipped to take over where Maurice left off? I know what he told me the other day, but what's your take on him?'

'Absolutely not.'

He took a small sip of bourbon. 'You sound very sure of that.'

'Because I am. Edgar is a self-described non-people person. He was – is – the tech side of the business. Maurice was the one who set up the jobs, worked the phones, led client meetings, things like that.'

Another 'Fuck' came out of his mouth, replaced by a final sip of bourbon. 'This is the problem working with CIs,' he said.

'Your CI,' I said, 'had a pregnant wife, David. If you're looking for sympathy, you're in the wrong place. Maybe you want to go visit Lisa Joseph and explain to her how much the death of the father of her unborn child sucks for you.'

He looked at me like he was not used to being spoken to like that. He raised his hand for another glass of bourbon. With his eyes still on me, he said, 'You don't mince words, do you?'

'I've also been told recently that I'm too sarcastic, and that this may be stalling my climb up the career ladder. I'm guessing you got your ass chewed out by your boss?'

He got quiet again. Then he said, 'Something like that.'

'Something like that' didn't ring true. So here I was, sitting with a federal agent who was close to apologizing for lying to Edgar and me and who was still continuing to lie to me. I decided to push it.

'Your bosses don't know about your investigation, do they?' When I didn't get an answer, I kept poking. 'You're working off the books, aren't you? Which means – in a not-mincing-my-words kind of way – you are completely fucked. And you got a good man killed.'

'You don't know that, Mr Donne.' His new bourbon came and he pulled it close to him. Like a security shot.

'You don't know that you didn't, David. It'd be one hell of a coincidence that your *investigation* has nothing to do with MoJo's murder. And without backup from your supervisors, you have really stepped in it. When MoJo's wife finds out about this, there's gonna be a line of lawyers waiting to crawl up your federal ass.'

He gave that some thought. 'She's an African-American woman.'

'What the hell does that have to do with anything?'

'We were trying to take down Duke Lansing,' he said, and again checked around to see if he'd been overheard. 'I can't tell you more than that, but Maurice was in a unique position to help us take down this low-life. I'm sure his wife would understand that.'

'Because she's black?' I asked. 'Her husband's dead.'

'There's no proof of a connection between that and what he was doing for me.'

'*That you know of.*' Another thought came to me. 'How are you going to explain this to the cops, David?'

He thought about that. 'I haven't thought about that,' he said. 'Fuck.'

'Yeah. Fuck.'

He brought his glass up to his nose, closed his eyes, and took a big sniff instead of a sip this time. 'The local cops don't need to be involved.'

If I had had some beer in my mouth when he said that, I would have spit it out. 'What the fuck do you mean, they don't need to be involved? They are involved.'

'With investigating his murder, not with what he was doing for me.'

'I gotta tell ya, David,' I said, 'that's gonna change tomorrow.'

'What does that mean?'

'If you do not go to the detective-in-charge with what you know about MoJo and Lansing, I will.'

'You already gave them the recording.'

'That's before we knew MoJo was working with you as a CI. Royce needs to know about that.'

'We're not ready to bring the locals in on this, Raymond.'

I put all my fingers except my two thumbs on my pint of beer. In about as level a tone as I could manage, I said, 'You have to stop with that *local* bullshit. You know about me, so you should know how I feel about this. I don't give one shit about your investigation. I do give many shits about finding out who killed MoJo. So if you don't inform Detective Royce about your involvement with MoJo by the end of my school day tomorrow, I will.'

'Then I'll charge you with impeding a federal investigation.'

'No, you won't,' I said. 'Because Royce will make . . . excuse me . . . a federal case out of it and counter-charge you with impeding a murder investigation. And since we're both aware your bosses know very little about what you're up to, I hope you have a good kayak for your trip up Shit's Creek.'

I wasn't sure about that whole 'counter-charge' thing, but Henderson was so upset at the moment I figured it would work to keep him on the ropes. Maybe that's something else whoever told him about me should have mentioned: I hate being lied to.

'What are you proposing, Mr Donne?'

'I'm not *proposing* anything. You tell Royce by three-thirty tomorrow or I will.' I thought a little more. 'And maybe I will have a bourbon.'

He finished his and ordered two more. We were quiet for a minute or two, so I took the time to check out the TV across the way. Another Yankee was on his way to the Injured List. Then something else occurred to me.

'Any truth to that missing kid story you sold MoJo?'

Again, poker was not in David Henderson's retirement plan. This time he clearly knew it. 'Actually, yes. There is a missing kid we are looking for.'

'And by *we* you mean . . .'

'Me,' he said. 'I have intel that one of the kids from Lansing's compound went AWOL. I figure I find the kid, he may be a source of more information.'

'Not to mention that finding missing kids is a good thing in and of itself.'

'He's sixteen. We don't consider him missing so much as a runaway. But, he's not turning himself in to any authorities yet, so . . .'

Oh, shit, I thought. He was talking about Harlan S., the subject of Allison's series.

'What?' he said to me. I guess my poker face wasn't working either.

'I just don't like the idea of using kids to get the grown-ups in their lives,' I said, knowing full well whose pants were on fire now. 'The kid's upset enough to run away and now you want to use him to help take down one of the assholes in his life. Like he hasn't been through enough. How'd you find out the kid was missing?'

'Why do you want to know that?' I would have asked that, too.

'Just makes sense that if you have someone inside Lansing's organization, you wouldn't need MoJo or the kid.'

'I never said I had someone inside Lansing's organization. I said we had intel.'

I took a sip of bourbon. My guess was Henderson's *intel* was MoJo; then Harlan pulled his disappearing act after MoJo told Henderson and gave Harlan Allison's contact info. Run-on sentences can be confusing. It was getting so I needed a scorecard to keep up with the players here, but I think I had it. And if I did have it, I should have told Henderson about Allison meeting with the kid she called Harlan, but that could come back to bite me on a few levels. And if Henderson wasn't hip enough to keep up with *New York Here and Now*, how was that my responsibility?

Shit. Although I knew how the conversation would go, I needed to talk with Allison about this. She was not going to agree to tell the feds or Royce that she knew – or would know soon – the whereabouts of a runaway who was associated with Duke Lansing and therefore may or may not be connected to MoJo's murder. I had to go home.

I stood up, downed the rest of my bourbon and pushed the half-empty beer bottle away. 'That's it for me, David,' I said. 'I'm done playing word games. I'll be calling Royce tomorrow at three-thirty to see how your conversation with him went.'

'Anything I can do to make you hold off on that?'

'You wanna extradite me to some black ops thing overseas, go for it. But you know the right thing to do here.' I stuck out my hand. 'You may be FBI, but you're still a cop.'

He looked at me without getting off his barstool. 'I'll be in touch. Soon.'

'Looking forward to it.' I pointed at the bartender. 'Be sure to tip like a real cop and not a fed.'

FOURTEEN

It took me twenty minutes to walk home and to halfway clear my head, partly from the bourbon I'd had and partly from the information Henderson had just laid on me. The air was cool and I could smell some of the salty East River in it. I took in as much as I could, imagining that with each exhale a little stress was leaving my body. It was a trick Allison had taught me. Sometimes it worked. Tonight I wasn't sure what it was doing for me.

When I turned the corner onto my street, I saw a large man leaning against a black Town Car, smoking a cigar, exhaling enough smoke to give people on the sidewalk a reason to put some distance between them and the smoker. *Oh boy.*

The cigar smoker was my Uncle Ray: Chief of Detectives, NYPD. Visiting me on a Monday night. This could not be good.

When he saw me, he took one more drag from his almost-finished cigar, threw the remaining two inches to the ground, and crushed it under his shoe. I had often wondered when I watched him do that if he was imagining that I was the cigar. It was feeling that way now.

As I usually did when greeting my uncle during an unexpected visit, I threw my arms open and stepped in for one of his enormous hugs. 'Uncle Ray,' I said as he enveloped me. He held me for twenty seconds and two hard pats on the back. That meant more than mildly annoyed.

'Welcome home, Nephew,' he said when he released me.

'What does that mean?'

'I heard you were in jail today. It's good to have you home.'

'How did you . . .' I stopped myself because I knew the answer. 'Someone at the jail recognized my name – our name – and called to tell you I was there.'

He patted me on the back again. 'You're finally getting it, Ray. You're not there yet, but you're getting it.' What he meant was that because we shared the same name, it was hard for me to do anything within the five boroughs – sometimes beyond – involving a uniformed employee of the city that did not somehow find its way back to him.

At least he wasn't here because Detective Royce had called him.

'I also got a call this morning from your favorite detective,' Uncle Ray said. 'Wanna guess what that was about?'

'The recording I found. I gave that to him as soon as I knew what it was.'

'Almost, Ray. You waited a little more time than you should have before calling him. If I didn't know better, I'd think you were considering whether or not to call him.'

I could have told him I wasn't sure what to do with the recording and that's why I waited, but again, I knew what his response to that would be. What I knew about chain of evidence I had learned as a kid from my lawyer dad and his detective brother. Come to think of it, most of what the instructors were teaching me at the police academy I had learned before graduating high school.

'So,' he said, 'your little excursion to Riker's today. I've never known you to be one to visit former students, Ray. And, honestly, I would not have thought much about it were it not for the call from Detective Royce.'

I was about to say something when he held his hand up. 'As soon as I knew that it was your school where the guy got the Wounded Knee treatment, I knew we'd be having this conversation soon. Actually, it took a little longer than I had predicted.'

I took a deep breath of the cool night air, and as I exhaled, I imagined a puff of gray stress leaving my body. 'It's not my fault that people trust me, Uncle Ray. And it's definitely not my fault that my uncle is the Chief of Detectives and sometimes people will take advantage of that.'

'No one takes more advantage of that than you, Nephew.'

'Only when I need to.'

'You seem to need to a lot.' He paused, and then let out a deep breath of his own. I wondered what he saw when he did that. 'You know I only get upset with your getting involved with these cases because I worry about your safety. And let's be honest, over the past five years, you've given me more than enough reasons to worry.'

'True.'

'And now there's Allison,' he said. 'With you two living together – in sin, I might add – you have to think of her, Ray.'

He was quoting my mother on that sin part. Uncle Ray was on

his second wife and thought it was smart of me to try living with Allison before making the big decision. 'Believe me,' I said. 'I do.'

'OK then.' He was using his Uncle Ray voice now, not Chief Donne. 'You guys still planning on coming out to the Island for Easter?'

'Unless we get a better offer.'

'That's funny. Keep it up, that sense of humor's gonna come in handy one day.'

'I'll see you on Easter, Uncle Ray.' He was about to bring me into a farewell hug when something occurred to me. Something I knew had a good chance of backfiring, but I decided to go for it anyway. 'That former student I was visiting at Riker's,' I said.

'Yeah?' he said.

'His name is Gabriel Ocasio. Goes by Gator. He got picked up on a possession with intent charge a few days ago right after he got back from Riker's.'

'Aren't those the kids you work with, Ray?' he asked. 'The ones who don't always think before they possess?'

I let that pass as I was about to ask for a favor. A big one. I explained to him the kind of kid Gator was and that although it wasn't past him to do something like this, I had the feeling he'd been set up to get him off the streets.

'Because . . .' Uncle Ray said.

'I'm thinking someone knew he saw the shooter a day or two before it happened. If he's on the Island, he can't do much with that information.'

My uncle considered that. It was another reason I loved the man. As much as he thought I should stay in my lane and avoid anything along the lines of police work, he knew my instincts were still sharp.

'So,' he finally said, 'you'd like me to find out who tipped off the cops that picked up your boy Gator?'

'If you don't mind'

'And after I procure this information, what do you expect me to do with it, Encyclopedia?'

I laughed. He was the one who'd bought me the entire *Encyclopedia Brown, Boy Detective* series as a kid, probably leading me onto this path of wanting to be the guy who figured things out.

'Give it to Detective Royce, of course,' I said. 'What else would I want?'

'It's the "what else" that gives me pause, Nephew.' About five seconds passed. 'But it's a good idea. I'll find out and get back to Royce on it when I do. But I will be expecting a much better bottle of Scotch for Easter this year.'

'I can do that. Thanks.'

We hugged again and he got into the back seat of the Town Car and it drove away. I took a few more deep breaths and went upstairs to see if my girlfriend was still awake.

She was. 'The freaking FBI?'

'I saw the badge and everything.'

'So you were right about him lying to you and Edgar the other day.'

'He's still lying. I'm not sure what about, but this guy's working off the books. It's like he's got a personal boner for Duke Lansing.'

'"Personal boner,"' she repeated. 'Is that technical jargon for cops or teachers?'

'Whatever happens next, I'm glad Royce will find out about Henderson tomorrow. I'm calling him at three-thirty unless he calls me first.'

Allison thought about that for a few seconds. 'I'm gonna give Royce a call tomorrow myself, Ray.'

'About what?'

'It may sound a little insensitive, but I'd love to do a piece from the killer's perspective.' She read the look on my face. 'From the vantage point, at least. The window. Didn't you ever wonder what it was like to commit premeditated murder, Ray?'

I nodded. As a cop, you couldn't ignore that feeling. What kind of person plans out a murder and then waits around to commit it? 'Yeah, sure. But what do you expect to get by visiting the scene of the crime? The window?'

'That's what makes it interesting. Didn't you tell me the other day that sometimes I'll find the answers before knowing the questions?'

I remembered saying something like that to her shortly after finding MoJo's body, but I was still somewhat fuzzy. 'Did I say that?'

'Well,' she said, 'this is kinda like that. Maybe.'

I had to admit it. She was good. Knowing her, she'd write a great piece. I'd be more excited about it if I hadn't known the victim, but I could see how this would interest readers, and I knew how much she needed to keep a story like this alive with fresh perspectives.

As for getting permission from Royce, that was on her and I told her so.

'Of course I'm gonna ask him directly,' she said. 'I'm not sure if he's still sore about the video I took, but involving you – no offense – would not be a good idea.'

'No offense taken. Good luck. Just do me a favor and call him early in the day so our phone calls aren't back to back. I don't want him thinking we're timing this stuff.'

'First thing in the morning, tough guy.' She pulled me in for a hug and a rather surprising squeeze of the butt. 'You ready for bed?'

I squeezed back. 'This journalism thing gets you kinda hot, huh?'

'Don't blow it by pointing it out, Ray. Just go brush that whiskey from your mouth and meet me in the bedroom.'

Like most obedient boyfriends, I did as instructed.

FIFTEEN

It turned out that I didn't have to worry about calling Royce. He showed up the next day at my school right after I'd finished lunch duty. I was sitting on the steps outside the building, soaking up a little sun, finishing an apple, and sucking a bottle of water dry. He pulled up in front of the building and walked over to me. He took off his blue suit jacket and held it in front of him.

'Got an interesting phone call from your guy at the FBI,' he said.

'I hate to disappoint you, Detective, but I don't have a guy at the FBI.'

'Special Agent David Henderson. They always love to mention the special part, you notice that?' He took a step closer. 'Please tell me you knew nothing about this until last night.'

I told him and asked why he didn't just call me for that information.

'Again, I wanted to see your face when you answered. Anything else interesting happen since I was at your place on Sunday?' He looked up at the sky. 'God, has it only been two days? You get a lot done in forty-eight hours, Mr Donne. Anybody else reach out to you I should know about? CIA? Homeland Security? NASA?'

I was going to point out that at least I was bringing out the sense of humor in him. I decided not to. 'I saw my uncle last night. He dropped by for a surprise visit.'

Royce nodded. 'Good. I brought him up to date on the case and told him how you were involved. Again. But, I did not ask him to go by your apartment and see you.'

'I think he's like you and just wanted to see my face when he told me to do my best to reduce my involvement in this case.'

'Do I need to swing by your buddy Edgar's and tell him the same thing? Give him the same warning about staying away?'

'No. Edgar doesn't know the truth about Henderson yet. Only what he told us the other day, which was mostly lies. Did Henderson tell you that his bosses don't know he's straying off the path?'

'Not at first, but when I asked him why my captain knew nothing about his interest in Maurice Joseph's murder, he kinda had to give up that tidbit.'

'So what do you do now?'

'Keep working the case. My supervisor is going to call Henderson's supervisor. and I wouldn't be surprised if Special Agent Henderson has to go shopping for some special new underwear this afternoon. Maybe some of that Mormon-strength stuff.'

I laughed and then looked at the building across the street where the shooter apparently did his work. 'Did you find anything over there?'

He turned around. 'Not much. No usable fingerprints, just some smudges where the shooter touched the window frame. It was a nice piece of information to have, though. We now know where the shooter was, but we got zip on forensics. We're going to re-canvass the neighbors, but the security cameras over there are either not working or in shit condition.' He turned back. 'I asked you a few days ago if you knew whether Mr Joseph was using again, remember?'

'Yes.' That was information I was not supposed to have and didn't want Allison's guy at the ME's to get burned. 'Why?' I asked.

'Turns out he was,' Royce said. And then he went on to tell me what I already knew. I did my best to act surprised and didn't have to try too hard to still be in disbelief.

'That's more than a little hard to wrap my head around,' I said. 'Like I told you the other day, I never saw any signs of MoJo using.'

'Toxicology reports don't usually lie, Mr Donne. Unlike FBI agents. I'm off to see Mr Joseph's widow now and find out what she knew about it.' He held up his hand. 'And before you ask: No, you may not come with me. Pregnant widow aside, his wife needs to be questioned. I'll do it at her place out of respect, but not with you there.'

He was right; I would have asked to be there. I was glad he saved me the trouble.

'One thing I can tell you, though,' he said.

'What's that?'

'I'm not sure if this was on your mind or not, but Mr Joseph was more than likely dead about five to ten minutes after he was shot. Even if you went up to the roof immediately after he was shot, you couldn't have done much.'

'Thanks,' I said. 'The thought had occurred to me.'

'ME said it was probably a crossbow. Like the one the guy uses on that walking zombie show. They pack one helluva punch.'

'I saw what they could do up close.'

'Right.' He turned to head off to his car and then stopped. 'Your girlfriend called me this morning, by the way.'

'Really? What about?' I was getting a lot of practice playing dumb today.

'She wanted access to the crime scene.' He pointed over at the building across the way. 'The window where the shooter was, not your roof.'

'She may have mentioned something along those lines. What'd you say?'

'I told her I'd think about it. Who knows, maybe some fresh eyes'll help out. I'll probably say yes, but what's the fun in doing that right away?'

I stood up and stretched. 'Your call, Detective. But thanks ahead of time.'

'No problem,' he said. 'I'll have to go with her, of course, so I gotta see how my schedule plays out.' He started again toward his car. 'Good reporter, your girlfriend,' he said without turning back.

'Yes,' I agreed.

'You guys deserve each other.'

I agreed with that, as well, but not knowing whether it was a compliment, I didn't say so out loud. He got into his car, did an illegal U-turn, and headed off to speak with a dead man's widow about his drug usage. With the sun heating me up, I wanted to walk to the river. Breathe in some of that brackish air and watch the water go where it goes. Somewhere far from here.

That would have to wait. I had a few more hours in my day left.

I was outside in the playground doing dismissal when my phone rang. Edgar.

'What's up, Edgar?'

'There's another memorial.' I could hear the stress in his voice. 'Another one.'

'OK, relax,' I said. 'Where and when?'

'Tomorrow. Up at the rehab house. Newer Leaves.'

'That's cool,' I said. 'How'd you find out?'

'I just got off the phone with Lisa. They called her this morning. It's not a big deal, but they asked her to come up and she asked me to drive her. Her mom and sister are leaving to go back home tonight.'

'I hope you said yes.'

'I did,' he said. 'I also said you would come along.'

A few years ago, I would have asked Edgar why he would say such a thing. Volunteer me without asking me first. Now, I knew better.

Raymond Donne: Emotional Support Human, Will Travel.

'How far upstate?' I asked, figuring I might be able to go up and then come down for some school time.

'At Newer Leaves. Just above New Paltz,' he said. 'Two-hour drive.'

So much for doing both the memorial and school the next day. I hadn't taken a day off all year. Looked like that was about to change. 'OK, man. What's the plan?'

He told me, I agreed, and he promised to bring coffee and a half-dozen of my favorite donuts. I know: cops and donuts. But I wasn't a cop anymore. I told him I'd see him in the morning and headed back inside to finish up some paperwork and tell Ron Thomas I'd be taking tomorrow off.

And then my phone rang again. Allison.

'Hey,' I said. 'What's up?'

'I hear you just spoke with Royce.'

'I did. How'd you know?'

'He just called me. What'd you say to him?'

'Nothing he didn't already know. He did most of the talking. He told me about MoJo's tox report and that he was leaving to go speak with Lisa. He also told me you called him this morning about your crime scene visit. He told me he was probably going to give you permission.'

'He did,' she said. 'He's going to give me ten minutes some time tomorrow after he figures out what his day looks like.'

'That's great,' I said and then I told what my next day was looking like.

'Oh, man. I'd love to go to that, Ray. That place was a big part of MoJo's story.'

Story? 'You mean his life, right?'

'You know what I mean.' She was silent for a bit. 'Well, whatever you said to Royce – or didn't say to Royce – thanks.'

'You're welcome. I'll see you tonight for dinner, right?'

'As far as I know,' she said. 'I need a nice quiet evening at the apartment. No LineUp, no stories to submit. Just me and the love of my life.'

'Is he bigger than I am?'

She laughed. 'That was good, Raymond. See ya later. Love you.'

'I love you back, Allie.'

I got through the next hour with no more phone calls or surprise visits.

Make that fifty-eight minutes.

'He said Maurice was using, Ray. That he had fentanyl and heroin in his system. Excuse my language, but what the fuck?' Detective Royce had just left Lisa's.

'I know, Lisa. He dropped by school to talk about a few things.'

'Ray, I am not just talking as Maurice's wife, I'm talking as a licensed drug counselor: he was not using.' She paused as if she were about to say something else. I waited. She had just been given some pretty harsh news and maybe was using the time with me to process it. When she didn't speak again, I did.

'What is it?' I asked. 'I mean, what *else* is it?'

I could hear her breathing on the other end. 'Thank God my sister and mother left this morning, Ray. I don't think I have the strength to hide something like this from them.' More deep breathing. 'After the detective left, I went through Maurice's stuff again. In his area of the bedroom.'

'And . . .'

'And I found some bags of heroin, Ray. They were hidden in the back of one of the drawers in that little desk he had.'

Dammit. 'I'm sorry, Lisa. I don't know what to say.'

'Detective Royce also told me about what they found in Maurice's pockets.'

'Yeah,' I said.

'Did you know about that, Ray?'

'After the fact, Lisa. And I certainly wasn't going to be the one to bring it up to you. I figured the cops would do that soon enough.'

'You got that right.' She started crying now. I waited patiently on my end until she was ready to speak again. It didn't take as long as I had thought. 'What'd they tell you about the bags of heroin they found on him?'

'The cops didn't tell me anything,' I said. 'I found out through Allison, who was told by someone she knows in the medical examiner's office.'

'You know anything about how street heroin is packaged?'

'A little. Why?'

'The bags I found in Maurice's desk had little dice printed on them.'

'Dice?' I asked. 'Like . . . rolling dice?'

'Yeah, two of them. Double-eights. You ever see that before? Eights? On dice?'

'Only real dice I've seen go up to six. When I was on the street, drugs were mostly marijuana and crack. Most of that came with labels. Heroin's just become big again in the past ten years. But, yeah, the dealers package their stuff so it stands out from others. If people like your stuff, they remember the bags.' I was telling her stuff she probably already knew.

'Then we need to find out who was dealing heroin with double-eights on them.'

We? 'I'm sure the police are looking into that, Lisa,' I said.

'Screw the police, Ray. They're gonna think Maurice was back on the junk and write him off as another victim of the drug trade. One more addict who couldn't handle rehab. You know that.'

'I also know Royce,' I said. 'He'll look into it. He's a thorough investigator.'

'I didn't like the way he was looking at me when I told him Maurice was not using. It was like he thought I was lying to cover up. Just another junkie's wife.'

'I'm sorry but that's how cops think, Lisa. You've dealt with enough of them to know that.'

'But this is Maurice we're talking about.'

'You're preaching to the choir,' I said. 'I just don't think there's much we can do right now. We have to let—'

'Don't you still have people on the street? Maurice told me about all the stuff you've been getting into since you left the PD. You must have people you can go to and look into this.'

My God, I thought. *Between her and Edgar, I wasn't sure how much more tugging my heart could take.*

'Let me ask around a bit,' I said, thinking, of course, about Tio. 'I may know some people who know people. But no promises.'

'I won't ask for any, Ray. And I do appreciate this.'

'I'll make some calls. And I'll see you tomorrow around ten with Edgar.'

'Thank you for that, too. I don't think he would go without you.'

'He's a work in progress, Lisa.'

She laughed. 'He is at that, Ray. Thank you.'

'Thank me when I find something out. See ya tomorrow.'

SIXTEEN

I had a few hours before I needed to be home if I wanted to have dinner with Allison. Lisa was right; I did still have some people on the street I could reach out to. And there was nobody more in the know than Tio. I took the fifteen-minute walk from school to his pizza place.

Boo had a booth all to himself off to the side. The table was covered with spreadsheets, a laptop, and what looked like a few menus from the local competition. Another young man was in the kitchen working the ovens, and a girl of maybe sixteen was working the phone. A mom and two kids filled up another table, eating some slices. A few customers were waiting around for their takeout orders. I was the only white person in the place and had arrived just as the dinner rush was beginning.

'Yo, Teacherman,' Boo said in his usual greeting to me. 'You slumming it tonight or something? Or you just cravin' some of my eggplant parmigian?'

I reached out my hand and shook his as I slid in across from him. If I hadn't known better, I'd have thought he was doing his taxes.

'What's with all the paperwork?' I asked. 'You finally taking over?'

'Think I can't?'

'No.' I leaned forward and whispered, 'I think it's about time.'

He smiled at that. I'd known Boo for as long as I'd known Tio – although he'd grown at least a foot-and-a-half since then – and I knew that to get him to smile was a major accomplishment. 'Tio expecting you?' Boo asked.

'No. Something just came up and I figured I'd swing by and see if I could get a few minutes with him.'

Boo looked back down at his papers. 'That what you figured?'

'It's what I was hoping, anyway.'

I waited a while as Boo considered that. We both knew I should have called first, but I thought with Tio dropping by my place of business unexpectedly the other day, maybe our relationship was changing. What I was feeling from Boo was maybe not.

'He's not around tonight, Teacherman,' Boo said. 'You got a message you wanna leave?'

I leaned back and let out some air. I had hoped this would go smoother.

'You don't wanna deal with me?' he said, eyes on his laptop. 'Afta all we been through together?' He did sarcasm well. I should put him and Royce together some day.

My turn to smile. He was right. I could tell he wasn't the little kid I'd met all those years ago. He may not be Tio yet, but it was as good a time as any to trust him.

'What do you know about the Brooklyn heroin trade?' I asked.

He didn't flinch. He just tapped some keys on his laptop, checked something on his spreadsheets, and pushed a menu at me. 'You like this one?'

I looked at the menu. It was fine and I said so.

'How about these?' he said, sliding the other ones across the table.

'I don't know, Boo,' I said, opening each of them up and reading the offerings. 'They all look the same to me.'

He nodded. 'That's what I'm thinking,' he said. 'We need a menu that stand out. Something that says we're not like others. We better.'

'You doing the numbers and the marketing now?'

He shook his head. 'Why you wanna know about heroin? This got something to do with your boy that caught an arrow someone shot in the air the other day?'

I didn't know how to answer that. I had come here seeking some wisdom from Tio and here I was with his protégé, and I was unsure how much to say.

'That's OK, Teacherman. Your silence answer the question.' He closed up the laptop, stacked all the spreadsheets together and made a neat pile of them on top of the various menus. 'I know some. What do you wanna know?'

I guessed I was trusting him. 'Double-eights.'

'Add up to sixteen. Even you know that.'

'They were on some bags of heroin that were found in MoJo's possession. He was the guy killed by the arrow last week. Dice with double-eights.'

'You wanna know who's dealing H with double-eights on it?'

'That's exactly what I want to know.'

'The cops wanna know this, too? Or is this between you and Tio? And me.'

'I'm not sure what the police want to know, Boo. I just know MoJo's wife – widow – asked me to look into this. She's holding the belief that her husband was not using anymore.' I explained to him that Lisa had experience with this kind of situation.

He looked me in the eyes and seemed to be assessing me. Damn, this kid had grown up. 'Whatta you think?'

A great question. 'I don't know at this point, Boo. I don't want to believe he was back on the stuff, but I don't wanna sound like a rookie, either.'

He nodded. 'I feel ya, Teacherman. You caught between being a friend and some hard truth about that friend.'

'I don't know if it is the truth.'

'And what if it is?' he asked.

'Then that's what I tell his wife.'

He waited a few seconds. 'Whatchoo gonna tell the police?'

'Nothing,' I said. 'Let them find their own truth.'

Boo considered that. He rubbed his temples like a man struggling to make a decision. There was nothing for me to do except wait. Finally he said, 'Let me make a call.' He got up out of the booth and walked through the kitchen. I sat there realizing that the smells and sounds of food were making me hungry. Maybe I'd bring something home from here for Allison and me.

Boo came back in about five minutes. 'Made two calls, Teacherman. One to Tio.' He looked around. 'Just 'cause I *can* run this place, don't mean I do. Had to ask for some time off. When I told him it was for you, he said take it and he'd settle up with you later.'

'And the other call?'

'Me and you gonna have some dinner and then we taking a field trip.'

I called Allison and left a message that our quiet evening at home was going to have to be rescheduled.

Boo and I were on the L train heading to Bushwick Avenue. After our meeting at Tio's pizza place, he had barely spoken a word to me except to remind me which stop we were getting off at and to keep my mouth shut as much as possible when we got there. At the moment, he had his eyes glued to his phone, probably playing one of the myriad of games available to young men of his age. I took a look at his screen and smiled. I could not have been more wrong.

'Somethin' funny, Teacherman?' he asked, without taking his eyes off his phone.

'Nah, Boo,' I said. 'Not funny. Just surprising.'

'What so surprising? That I'm readin'?'

'Sorry. It's just that most times I see teenagers on the train—'

'I ain't most teenagers,' he cut me off. 'Didn't you just see me at the store? Ya think I'm one a them knuckleheads can't go an hour or so without answering the call of duty or some shit?'

I had insulted him. 'I'm sorry.' In all the years I had known him – even when he was a 'kid' – I had never once thought of Boo as less than highly intelligent. And, yes, he had just proven that back at the pizza place.

'That's like me lookin' at you and thinking "Oh, there goes another white man home to his wife and two-point-three kids out in the 'burbs."' Now his eyes were on me. 'Guess I'd be wrong about that, right?'

'Pretty much.' I was afraid I'd crossed a line and he was going to stop talking altogether. Again, I was wrong.

'Besides,' he said, tapping his phone with his index finger. 'This here's Langston Hughes. You ever hear of him?'

'I teach middle school, Boo. Of course I've heard of him. I've taught his poems.'

'Thought you guys only taught stuff written by white men that been dead for a hundred years. Or am I wrong 'bout that?'

'With me you would be,' I said. 'I've taught Langston Hughes, Toni Morrison, James Baldwin. I even throw in some Tupac and Missy Elliot from time to time.'

He nodded. 'You ain't one a them white teachers think they cool teaching black artists, though. I can tell.'

'How can you tell that?'

'Way you talk to Tio,' he said. 'Way you talk to me.'

'How's that?'

He was looking for the right words. 'With respect,' he came up with. 'Like I may not know what you know, but I'm smart in my own ways. I know things you don't. Shit, that's why we on this little trip right now. You got something to learn and you came to Tio – and now me – to get schooled.'

He was right. I had the urge to stick out my hand for a fist bump, but controlled myself. *That* would be a white guy thing. Instead, I said, 'So what are you going to do when you're done working with Tio?'

'Whatta ya mean by that?'

'You're what now? Nineteen? Tio told me you have your GED and here you are riding the L train reading poetry. Then there's all that stuff back at the pizza place. The numbers, the menus. There must be something more you wanna do.'

He looked down into his lap and shook his head. 'This ain't one a them "Where do you see yourself in five years?" questions, is it? That's one a the reasons I did the GED and not the regular sit-through-high-school-classes diploma thing. Too many questions like that.'

I almost apologized again but decided against it. I had asked a question I wanted an answer to. I asked the same thing to all my graduating eighth-graders.

'You gonna stay at the pizza place the rest of your life, Boo?' I asked. 'There's nothing wrong with that, I'm just asking.'

He looked down at his phone again. 'What? You worried about me having a dream deferred, Teacherman? It ain't like that.'

Quoting Mr Hughes to make his point. Nice. 'What is it like?'

He shrugged. 'I'm good where I'm at right now. Still learning from Tio.' He looked me dead in the eyes. 'I'm good.'

The way he said those last two words made it clear the conversation was over. And for the third time in less than five minutes I was proven wrong when he mumbled something I couldn't quite make out.

'What's that?' I asked.

'Said I'm also taking a cooking class. Over at the Culinary.'

'Shit, Boo. That's great. After that you can—'

'Shhh,' he said, his index finger touching his lips. 'This our stop.'

We walked in silence the two blocks to the bodega where we were supposed to meet with Tio's . . . I don't know . . . colleague? As we crossed the street, I saw a huge black guy – twenty maybe? – sucking on one of those vapor things that are all the rage these days. He and Boo exchanged a complicated handshake and, glancing at me, the guy said, 'You sure he's OK, Boo? He looks like a cop.'

'Used to be, Missouri. Now he's a teacher.'

The guy was wearing a St Louis Cardinals baseball cap and a Kansas City Royals sweatshirt. His black sweatpants had the word *Mizzou* running down each leg.

'I can see where your allegiances lie,' I said. 'That why they call you Missouri?'

'No,' he said. 'They call me Missouri 'cause I love company.' He smiled at his own joke and put his fist to his chest. 'I'm from Ferguson, man. Left just before that cop killed Michael Brown.' He waited for a response. I gave him none. 'So, yeah,' he continued, 'I'm from the Show-Me State. You got something you wanna show me?'

I reached into my pocket, pulled out my cell phone and handed it to him. Boo told me to expect that. I raised my arms just in case he wanted to search me.

'Nah, you a'ight, man. Tio and Boo say I can trust you, I trust you. Just these other guys we gonna go see, they don't want no strangers – 'specially Caucasian strangers, no offense – with cell phones comin' a their game, you feel me?'

I nodded. 'I feel you.'

He and Boo smiled at that. A white guy saying he feels you must sound pretty funny. It did to me.

'Let's go then.'

We were outside the building in less than five minutes; it was a four-story brownstone that had seen its best days about three weeks after it was built. If what I guessed was true, each floor had three apartments and – even given the condition of the building – each went for a few thousand a month, given how close they were to the subway. We went around the back through a small alleyway that smelled like garbage, piss, and something with a lot of fur had died recently. When we got to the back entrance – which looked like the doors to a storm cellar – Missouri knocked twice, then three times, then twice again.

'What's the deal here again?' I asked.

Missouri blew out some vape smoke. 'My cousin's the super a the building. He's got a basement apartment. Not much, just a room, a hot plate, and a bathroom with a shower stall. The other part of the basement's a . . . recreation area, ya might call it.' He took another puff. As he let that one out, he said, 'That's your last question for awhile, Teach. Like the man said, you need to be seen more than heard.'

I nodded my understanding and the cellar door opened a few inches. A voice said, 'Missouri Man,' and then the door opened wider. When the owner of the voice looked up and saw Boo, he nodded. When he saw me, he said, 'You bring Eminem whichoo?'

We all laughed at that; I was the only one who sounded less than amused.

'Nah,' Boo said. 'This Tio's man, Raymond. S'all good. He here to learn.'

I got a good look at the voice as he stepped up to join us: he was black, about six feet tall, all dressed in red sweats with white high tops and a backwards blue baseball cap. He took the time to look at me, too.

'Any friend of Tio's,' he said, and opened the door to let us inside.

I followed Missouri and Boo down a barely lit set of steps. The Voice stayed at the door. 'Watch y'all's steps now,' he said. 'I'm the only nine-one-one 'round here and I'm just as fast as the real one.' He chuckled at his own joke as we descended. The metal door shut behind us.

According to what Missouri had just described, I assumed we were stepping right from the stairs into the 'recreation area.' Some work lights hung from the six-foot ceiling above a piece of plywood on the floor that was at least eight feet by eight feet. Most of the players in the room – seven, eight? – were slouching, careful of the low ceiling. The air in the basement was a mixture of must, something lemony, sweat, and testosterone. I was again reminded of the boys' locker room at school. The area contained two unoccupied chairs – metal and folding – and a teenager stood off to the side manning a cooler and a stand of bagged snacks.

All eyes – eight pairs from what I could now make out – turned to see who the newcomers were. When that was established all sixteen eyes settled on me. If I had a dollar for every time I was the only white guy in a room, I'd probably have enough to get in a few rolls of this dice game.

'He cool,' Missouri announced. 'Friend of Tio's.' He raised his hands like he was preaching. 'Don't ask, don't tell.'

With that, everyone went back to the game, which, as we got closer, I could see involved three dice: a pair of reds and one blue. If the colors meant anything, I didn't know what, and I knew enough not to ask. I watched as the roller, clad in a Yankees jersey and blue jeans, shook his hand up by his ear, whispered something to the dice, and rolled. Nobody reacted so I figured the roll didn't mean much.

'That's Clack Clack,' Boo whispered to me. 'He always come with a lot of cheese.' He rubbed his index finger and thumb together in case I didn't get the lingo. 'Don't always leave with all that much, though.'

I nodded as Clack Clack picked up the dice again, went through the same motions as before, and rolled. This time the other men murmured amongst themselves. This roll had some meaning behind it.

'That's a point,' Boo whispered. 'He got a pair a twos and a four. Four's the number to beat now.' The next guy picked up the dice and rolled them between his hands like he was warming them up. He was wearing a white collared shirt and dark pants, like he'd just gotten off work. His shiny new shoes were as out of place in that basement as I was. 'That's Trips,' Boo said. 'Wall Street boy. He roll more triples than anyone I ever seen. Triples hard to beat. Three sixes you automatically win.'

I did the math – one sixth times one sixth times one sixth – and whispered, 'One out of two hundred and sixteen chance of rolling a triple six. That's less than half a percent.'

'See,' said Boo. 'There's somethin' I didn't know.' He paused and added, 'Not sure I need to.'

I watched as Trips, as if on cue, rolled and all the guys let out a slur of words, the slurriest coming from Clack Clack, who apparently had just been beaten by a triple.

'Damn, Trips,' he said. 'How you do me like that?'

'Good Lord loves me, Clack,' Trips said. 'Loves me like a rock.' Trips picked up the money off the plywood and handed the dice to the guy next to him. Boo touched me on the arm.

'That's the guy you wanna talk to, Teacherman,' Boo whispered. 'Hex.'

'Hex? Does he do a little voodoo on the dice or something?'

'You can ask him after he lose,' Boo said. 'Shouldn't be too long a wait.' He looked over at the kid with the cooler. 'Why'nt you get Missouri and me a water while we're waiting.'

'Sure.' I ducked under a work light and walked over to the kid at the cooler. 'Three waters, please.'

The kid reached through the ice – I noticed a few beers in there – and pulled out the waters. I hated that crinkling sound the plastic bottles made as he handed them to me. 'Fi'teen dollars,' he said.

'Fifteen dollars?' I said. 'Five bucks a water?'

'White man can divide,' he said. 'Ballpark prices, m'man.'

The last time I had paid ballpark prices for a drink, I was pretty sure was at a ballpark. 'Anybody ever walk out and get their own water at the corner?'

'Not sure,' the kid said. 'If they did, they ain't come back in.'

I reached into my pocket and pulled out a twenty. The kid gave me back five ones. I turned to go back to the game and he said, 'What, no tip?'

I looked over my shoulder. 'Don't ride between subway cars.'

As I walked back over to Boo and Missouri, the guy they called Hex had just finished rolling the dice. 'Got damn,' he yelled with his mouth inches from the ceiling. 'Tell me, God,' he screamed. 'Why you love Trips so much and hate me? Why?'

Trips and the others all laughed. Within a few seconds, Hex joined in with them. He bent over, picked up the dice and handed them to the next guy. 'Be careful now, Polo. Somethin' wrong with them bones, boy.'

I handed Boo the water and he said, 'Hex just rolled a 1, 2, 3. Automatic loser.'

I considered telling him the odds of that and decided not to.

When I gave Missouri his water, he thanked me. 'Now Hex gonna go outside. Either he gonna blow off steam and hit the pipe, go

home and lick his wounds, or tap the money machine at the bodega
on the corner. Depends on the kinda week he had.'

I figured that to mean how much Hex had made slinging heroin
along this part of the L Train route. I didn't like that the info I was
looking for was going to be given to me by a drug dealer, but
when you're looking for the person who sold heroin laced with
fentanyl, you're not going to find the answers at the library.

Hex made his way over to the three of us, and bumped fists with
Boo and Missouri. Then he looked at me. 'You get off at the wrong
stop, Magnum?'

'This here's Raymond,' Boo said. 'Tio'd like it if you spoke
to him.'

'Tio'd like if I spoke to him,' Hex repeated. 'Since when I do
what Tio like?'

That question was met with silence, as if Boo knew the answer
would come to Hex if he just took the time to think on it. I've done
the same in my class. If you wait long enough, most kids can
answer their own questions. While Hex was considering the plusses
and minuses of the situation, he looked at my unopened water bottle.
'You gonna drink that?'

I handed him the bottle and kept my mouth shut. Hex unscrewed
the top of the bottle and chugged down the water like a college freshman
on a beer-drinking dare. When he finished it, he screwed the lid back
on, handed me the bottle, and said, 'Make sure you get your nickel
back on that now. That way it only four-ninety-five a bottle.'

Again, we all laughed. Hex continued. 'Let's go outside for some
air.' We all followed Hex as he made his way up the stairs and 911
let us out. I tossed my empty to the guy selling water. *There's your
tip, son.* After being in the basement for almost half an hour, the
outside air came as . . . well, a breath of fresh air.

Without even thinking, the four of us ended up in a square in
the alley between buildings. The air stopped feeling fresh again.

'Whatchoo wanna talk about, Magnum?' Hex asked me.

I looked at Boo, then Missouri. They both nodded. I wasn't used
to keeping my mouth shut and even less accustomed to having to
ask for permission to speak.

'A friend of mine was killed the other day,' I said. 'You might've
heard about it. Shot by an arrow on top of my school's building.'

'Read about that in the news. Some real cowboy-and-Indian shit.
What's that got to do with me?'

'Turns out he had heroin laced with fentanyl in his system. If he hadn't been shot by the arrow, he probably would've OD'd up there.'

'Again,' Hex said. 'I don't feel what that's got to do with me.'

I swallowed before saying, 'He used to buy off you. You used to sell him—'

'Whoa, whoa, whoa, Mister PI. I ain't know this guy up on your roof and if I did I sure didn't sell him whatever you think I sold him.' Hex turned to Boo. 'This what Tio sent this guy here for? To jack me up? Catch me saying I sold someone some Murder Eight?' He took a step toward me. I held my ground.

'Chill, Hex,' Boo said. 'Ain't nobody jacking you up. All he wants to know is—'

'If you didn't sell the fentanyl to him, I need to know who did,' I interrupted. 'Victim's name was Maurice Joseph. You might have known him as MoJo.'

That took about five seconds to sink in and when it did, Hex said, 'Ah, shit, man. That was MoJo? I didn't know it was him. They didn't say that name in the newspaper. Damn, man. That's some weird fuckin' shit right there.'

I guessed in Hex's world, murder by arrow on a school rooftop only becomes 'weird fuckin' shit' when you knew the victim. We were silent for a while as Hex pondered the sky. He let out a long breath. 'I ain't . . . conducted business with MoJo for a few years now. He told me he was done with that shit. I heard he got – had – a kid comin' and his lady was giving him all kinds of shit about shapin' up and whatnot. This ain't on me, Magnum, and you can tell all your cop friends that.'

'I'm not a cop, Hex. And I'm not a private investigator. I'm a school teacher who was friends with MoJo, and I promised his wife I'd check some shit out.' I let him think on that before asking, 'If someone *was* conducting business with MoJo, you have any idea who it might be? Packages his shit with dice, specifically double-eights.'

'What? You think 'cause I'ma businessman, I know all the other businessmen in the same business?' He challenged me with his eyes, but I knew he knew what – or who – I was talking about. 'You know all the teachers in the teaching system, Magnum?'

'I think,' I said, holding his gaze, 'that a smart businessman such as you would know his competition. Especially along the L train. Tio thought you'd know, too. He said if anyone would, it'd be you.'

Obviously flattered by that, Hex paused and said, 'Tio say that?'

'Word for word.' Truth was, having not spoken directly with Tio, I had no idea what he had said.

Hex looked at Boo who said, 'Heard it myself, Hex. Tio knows you in the know.'

Hex nodded. 'Respect,' he said. 'If MoJo's been buying on the L, it ain't from any of my boys. We may be what you call competition, but we keep in touch and all. Making sure we don't shit in someone else's pot, ya feel me?'

I nodded. He went on.

'Only guy I don't check in with is out in Canarsie.' The last stop on the L train. 'This guy some Casper the Friendly Ghost-looking motherfucker. I heard he mighta been putting dice on his merch.'

'Pretty white, huh?'

'So white they call him Al. Like in Al Bino. His skin so pale you can see his internal organs, know what I'm sayin'? Got them pink eyes like those white bunny rabbits.' He gave a fake shiver. 'That kinda white freak even me out.'

Guy like that shouldn't be too hard to get info on. 'You don't happen to know—'

'We never exchanged business cards, if that's what you gonna ask next.'

I was silent for a few beats, taking the opportunity to look at Missouri and Boo. Neither one of them seemed to have anything to add to the conversation, so I stuck out my hand to Hex. 'I appreciate your help.'

'Yeah, yeah, yeah,' he said. 'You be sure and tell Tio I helped you out.'

'I will.' The three of us were about to head off when I thought of one more thing. 'Hey, Hex,' I said.

'Yeah?'

'Just out of curiosity. Where'd you get the name?'

'When I'm not doin' business, Magnum, I'm playing dice. Don't play pool, no fantasy football bullshit, and I don't bowl. I'm a dice man.'

I gave that some thought and it hit me. 'Hexagon.'

He pointed at me. 'I thought you was too smart to be a cop.'

SEVENTEEN

'I can take care of myself,' Allison said when I returned home and apologized for the late change of plans. 'I heated up some leftovers and watched a chick flick.' She was cleaning off a few dishes. 'You learn anything useful on your field trip?'

'More than I expected about dice games,' I said. 'A little bit about who MoJo may have gotten the heroin from. It was amazing how offended this guy Hex was by my even suggesting he was selling heroin laced with fentanyl.'

'I'm not surprised, Ray. Any self-respecting dealer suspected of lacing his heroin with fentanyl is not going to stay in business very long. You lose a lot of customers that way. Literally and figuratively.' She finished washing her last dish, turned around and leaned on the counter. 'You know anybody out in Canarsie?'

'I'm sure I do but none that come right to mind,' I said. 'I'll give Billy Morris a call in the morning.'

Billy and I used to work the streets together in Williamsburg when we both came out of the academy. Our relationship ran the way many cop relationships go: we went from inseparable, to separated, and eventually to a couple of guys who got together over beers once in a while, telling stories that just got bigger and better with each retelling.

Never, Billy once told me, *let the truth get in the way of a good story.*

'There is something, though,' Allison said.

'What's that?'

'If MoJo didn't buy from his usual dealer, this guy Hex, then maybe he didn't buy the heroin at all. Why would he go to a dealer he doesn't trust? That's – and MoJo is a case in point – risky business.'

I thought about that. 'So someone *gave* the heroin to MoJo? Someone he trusted enough to take drugs from?'

'That's one possibility,' she said. 'Put your police cap on, Ray.'

I did. The first thing I came up with was, 'It's highly unlikely that someone stashed the stuff on MoJo without his knowing

because that'd be kinda hard to do before or after he was shot.'
Even I could tell I was searching for an improbable possibility.

'True.' She wasn't buying it, either. 'It's also possible MoJo took
the stuff off someone else, the temptation was just too much and
got an unexpected jones for a hit, and—'

'Edgar said MoJo was a sponsor for some of the members of his
support group. He could have been protecting someone else.'

'I can see that,' she said. 'But that still doesn't explain—'

'How the heroin and fentanyl made it into MoJo's system.' I
walked out onto the balcony, careful to leave my police cap on.
I looked out at the skyline. 'Is it too late to call your guy at the
ME's office?'

Allison put her hands on my shoulder. 'It's almost ten. My guy
at the ME's office does have a life outside the ME's office, Ray.'

'I'd like to reach out to him tomorrow. Can I do that directly or
do I have to go through you.'

'I'll call him in the morning and tell him you'll be calling. Or I
could ask your questions for you.' She paused, studied my face,
and shook her head. 'But you don't want me to do that.'

'I don't. My questions; I should be the one to ask them. And the
way it usually goes is that more answers will lead to more questions
and I don't want to play phone tag.' I pulled her close. 'You OK
with that?'

She squeezed me. 'Just remember, Ray. This is *my* guy at the
ME. You can't have him. I'm just loaning him to you for a while.
You can get your own guy.'

'That's funny.'

'I do what I can.' She broke from the hug. 'Wanna see my latest
article before I upload it to the site?'

'I'd be honored,' I said.

'Grab a couple of beers and I'll meet you back here in a minute.'
Again, I did as I was told and read Allison's latest.

FROM WHITE NATIONALIST TO AMERICAN TEEN
A YOUNG MAN'S JOURNEY OUT OF NYC WHITE SUPREMACY
Second in a series by Allison Rogers

Harlan S. enjoys skipping stones. Up here along the Hudson
River, close enough to hear the traffic rumbling across the

George Washington Bridge as it moves into and out of New York City and New Jersey, it's not easy to find good, flat skipping stones. But that doesn't stop Harlan from looking and using what he can.

'My dad used to take us camping upstate,' he tells me. 'We'd fish and hunt. The only supplies we brought were our guns, fishing rods, sleeping bags and our tent. Everything else we needed, we took from the land. He used to tell us that was the only way we'd survive if there were ever another war because the next war would be the last war.' He pauses to let out a breath. 'When we weren't gathering wood for the fire or hunting for food or swimming in the lake, we'd skip stones.' He looks up at the line of trucks coming over the river into Manhattan. 'Once I saw my dad skip one seven times. I thought it was the coolest thing I'd ever seen.'

Listening to Harlan speak about his father, a White Nationalist, I can hear the little boy who once looked up to his dad, like all little boys should. Now, Harlan is hiding from his family, afraid to go back to the world in which he was raised. A world where little boys and girls are carefully taught to hate those who don't look like they do, pray like they do, think like they do.

He finds a pretty decent flat stone and sidearms it into the river; it skips four times. Not bad, but it's not seven.

When I ask where he wants to go from here, Harlan shrugs. 'Out west, I guess. Somewhere I can finish up school, work outside, maybe go to college. Maybe even back upstate.' He looks north up the Hudson. 'Maybe I can get a job along the river while finishing up school.'

Now that he's away from his family, I can't help but be curious: why doesn't he just leave New York and start all over?

'I'm sixteen,' he reminds me. 'My mom has some people out in Colorado and Wyoming, but I'm having trouble tracking them down. They kinda . . . disowned us because of my dad's – our family's – beliefs. I use the computers at the libraries when I can, and tried to look them up. I called a few times, but I don't know if they're the right ones because no one's calling me back.'

If they invited him out west, would he go?

'I'm not sure,' he says. 'I left without saying goodbye to

anyone. I'm not worried about my parents, they'll be fine, but I have two little sisters. I need to make sure they're OK. My dad's been on edge lately, really getting more and more angry.'

At? 'The government,' Harlan tells me. 'The schools, the media, the Jews, Blacks, Asians. Socialists. Hell, he's angry at everyone these days.'

He picks up another stone, but even I can see this one is not made for skipping. He rolls it around in his hand for a few seconds like Mariano Rivera deciding just how nasty a cut fastball he's going to deliver. Finally, Harlan rears back with all he's got, leg kick and all, and throws the rock halfway to New Jersey.

'My sisters,' he repeats. 'I gotta make sure my sisters are OK.'

I ask him if he wants to have dinner with me so we can talk some more. I try to tempt him with burgers, pizza, Thai food. Has he ever had Thai food?

He says that the shelter where he's staying tonight has him on supper duty and he has to leave me soon. 'I gotta set the tables and serve the meal tonight. I don't mind. I used to do it at home all the time. Only difference is that tonight I gotta do it for fifty people, not five.' Another pause. 'And for people who don't look like me.' He thinks about it and says, 'Tonight's Fried Chicken Night. Maybe that's something I can learn to do. Cook. I can do that anywhere.'

As we go our separate ways until next time, I can't help but be impressed by the thing I hear most in his voice. Through all the fear and worry about his sisters, one thing comes out in every word he speaks.

Hope.

'Wow,' I said when I was finished. 'This is what you were doing today?'

'Yep. You're not the only one who's meeting interesting people these days.'

I reread the last paragraph. 'Most writers cannot interview a kid who's run away from his White Nationalist family and end on a note of optimism, Allie.'

She raised her beer bottle for me to toast. 'I am not most writers, Raymond.' She squinted at me. 'I thought we had established that.'

'We did,' I said. 'I mean I know that. Was this meeting planned?'

'He called me this afternoon and said he had a few hours before having to get back to his new shelter. Not too many things with Harlan can be planned these days.'

I looked at the beginning of the piece again. 'Is he staying up by the GW Bridge?'

'He didn't say, and I didn't ask. And before you ask, I didn't bring up Duke Lansing, either. I figure I'll wait for the next interview. If there is a next interview.' She took another sip of beer. 'So, is it ready to post?'

'You need to ask? It's great.'

'Just being polite.' She pressed a few buttons and the laptop made a whooshing sound. Her piece on Harlan was out there for the whole world to read. 'Now, my day is officially over.'

'Before I get ready for bed, I think I'm gonna give Billy Morris a call tonight instead of waiting until tomorrow.'

'Billy? It's after nine. He doesn't pick up his phone after nine, even I know that.'

'I'm planning on leaving a message. I have a question that I guess can wait until tomorrow, but I wanna be his first call in the morning.'

'OK.' She kissed me on the cheek. 'Don't be late if he somehow picks up.'

'Voicemail and brushing my teeth, Allie.'

I stepped back onto the balcony to make the call. Sure enough, his voicemail picked up and I left a message asking him to give me a call first thing in the morning.

EIGHTEEN

First thing in the morning, my cell phone went off. Billy Morris.

'Mornin', Partner,' he said. 'First thing enough for ya?'

'Yeah,' I said, rubbing the sleep from my eyes. 'You can run a wake-up service when you retire.'

'Still having too much fun to think about retiring, Ray. Plus those girls of mine seem to be set on going to college and they're much smarter than their old man. They ain't gonna settle on a state school and just a bachelor's.'

I rolled over to see if the phone had awakened Allison. She wasn't there and I realized the shower was running. 'You married smart, Billy. Good thing the girls got your wife's genes.'

'And my wife still looks good in those jeans, son.' An oldie, but goodie. 'Now, what can I do you for?'

Almost right to the point. 'What do you know about the Canarsie drug scene?' I asked. 'With an emphasis on the heroin trade.'

'Whoa, son. I thought you were calling to get together or some shit. What's this line of inquiry about?'

I loved when Billy talked Cop. 'Just like I said, I need to know what you know about Canarsie and drugs.' I knew I'd be telling him the whole story soon.

'About as much as you know about the National League Central, I'd suppose. I got a little bit of knowledge but I'm more of a Brooklyn West kinda guy. You know I'm dealing mostly with The Chosen People these days.' He meant the Jewish communities in Sunset and Borough Parks. He may have three bars on his uniform these days, but he was still a street cop and it didn't matter where those streets were. Blacks, Hispanics, Asians, West Indians, Orthodox Jews: Billy Morris was the United Nations of cops. 'But I got some of my peeps over there,' he said. 'Whatta ya need to know?'

I told him what I had learned last night about the 'Albino' guy who was maybe dealing heroin at the end of the Canarsie Line. I also told him where I got the info and how the whole thing got started last Thursday on the roof of my school.

'Damn,' he said. 'I heard about that. Shoulda known that was your place of work. You just keep on steppin' in it, don'tcha son?'

'I walk where I walk, Billy.'

'Right. Anyway, I may know someone who can help ya. What's your schedule look like the rest of today?'

I told him about the memorial for MoJo upstate and that I hoped to be home in time to have dinner with Allison.

'Speaking of whom,' he said. 'I've been reading her stuff. She's really good, son. You gonna put a ring on her finger soon?'

'You been talking to my mother again, Billy?'

He laughed. 'I'm just saying, smart and beautiful is a helluva package for guys like us, Ray.'

'You're preaching to the choir. So, what about your guy?'

'Keep your cell phone on and on ya at all times. I'm gonna reach out now – he keeps the same hours we do, only more of them – and I'll ask him to get back to you with anything solid before the end of business today. If you don't hear from him by tomorrow – let's say noon – holler back and I'll put a fire under his butt for ya.'

'I don't need anybody's butt on fire. I just need some info here.'

'I gotcha, son. My bet is he'll get back to ya sometime today. Just bring your phone to bed with you. Richie works a long day.'

'Richie.'

'Richie Hebner, my guy over in Canarsie. You'd like him. He's one of us.'

'Good looking and loyal?'

'You just described my dog, Ray. But, yeah, you feel me.'

Now how come that sounded natural when Billy Morris said it? All those extra years on the streets, I guessed.

'Thanks, Billy,' I said. 'I really appreciate this. Next round's on me.'

'You know what I always say: we're all gonna die a beer up or a beer down, Ray. But I will take you up on that as long as it's soon. Let's do The LineUp with the ladies. It'll be nice to see Mrs Mac again, and you and I do not see each other enough. One barbecue a year just don't cut it.'

'I hear ya,' I said. 'Talk to you soon, man.'

'If not sooner.'

An hour later, I was shaved and showered, and dressed for a casual outside memorial service. Allison checked me out. 'Not bad. You sure about the no-tie look, Ray? Nicer shoes, maybe.'

'It's informal, Allie. And I don't think I have nicer shoes.'

'I'll put that on our shopping list.'

That was the first time I had heard *we* had a shopping list. I was about to comment when my phone went off. I didn't recognize the number, and considered not answering because Edgar was due to pick me up any minute. I pressed the green circle anyway, thinking there was a small chance it was Billy's guy calling me already. It was.

'Raymond,' he said. 'Richie Hebner, Billy's friend from Brooklyn South.'

'Richie. Didn't expect to hear from you so soon.'

'Just wanted to check in. Billy doesn't ask for enough favors so when he does, I wanna get right on it.'

'He does bring that out in people. You don't have any info for me yet, do you?'

'I'm ninety-nine percent positive I know who you're talking about. Not many guys fit the description you gave Billy. The one I'm thinking about's got about as much whiteness as the NBA, know what I'm saying?'

'Yeah.'

'I just wanted to touch base, let you know I'm on it. When I find out more, I'll give you a call and we can meet. Not the kinda stuff I usually like to talk about on the phone. Let me see what I can dig up today and maybe we can meet tomorrow?'

'Tomorrow works,' I said if only because that's what he offered. Sooner would be better, but I didn't say that. 'Thanks.'

'Thank me tomorrow, man. Keep your phone on, OK?'

'It always is, Richie.'

'Billy told me that about you. Tomorrow then.'

'Thanks again, Richie.'

NINETEEN

The drive north to Ulster County took an hour and a half. We had the windows rolled down as the temperature was now in the low seventies. There are few more pleasant smells than springtime in the Hudson Valley. The mix of freshly cut hay and horse manure – yes, horse manure – could easily make you forget you were less than ninety miles from the city. I knew from previous trips up this way that the smell of fresh apples would be permeating the air come September.

The ride was made more enjoyable because Edgar had treated himself to a new car right after he retired from his city job. He had figured out how to write it off on his taxes as a 'company vehicle' and had spared little expense. Of course, he had an amazing audio system – which now was being under-utilized since Lisa was napping in the back. It also had the latest in GPS technology, hands-free cell phone/blue tooth capability, and mobile WiFi. If Bill Gates has a weekend car, I'm sure it's something like this.

As we took the New Paltz exit, I was reminded of my student

Frankie who had taken his kid sister up here some years ago to hide them both from his father's killers. Frankie's father was the first dead body I'd come across after leaving the NYPD. I had helped track the kids down, but as was often the case back then, I was about a day late and two dollars short. It all worked out in the end, though. Except for a couple of more dead guys.

We took the only road through the college town, turned north onto Route 32, and Edgar said, 'It's going to be about nine more minutes. You hungry?'

'I'm good,' I said. 'We'll see how Lisa feels when she wakes up.' I looked at the digital clock on the dashboard. It was eleven-thirteen. 'Memorial starts at one, so we can eat if she has to.'

'It's nice of Newer Leaves to do this for MoJo,' Edgar said. 'It would mean a lot to him the way he went on about this place.'

I agreed; Lisa had half of MoJo's ashes in her bag. She had made bread dough and rolled the ashes into it in order to feed the fish in the lake on the grounds of Newer Leaves. It was a Chinese tradition that she had read about years ago. The other half of the ashes had already helped feed some of the bass and sunfish in the East River, not far from their apartment.

'Oh, my God,' Lisa said suddenly. 'Please tell me I was not dreaming and that that sign back there said barbecue.'

Edgar punched some buttons on his GPS. 'Yessiree Bob. You want me to—'

'Don't even ask, Edgar,' she groaned. 'I've been craving barbecue for the past few days but was just too . . .' Her thoughts drifted off. 'Just let's go.'

'Yes, ma'am,' Edgar said. 'You up for some barbecue, Ray?'

'Edgar,' I said. 'Has anyone ever answered "No" to that question?'

About an hour later, we were back in the car with at least one answer from today's trip: a seven-month-pregnant woman could definitely eat a pulled pork sandwich, a half-rack of baby-back ribs, and a half-pint of coleslaw. Edgar and I did pretty well ourselves, but Lisa had to be helped into the backseat of the car.

'Let's just sit for a while,' she said. 'I need a little while before I even think about going anywhere.'

We rolled down the windows – the temp was pushing eighty now – and waited for Lisa to give us the go-ahead. We had about a half-hour before the memorial started. I used some of the time to step out of the car and call Allison.

'Hey, tough guy. How's that fresh Hudson Valley air treating ya?'

'Pretty good.' I told her about lunch and how we should come up here sometime – just the two of us. 'I know how much you like hiking.'

'About as much as you like paperwork. Give me a porch swing and some boat drinks and I'll be fine.'

'You still going to the crime scene?'

'Yes. And now that they're done collecting evidence, I was able to persuade Royce to give me half an hour instead of ten minutes.'

'How'd you do that?'

'I reminded him that my boyfriend had given him a pretty strong piece of evidence in the case and since they had already processed the crime scene, it wouldn't interfere with an active investigation. And I think his day was kinda slow.'

She continued. 'I still wish I'd gone up today with you, but I promised my partners I'd visit a few of the new brunch places on the Upper West Side for the website. Which is another reason I want to go to the crime scene. If nothing else breaks, I'll have to move MoJo to the back burner. At least today I can keep the story moving forward.'

'Royce say anything else about the apartments? Anything else about the guy Gator ran into? The Unabomber guy?'

'Not much, they canvassed the whole building and came up with nothing. But I had the feeling he was holding something back.'

'Like what?'

'Like something that would stop me from putting MoJo on the back burner.' She paused. 'Speaking of which, I'm supposed to meet Royce in about an hour, so . . .'

I could hear the sound of her fingers skipping across the keys of her laptop. I did not have her full attention.

'So what are you going to do?'

'What makes you think I'm going to do anything, Ray?'

'Because I know you, and I know how you get when you think you know there's an answer out there waiting to be found.'

'An answer to what?'

'I don't know, but I'm sure you'll find that, too.'

'You getting all philosophical on me again, Ray? Been reading Jean-Paul Sartre behind my back? It sounds like you're telling me I'm gonna find the answer before I even know what the question is.'

'If anyone can, Allie, it's you. I'll see you at home sometime around six or seven depending on how the traffic is into the city.'

'Maybe you can bring back some of that barbecue on the way home?'

'That might work.'

'Make it work, Raymond. You've got my mouth watering.' She waited a beat and added, 'Before you think too much of yourself, I'm talking about the food.'

'Never a doubt in my mind what you were talking about, Allie. Love you.'

'I love you, too, Ray. Tell Edgar I said to drive carefully.'

'Will do.'

'Oh,' she added. 'Bring me back some literature from Newer Leaves. I'm thinking of doing a piece on the whole opioid crisis: from users, to where they get their drugs, to the justice system and rehab.'

'I'll see what I can pick up.'

When I got back in the car, Edgar asked, 'What'd Allison say?'

'Told me to tell you to drive carefully.'

He mumbled something, Lisa mumbled something, and we were off. Five minutes later, we were pulling into a long driveway that lead up to a huge white house that could only be described as a mansion. *This was rehab?*

'Is this where the president lives?' I joked. Nobody laughed.

'Welcome to Newer Leaves,' Lisa said. 'This is what happens when a wealthy donor with a family history of substance abuse leaves you his house and property in his will.' She let out a long, yet somehow polite, burp. 'There are about forty acres and almost as many rooms. At any given time, they might have two-dozen clients residing here. Each resident gets a roommate.'

I had almost forgotten that Lisa was a substance abuse counselor and this was where she and MoJo had met. We were a long way from their apartment in Brooklyn.

'This was my first full-time job after I got my graduate degree,' she said. 'They have a whole floor for the live-in staff. That's how they get away with paying us so little. They gave us room, meals, and a small stipend. I could've moved back home and lived with my folks in Queens and worked for the city, but this was too good to pass up.'

'How did MoJo end up here?' I asked.

'He fit the profile,' Lisa said. 'He was a repeat *non-violent* offender. He passed the interview and the background check. Since he was unmarried, he had no problem signing up for the two years.'

'Two years,' I repeated. 'Damn.'

'Yep. The first six months, no contact with the outside world. None. No letters, no phone calls, no texts, and definitely no visits.'

'What about guys with kids?'

'Same rules for everyone, Ray. You know them when you sign on. If you can't handle the rules, there are other places to go.'

'That's gotta be tough on the kids, though. How do they handle that?'

'We counsel the whole family. And not seeing your dad while he's in recovery is better than seeing your dad drunk and possibly abusive toward you and your mother.'

She had a point. 'What about after six months?'

'The residents can receive emails and texts. If that goes well, and the men are working the program, they start earning phone privileges.'

'When do they get to see their families?'

'After a year. One monthly visit for three months, then two monthlies for another three months, and then weeklies after that. Those last six months come with family therapy.' She took a deep breath and let out a long, whispering burp. 'We don't just drop them back into the family milieu without lots of preparation. For everyone. Imagine your dad being out of the house for two years and then he just drops back in.'

I thought about making a joke about how many times I had wished my father would go away for a while, but this was not the time or place for humor.

I looked around as Edgar pulled into the parking lot. There were about ten other cars already there. Half of the cars were pickups.

'Must cost a fortune to maintain this property,' I said.

'That's another part of what makes this place work, Ray,' Lisa said. 'All the residents must have jobs provided by the organization. One of the options is landscaping. Newer Leaves is also the name of the company they run. They do landscaping all through the lower Hudson Valley; the men make a small salary and the rest comes back to the facility. Others do restaurant work and work in the kitchen here. It's the same with carpentry, plumbing, and electrical work. Everything they do in the outside world comes back here and keeps the place running.'

'Sounds like a socialist's dream.'

'They even have some lawyers and accountants in residence,' she explained. 'You know as well as I do that drug abuse doesn't give a shit what color your collar is.'

'Interesting way of putting it.'

'True that. If only the government could get more on board with this type of approach, we'd see a lot fewer of our young men behind bars.'

Edgar mumbled something again. I asked him to repeat it.

'Too many people make too much money off the prison system,' he said, more clearly this time. 'That's why good people like MoJo end up in jail.' He put his hands together in front of his mouth as if he'd said too much. 'Sorry, Lisa.'

'You're preaching to the choir, Edgar. Places like Newer Leaves threaten the established way of fighting the "War on Drugs." The only winners in that war are the prison owners and the politicians in their pockets.'

'Well,' Edgar said, 'I'm glad this place is here.' He turned to me. 'This was the first security job MoJo and I did together.'

'How'd that come about?'

'After we met at the tech show, he told me about this place and how they were applying for a grant they could only get if they had a properly installed security system.'

He got out of the car and I followed his lead. He opened the back door for Lisa and she was able to get out by herself. We all stretched and looked around.

'They still have a lot of valuable things inside,' Edgar went on. 'Left over from the original owner. Paintings, other artwork, furniture. They figured a place this far away from town was ripe for the picking. The state was also concerned about some of the residents walking off with stuff.' Edgar pointed to the house. 'We put in window alarms, door alarms . . .' He spun around and pointed to the gate and the surrounding fencing. 'We also put in some motion detectors along the perimeter and security lighting.'

I again was struck by how much it felt like I was on the set of one of those home shows – real estate porn, I called them – Allison liked to watch on the rare lazy weekend. I was also surprised by something behind the house.

An archery course set-up.

Just as I was making a mental note to tell Royce about this, a man in a seersucker jacket and blue jeans came up to us. No tie, he had his blue shirt collar unbuttoned, his hair and gray beard trimmed short, and a pair of boots that would fit in well in Allison's hometown in Missouri. It was Eddie Price from the other night.

'Lisa,' he said, his arms open wide. 'We are so glad you have allowed us to celebrate Maurice this way and that you and your friends could make it up all the way from the city.'

He and Lisa exchanged the kind of hug that said, 'I'm glad to see you, but one of us is pregnant.' The guy pointed. 'Edgar, right?'

He nodded. 'Yes,' he said. 'Nice to see you again, Mr Price.'

'Eddie. And you, Edgar.' They shook hands. Mr Price looked at me and said, 'Nice to see you again, Mr Donne.' Without all the noise from the bar, I placed his accent somewhere just east or west of the Mississippi River. I also thought I recognized his voice from somewhere.

'Lisa said she was bringing Maurice's sponsor from the school, so I checked the name on the paperwork. I also googled you. I didn't know who you were the other night. I can see why he wanted your help with the community service. Thank you for helping Maurice back into society.'

'He's been more than worth it, Mr Price, believe me.' I caught myself using the present tense. I didn't bother correcting myself.

'Please,' he said. 'Everyone calls me Eddie.' Eddie looked over his shoulder, back at the house, and then at his watch. 'We should probably go in now. We'd like to get started at one o'clock sharp.' He turned to Lisa. 'No offense, but some of our guys are due back at work and . . . well, you know how some of our employers can be.'

'I do, Eddie,' Lisa said. 'Thank you again for all of this.'

'You and Maurice are family, Lisa. You know that. This is the least we could do for you both.' To all of us, he said, 'Please, follow me.'

As we made our way toward the house, no one else seemed to pay any attention to the archery set-up in the back. Maybe it was just my mind going places it shouldn't be, but with the exception of last Thursday, I couldn't remember the last time I had seen anything involving archery. Now two times in less than a week?

Lisa grabbed my hand. 'They're very strict on the schedule around here. Eddie likes to say, "Structure is the key." If he says something starts at one o'clock, it starts at one o'clock. Any break in the schedule can be an excuse for abuse.'

'Self-help tips that rhyme,' I said. 'My favorite.'

'He's right, though. One of the things that keeps Newer Leaves running so smoothly is the tight schedule. Wake-up's at seven thirty. Breakfast at eight. You're out the door or working your shift on-site at nine. If you're currently between jobs or assignments, you're in one group session or another. Most substance abusers don't have schedules while they're actively using. That's one of the first things they learn here.'

'What about those who don't learn it?'

'They're given more training and workshops. If they can't get with the program in six months, we – Newer Leaves – have to make room for someone else.' We made our way to the front door, which was being held open by Eddie. 'You can't imagine the waiting list for this place, Ray.'

I took one more look around while Edgar and Lisa stepped inside. *Yeah,* I thought. *I think I can.*

TWENTY

At exactly one o'clock, Eddie Price stepped up to the podium, which was set up on a multi-purpose stage. The room we were in probably hosted many parties back in the day. There were tall windows with heavy shades, shiny wooden floors, and lights hanging from the ceiling that may have cost close to what Edgar had paid for his car. *If I breathed in deeply enough would I smell the ghosts of rich people past?* Eddie welcomed us all, thanked everyone for coming and for being prompt. That last part brought a smattering of chuckles. He mentioned the weather, how springtime always brought with it a sense of renewal, and how we shouldn't look at today as a day to console one another over the loss of Maurice Joseph but as an opportunity to celebrate his life and successes.

The way he said Maurice's name finally put the pieces together for me as to how I recognized Eddie Price. He was the guy MoJo had been recording – accidentally or on purpose – with his spy pen.

Now I was thinking it must have been an accident. Why would MoJo be secretly recording the guy who ran the place that was helping him put his life back together?

Eddie Price finished up and a couple of residents spoke about MoJo and his positive influence on them. Then Eddie asked Lisa to come up to the microphone. I don't usually think of pregnant women as walking with grace and poise, but Lisa Joseph did just that.

'It is not an exaggeration,' she said when she got to the mic, 'to say that Newer Leaves gave Maurice his life back. And, you all' – she took the whole assembly in by holding up the palms of both hands – 'played a big part in that. Not only in giving him another chance, but in giving *us* a chance.' She placed her palms on her belly. 'And you can see how that worked out.' Polite, slightly awkward laughter came from the crowd.

'I look out at you all,' she continued, 'and I'm glad to see many familiar faces, but just as importantly, many who are not familiar. Those who I do know understand how much work it takes to start again, as many of you have. Maurice and I were – and are – very proud of you.' She paused to take a breath and look up to the ceiling. 'Those who are newer here and never had the pleasure of meeting Maurice, please heed the message my husband's life represented: Working works. Passion works. Love works.' She put both hands on her stomach. 'We all thank you.'

Everyone applauded and Lisa was helped off the stage, back to her seat by Eddie Price. Eddie asked Edgar if he'd like to go up and say a few words as Maurice's business partner and Edgar shook his head. Edgar and public speaking were not compatible yet. Eddie went back up to the podium.

'That concludes the indoor part of our service,' he said. 'Anyone wishing to join us at the lake for a ceremonial feeding of the fish are welcome. Afterwards, we will gather in the main dining room for some light snacks and beverages. Until exactly three-fifteen.' More chuckles. If he ever left this place, I thought, Eddie Price had a career in the cruise ship business. 'Thank you all again for coming.'

Lisa was the last person to toss a ball of dough containing her husband's ashes into the lake. She explained that a Chinese friend of hers had introduced her to the ancient tradition. One after another, the balls were eaten by the fish, ensuring a part of Maurice Joseph's legacy for years to come. I couldn't help thinking that when the time came and I was no longer breathing, I had given my sister Rachel explicit instructions to spread my ashes around the infield at Yankee Stadium. I was sure her NYPD husband, her Chief of Detectives uncle, and a decent lawyer could get her off with a temporary insanity plea.

On the way back to the house, Lisa said to me, 'I saw you noticing the archery setup in the back.'

'You saw me noticing that, huh?'

'It's a therapeutic tool, Raymond. It takes a great deal of concentration and focus to be able to hit the target.' She paused as I guessed she realized someone must have used that kind of focus on her husband; someone who considered Maurice more of a target than a real live human being with people who loved him. 'It's a very mindful experience, shooting an arrow. You need to not only control your breathing and your body, you need to be able to . . . your whole world becomes the bow, the arrow, and the target.'

I'd only known Lisa as MoJo's wife, but I was starting to see what made her such a great counselor. The ability to shut out what had happened last week to her husband – and how it had happened – was admirable. I'm not sure I could do that if anything of the sort ever happened to Allison or Rachel. What I knew of myself was I'd want revenge, to hurt someone. Lisa didn't have that bone. Maybe that was another boy thing.

'I'm going to stay out here, guys,' Lisa said to Edgar and me. She looked over at a wooden chair that had a great view of the southern part of the Catskill Mountains. 'I'll grab a seat. Can you get me a seltzer or club soda?' For the umpteenth time that day, she touched her stomach. 'Something with bubbles.'

Edgar said, 'Absolutely,' and we went back inside the mansion. After asking directions, we found the main dining room and the beverage table. Eddie Price was standing there speaking with a light-skinned black man in light green overalls and a blue work shirt. They were both drinking something clear out of plastic cups.

'I distinctly remember telling the maintenance staff,' Eddie Price was explaining, 'to remove the targets before the service. If Lisa has seen them . . .'

'She has,' I said, interrupting. 'It's OK. She actually explained to me how they were used in the therapy here. Everything here reminds her of Maurice, Mr Price. You can't avoid that. She's very grateful for the service.'

Eddie Price considered that as I poured some club soda into plastic cups for Lisa, Edgar and myself. I handed two to Edgar and motioned with my head for him to take them outside. I turned back to Price.

'That may be all well and good, Raymond,' Price said. 'But when I give an instruction, I expect it to be followed.'

The man in the overalls said, 'I'll have them removed immediately, Mr Price.'

'No, no, no. That will only bring more attention to them.' He took a sip of his seltzer as if he wished it were something stronger. 'Just get back to the garden and . . . I don't know . . . be more attentive next time.'

The man left, leaving me alone with Eddie Price. Not being one for awkward silences, I said, 'Lisa told me you run a tight ship here.'

'I have to,' he said. 'My guys depend on me. Most of them come here with completely disordered lives. That's how Maurice was when he first showed up. Without the constant structure and vigilance, the program will not work.'

'I get it. I wish I could get more consistency from the teachers I work with. Most of them are not on the same page. Some are reading completely different books.'

Price smiled. 'That's the problem with public education. Structure starts at the top and – with all due respect – your union does not allow for some measures that need to be taken to develop that structure.'

I was sure he was right. 'I'm sure you're right. What's your success rate here?'

'Define "success,"' he said.

I had to think on that. 'What're your recidivism numbers? How many clients return after leaving?'

'Zero.' He must have read the amazed look on my face. 'We don't accept returnees, Raymond. When you enter Newer Leaves, you commit to two years. Some need more time; some – like Maurice – need less. But once you are officially discharged, there is no readmission. You either have what it takes to work this program or you don't.'

'Working works?'

'Exactly.'

'If you don't mind my saying, that sounds kind of strict.'

'It is. Purposefully so.' He rubbed his lower lip. 'If our guys think they can leave before they're prepared to reenter society as productive, drug-free members, they won't take the program seriously.'

'One and Done,' I said. 'Or Two and Through in this case.'

He smiled again. I guessed I was pleasing him. 'It works,' he said.

'How do you know?'

'What do you mean?'

'If the guys can't come back, how do you know it works? How do you know they're not in some other program somewhere else? Or out in the world using.'

'We do follow-up. We place them with programs and people like you and stay in communication with them and their sponsors.'

'And you've never had a former resident slip?'

Just as he was about to answer me, his phone went off. He took it out of his pocket, looked at the number, and said, 'I have to take this, Raymond. Excuse me.'

He walked away. By the tone of his voice, I could tell he was either unhappy with the caller or the direction our conversation was heading. Or both. I went back outside to check in on Lisa and Edgar. They both seemed to be lost in the view. I enjoyed it with them for a bit and then told Lisa about my talk with Price.

'I should have warned you, Ray,' she said. 'Eddie doesn't take well to people questioning Newer Leaves's methods of success. I hate to say this about him because he does help so many people, but there are some he just can't reach. He can't seem to admit to that, but some users are treatment-resistant.'

'And he doesn't acknowledge that?'

'Doesn't and can't.'

'I guess that could be considered admirable.'

'It could be. It kills him that he can't put down one hundred percent success rate on his grant applications. No one would believe those numbers.'

'Nobody's perfect,' Edgar chimed in.

Lisa feigned shock and put her index finger to her lips. 'Shhh, Edgar. You don't want that getting around.'

Somebody cleared a throat. Seeing that it was not one of us, I looked over and saw another man in the same green overalls outfit as the guy Price had been reaming out inside. He walked over to us with great caution and said, 'Hey, Ms Hamilton.'

It took Lisa a few seconds until she said, 'RV. I've told you to call me Lisa.'

The guy stuck his hand out. 'Lisa.' He checked Edgar and me out. 'Sorry I couldn't make it to the service. I was clearing some of the brush from the back woods. We're putting in some benches back there. One of them will have MoJo's name on it. That was my idea. You know how he liked it back there.'

'Nice,' Lisa said. 'These are friends of mine and MoJo's. Ray and Edgar.'

We shook hands and I said, 'Nice to meet you, Harvey.'

He gave me a small smile. 'Everyone calls me that at first,' he said. 'It's RV.'

'RV?'

Lisa stood up. 'Reggie is one of the full-timers here at Newer Leaves, Ray. He's a former resident and now stays on as maintenance. At first, there wasn't any room for him inside, so he lives near the woods.'

'In a recreational vehicle,' he said. 'That's why they call me RV. Also, my name's Robert Valentine, so it kinda works both ways, y'know.'

I nodded. 'Cool.'

'Yeah. I gotta satellite TV and WiFi setup. MoJo helped me with that.'

Edgar asked, 'What kinda setup ya got?'

RV explained. Edgar nodded, but he might as well have been speaking French for all I understood. It took no time to realize, though, that he and Edgar literally spoke the same language. I had a feeling RV might've tested on the spectrum, as well.

'I'm real sorry about MoJo, Lisa,' RV said. 'I mean I just saw him, y'know.'

Lisa's face went quizzical. 'No, RV. I didn't know. Were you down in the city?'

RV looked more uncomfortable now. He kicked at the grass. 'Ah, I talk too much sometimes. But he didn't tell me it was a secret.'

'When did you see him last?' Lisa asked. When RV stayed shut, Lisa kept going. 'RV, it's not like you're going to get him into trouble now.' She paused and slowed down. 'When did you see MoJo last?'

Still looking at his feet, RV said, 'Last week. He was up here Thursday night. I came across him right out here. He said he was doing some security work for Eddie. Checking the perimeter, he said.'

'Wednesday night?' Lisa said, and I could tell we were both thinking the same thing. And then it hit Edgar.

'MoJo was up here the night before he was killed.'

TWENTY-ONE

'MoJo said that?' I asked RV. 'That he was up here doing security for Eddie?'

'That's what he told me, yeah.'

I turned to Edgar. 'Did you know about this?'

He shook his head no. Lisa had already answered the question. So why was MoJo up here without his partner or his wife knowing about it? My mind immediately went back to the video MoJo had secretly recorded of Duke Lansing. Edgar hadn't known about that job, either.

I looked back at RV. 'Did you tell anyone up here that you ran into MoJo?'

RV shrugged. 'Didn't think there'd be a reason to. If he was working for Eddie, then Eddie woulda known already, right?'

'Right,' I said. 'Let's keep it that way for now. OK?'

RV nodded. 'Whatever's best for MoJo.'

Royce was going to love this. Not only did I have to tell him about the archery range, I had info that MoJo had been up here the night before he was killed. He was going to think I'd come up north playing cop again when all I was doing was attending the ceremony. I wondered what the odds were that Royce would believe that. Probably about the same as Uncle Ray's believing it.

'I should probably be getting back to work now, Ms . . . Lisa,' RV said.

Lisa reached out and touched him on the shoulder. 'Good to see you again, RV.'

'You sure I didn't do anything wrong telling you 'bout MoJo being up here?' He looked at me after asking the question.

'I'm sure,' Lisa said. Then reading the look on RV's face, she said, 'Ray's not a policeman, RV. He's a friend from the school MoJo was working at.'

'Oh,' he said and gave me a good long look and a real smile this time. 'You sure do look and sound like a cop.'

'I get that a lot,' I said and offered him my hand. 'Take care of yourself.'

'Roger that,' he said. 'Nice to meet you, too, Edgar.'

'Yeah,' Edgar said, distracted. He was obviously mulling over the possibility that this was twice his partner was working without his knowledge. 'Let's go, Ray,' he said. 'Lisa, you ready?'

'I'm getting tired,' Lisa said. 'So . . .'

We said goodbye to RV again and headed off to Edgar's car. Lisa held onto my arm as we walked. We were about twenty feet away from the parking lot when we ran into someone else I'd met the other night. Dennis McLain. As with Eddie Price, now that we were in the open and not a noisy bar, I could hear that his accent was more upstate New York than New York City.

He gave Lisa a careful hug. 'Again, I am so sorry. MoJo was a great guy.'

'I know, Denny,' she said. 'That's why I married him.'

Maybe this is what happens when you've been mourning a loss and consoled by others non-stop for a week. You develop a weird kind of sense of humor that has nothing to do with being funny and everything to do with not letting the tragedies in your life define you. That's not something you pick up in social work school; that comes from a much deeper place.

It turned out MoJo had told Denny about both of us. Lisa explained to Edgar that Denny – Dennis T. McLain, Esq. – was the attorney for Newer Leaves. And, as the old commercial used to say, he was also a client.

'Saved my life,' he told us. 'The weekly meetings keep me going.'

'That's another thing,' Lisa explained. 'Newer Leaves has weekly support meetings.' I knew all this, but I let her explain. 'Nothing too AA, just guys keeping in touch with one another and sharing stories of Lanel.'

'Lanel?' Edgar asked.

'L.A.N.L. Life After Newer Leaves. They do three weeklies up here at the mother ship and others around the area. Maurice attended the one in Greenpoint by our apartment and sometimes the one in Park Slope.'

Park Slope, Brooklyn, not only had a different zip code than Williamsburg, Brooklyn, but a much higher average yearly salary. Brownstones in the Slope went for well above eight figures. Think Woody Allen Brooklyn, not Spike Lee Brooklyn.

'I'm sorry I missed the service,' Denny said. 'I had an appointment across the river that went longer than it should have. I don't have to tell you what happens when you get a bunch of bureaucrats and lawyers in the same room.' He stuck out his tongue and made a fake gagging noise. I love it when lawyers try to be like the rest of us. 'We're working on a grant for Newer Leaves. Nothing too big, but it will allow us to sell the maple syrup we get from the back twenty. More of a public relations deal than actually making any real money. But, that doesn't stop five different state agencies from getting involved and creating hurdles.'

'I work for the city,' I said. 'I've been jumping hurdles for the last ten years between the NYPD and DOE.'

'Yeah,' Denny said. 'Maurice told me you were a cop and now you're a teacher.'

'That's me.'

'Always chasing the mighty dollar, huh?'

'I might be a people person, I'm not sure.'

'Least you got a good union behind you. Lot of people bash the unions these days, but I bet you don't see a whole bunch of them lining up for your job.'

'Not outside my door,' I said. 'Or the precincts.'

He pointed at me. 'That's what I keep telling people. We need the unions so we can attract people like yourself to jobs that – let's be honest – most folks wouldn't think of doing and couldn't think of doing without.'

'You sound like you're running for office.'

Lisa laughed. 'I left that out, Ray. Denny is on the ballot for state senator from this area. Moved his family up here from Queens after his two years at Newer Leaves, opened a private practice, and is now getting into politics.'

I thought about the regional demographics: a couple of local liberal college towns combined with more conservative rural areas. That's a tough tightrope to walk for any politician and I said so.

'That's what makes it fun, Ray,' McLain said. 'Listen, at the end of the day, we all want what's best for New York and the Hudson Valley. Sometimes folks up here feel ignored because of all the attention you city people get.'

'City people like you used to be?'

He put his finger to his lips. 'Shh. I wouldn't want that getting around. Actually, I use my Queens' background and current residence as a bit of a bridge between Downstate and Upstate.'

'Is it working?'

'I'm neck-and-neck with my Republican opponent. Who' – he leaned in and stage-whispered – 'I sometimes go hunting with.'

'Scandalous,' I said.

'Don't get too many scandals up here. State senate race usually comes down to gun control, reproductive rights, and taxes. I'm slightly left of center, my opponent is slightly right. I hate to say it, but the more old folks who . . . go elsewhere, the better the numbers look for me.'

'By "elsewhere" you mean . . .?' said Edgar.

Denny smiled. 'Heaven or Hell.' He paused. 'Or Florida.'

Lisa cleared her throat, which I took as my cue to check my watch. 'We need to hit the road, Denny. If we don't leave now we're gonna make it just in time for that traffic in the Bronx.'

'One thing I don't miss about the city,' he said and shook hands with Edgar and me. He gave Lisa another careful hug and a kiss on the cheek. 'Be well, Mama,' he said. 'You'll let us know when the little one comes?'

'Of course.'

Ten minutes later I had a take-out bag filled with a barbecue dinner for Allison and me. Twenty minutes later we were on the thruway headed home. Lisa had fallen asleep in the back seat, so the ride south was quiet. Edgar had his eyes on the road and his hands at two and ten. I could tell he didn't feel like talking. I kept myself busy mentally, reviewing all the major league baseball players coming off bad seasons or injuries last season. The Yanks and Mets had their shares.

It did not escape me that my brain at the moment was filled with the idea of comebacks and redemption.

TWENTY-TWO

B y the time I got home, the sun was behind the city and Allison had all the windows open. She was on the back deck, watching the sunset, a glass of white wine in her hand. I cleared my throat so I wouldn't startle her. She turned and I raised the bag of barbecue I'd brought home from the wild. She raised her glass in a toast. To me, maybe, but more likely the bag of food I was holding.

'You want me to warm it up?'

She gave me a hungry grin and wiggled her fingers in a come hither way. 'Just bring it out.' I went to the fridge, grabbed a beer, went over to the cabinets to pull out two plates, and got a roll of paper towels for napkins. I had to put the bag of barbecue between my teeth to manage everything.

'There's next year's Christmas card,' Allison said, taking the bag from my teeth and giving me a kiss. 'How was the traffic, honey?'

'Ugh,' I said. 'This city needs less cars and more moving people.'

'Look at you. Almost correctly quoting lyrics from the eighties.' She placed the food on the small patio table and finished her wine. 'Don't you dare open that bag until I get back.'

By the time she returned, I had finished half my beer and, against her direct orders, had equally divided the barbecue between the two plates. She sat down and we ate in silence for a few minutes before she spoke.

'How was the service?'

'Not too much God stuff. But the way people talk about Newer Leaves, you'd think it was a religion.'

'I heard about them a while ago,' she said. 'I was thinking of doing a piece on them when I was still with the paper.'

'You could do one now. You mentioned it the other night.'

'My partners want to stay focused on more city-ish stuff. That's our . . . niche.'

I took another bite of rib and followed it with the last of my beer. I stood up. 'You tell them about focusing on former clients who live in the city?'

She finished her wine. 'It's possible.'

'It's another way of keeping MoJo's story moving forward.'

'I'm too tired to think about it,' she said. She handed me her empty glass. 'While you're up, this'll help me think better.'

I leaned in and kissed her. 'Whatever you say, Allie.'

'That's what I love to hear.'

I came back and Allison was piling up the remains of our meal. We were in the habit of whoever cooked, the other cleaned. Since I had technically provided the meal, it fell to her to clear the table. When she came back outside, the sky behind the city was a fading orange and the breeze had picked up a touch.

'How was your trip today?' I asked. 'To the crime scene.'

She paused looking for just the right word. 'Enlightening.'

'In what way?'

'It's hard to explain. I'm still processing it before I put the words down. I've never studied a location where a murderer waited for his victim. It reminded me a bit of sitting with my dad in his hunting blind back home. We'd wait for hours sometimes until he was ready to shoot a deer.'

'Only here,' I said, 'the prey was human.'

She gave me the Shut-Up look. 'I know that, Ray. That's what made it so . . . I hate the word weird. It was . . . almost surreal. What kind of person does that? It's the textbook definition of premeditated. After a few minutes, I could almost feel it. Someone – maybe someone evil – was in the same place I was about to commit an evil act.'

'Are you saying you could feel the killer's presence?'

'If I hadn't known what had happened from that window, I don't know if I would've felt anything. But it's in the knowing, isn't it?' She paused for another sip. 'Since I knew what had happened there, I kinda did feel something. I just need to be a good enough writer to get that down on paper.'

I put my arm around her. 'You are a good enough writer, Allie. But I was a cop for five years. I was constantly asking myself why people did the things they did. Lucky for me, that wasn't part of the job description. I didn't have to know why, just the who.'

'And how did that make you feel?' she asked.

'We doing therapy, now?'

'No. Not really. But how did it make you feel? You told me yourself that you could have gone back to being a cop.'

'I also told you I didn't like the feel of sitting on my ass all day or the smell of paperwork and fingerprints.'

'Yeah,' she said. 'I remember that answer. That was a while ago. I know you so much better now and I know that's not the whole answer. *You* know it's not.'

'Wow,' I said. 'We *are* doing therapy.'

She gave me a playful slap on the arm. 'It's not therapy because I understand you more now that we're closer. It'd be therapy if I didn't.'

She had a point. Again. I processed it by sipping from my beer. Amazing how that almost always seemed to help.

'Yes,' I said.

'Yes, what?'

'Yes,' I repeated. 'Not knowing why people did the things they did bothered me. Yes, not being able to get out of the gray and into the black and white bothered me. Yes, I could have done some good if I'd gone back to being a cop, even if it was behind a desk. And, yes, I believe I do more good now that I'm a teacher.'

Allison looked at me as if we'd just met. 'Wow,' she said. 'That is the most you've ever said about that subject. At least to me.'

I let out a deep breath. 'It's the most I've ever said about the subject to anyone. Myself included. You sure this isn't therapy?'

She squeezed me tighter. 'I'm sure, Ray. This is what couples do. They talk about things and unexpected stuff comes up.'

'If you weren't such a kickass reporter, I'd say that you were in the wrong business.'

'Now that's how a boyfriend is supposed to talk. Was that so hard?'

Another sip. 'No. No it wasn't.'

'Good for you.' She kissed me. 'I was researching deaths by arrow today.'

'Yeah,' I said. 'You said you found nothing in the city for almost ever.'

'Just that guy out on Long Island back in 2006 and the Jersey thing a few years ago. Not a popular way to commit murder.'

'What's your point?' I asked. And realized the accidental pun, which we both decided wisely to ignore.

'It got me thinking about another angle on the story,' she said, and took a sip of wine. 'Before you say anything, I know it's a bit morbid, but I started thinking about unconventional ways of killing people.'

I considered that, squinted at her, and said, 'But we're OK, right.'

'After all that nice stuff you just said, yes. For now. You know what the three most common ways of committing murder are in the US?'

'Number one is guns.'

'Right.'

'Second . . .' I thought back to my time on the streets. 'Stabbings.'

'Yep.'

I had to think harder now. There's murder in real life and then there's murder on TV and in movies and books. 'Poisoning?'

'Suffocation,' she said. 'Mostly physical strangling and that's usually by people who knew the victim. Quote, unquote: loved ones.'

I took a sip. 'So your piece would be on . . .'

'The uncommon ways people do away with one another. I hate to say it, but MoJo's murder was an extremely rare, and not that efficient, means to an end.'

'Efficient enough,' I said.

She waved that off. 'That came out wrong and you know it is not what I meant. The more I thought about the way Maurice was killed, the more I thought that there were only really two advantages to the method. The first being it's a pretty silent way to do it. No one hears an arrow, right?'

'Not unless you're really close to one, I guess. What's the other advantage?'

She took a deep breath. 'This is clearly speculation on my part. But what if someone wanted to send a message?'

I felt my forehead crease and my eyebrows come together. 'What kind of message?' I asked. 'And to whom?'

'That's as far as I got, Ray. It may be my imagination getting the better of my journalistic instincts.' Another sip of wine. 'I'm trying to set up a meeting with a forensic psychologist over at John Jay this week.'

I told her about the archery course up at Newer Leaves and what Lisa had told me about its use in therapy.

Allison nodded. 'I can see that. Mindfulness, staying focused, and whatnot.' She got up and stretched. 'Do you know what piquerism is?'

'Isn't that,' I said, 'a style of painting that uses a lot of dots? *Sunday in the Park With George?*'

'That's pointillism. Piquerism is a sexual fascination with piercing the human skin. Your own, or more commonly, someone else's.'

It came back to me now, at least a little bit. 'I heard about that at the academy in a criminal psych class. It's why some serial killers stab their victims over and over again. The blade becomes a substitute for the penis. What does this have to do with MoJo? You think some sicko's out there shooting people with arrows and getting off on it?'

'No,' she said. 'That would be on the news. It just came up in my research. Did you hear about the body the police found along the Hudson last week?'

I had, but it took a while to recall, as I had actually been at another murder scene this week. 'Yeah,' I said. 'Guy got hit in the head and fell into the rocks along the river. Official cause of death was blunt-force trauma, right? He never made it to the water.'

'You know my friend at the medical examiner's office, right?'

'The one who told you about the drugs they found on MoJo?'

'That's him. He called me this morning after you left and I took a quick trip over to his office. He was able to tell me they are about ninety-percent certain that the blunt instrument that caused the blunt-force trauma was not always so blunt.'

'I'm not following you,' I said.

'Based on the shape and depth of the head wound, they think it was an ax.'

I thought about that. 'Axes do have blunt sides, Allie.'

Is this what other couples talk about while sharing after-dinner drinks on a balcony in the fading sunset?

'No, he got hit with the business end, Ray. A very dull and possibly very old business end. It only penetrated four centimeters into the lower part of the skull. Not too deep, but deep enough where the victim bled out.'

'So the killer found what was around and used it on his victim. Happens all the time. Most murders are not thought out. Find an old ax, use an old ax. Is that all your friend at the ME gave you?'

'Not every reporter's friend at the ME gets access to crime scene photos.'

'And yours does?'

She sipped and nodded. 'I wasn't allowed to make a copy – you don't wanna know what I'd have had to do for that – but he did show me one interesting photo.'

'Interesting in what way?'

'On one of the rocks where they found the body, somebody had scrawled the Roman numeral one. One horizontal line connected to two vertical lines.'

'Sounds like graffiti to me.'

'That's what I thought, but my friend told me the marks had been made fairly recently. There was still rock dust around the number.'

I let that sink in. 'That's interesting.'

'Wanna know something else interesting?'

'Why do you tease me this way, Allie?'

'Sorry. It's kinda fun, but given the circumstances . . .'

'What is it?'

'When I was at the crime scene earlier today, I took some photos on my phone.'

'Royce allowed that?'

'He didn't know.' She reached into her pocket, pulled out her phone, and went to the camera app. She swiped a few times and handed it to me. 'What do you see there, Ray?' She pointed at the picture on the screen. 'To the right of the window.'

I looked at where her finger pointed. The Roman numeral two: two horizontal lines connected to two vertical lines. An uncomfortable chill went up my spine.

'Holy shit,' was all I could think to say.

'I didn't think anything of it until I saw the crime-scene photos from the Hudson. I thought this' – she pointed at the numeral on her phone – 'was a gang thing or, like you said, just random graffiti. Now I don't know what to think, but I'm going to see Royce tomorrow morning.'

I was quite often amazed at how my girlfriend's brain worked. She would have made a great cop – except for her stubborn refusal to see the world in black and white. Nobody is all bad and nobody is all good. Sometimes a cigar is more than just a cigar.

But sometimes horizontal and vertical lines are just horizontal and vertical lines.

And sometimes they are Roman numerals that just might connect two murders.

TWENTY-THREE

S ometime during the dark of night, Allison got up without waking me and found just the right words she'd been searching for only hours before. When I woke up, I got to read them along with about a thousand other people.

A KILLER VIEW

What's it like, lying in wait to commit murder?

What goes through the mind of the killer? How does their body react? How does it feel to know that at any moment you are going to be responsible for one less soul living on this planet? Does your breathing get quicker? Deeper?

It's early afternoon and I'm looking out of the fifth-floor apartment window from where, last Thursday, an unknown archer released an arrow that killed Maurice Joseph, a middle-school aide who was working on the school's rooftop across the street, tending to his hydroponic garden and his pigeons. I estimate the distance between this window and the spot where Mr Joseph's body fell to be around fifty yards.

According to a hunting expert I spoke with, once the archer released the arrow, Mr Joseph had about half a second before it entered his body. That's factoring an average arrow speed of three-hundred-feet per second. That's a little less time than it takes to sip from a cup of coffee and a little more than a blink of an eye.

Isaac Newton would have been perversely proud. All three of his laws of motion were in play: an arrow at rest stays at rest until it's released; the pullback on the arrow equals the spring when the grip is let go; the force of the arrow that ended Mr Joseph's life was equivalent to its mass times the acceleration.

Still, I am looking out of the window where last week someone took aim and ended a life. I won't be thinking about Mr Newton or physics until much later.

Below me, on the busy avenue, a young man walks by, possibly on the way to the bodega on the corner for a cup of coffee, or maybe to the subway. Two neighborhood women – side by side – are talking just a little too loud as they push matching strollers on their way to the playground in the court-yard of the houses. Cars go by, windows rolled down, playing loud music in defiance of last week's unexpected visit from Old Man Winter.

Ask any middle-school science teacher and they'll tell you all about the potential energy and the kinetic energy of the arrow that ended Maurice Joseph's life.

But what about Mr Joseph's potential? He was up on that roof as part of his re-entry into society after months in a drug rehabilitation program. He was changing lives – his own included – by teaching hydroponics, organic gardening, and animal care. His wife – now his widow – is due to have a baby in less than two months.

No amount of science can measure Maurice Joseph's poten-tial energy. No understanding of the Archer's Paradox – the natural bend of the arrow when released will affect its flight and accuracy, so never aim directly at your target – will soothe the future pain of another fatherless child in this, the greatest city in the world.

Hooke's Law: the weight of the draw is proportionate to the length of the draw. More physics. Was the killer's heartbeat increasing in direct proportion to Mr Joseph's heartbeat decreasing? Did they sweat more the farther they pulled back the arrow? How does any knowledge of physics play into the metaphysical?

Maurice Joseph is the first murder victim by arrow the city can recall. This will ensure that his death will be remembered longer than most other victims' deaths by violence – drug overdose, vehicular accident, suicide, or something boring like cancer.

There were so many things the killer had to take into consid-eration before shooting the arrow across the street: wind speed and direction, humidity, air pressure, the trajectory of the arrow's angle. So many factors. Those who knew Mr Joseph well said he had three major factors in his life: his unborn daughter, his wife, and his recovery.

We can only hope that Mr Newton's third law will apply here. For every action, there is an equal and opposite reaction: the killer of Mr Joseph will be caught and brought to justice.

Meanwhile, I am looking out of the window where just last week a killer lay in wait and a life was taken.

Allison Rogers for *New York City Here and Now*

'Holy shit,' I said, about half a minute after reading the last sentence. 'Where the hell did that come from?'

Allison took a sip of her coffee. 'I couldn't fall asleep last night. I kept seeing the school roof from the window. I kept seeing the arrow flying across the street and hitting Maurice. I got out of bed, turned on the laptop and it just came out.' She paused and looked at the article on my laptop. 'It usually doesn't work that way.'

'I'm not sure what to say. Would it sound like I was kissing your ass if I said it was poetry?'

'I don't know,' she said. 'Let's see what happens when you say it.'

'It's fucking poetry, Allie. Absolutely fucking poetry.'

She pretended to give that some thought. 'That feels pretty good, Ray. I didn't realize how much my ass needed kissing. It's nice.'

'Keep writing like this and I'll pucker up anytime.'

'Ha. That's what they all say.'

I decided against asking who *they* were. Instead I said, 'This will keep MoJo's story from fading away soon. You gonna bounce that Roman numeral idea off Royce today? I think he needs to hear it.'

'I think so, yeah. I'm planning on taking a page out of your teacher's handbook.'

'Which page would that be?'

'The one where it says to throw everything you can at your students and see what sticks,' she said.

'I like that page.'

She finished her coffee and got off the futon. 'I'm gonna shower and then call Royce. Soon as I know he's in, I'm heading over to talk about the Roman numeral thing.' She looked at the clock on the laptop. 'You gotta get going.'

I stood. 'Yeah. Call me later and let me know what Royce says.'

'Will do, tough guy.'

I brought her into a hug. 'Holy shit, Allie. You are good.'

'Say that one more time and you're coming into the shower with me.'

'That would make me late for school.'

'What are you now? A Boy Scout?'

'A horny Boy Scout who doesn't want to get into trouble with the Scout Master.'

'Just tell him you were getting laid in the shower.'

'Then I'd have to explain to him what "getting laid" means.'

She laughed, broke the hug and said, 'Later then?'

'Absolutely.'

I was heading back into the school after letting all the kids in when I saw my principal waiting for me at the top of the stairs, holding a rolled-up newspaper in his right hand. If I were a dog who had just taken a shit on his carpet, I would have been nervous. Now I was just curious. Ron doesn't usually come out of his office this early.

'Morning, Ron,' I said as I reached the top step.

'Ray. I guess you've been too busy to see the paper this morning?'

Only my boss could make doing my job sound like a bad thing.

'That would be a good guess, Ron. What'd I miss?'

'There's been another murder.' He sounded like an Agatha Christie character.

I wasn't sure why he was telling me this. We lived in – well, *I* lived in – New York City. Things were always getting better, but there were hundreds of murders a year in New York City. Instead of asking why he was bringing this to my attention, I decided to wait. I didn't have to wait long.

'The police found some poor son of a bitch under the Williamsburg Bridge last night. Or early this morning. Sometime around midnight.'

'Damn,' I said. 'That's too bad.' *And . . .?*

'He was speared, Ray.'

That got my attention. 'What?'

'You heard me,' Ron said. 'Speared. Like in the movies. Like how MoJo got shot by an arrow; this guy was speared.'

And another victim had been axed. Tomahawked? Jesus.

I didn't know what to say, so I said, 'May I see the paper?'

He handed it to me and I read the article. No photos, but the reporter clearly stated – three times – that the victim had been speared. It was a through-and-through injury; the weapon had been left next to the body. The very last line of the article was the one that had Ron upset.

Because of the manner of death, a police spokesperson said they were looking into a possible connection between last night's homicide and the killing last Thursday of Maurice Joseph, who died as the result of an arrow shooting as he worked on the rooftop of a Brooklyn school building.

I read the article again and then handed the paper back to Ron. There was, of course, nothing in the article about Roman numerals. I wondered if Allison had gotten in touch with Royce and how the conversation had gone. I also found myself wishing I were in that conversation.

'If I get any calls from the cops or papers today—' Ron began until I interrupted.

'Transfer them to me,' I said. I went up to my office and called Allison. It went to straight to voicemail. 'Call me after you talk to Royce.'

I was in my office preparing some faxes that needed to be sent to the district office by the end of the day when my walkie-talkie summoned me. It was Mary from the main office.

'You have a Mr Henderson here to see you, Ray,' she said. 'He didn't tell me what it's regarding.'

When I got downstairs, Henderson was on his cell phone, pacing outside the main office. He was wearing the same suit he had on the last time we talked. When he saw me, he said goodbye and stuck out his hand.

'Mr Donne,' he said, 'I hope I didn't take you away from anything important.'

'Just paperwork,' I said. 'You know how that is. What's up, David?'

He looked around the hallway. 'Can we talk?'

'Yeah. Let's go up to my office. I've got about two—'

'How about outside the building?' he said, more than a touch of paranoia in his voice. 'Someplace we can have a cup of coffee or something.'

OK. 'Yeah. I know just the place.' This was Williamsburg, after all.

As we headed for the door, we saw Ron Thomas in the hallway. He'd already left his office twice in one day. Maybe he was checking for his shadow, signaling another eight weeks of school. When he saw me with Henderson, he walked over.

'Everything OK, Ray?' He eyed Henderson nervously. He probably thought Henderson was from the Department of Ed. Or worse. Another reporter.

'Yeah, Ron. Just going out for a bit of fresh air with—'

'David Henderson,' David said, and then surprised me by taking out his official ID. 'Special Agent, FBI.'

'FBI?' Ron repeated as if Henderson had just said 'Citizen of Venus.'

'What does the FBI have to do with us?' I could see the possibilities running through Ron's head – none of them were good.

David didn't miss a beat. 'Ray and I are old friends. From his time on the job. We're discussing a possible visit to the school. Part telling your students what the FBI does – community outreach kind of thing – and part explaining to them the path to a career with the bureau.'

David Henderson. Olympic Gold Medalist in Lying.

'That's a great idea,' Ron said. He looked at me. 'This is the kind of thing I should know about, Ray.'

'I wanted to speak with David first,' I said, adding onto the lie. 'I wanted to make sure it was a bit more . . . structured before presenting it to you.'

Ron nodded thoughtfully. 'I like it, Ray. Be good for the school's image. Let me know what you come up with.' He shook David's hand again. 'And thanks, Agent Henderson.'

'Thank you.'

'You not only lie well,' I said as we walked down the outside steps, 'you lie quickly. Makes me wonder if I should even ask why you're really here.'

'That is why I'm here,' he said. We got to the sidewalk. 'Which way?'

'There's a good coffee place a few blocks up. A bit trendy for my taste, but since the government's paying . . .'

A few minutes later, we got our coffees and decided to sit on the bench outside. Part of being a trendy Brooklyn coffee shop is having the mandatory bench outside.

'What's up, Special Agent Henderson?'

He ignored that. 'First off,' he began, 'I shouldn't even be talking with you.'

I stood. 'That's fine with me. I'm at work and have stuff to do.'
I took a step back toward the school.

'Sit down, Mr Donne,' he said. 'Please.'

I did. 'I'm gonna tell you this once, David. I even smell you
lying to me, I go back to my school and the first thing I do is call
the New York field office and have a talk with your supervisor.'

He took a deep breath. 'I'm not here to lie to you.'

'Says the guy who's been doing a lot of that since we met.'

'I understand why you feel that way and you have every right
to. But I'm here to come clean.' He paused. 'I also need your advice.'

An FBI agent needs my advice? Take that, Mrs Fletcher.

'Talk to me.'

After a sip of coffee, he said, 'I wasn't completely honest with
you about my relationship with Maurice Joseph.'

I smirked. 'No shit.'

'He *was* working with me on gathering intel on Duke Lansing.
What I should have added is that I do have someone on the inside.
The problem is, I'm not sure how much I can trust him, which is
why I asked Maurice for help.'

'I asked you the last time we spoke,' I said. 'What did you have
on MoJo that would make him do something so risky?'

'Nothing on him, really.'

'Meaning?'

He took another sip. 'I've got information that someone at
Newer Leaves is distributing heroin.'

'To the residents?'

'And others. I'm not proud of this, but I used Maurice's attach-
ment to Newer Leaves as . . . leverage to get him to help me with
Lansing.'

I looked at my feet. 'You telling me that you promised not to
investigate the info about someone dealing at Newer Leaves if MoJo
went along with your plan? You knew how much that place meant
to him and how far he'd go to protect it.'

'Yes.'

I looked him in the eyes. 'Your lack of pride here is well deserved,
David.'

'What I didn't know was Maurice would look into who was doing
what at Newer Leaves by himself. He found out stuff he then shared
with me. Info I did not have.'

I thought back to the spy pen that MoJo had used to record Eddie

Price. We had originally considered the very real possibility that MoJo didn't know he was recording at the time, that he was just using the old piece of technology as a pen. That didn't seem to be the case anymore. Not if MoJo were up at Newer Leaves looking for a possible drug dealer. I kept that to myself for now.

But it was my turn to reveal something. 'Does it have anything to do with bags of heroin with double-eights on them?'

'How the fuck did you—?'

At the risk of sounding like a cliché, I said, 'I have sources, too.'

'You know he had them in his possession at the time of his death?'

And in his system.

'Yes. Did he tell you where – or who – he got them from?'

'No. But I have someone looking into it.' *Me, too.*

'So I'm guessing,' I said, 'that you are now thinking MoJo's murder probably did have something to do with the work he was doing for you or what he found up at Newer Leaves.'

He gave me a pained look. 'That is a distinct possibility, Mr Donne.'

'Distinct? What other conclusion can you come to, Agent?'

'If you asked me that question yesterday, I would have said it was more than a distinct possibility. It was the conclusion I was working on.'

'What happened between yesterday and now?'

Another pause, another sip. 'You hear about the DB they found by the river last night? The spearing victim?'

DB: cop-talk for dead body. Another way we distanced ourselves from the ugliness the job often threw our way. 'I just read about it in the paper.'

'There was also a guy killed by an ax the week before Maurice was killed. The police are saying a blunt instrument, but a guy I know said it was an ax of some sort.'

I stayed silent. There was no need to tell him too much of what I already knew. The more he told me, the better.

'Are you saying they're all connected?'

'I think we may have a serial killer out there is what I'm saying.'

Whoa. This was turning into a movie.

'Go on,' I said.

'We have three murder victims all killed in uncommon ways.

More so to the fact, they were all murdered by what we can consider Indian – Native American – weapons. An ax, an arrow, a spear.'

'That sounds like a connection to me.' And he didn't seem to know about the Roman numerals. 'You speak to Royce about your theory?'

'Not yet.' He cleared his throat. 'I wanted to bounce it off you first.'

I was about to ask why me, but I knew. 'Keeping it on the down low and doing a sanity check?'

'Exactly.'

I took a sip of coffee and went over everything Henderson had just told me. It must have been a minute before I spoke.

'You need to go to Royce with the serial killer theory,' I said. 'It doesn't sound crazy, but it does seem to argue *against* MoJo's getting murdered because of the work he was doing for you or what he found out about Newer Leaves.'

'I thought of that. They can't all be true.'

'And keep the connection to Newer Leaves between us right now. If it was important enough to MoJo to keep that from getting out, I want to respect that. Let me ask around up there. I met some of the folks the other day at the memorial.'

Henderson let out a breath I didn't know he was holding. 'I appreciate that, Ray. Keep in mind, though. I'm purposely not asking you for anything but advice here.'

'I hear ya, David. And there might come a time when Royce needs to know about what may or may not be happening at Newer Leaves. Now is not that time.'

'Right.'

With nothing more to say, I stood and looked down at Special Agent David Henderson. 'How's your ass, by the way?'

'Excuse me?'

'I'm guessing after Royce called your boss, you got chewed out a bit. On the rare occasion that happens to me, it's usually in the region of my buttocks.'

He laughed and stood with me. 'Not too bad, I guess. My boss, she's not too happy with me, but she seemed to understand. Let's just say I'm on a bit of a tight leash for the foreseeable future.'

'I've been there,' I said.

'I'm not surprised.'

I pulled my phone out and checked the time. I had to get back to school. I also asked him to keep me in the loop. I thought I deserved that much. He agreed and shook my hand.

'I'm sure we'll be in touch soon,' he said. 'This whole "keeping you in the loop" thing works both ways, right? You'll let me know what you find out?'

'Roger that,' I said and went back to work, leaving him to finish his coffee.

TWENTY-FOUR

'Uncle Ray.' I had just sat down for the first time that day and was about to enjoy a lunch of rice and beans from the Dominican place down the block. 'You're not changing Easter plans on us, I hope?' Secretly, I hoped he was calling to tell me Easter plans had been canceled. Jesus coming back to life and a big bunny hiding eggs wasn't a holiday; it was a network sitcom.

'You know what really infuriates me about you, Nephew?'

'I could guess,' I said, adding some hot sauce to my beans. 'But that would take too long, so why don't you tell me what it is.'

'You were such a good fucking cop, who has unfortunately decided his time would be better spent teaching kids who are just gonna end up dealing with the authorities someday.'

I agreed with half of what he had just said. He had conveniently left my injured knees out of his assessment. 'Thanks?'

'You were right about your boy Gator.'

'How so?'

I could hear the frustration in his breath as he let it out. I believe it truly bothered him that I was right sometimes. 'I had some of my guys check around the houses the other day. Where Gator lives?'

That was more than I had asked him to do. 'And . . .?'

'And they found the knucklehead who gave the stuff to Gator to hold.'

'How'd they do that?'

'Good old-fashioned shoe leather and knocking on a shitload of doors. And let's just say the guys I had go over there were not sent because they're overly polite.'

I chose not to pursue that. 'OK. Who was he? What'd the guy say?'

'Knucklehead's name doesn't concern you. What does concern you – and by that I mean mind your own fucking business and leave it to Royce – is that he told my guys "some white guy in a pimped-out pickup" came up to him, asked if he knew Gator, and when he said he did, gave him a bag and five bills to give the bag to Gator.'

'Just like that?'

'The guys asking didn't know Gator by name. Just what apartment he lived in and the whole overbite thing, right?'

'Right.'

'So our guy has no idea what this is about and figures he's doing Gator a favor and making five hundred at the same time, what's to lose?'

'So he didn't know Gator was being set up?'

'Not that he said and he woulda said because my boys really sweated the guy, Raymond. I think our guy just got blinded by the easy five bills.'

'So whoever gave . . . the knucklehead the bag more than likely called the cops on Gator. Told them he was holding.'

'There ya go again, Raymond,' my uncle said. 'Acting like a smart cop.'

'Any idea who the generous donor was?'

'Not as of yet. We have the nine-one-one recording about Gator, traced the call to one of the few working payphones on the avenue, and our messenger didn't think to pay attention to the license plate of the vehicle.' Uncle Ray paused. 'He did say it was red, though. With high headlights.'

'That's a big help. What happens now?'

'I told you, Nephew. I gave the info to Royce and you're to stay out of it. My guess is he's gonna interview the knucklehead himself, check for any surveillance video featuring a redneck pickup truck and keep his fingers crossed. I'm just calling because as much shit as I give you when you do stuff like this, I wanted you to know you were right and to tell you again what a damn shame it is you're not a cop anymore.'

'I meant what happens to Gator now?'

'Royce is gonna try and have a chat with him and his lawyer tomorrow. Royce called the ADA and it sounds like they'll be able to reduce the charges to something like being dumb enough to take a bag from someone you hardly know.'

'Is that enough to get him out of Riker's?'

'Everything goes right? My guess is in a few days. Ignorance is no excuse for breaking the law, but your boy did come up with some important information. That'll play well with the judge and I don't see a real problem here.'

I thought about that. 'So nothing yet on the vehicle or the guys who dropped off the bag?' That was met with silence from my uncle. 'What is it, Uncle Ray?'

'The kid who took the bag and passed it to your boy?'

'Yeah?'

'Said the guy had a tattoo on the back of his hand.'

'Really,' I said. 'Of what?'

'I shouldn't be telling you this, Ray, but it was red, white and blue.'

'The American flag? That's kind of a common tattoo, I'd think.'

'Not when it's shaped like a swastika.'

'That's what the kid said? It was a swastika?'

'Turns out our knucklehead paid some attention in school.'

'Man.'

'And there's another thing.'

Uncle Ray could be such a tease. 'What's that?'

'The bags your boy Gator was holding were labeled. Specially tagged.'

Holy shit. I thought about letting him tell me, but decided to take a shot at either impressing him, confusing him, or pissing him the hell off. Maybe I'd hit the trifecta.

'Don't tell me,' I said. 'Double-Eights. Dice'

Two beats of silence. 'How the fuck did you know that?'

'I can't tell you that right now. It would get certain people in trouble.'

'Certain people you live with, Ray?'

'I'm pleading the Fifth on this one, Chief. For the moment.'

I could tell by his silence the shade of red his face was turning. 'You're not gonna get a lot more of these moments, Nephew.'

'Thanks, Uncle Ray.'

'Yeah,' he said, but not in a nice way. And just when I thought he was going to chew me out some more, he added, 'You know it's never too late, Ray.'

'For what?'

'For you to return to the fold, Boyo. You know you want to. I can hear that now more than ever.'

I did not expect this discussion again. 'I really don't, Uncle Ray. Despite what you may think, I feel those of us teachers who take what we do seriously make your job that much easier. We wanna get to these kids before you do.'

'Ahhh, I know you do, Raymond. I'm just putting it out there. Again.'

'And that's why I love you, Uncle Ray.' I looked at my watch. 'I gotta go. Thanks again and I'll see you at Easter.'

'Don't forget the Scotch. And after this conversation, it just aged two years.'

'Wouldn't dream of anything less.'

I couldn't keep from thinking about White Nationalist Duke Lansing, sixteen-year-old Harlan S. from Allison's series, and now a drug courier with a red, white, and blue swastika on his hand. And Double-Eights.

Ask any good cop and they'll tell you they don't believe in coincidences. Uncle Ray was right about one thing. In that respect, I was like most cops.

During the last period, my cell phone rang. It was Richie Hebner.

'I found your translucent, drug-dealing white-ass scumbag,' were the first words out of his mouth.

'That was quick.'

'Yeah, well, I guess there's not too many guys who look like that slinging heroin on the mean streets of Canarsie.'

'I would imagine not. I assume you got a name?'

'Albert Biancotto. Which clearly gave rise to his professional name,' Richie said. 'Al Bino.'

'You are shitting me,' I said, remembering that's what Hex had called him the other night outside the dice game.

'I shit you not. I ran him through the system and – quite to my surprise – the guy's got no record. Drugs, possession, jaywalking. Nada. He doesn't even have a traffic ticket, probably because Albert Biancotto doesn't own a car, at least not one registered in his name. Nor does he seem to have a permanent address.'

'Is he really an albino?'

'I'm not sure,' Richie said. 'But my guy who knows him says he's whiter than professional hockey.'

'So,' I said, 'with no record, how does your guy know Biancotto?'

'Al spends just about all his time on the streets talking with young men who do have records for dealing. If guilt by association were a real crime, this guy would be doing hard time upstate. And the guys he associates with, they are not what you would call discriminating dealers, Ray.'

'How do you mean?'

'They deal whatever the flavor of the month is. Crack, weed, Ritalin. Right now, the drug of choice, as you know, is opioids, and heroin for those who can't scrape together the cash for opioids.'

No surprise there. 'Did you find out anything about the double-eights?'

'Oh, yeah,' he said. 'You're gonna love this.' Meaning I was not going to love this. 'Tell me, Mr Donne, what's the eighth letter of the alphabet?'

I did that real quick. 'H.'

'Right. Now double that.'

'Two H.'

'Or HH.'

That was not the same mathematically – two H is two times H whereas HH is H times H – but I didn't want to teach a math lesson here. 'OK,' I said. 'HH. So what?'

'Whatta you know about the White Nationalist movement? Or neo-Nazis?'

'A bit more than I did a week ago before MoJo was killed. Why?'

'HH, Ray. *Heil Hitler.* Half the white boys in the movement's got that tattooed somewhere on their lily-white supremacist bodies. This guy, Biancotto, puts it – very discreetly for a drug-dealing racist, I might add – on the bags of whatever it is he's not getting caught selling.'

He let that sink in for a bit. 'I take it you never heard of the CCC?'

I ran that through my brain. 'The Civilian Conservation Corp? It was part of The New Deal back in the thirties that put unmarried guys to work out west. What does that have to do with this?'

'Absolutely squat, Ray,' Richie said. 'Nowadays, here in the Borough of Kings, it stands for the Canarsie Christian Crusade.'

'Jesus. Tell me that's not what it sounds like.'

'If it sounds like the KKK, then I can't do that. And I'll give you three guesses who's an active member of the council, and the first two don't count.'

'Al Biancotto.'

'Ding ding ding.'

Shit, I thought. *Does everything about MoJo's murder involve White Nationalists?*

'Now,' Richie said, 'there's an ugly rumor out there about the CCC.'

'Uglier than being White Supremacists.'

'Oh, yeah. It's only a rumor, but talk is they got someone in their group who puts heroin out there on the streets that's not always pure heroin. It's mixed with fentanyl.'

'On purpose?' I said. 'Why would they do that? They're killing off their base.'

'They're not putting it out for their base, they're putting it out for other dealers' bases. Bases of a certain shade, if you get my drift.'

I thought on that. 'They're putting fentanyl into the bags of heroin sold to non-white users in the hopes they'll OD?'

'You catch on as quickly as Billy said you would. That's some evil shit right there, huh?'

'Evil's not the word. That's old-time Nazi.'

Richie let out one of the most humorless chuckles I'd ever heard. 'That's a good way to say it, Ray. A real good way.'

'So,' I said, 'no address for this guy?'

'Not a residence, no. But I do know where he spends most of his indoor time when he's not on the streets supervising. Some kind of computer shop in Canarsie. You got a paper and pencil?'

More than I could count. 'Shoot.'

'It's at the end of the subway line. It's called *The Last Stopp for Lap Topss.* You're gonna love this clever part. The *Stopp*'s got two Ps and *Laptopss* got two Ss. What's that? A palindrome?'

'Almost an anagram,' I said. 'One more **t** than there should be.' I agreed that it was clever. For a neo-Nazi. I also asked if he had any more info for me.

'No,' Richie said. 'No more info, but I do have some good advice for you.'

'What's that?' I asked, knowing the answer already.

'Stay away from this guy, Ray. Billy told me how much you like to play PI. This Biancotto's the real deal. The fact that we got nothing on him proves that.'

'I'm not planning on paying him a visit, Richie.'

'Billy told me you'd say that. But if you decide to – and again, I'm saying please don't – do me a favor.'

'What's that?'

'Bring some backup. You're gonna need it.'

I considered that. 'Thanks, Richie. For the info and advice.'

'Use them both with caution, Ray.'

'Will do. And, hey, you should swing by The LineUp some Wednesday night. I work the sticks once a week. Beers are on me.'

'I might just do that. I'm a big fan of the barter system. See ya later, Ray.'

'Absolutely.'

Backup?

I'm a schoolteacher. A dean. Where the hell was I going to get backup if I made the unlikely and inadvisable decision to take the L train out to Canarsie and have a talk with Albert Biancotto?

Oh, right.

TWENTY-FIVE

After all the distractions of the past week, it felt good to be at my desk with the kids dismissed, the teachers gone, and just the cleaners and me in the building. I took the opportunity to finish up some paperwork, send some emails, fax some forms to the mother ship in downtown Brooklyn, and throw some crap out that had been building up in the office over the past few weeks. I felt a little like I was back in college, putting off studying for a test.

At five o'clock, Allison called. 'Been real busy, Ray. Had my meeting with Royce, then the *Here and Now* staff got together for lunch, my mom called and we ended up on the phone for almost two hours. I had to hang up because my phone died. At least that's what I told her. She still doesn't know I can talk while charging my phone.'

'Everything OK with your folks?' Phone calls between Allison and her family in Missouri were often, but brief. Two hours would add up to a month of calls.

'My dad fell and broke his pelvis,' she said. 'He's gonna need surgery and lots of rehab. I might head out next week and spend some time with them.'

'Sorry about that,' I said, knowing the older Allison's folks got, the more she missed them. Dad's broken pelvis or not, she'd be looking forward to the time back home.

'Where are you?'

'Still at my desk,' I said. 'How was your talk with Royce?'

'He was not pleased that I had taken some photos during my trip the other day, but I told him about the Roman numerals. He found that interesting enough that he allowed me to ride over to the new crime scene with him. It's not his case, but he wanted to check it out.'

'And?'

'We didn't find anything connecting the other murders to last night's.' A pause, then, 'Not at first.'

I waited. 'You teasing me again?'

'Royce called the detective-in-charge of the new case and told him about the Roman numerals. On closer inspection of the murder weapon – the fucking spear – there were three vertical lines on the staff, connected by two horizontal lines.'

'Roman numeral three.' Then I told her Henderson's serial killer theory. 'Pretty hard to wrap my mind around.'

'I had a math teacher back in middle school who used to tell us "Two does not make a pattern. But when there's three . . ."'

'I said the same thing to my kids when I was in the classroom. They taught us something very much like that in the academy, too.'

'Royce said something else, too. Unlike MoJo, the other two victims were killed somewhere else and their bodies were moved to where they were found.'

'To make sure they were found,' I said.

'That's what Royce and the other detective are going on.'

I told her about what my uncle had confirmed about the bags of heroin Gator had been caught holding.

She was silent for a bit. 'This is getting weird, Ray.'

'Ya think?' Then I said, 'Where are you now?'

'Waiting on the G train to take me home to my live-in boyfriend.'

'Very cool. I'll be back by seven and pick up something for dinner then.'

'I could use that,' she said. 'And maybe another shower.'

'Feeling dirty?' I said, trying my best to sound flirtatious. I really just needed some healthy skin-to-skin contact.

'In more ways than one, tough guy.'

I called it quits around six and headed out of the building. Standing against a very nice blue car were Dennis McLain and – what was his name? – RV, from Newer Leaves.

They both stood up straight when they saw me. McLain spoke first.

'Mr Donne. We were told you were still inside.'

'By whom?'

'A Ms Josephine Levine. Seems she puts in late hours, too.'

'Giving the taxpayers their money's worth.' I shook both of their hands. McLain was wearing a blue suit the exact color of his car. 'What brings you down to Brooklyn? Or back down, I should say.'

'Fundraiser,' McLain said. 'I think I tapped the well up north about as dry as it's gonna get, so I have some old friends throwing me an event down here.'

I turned to RV. 'Hey, man. How's it going?' His outfit was a black jacket and pants. The work boots I'd seen the other day had been replaced by a pair of dress shoes.

He looked nervous. 'Good. I guess. I don't like the city that much.'

'A little too different from your neck of the woods?'

'Something like that,' he said. 'Yeah.' A truck went by and startled him.

'If I knew you were having an event,' I said to McLain, 'I might've dropped by, but I have other plans.'

'Just as well,' he said. 'It's more of a private dinner. A club I used to belong to in Ozone Park. Kind of a church thing.'

'Yeah. My dad used to belong to Knights of Columbus on the Island.'

'Then you know what I mean.'

'What brings you by the school?'

'Actually,' he said, 'I'm here to see you.'

'Really?' *Maybe he did want some of my money.*

'Yes. I don't mean to sound crude, but we have another client up at Newer Leaves who's ready for placement and . . .'

'Since a spot just opened here, you figured you'd ask?'

'Is that horrible?'

'Not at all,' I said. 'But it's too late in the year to get that ball rolling. Means a lot of forms, background checks, all that fun stuff.'

He laughed. A paperwork joke between the guys. 'The fall then?'

'Almost definitely. I think MoJo would like that, Denny.'

'Speaking of whom.' McLain took me by the elbow. 'Excuse us, RV.' We walked closer to the school and he lowered his voice. 'Did Maurice by any chance mention anything to you about Newer Leaves?'

'Lots. Can you be more specific?'

We took a few more steps. RV looked more uncomfortable the farther we got from him. 'There have been some rumors among the men. About drugs finding their way into the house.'

I shook my head. 'MoJo said nothing to me about that.'

'Are you sure, Ray? All it takes is a few rumors in the wrong ears for a place like Newer Leaves to get some unwanted attention.'

'From whom?'

'Let's just say there are some . . . special interests up in my district who'd like to see Newer Leaves somewhere else. You've heard of NIMBY?'

'Sure,' I said. 'Not In My Backyard.' I also heard him say 'my district.'

'There's been some talk at the town halls. Some vo— folks – are afraid of the type of people Newer Leaves brings in. You noticed the racial makeup the other day.'

'I was impressed with the racial makeup.'

'Not everyone thinks like you and I do, Ray,' he said. 'The demographics up there still skew mostly white. A lot of people want to keep it that way.' He patted my shoulder. 'But I'm glad Maurice didn't say anything to you. I know he trusted you.'

'Sorry I couldn't help.'

'But you did.' We walked back over to RV. McLain shook my hand again. 'Thanks again, Ray. We'll talk about the fall.'

'Yes.' I shook RV's hand. 'Are you a member of this club, RV?'

He didn't understand the question at first. When he did, he said, 'Oh, no. I just drive Mr McLain sometimes.' I guessed that RV must have been the associate who drove Price and McLain down to Maurice's benefit the other night.

McLain patted RV on the back, signaling him to get behind the wheel. 'Let's talk soon, Mr Donne.'

I held the door for him. 'Let's do that.' I shut the door and they drove away.

By the time I got home, Allison already had the table set. I had picked up some baked ziti and a salad; she'd picked up some wine. We opted for the wine first, put on some Sinatra and ended up in the shower before eating. After we dried off, we hit the futon, ate our pasta, and fell asleep, happy and fed, with Frank in the background.

TWENTY-SIX

'You want a ride to work?' Allison asked. 'I have the company car today.'

'Sure, great.' I was just tying my sneakers. 'Anything special on your plate?'

'I've got some interviews in different parts of the city; I asked for the car and no one had anything else, so it's mine for the day.'

'I don't think I've had a ride to school since high school,' I said.

'Just don't develop any mommy issues.'

'After last night, not a chance.' I grabbed my backpack.

'I would hope not,' she said. 'Now get a move on. You don't want to be late.'

'How'd your talk with the FBI go?' Ron Thomas asked as I left the lunchroom.

I had forgotten about that particular lie. 'Good,' I said. 'Agent Henderson has some smart ideas about raising awareness and a possible career talk with the kids.'

'That's a great idea, Ray. We should do a whole career day here.'

'Maybe we can put something together for the eighth grade after one of the graduation rehearsals.'

'Now you're thinking like an administrator.' I let that slide. 'Make some phone calls and let me know what you come up with. Good thinking, Ray.'

And then he was gone.

I went to my office and called to thank Billy for putting me in touch with Richie Hebner and to see when he was free for some beers.

'I'm free today, partner,' he said. 'How about we go out to Canarsie, meet this Al Biancotto guy, and then go for some beers.'

That was quicker than I had expected, but I knew enough that between work and his family Billy didn't get a lot of free time. 'Let me get back to you on that?'

'Gotta check in with the missus?'

'More like an FBI agent. I'll call you back.'

'CCC?' Henderson said. 'Out in Canarsie. Let me run that past the guys in the joint task force, along with this Biancotto guy's name. But, yeah, I can make a trip out there today. Just let me clear it with my field director. I'll call you back.'

After playing phone tag for about an hour, my 'backup' met me at four thirty in front of the entrance to the L train a few blocks from my school.

'Billy,' I said, 'meet David. David, Billy.'

They shook hands and Billy said, 'So you're the Special Agent, huh?'

'Yeah.'

'Just like Mulder and Scully? *The X Files?*'

'You know, Sergeant Morris,' Henderson said, 'that joke was hysterical the first hundred times I heard it. Now, not so much.'

'I knew you guys would get along,' I said. 'C'mon. We got a train to catch.'

Even though Billy and Henderson both had cars, I suggested we take the train. That way we didn't have to deal with any traffic and there'd be no argument over whose car we were going to take. If we compromised and took two cars, that would give the impression that we were rolling up on Biancotto and that's the last thing I needed. This was not to be a show of force. I wanted information; that was it. The subway was also neutral territory, and I didn't want either of these guys feeling superior to the other because he was the one driving.

My plan was simple: I just wanted to find out if Biancotto had
been dealing to MoJo again. That's not the kind of question you
could just call up and ask a guy, even if you did have his number.
It was the kind of question you could ask a guy if you went to see
him directly; ask nicely, with an NYPD sergeant and an FBI Special
Agent as backup, both of whom were carrying and kind of owed
me. I also wanted to know – but was not sure about getting the
answer to this one – why MoJo was in possession of Biancotto's
merchandise if, as I was hoping, he was not using again, and why
that merchandise was laced with fentanyl?

See? Simple.

I explained all this to my companions during the subway ride
and they didn't question me. At least not out loud. What they were
thinking could have been a whole other story. Billy Morris had
known me for years and was not one to doubt me. I'd just met
Henderson a week ago, and he and I both knew who had to earn
the trust back in this relationship. Either way, it was the only plan
I had, and these were the only two guys I knew who could help me
out on very short notice. When Allison called and asked what I was
doing, I half-lied and told her I was getting together with Billy. OK,
more than a half-lie. Closer to ninety percent. I didn't see any reason
to worry her, and chances were real good I'd be home not too long
after dinner.

The ride took less than half an hour. I found it charming that outside
the Canarsie subway station was a sign welcoming us to this part
of Brooklyn and featuring a drawing of the Native Americans who
we had stolen the land from. Canarsie was one of those parts of
Brooklyn that looked pretty much the same as it had twenty, thirty,
forty years ago. I was sure that would change soon. There were
some signs of residential and business improvements – read that as
'gentrification' – around the L train station, as it provided a straight
shot into lower Manhattan for two dollars and seventy-five cents.
But when we found Al Biancotto's place, it clearly hadn't changed
much since Reagan was in office.

The faded and ripped blue awning above the store still read 'ABC
The Last Stopp for Lap Topss.' I'm guessing ABC stood for Al
Biancotto's Computers.

As Richie had led me to expect, there was Al standing outside
the store, under the ancient awning, which was flapping in the

slight breeze; he was talking to a young white kid in a sweatshirt, knee-length shorts, and a blue baseball cap. With them was a tall bald guy in sunglasses, a flannel shirt with the sleeves rolled up, and jeans. Al was wearing a long-sleeved T-shirt and shorts, and had the whitest legs I'd ever seen on someone this side of an albino. He was also wearing sunglasses and one of those wide-brimmed white hats you usually see on old men using metal detectors to look for hidden treasure on the beach. I couldn't hear what he was saying, but his hands didn't look happy.

I turned to Billy and Henderson. 'You guys stay here. I'm gonna go over and talk with him.'

'What if he tries something?' Billy asked.

'Then your being over there just gives you a better view of him trying something,' I said. 'If anything goes down, you're across the street. This goes the way I want it to, I'm back in five minutes and we're back on the L to Williamsburg.' Before he could ask I said, 'And I don't answer negative questions, just use your best judgment.'

I headed across the street. I was about halfway there when a car beeped at me, drawing Al's attention. He gestured with his head toward me and the two guys he was conversing with flanked him. This was not the first time strangers had approached the boss outside his place of business. When I got close enough, I could smell the sunblock and cocoa butter. I could also see the blue veins that crisscrossed Al's legs, arms and hands like a road map. It was hard to tell how old he was. With so little color in his skin, he could have been anywhere between thirty and sixty.

He looked me up and down and said, 'You're new.'

'As compared to . . .?'

'The other narcotic guys they got working around here.'

'That's because I'm not a cop.'

He looked over my shoulder. 'Well, your two friends definitely are so what does that make you?'

I took a step closer and shrugged. 'Someone who has friends who are cops.'

He smirked. 'Should I be impressed?' he said. ''Cause I gotta be honest, I don't feel all that impressed. I got lots of friends who are cops.' He slapped his boy on the arm and they had a good laugh. The bald guy stayed shut.

When they settled down, I said, 'I'm here to talk about MoJo.'

Al considered that. 'You friends with him, too?'

'I was. I'm also friends with his wife, Lisa. You know her?'

'I know she's a colored woman,' he said. Then added, 'Excuse me. *African American.* I forget to be politically correct sometimes.' Again with the laughter.

'She's concerned he was using again,' I said, going for direct, not waiting for the chuckles to die down this time and not wanting this conversation to go any longer than it had to. 'You know anything about that?'

Al tipped his sunglasses and exposed a pair of blue eyes that were so light they made me think he may have worn those glasses indoors, too. The rumors that his eyes were pink were greatly exaggerated.

'For a friend of MoJo, you sure do sound like a cop,' he said.

'I'm a teacher. MoJo was working at my school when he was killed. They found fentanyl in his system and his wife wants to believe that he was not using anymore because that's what he told her.'

'And that would be the first time that a white guy lied to an African American woman to get some dark pussy, right?' More laughter.

This guy needed a beating. Not now and probably not by me, but he needed a beating. I tried again. 'Were you selling to MoJo again, Al?'

'First of all,' he said, 'people I know call me Al. You can call me Mr Biancotto. Second, I stopped selling to MoJo years before he knocked up the colored woman he called his wife. I wouldn't have taken his business after that. I don't mind my kind dipping the wick in the dark wax every once in a while – who can blame them, right? – but when they start procreating, adding to the mixing of the races, I draw the line.' He slid his glasses back. 'So the answer to your question, friend of MoJo, is no. I was not selling to him.'

'Any idea why he had sixty bags of Double-H on him?'

The glasses came all the way off now. 'The fuck you say?'

'Sixty bags. Your tag. Cops found heroin and fentanyl in his system. They also found a heroin/fentanyl mix in the bags.'

That got his full attention. 'I know you don't know me real well, friend' – he took the last step there was to take between us – 'but I am not one to fuck with. I believe you sorta know that or you wouldn'ta brought Starsky and Hutch across the way there, but I'm not sure you get the whole meaning of that statement.'

I held my ground and looked over my shoulder. Billy looked ready to pounce. I slowly raised my hand, telling him I was fine.

'Listen, *Al*,' I said. 'I did not come here to fuck with you because I know that would be a stupid thing to do. I came here to get an answer for a friend. I believe you just gave me the answer I was looking for. I hear you're a man of your word' – I hadn't heard that, but it couldn't hurt to say it – 'so I believe you. I just gave you some info you could probably find helpful. Someone is out there distributing fentanyl under your label.'

He gave that some thought. So did I, and I was pretty sure we were thinking the same thing. If we were, it could be helpful for the good guys.

'OK, friend,' Al said when he was done thinking. 'I heard you and you heard me. I think we can consider our conversation done here.'

I was about to agree when something else occurred to me and I decided to push my luck. 'Any of your guys,' I said, 'have a tattoo on his hand of a red, white, and blue swastika?'

'Why you wanna know that?'

I told him the story of the guy who dropped off the package that got Gator sent away to Riker's and how that guy was probably involved in MoJo's murder. This time, it didn't take long for an answer.

'Lots of my guys got tattoos of lots of stuff,' he said. He turned his arms over so I could see a black H on each of them with *CCC* running across the horizontal line. His boy rolled up his sleeves. I counted two Confederate flags, two pairs of SS lightning bolts, and a swastika. The lightning bolts looked like prison ink. The bald guy just stood there with his arms behind him. He wasn't gonna show me shit. 'And, yeah, we put our beliefs in ink. I don't keep track of how they decide to represent, so . . . But I will tell you this. If you're thinking I put the hit out on MoJo, take that shit somewhere else. Just 'cause I don't like who the man decided to procreate with, don't mean I'm gonna risk all I got by ending him. One of my guys did that, they had their own beef with MoJo – got nothing to do with me.'

He looked across the street. 'Make sure your friends understand that. I'm not looking for no more visitors around here.' He leaned in closer so I could get a good look at his gray-blue eyes. 'Things could get ugly if that happens. And that ain't going to be good for no one.'

As he slid his glasses back into place, I said, 'I hear ya. I appreciate your time.'

Al Biancotto gave me a creepy smirk. 'Call next time,' he said. And one last time, I listened to him and his boy laughing as I walked away. Fun job these guys had.

When I got to the other side of the street, Billy had one of his trademark grins on his face. 'Well,' he said, 'that seemed to go just fine.'

'On what do you base that?' I asked.

'By the fact that you're walking back here under your own power and we never moved from our position of observation.'

'There is that.'

'What did he say?' David asked as we walked back to the subway.

I gave them the story and as it was pretty short to begin with, they got it all. When I was done, Billy said, 'So not a candidate for Canarsie's Man of the Year, huh?'

'Nope,' I said. 'But there is that silver lining.'

'Do tell,' Billy said.

We kept walking to the L train. 'When I was kid,' I began, 'my uncle rented this place way out east on the Island. In Quogue. At the time it was the only one-syllable stop on the Long Island Rail Road.'

Billy turned to Henderson. 'In case you haven't picked up on it, Ray here is a word nerd. Tell the story, Ray.'

We began climbing the stairs to the train. 'I used to go hiking along the cliffs overlooking the water, getting as close to the edge as possible without falling. Every once in a while, I screwed up and I fell. Rolled down into the beach area and came up with a mouth full of sand, but no real injury.'

'Yeah?'

'One day,' I went on, 'I was walking, and I found what looked like an old faded football, so I kicked it.' We went through the turnstiles. 'It wasn't old, and it wasn't a football. It was a beehive. As it tumbled down the cliff, I saw about a hundred bees flying out, and they were not happy.'

Henderson said, 'They come after you?'

'They had no idea who kicked them. They were just pissed off and were probably going to go after the next person they ran into. Some innocent person on the beach more than likely.'

The next L train toward the city was pulling in as Billy asked, 'What the hell does that have to do with what just happened?'

We got on the train, and since this was the first stop going our way, easily found three seats together. 'I think,' I said sitting between the two, 'I just kicked a beehive. Now we just gotta see who the bees go after.'

TWENTY-SEVEN

We were about to go for those beers when my cell phone rang. It was Allison. 'Can you meet me at the precinct?' she asked.

'What's the matter?'

'You need to see something.'

'But you're OK?'

'Yeah. Just get here as soon as you can.'

I looked at Billy and Henderson. 'Go,' they said in unison.

When I got to the Ninetieth Precinct, Allison was outside with Royce and a uniformed female officer who was taking pictures of the company car. I went right over, put my arm around Allison, and said, 'Someone break in?'

'No.' Allison walked me over to the driver's side window and pointed at where someone had drawn an upside down arrow. 'I found that after my last interview.'

'What's it mean?' I asked, knowing the answer would not be good.

'The first thing it means is someone's following me.' She held up her phone as Royce joined us. 'And . . . I looked it up. Most upside down Native American symbols represent death.'

I turned to Royce. 'So this is a threat?'

Royce said, 'That's how we're treating it, yes.'

I looked at the car and noticed some fingerprint powder on the windows and door handles. That was optimistic of them. All I saw were smudges, and whoever had drawn the arrow never had to touch the car. Try as they might, the cops would come up empty.

'Can we drive it home now, Detective?' I asked.

The uniformed officer with the camera took one more picture and said, 'OK by me, sir.' She raised the camera. 'Not much here.' *See?*

'Go ahead,' Royce said. 'Call nine-one-one immediately if you suspect anything.' He looked at Allison. 'You want an escort home?'

'I'm with Ray. What could happen?'

Royce rubbed his goatee. 'I'm the wrong one to ask about that, Ms Rogers.' He looked at me. 'You might want to call your uncle. Have someone watch the front of your place for a couple of days.'

'You read my mind, Detective.' We shook hands. 'Thanks.'

I called Uncle Ray on the way home and he assured me he'd have a car outside our building within the hour. Forty-five minutes later, we were home and got a call from an Officer Paulson. She said she was down the block in a light blue four-door if we needed anything. She sounded very serious.

Neither one of us was very hungry, so we just snacked on some leftovers from the fridge. Allison was a little more shaken up about the arrow incident than I had first thought. We sat on the futon watching TV, and she was about as quiet as I've ever seen her. I was about to ask her if she wanted to go out for some air and some ice cream when my phone rang. Not recognizing the number, I said, 'Hello?'

'Raymond Donne?'

'This is he. Who's this?'

'Eddie Price,' he said. 'From Newer Leaves? We met the other day. At the mem— well, at both memorials. I got your number off of Maurice's paperwork. I hope you don't mind.'

I stood up. 'Not at all, Mr Price. What's up?'

'Do you have a moment to talk?'

'Sure.' I took the phone out to the balcony. 'Go ahead.'

He was silent for a few seconds, then said, 'I hope this doesn't sound weird.'

You don't know what passes for weird these days, brother.

'Try me.'

'Did MoJo mention anything to you about some . . . work he was doing for me up at Newer Leaves?'

'Not to me, no.'

'What about your friend Edgar?'

'You'd have to ask Edgar, Mr Price,' I said. 'If it were security work, wouldn't Edgar have been involved?'

'This was more of a . . .' He struggled for the right word. 'Personal matter.'

'Like I said, MoJo said nothing to me. Do you have Edgar's number?'

'I do. It's also on the paperwork as a reference. I'll check with him tomorrow.' It didn't sound like he was going to get much sleep tonight.

I waited for him to say more. When he didn't, I said, 'Goodnight.'

'Yes, goodnight, Raymond. Thank you.'

That made two people – three if I included RV – in two days who had asked me if MoJo had spoken to me about something to do with Newer Leaves. I went back inside and bounced that off Allison.

She lowered the volume on the TV. 'That is odd. At least McLain came right out and said what it was he wanted to know. You think it's the same thing? And if whatever Price had going on with MoJo was "personal," why ask you about it?'

'I don't know. People sometimes think I know more than I do, I guess.'

She turned off the TV and leaned back with her eyes closed. 'I wonder,' she said, 'where they get that idea from.'

I guessed she was feeling a little better.

Neither of us slept well that night. When that happens to me, I tend to toss and turn, hoping I'll drop off sometime soon. Allison's a pacer; I think most writers are. At around two in the morning, she got up to pace. I joined her half an hour later as she was staring out the kitchen windows.

'What're you thinking?' I asked.

'About MoJo and Harlan. What the hell was MoJo doing, Ray? Sneaking around for the FBI and now McLain asking questions?' I had no answer for that. 'And I haven't heard from Harlan in a while. I'm worried something happened to him. He was calling me almost every day.'

I put my arms around her. 'He's more than just a story to you, I know.'

'You figured that out, huh?' More staring. 'And what was that fucking arrow about? Is someone threatening me because of my pieces on MoJo or the series on Harlan?' She turned around. 'I am not you, Raymond. I'm not used to this shit.'

I pulled her into a hug. 'You don't get used to it, Allie. And it sucks that it happens when all you want to do is help people.'

'That is all I want to do. That's what journalism is supposed to do. Inform and help where we can. My mentor at MU drilled that into us.'

'Cops, teachers, and reporters,' I said. 'For every one on our side, there seems to be one on the other side.'

She squeezed me. 'Sucks is a good word for that.' She broke the hug and said, 'I'm not going to get any sleep tonight, Ray. Let's just sit on the couch.'

I took her by the hand and led her to the futon. 'I can do that.'

It turns out we did get a little sleep, maybe three hours. I was about to call in sick to work when I realized it was Saturday. We dozed in and out of consciousness for a few hours and by eleven were ready to get up. Allison had to get the car up to a colleague in Harlem, so we had a quick breakfast and I walked her to the car.

'You want me to go with you?' I asked.

'I'll be fine,' she said. 'Be back in a few hours.'

I went down the block and found Officer Paulson sipping a cup of coffee behind the wheel of her light blue four-door. We exchanged pleasantries and I asked if she wouldn't mind following Allison up to Harlem and then taking her home. After all, she had been instructed by my uncle to keep an eye on her. She said she would, and I jogged back to Allison to tell her the news.

'Oh, good. Now I've got an escort.' She got in the car. 'I don't like this.'

'Me, neither.' I stuck my head into the car and kissed her. 'Call me. I may be down by the river.'

I never made it to the river, because when I got upstairs, my phone rang. It was RV and he sounded more nervous than the last time I'd seen him.

'Can you meet me at Lisa Joseph's?' he asked. 'I have something I need to tell the two of you.' He paused and breathed heavily. 'About MoJo.'

'Should I call Detective Royce?' I asked.

Another pause. 'Maybe after I tell you, then you can decide?'

'OK. Give me ten minutes. You know where she lives?'

'I have GPS. I'll see you soon. I'll be outside.'

I went to the car service on the corner and the guy had me in front of Lisa's in just over five minutes. I got out and looked around for RV. I didn't see him, but I did see Dennis McLain. I walked over to him and he saw the look on my face.

He took me by the elbow. 'I figured you'd get here quicker if I had RV call you.'

'What's this about?' I asked.

He steered my attention across the street and said, 'See that man in the SUV?'

I looked across the street and noticed a bald man in shades sitting behind the wheel of a huge vehicle that had no reason to be parked on this street. 'I see him,' I said. And I recognized him: he was the bald guy standing with Al Biancotto outside the computer shop the other day.

'Good,' McLain said. 'Now he'll stay there if you do what I say.'

'What the fuck are you talking about?'

He squeezed my elbow harder. 'Come with me and Charles stays where he is. Don't, and Charles pays a visit to Lisa Joseph.'

'Where's RV?' I asked.

He laughed. 'Probably up at Newer Leaves. He works today.'

I looked across the street again and didn't like the way Charles was staring at Lisa Joseph's apartment. 'What do you want me to do?' I asked.

'First, give me your phone.' When he had it, he turned it off and tossed it into the street. 'Now, let's go for a drive.'

'What about Charles?' I asked.

'He'll stay there until I tell him different. Let's go, Raymond.'

TWENTY-EIGHT

Traffic was moving pretty well for a Saturday; we made it through the Bronx into Westchester in about a half-hour. Now that we were out of the city and around more trees, McLain got talkative. It may have also helped that he had me handcuff my wrists between my legs. He drove with his right hand on the steering wheel and his left hand holding a gun.

'I have to tell you,' he said, 'I have looked at this situation from every angle, Raymond, and I kept coming up with the same answer. You. You are the only person connected to the FBI, the NYPD, the media, and Newer Leaves.' He paused. 'And, of course, MoJo.'

'Did you kill Maurice?'

He kept his eyes ahead of him as we rode through the EZ Pass lane. 'Archery,' he said, 'is all in the mind, Raymond. The only one you are really competing against is yourself. Do the best you can, stay mindful of the process and your technique, and you'll come out ahead more times than not.'

'I'll take that as a yes.'

'If you're expecting a Scooby Doo moment, Raymond, I'm afraid you're going to be disappointed. We're not on this trip for an explanation. I'm just solving another problem. This one happens to be you.'

Less than an hour out of the city, we took an exit, made a series of complicated turns, and found ourselves on a ranch that looked like it hadn't been used in years.

'It may be a piece of shit real estate,' McLain said as we pulled up to an old barn, 'but it's mine. Technically, my dad's, but mine soon enough. Last time I saw the old guy he wasn't looking too good. All those years killing himself on the farm, and for what? No pension, no retirement, just Social Security and other taxpayer-supported entitlements.'

He leaned over and unlocked the handcuffs, leaving them dangling from my left wrist. 'Let's go,' he said, and we got out of the car. With his gun still on me, he pulled his cell phone out of his pocket and called someone. 'You can go,' he said. 'We're here.' He put the phone back and said, 'Your friend Lisa will be undisturbed.'

He unlocked the wooden door to the barn and motioned with the gun for me to go inside. He shut the door behind us and I realized he was right: the inside of the barn made it look even more worthless. A bunch of birds flew up into the rafters as we walked farther inside. Old farm tools were on the floor, a tractor from the deep past sat by itself in the corner, and sunlight came in through the openings in the walls and roof. It looked as if a strong wind might blow the whole thing over.

'But, as soon as we get some of those archaic zoning laws changed,' he went on, 'the price on these acres is going to skyrocket.'

'So much for being a man of the people, huh?' I said.

'All depends on which people you're talking about, Raymond. I happen to prefer the white ones with lots of money. And when I split this historic piece of Americana up into forty units, they'll be lining up with their trophy wives, private school kids, and checkbooks.'

'Making America White Again,' I said.

He laughed. 'Something like that.'

'So, I'm guessing MoJo figured out what you were doing at Newer Leaves. The rumors you and Price were so concerned about. The drugs.'

'Yeah,' he said. 'That's the thing about most junkies: they can't keep their fucking mouths shut. Eddie Price asked Maurice to talk to the guys, chat them up, see what they had to say. One of them trusted him too much and someone shot his mouth off. Even gave MoJo some of the merchandise he was supposed to sell for me. I figured I could trust these guys to sell some product and keep their mouths shut. Especially since I'm the facility's lawyer and I'm telling them I'm trying to keep the place open. I figured wrong and had to find a solution.'

'Killing MoJo and two other innocent people is a hell of a solution.'

'There're very few innocents out there, Raymond. You should know that better than most. All you've seen on the streets and in the school system. Innocent is just another word for not getting caught. As for me, I'm like most politicians. I'm just giving the people what they want. These people happen to want heroin.'

'And if a few die because of that?'

'You know the old expression: You can't legislate common sense. Besides, you don't think my opponent takes money from Big Pharma? Damn straight he does. I just get it in a different way. I've never taken a dollar from those companies.'

'No, you just reap the benefits of those who are addicted to their products.'

'That's very liberal talk, Raymond. You'd never get elected up here.'

'What was with the Roman numerals?' I asked.

'Trick I learned as a lawyer to use when things are going against you. Throw some diversions and distractions at the other side; it makes them waste energy trying to figure it out. The numerals were nothing but a way to connect all three killings. I wasn't sure the Native American aspect would be enough for the NYPD, so why not?'

'And the other two victims?'

'One homeless guy who picked the wrong place to sleep that night and one drunk who couldn't remember where he parked. Nothing like a good serial killer to keep cops off-balance.'

Fuck this guy. 'Eddie Price?'

McLain laughed. 'A bureaucrat. He knows his numbers and budgets and keeping his beds filled. And no imagination. He wouldn't dream someone from Newer Leaves was dealing. He's clueless.'

Before I could answer that, the door to the barn opened again. It was RV.

Judging by the look on McLain's face, I wasn't the only one surprised to see RV. He stepped into the barn and gently closed the door as if afraid to let it slam behind him.

'RV,' McLain said, putting the gun behind his back, 'I didn't call for you. You've done what I asked you to do. I told you I'd be driving myself today.' He sounded like a master speaking to his servant.

RV nodded. 'I, uh, know . . . that,' he barely got out.

'Then why are you here?'

RV looked at me. 'Why . . . is he here, Mr McLain? I thought you were meeting him at Lisa's apartment.'

McLain kept the gun behind his back as he took a step toward RV. 'That's really not your concern, RV. I don't need you today, so why don't you just go back to—'

'I'm, uh,' RV began. 'I'm not too sure about that, Mr McLain. Thing is, I'm not really sure about a lot of things lately.' He looked at his feet. 'And . . . I think you probably know something about that.'

'I don't know what you're talking about, but we can discuss it some other time.'

RV shook his head. 'No, I think I need to talk about it now.' He was sweating more than he should have been, like he was coming down from a high. 'I'm having weird dreams about stuff. Bad stuff.'

'That's a good thing to speak with your counselor about, RV. Why don't you do that, and I will touch base later?'

'What kind of bad dreams, RV?' I asked, desperate that he not leave.

'Mr Donne,' McLain said, 'I just told RV what to do.'

I looked at RV. 'Is that what Mr McLain does, RV? Tell you to do stuff?'

RV gave us a pained face. He was thinking hard on something. 'Sometimes,' he said, 'I think . . . I think that's what the dreams are about.' He looked at me. 'You know, before I came to Newer Leaves, I used to have these real bad blackouts from drinking and drugging. I'd do stuff I couldn't remember the next day.' He started tapping his head with his fingertips. 'Once I got into a fight outside a bar and they said I hurt some people real bad. That's what got me sent to jail and then the program.'

'And that's why you're doing so well now, RV,' McLain said.

I turned to McLain. 'He doesn't look like he's doing so well.' Back to RV. 'How are you feeling, RV?'

'Mr Donne,' McLain said, 'right now, this is between you and me.' He glanced behind himself at his gun. 'I don't think you want to bring RV into it.'

'Stop thinking for me!' RV shouted. 'Everybody does that. Thinking for me. Telling me what to do.' He tapped his head harder. 'I can think for myself.'

'Sure, you can,' McLain said. 'I just need to finish up with Mr Donne, then—'

'You gave me drugs!' RV shouted and pointed at McLain. 'Why did you give me drugs, Mr McLain? You were supposed to be . . . to be helping me.'

'I was helping you, RV. Helping you forget.'

'Forget what?' I asked, making McLain turn to me. He forgot about hiding his gun now and it came out from behind him.

'Helping me forget what?' RV asked.

McLain was getting flustered, not knowing which one of us to look at. He chose me and that turned out to be a mistake because as he did, RV took his own pistol out from behind him and pointed it at McLain.

'Forget what, Mr McLain?'

Then McLain made his second mistake and turned his body and his gun toward RV. RV fired six times at McLain. McLain never got a shot off before he collapsed. I rushed over and removed his gun from his hand.

'Bad things!' RV screamed again. 'Bad things!'

I threw McLain's gun into the corner of the barn and stepped over to RV. He had emptied his gun firing at McLain, so I didn't think I was in much danger. I held out my hand, RV gave me his gun, and fell to the floor of the barn. He crawled up into a fetal position and kept repeating those two words over and over.

'Bad things. Bad things.'

TWENTY-NINE

When the state cops were through with me, they released me to my Uncle Ray – who just happened to know the CO at the trooper barracks – who took me home. Not home exactly: the Nine-Oh. Allison and Edgar were on their way. Detective Royce brought my uncle and me into an interview room where the three of us sat at a cold metal table. Royce was holding a legal pad and computer printouts. 'Some good news, at least.'

'What's that?' I asked.

He held up a sheet of paper. 'The ME says that the drugs found in Mr Joseph's system more than likely came from the arrow that killed him.'

I leaned forward. 'Excuse me?'

'It was the proverbial poisoned arrow,' Royce said. 'Doc thinks Joseph maybe lived another five minutes after being shot, which means—'

'His heart was beating for another five minutes,' I said.

'Allowing the heroin and fentanyl time to enter his blood stream. They tested the arrow. It had the drugs on it. You were right. He was clean when he died.'

Some comfort for Lisa. 'McLain,' I said. 'He figured if MoJo had told anyone about what he had found out at Newer Leaves, it would be discounted as coming from the mixed-up mind of a relapsed addict.'

'Crazy like a motherfucking fox, McLain,' Royce said. 'But smart.'

'What about RV?'

'State's not sure yet. Best guess, based on what he said and his behavior, McLain gave him drugs, and drove him down here to do the other two murders.'

'Knowing RV's history and that he would not remember committing violent acts during a blackout.'

Royce nodded. 'We'll have a blood test, maybe an interview in a few days, if he's up to it. But that's where the smart money is.'

'McLain had a guy with him,' I said. 'Outside Lisa's place. I saw the same guy the other day out in Canarsie with a known heroin dealer.'

My uncle grunted. 'What the fuck were you doing out in . . .' My uncle held his hands up. 'Never mind. I don't wanna know.'

'You think the guy might be McLain's supplier?' Royce asked.

'Smart money,' I repeated, and he wrote down what I knew about Al Biancotto and the bald guy named Charles. When I was finished, he asked, 'Anything else you care to share with me before you go?'

I thought about that. 'No. I think I'm good.'

The three of us left the interview room together, but I was the only one who got hugs from a beautiful lady and a stressed-out Edgar.

'Can we go home now?' Allison asked.

'Yeah,' Edgar said. 'Can we go home?'

I said goodbye to Royce, hugged my uncle and thanked him for coming to get me upstate. Allison, Edgar, and I went home.

Edgar took us from the precinct to the small market on the avenue. I told him we'd see him tomorrow at The LineUp. Allison and I went into the market and did something we rarely do: picked up a pre-cooked chicken, prepared mashed potatoes, and one of those ready-to-eat salads. We would pop the bird and the potatoes into the oven, put dressing on the salad, compliment each other on our cooking skills, and go to bed.

Allison had the good idea to hit the liquor store and pick up a couple of bottles of wine. I went upstairs to set up the dinner. That took about ten minutes and Allison hadn't returned yet. I figured she was talking with the owner of the liquor store about some new Chardonnay or something. He had a habit of getting her involved in long conversations about wine. When another ten minutes passed, I called her cell from my landline and it went straight to voicemail. That was unusual.

I was hungry and went downstairs to rescue her from another long conversation. When I got outside the apartment, I noticed a cell phone on the sidewalk by our front door.

Allison's cell phone.

I ran to the liquor store and the owner told me Allison had not been in. I went into every open store within two blocks of the apartment and Allison was nowhere to be found.

Her phone buzzed. It was a text from her.

'*I'm OK,*' it said. '*They said you'll be hearing from me.*' They? '*Who's they?*' I texted.

Then another text came in. All this one said was, '*She loves you, tough guy.*'

Fuck.

THIRTY

Whoever had taken Allison must have followed us from the precinct. The police – including Detective Royce – were now going from door to door interviewing anyone who may have seen anything. As of now, no one had.

All I knew was that my girlfriend was gone, and no one was admitting to seeing shit. Royce told me to go back upstairs and wait, but he knew I wouldn't. I paced back and forth, up and down my block. Using Allison's phone, I called a bunch of people on her contact list on the off chance they'd heard from her. I knew it was an exercise in futility but, short of knocking on doors, it was the only thing I could do to keep from going crazy.

Royce came out of the McDonald's on the corner and walked over. The look on his face was as close to sympathetic as I'd ever seen from him.

'How you doing?' he asked.

I shook my head. 'Not good. Still nothing?'

'We'll expand the canvass area, see if that helps,' he said. 'I hate to ask you this again, but you're sure you saw nothing suspicious when you were driving here or when Edgar dropped you off?'

'I wasn't looking for anything, Detective. There was no reason to.' Clearly there had been. We just didn't realize it until it was too late.

'I hear ya,' Royce said. 'I just saw you on the phone. Nothing?'

'I didn't expect anything, but . . .'

Then it hit me who my next call should be to. He picked up after two rings.

'Nephew,' Uncle Ray said. 'You keep this up and I'm—'

'Allison's been kidnapped, Uncle Ray. From in front of my fucking apartment.'

It takes a lot to shock Uncle Ray. This seemed to do the job. He was speechless for a few seconds. 'OK,' he said. 'I'm back at One PP. I'll be at your place in ten minutes.' I heard him tell someone to bring the car around and do it quickly. 'You got cops there already, I assume.'

'Royce is here. We've got lots of uniforms working the scene.'

'You're about to have a whole lot more,' my uncle said. 'Put Royce on.'

I handed the phone to Royce. 'Yes, Chief,' he said. 'Already done, sir, and still working on it. I understand.' Pause. 'I won't go anywhere until you get here.' Pause. 'You're welcome, Chief. I'll see you in ten.'

Royce handed me back the phone.

'What did he thank you for?'

'Doing my job, I guess. You do know he's quite fond of your girlfriend.'

'Yeah.' I could feel my eyes starting to fill up. This was no time for that. 'I do.'

Royce looked around the intersection. He did one of those three-sixties he'd seen me do on the school roof right after MoJo had been killed. 'If I know Chief Donne, this corner's gonna look like the Saint Paddy's Day parade in about twenty minutes.'

'He does like to do things big.'

'That's good for this kind of thing. We'll have all those cops to help us, the media will turn up, this is gonna be a big deal. Hopefully, all the attention will bring someone to say they actually saw something helpful.'

'Along with the usual nut jobs and attention-seekers.'

'Can't have one without the other.' Then he did something he'd never done in all the years I've known him. He put his hand on my shoulder. 'We're going to find her, Mr Donne. Believe that.'

I looked the detective in the eyes. 'I do, Royce,' I said. 'I have to.'

Sometime later, my uncle walked up. He was alone so I figured he had told his driver to stay with the car. Five minutes after he arrived, the intersection of Greenpoint Avenue and Leonard Street did, indeed, look like Saint Patrick's Day.

He saw Royce a few feet away, finishing up with a uniform. Uncle Ray gave him a face that said *Give me something*.

'A guy who was sitting on his fire escape,' Royce said as he walked over with his walkie-talkie and pointed it across the street, 'says he saw a woman matching Allison's description getting into a van. It seemed to him she didn't want to get in, but it all happened so fast.'

'What kinda van?' I asked.

'Guy said it was silver. Or white. Or possibly gray. It either did or didn't have a logo on the side for some sort of business.' He paused. 'Our eyewitness was taking advantage of the nice weather to enjoy a taste of Mother Nature's gift to Jamaica.' He put his index finger and thumb to his lips. 'He did say the plates were yellow and blue, so it's a New York vehicle. It's not much, but it's something.'

It wasn't much, and I didn't think it came all that close to something. And with at least a twenty-minute head start, the white-silver-gray van with or without a logo on its side was probably miles away by now – either on its way upstate, out to Long Island, maybe even hiding in plain sight across the bridge in Manhattan with thousands of other similar vehicles. My head was pounding. I took a deep breath and tried to calm down.

When that didn't work, I turned around and kicked the metal garbage can that was sitting on the corner. It hurt like hell, but I had to do something.

'You know that doesn't help, Raymond,' my uncle said.

'Yeah,' I agreed, feeling like an ass. 'But at least it hurts like hell.'

Royce looked at us both and wanted to say something. Whatever it was, he decided against it and took out his notebook instead. What he did say was, 'Tell me again what Allison had on her. Not what she was wearing, I have that, but in her possession.'

I'd told a cop earlier, but I figured this was Royce's way of protecting any more of the city's property from being taught a lesson by my foot.

'Her work bag,' I said. 'Notebooks, pens and pencils, her laptop. Maybe her video drone, but I doubt it. I'd have to check upstairs for that.'

'The wonderful video drone.'

As he said that, Edgar pulled up in front of my apartment, almost exactly where he had dropped Allison and me off less than an hour ago. Along with his expansive knowledge of technology, Edgar was also an Olympic-class finder of parking spaces.

He walked over to where Royce, Uncle Ray and I were standing. 'Ray,' he said, 'I just heard.' He looked at Royce and my uncle and knew he couldn't say he found out through his mostly illegal police scanner. 'What the heck happened?'

I filled him in on the details and he got quiet.

'Mr Martinez,' Royce said, 'how did you get through all the squad cars?'

He gave an embarrassed shrug and glanced at my uncle. 'I showed them my business card and told them Chief Donne was expecting me.'

Royce grinned. 'Did you notice anything suspicious before when you drove from the precinct to here?'

Edgar shook his head. 'I didn't even think to look. I probably should have.' He turned to my uncle and stuck out his hand. 'Hello, Chief Donne. Sorry for the lie.' For Edgar, each time he saw my uncle it was like meeting Mickey Mantle.

'Hey, Edgar,' my uncle said. 'Don't worry about it. You got any ideas here?'

Edgar gave that some heavy thought. The Chief of Detectives had just asked for his opinion. 'You tried her phone?' he asked.

I held it up to show him.

He thought some more and then said in a voice above his usual volume, 'Darn it!'

'What?' I asked.

'Her laptop.'

'What about it?' Royce asked.

'Does she have it with her?'

I stepped in. 'As far as we know, Edgar. Why?'

He reached into his bag and pulled out his laptop. 'I should be

able to find her computer using the Find My device on her computer.'
He leaned on the hood of his car, punched a bunch of buttons and
waited. After a while, he said, 'Dammit!'

'What's the matter?' I asked.

'Someone turned the device off. Unless they turn it back on, it's
no good.'

'Shit,' I said, loud enough to attract the attention of a few cops.

'All right, boys,' my uncle said. 'Let's bring it back together
here.' Royce, Edgar and I faced him like we were in a huddle in
a pickup football game. 'We know that Allison's been abducted.
We know her computer's not going to help us find her. We have
the slightest piece of info to go on about a van that could be thirty
to fifty miles away in any direction.' He paused. 'Anything else we
have that I don't know about?'

We all thought about that. I said, 'She'd been writing about this
kid. She's been calling him Harlan S., but that's not his real name.
According to him, people are looking for him, so he's been bouncing
around a lot.'

'How does she contact him?'

'She doesn't. He contacts her, sets up a meet, she goes.'

'OK,' Uncle Ray said. 'So it's a possibility that whoever's looking
for this Harlan S. might have taken Allison, thinking she knows
where he is. Does she?'

'No,' I said. 'He called her from a different phone each time and
they met at a different location each time. The kid knew how to
stay below the radar.'

Uncle Ray said, 'Fuck.' Then he turned to Royce. 'You gave her
access to the crime scene. Anything there?'

Royce shook his head. 'Just what you know already. She's the
one who made the connection to the Roman numerals.'

'So,' Uncle Ray said, 'there's also the possibility that whoever
took Allison did so as retaliation for helping us with the case.'

Now it was my turn. 'Fuck.'

The four of us stood in silence for about half a minute.
Surprisingly, it was Edgar who broke the silence. He turned to me.
'Was there anything else she was working on? For the website?'

I ran that through my brain for a bit. 'She was doing some
restaurant features and a report on dating apps for college students,
but—'

'Nothing worth snatching a journalist for,' Royce said.

'No.' Then something came to me. 'After we realized what MoJo was looking into, she was thinking about doing a piece on the various ways opioids are distributed in the city. Legal and non. She was interviewing doctors, users, and some dealers on the street. It's possible she hit on something.'

'Did she tell you anything?' Royce asked.

I shook my head. 'She was always tight-lipped about her work until it was published or she needed my opinion on something, so I don't know.'

'And again,' Edgar said, 'that would all be on her laptop and she didn't wanna save any of her stuff in the Cloud because she was afraid of people hacking into it. She did save it on a flash drive, but she always kept that with her. I told her to keep a copy at home, but . . .'

Again, thirty seconds of silence. This one was broken by my uncle.

'So we go back and talk with all the people we know she's spoken with in the last seventy-two hours. With any luck, one of them turned her onto something or someone else we don't know about and we go talk to them.' He looked up and spun around. 'I'm gonna put a rush on seeing what any of these traffic and surveillance cameras got on 'em.' He turned to me. 'You ready to go upstairs yet, Ray?'

I shook my head. 'I think I'd go crazy up there alone.'

'I'll go with you,' Edgar said. 'For a walk,' he added. 'Not crazy.'

'Thanks, man. How about you just pace the streets with me for a while?'

'I can do that.'

Royce asked if Allison's phone was fully charged. 'Close enough,' I said.

'Keep it on you and I'll be in touch.'

'Thanks, Royce. I appreciate it.'

'Thank me when we get her back. All bullshit aside,' he said, 'she's one of the good ones, Mr Donne. Trust me when I say that any rock I come across is going to be turned over.' He looked at my uncle. 'And I'm not just saying that because Chief Donne is three feet away.'

That got me to smile. 'I feel ya, Royce.' I shook his hand and hugged my uncle. I turned to Edgar. 'You ready to pace?'

*   *   *

We got as far as the church when my phone rang. I looked at it optimistically but did not recognize the number. 'Hello?' I said, not knowing who or what to expect.

'Is this Ray?' a female voice wanted to know. 'Raymond Donne?'

'Yeah. Who's this?'

'It's Robbie,' she said. 'Robbie Roznowski? I work with Allie at *Here and Now*. I was monitoring my police scanner and just found out what happened. This is just horrible. Is there any news?' Then she added, 'Any new news, I mean?'

'Just what you heard on the scanner, Robbie.' I was starting to put a face to the name. They had an opening party a few months back and I met all her co-workers, but I'm not always good with connecting names to faces. She sounded like she may have been the one Allison told me reminded her a bit of Edgar; she thought the two should meet. Apparently, Robbie was also not too skilled in social situations, but technically savvy and a top-notch researcher and fact-checker. 'Have you heard anything?'

'No,' Robbie said. 'But we want to put it online.'

What? 'Like for a story, you mean?' I did not hide my disgust.

'Not like that, Ray. I mean for our readers to know what's going on. We have more than one thousand subscribers now. That's a thousand more sets of eyes keeping a lookout. We can also get the more mainstream media involved. Most of us still have lots of connections out there.' She paused for a second to breathe. I picked up that she pronounced *mainstream* the same way the former governor of Alaska had. 'Allie told us about your attitude toward the press – sometimes – but this is one of those times we can really help. No matter what you think, we do stick together. When something bad happens to one of us, it's an attack on all of us.'

I let that sink in and decided she was right. Desperate times and all that. I told her everything I knew – including what Allison was wearing and what the cops were doing. I even threw in the vague description of the van – and she promised to get it on their website and to as many other media outlets as she could.

'Thanks, Robbie,' I said. 'Hey, if she kept a record of who she was talking to the last few days, reach out to them or send me their numbers.'

'Will do. Keep me in the loop, Ray. It's the only way we can help. I'm gonna post this right now along with a picture of Allison and the number of the police tip line. Do you want to add a quote from you?'

I declined firmly enough so she knew not to ask again. I thanked her for her efforts, we said goodbye, and I filled Edgar in on the conversation. He seemed pleased.

'This is what social media should be used for,' he said. 'Not spewing that horse manure Lansing and his group put out there.'

'Yeah,' I said. 'Right.'

Edgar looked at me as I slid the phone back into my pocket. 'Sorry, Ray,' he said. 'I know this has to suck. A lot.'

'Yeah. I can't imagine what's going through Allie's mind.' Actually, having just been abducted myself, I could. 'It's gotta be freaking her out.'

'I know I would be if I were her. Then again, she's a pretty tough customer, Ray.'

'That she is, Edgar,' I said. 'That she is.'

THIRTY-ONE

There have been two mornings in my life where I've awakened hoping the events of the previous day had been a dream: the day after my father's fatal heart attack, and the day after nine-eleven, which forever changed the word impossible.

This was the third such day.

The alarm went off like it always does at six-thirty – on Sundays we turn it off and smile – I rolled over and Allison was not there. No dream. Sometime last night, someone had taken her away. To accent that point of reality, Allison's phone went off. I had gone to bed holding it and it was still in my hand.

Ron Thomas. I already knew what this was going to be about. I thought about not answering, but knew he'd just keep trying until he got me.

'Hello, Ron,' I said. I was now feeling the headache from last night.

'Ray,' he said. 'I couldn't reach your phone, so I tried Allison's. I am so sorry about what happened. It's all over the front pages, the radio and morning TV.' Say what you want about journalists – and a lot of it has been said by me – but when something happens to one of their own, they band together. 'How are you doing?'

'I'm in shock, Ron.' *How are you doing?* 'I'm still processing it.'

'That's why I'm calling, Ray. I think you need to stay home tomorrow.'

Right. 'I don't know, Ron. I can't do much from home and I think that's gonna drive me crazy. I may need something to distract me.'

He cleared his throat. 'Your job is not something that distracts you, Ray. It's something you do to the best of your abilities.'

Said the man with the forty-eight-inch high-definition TV in his office.

'Normally, I'd agree with you, Ron, but tomorrow I think it's best I come in.'

'And I'm telling you the opposite, Ray.'

I rolled out of bed and stood up. It hurt to do so. Lying in bed for hours with your body in stress can do that to you. 'Ron,' I said, 'with all due respect, you can't tell me not to come to work.'

'Actually, Ray, I can.' I heard some papers being shuffled on his end. 'It says in your contract that, and I'm quoting here, "If there comes a time when an administrator determines any teacher is unfit for duty in such a way that it creates an undue risk of danger to the school environment, said administrator has the authority to insist that teacher remove himself from the school grounds until further notice."'

'It actually says that in the contract?'

'You want me to wait while you get it?'

'You think I know where my fucking contract is, Ron?'

The silence that followed could not be cut by a knife. You would probably have needed a chain saw. Maybe a laser.

'Due to the current state of your mind, Ray,' Ron said, 'which goes to prove my point, by the way, I'm going to ignore that. But I will repeat: I am officially directing you to remain away from the school until further notice. Due to the unusual nature of the situation, I will not dock you any days from your sick bank, but you are not to come to work. Is that clear?'

'How many reporters called you this morning, Ron?'

'Is that clear?' he repeated. 'Mister Donne.'

'Yes, Mister Thomas,' I said. 'It's clear.' I hung up. Two deep breaths later the phone rang again. I didn't recognize the number. 'Hello?'

'Ray?'

'Yeah.'

'Josh King, Ray. I used to work with Allison at the paper. We met a few years back at a Christmas thing.'

'OK.'

'How are you feeling, Ray?' he asked. Before I could answer, he asked, 'Have you heard from the kidnappers?'

'Fuck you, Josh King.' I hung up.

So that's the kind of day this was going to be. Not knowing which calls to answer and which ones to let go to voicemail. I went in to the living room and sat on the futon. Judging from the view out the window, the way the rising sun was reflecting off the skyline, it was going to be another beautiful day in the greatest city in the world.

I turned on my laptop and went right to Allison's website to see what Robbie had posted during the past few hours.

Holy shit. Allison had posted something since last night!

ALLISON ROGERS: SPECIAL REPORT FROM THE FIELD

For the first time in recent memory, I woke up this morning not knowing where I was. Most mornings, I wake up next to my boyfriend in the one-bedroom apartment we share in Greenpoint, Brooklyn. Other mornings, maybe it's a hotel room if I'm away for work, or my parents' home in Missouri if it's the holidays.

This morning, I have no idea where I am.

I do know, though, I am not here because I want to be.

I am here because someone else wants me to be. I am, for the first time in recent memory – maybe ever – a means to someone else's ends. That much I do know.

With my eyes still closed, I take in a deep breath and a pleasant thought manages to sneak in. It reminds me of being at sleep-away camp with my cousin when we were teenagers. I only went for two summers, but I'll never forget the smell of early August mornings coming through the screened windows; the smell of last night's rain; the smell of the trees waking up.

I swore back then if I had tried hard enough, I could have smelled the sunrise, felt it in my lungs.

This is not that smell. This smells of fear. Fear and anger. I know enough to realize the fear is not only mine; I need to wake up a little more to remember whose anger it is. Maybe I need to breathe a little deeper.

Then I remember. The men who took me last night, who took me from the perceived and apparent safety of where I live, were filled with anger. Anger, they told me last night, at the government mostly. Anger at the people who were taking their country – their way of life – away from them and anger at the people who were letting them do it. With all that anger inside you, one of the men told me, there's not much room for much else. That much is true.

I sit up and look around the large room where I spent the night. As soon as I'm no longer horizontal, my head starts to swim and my eyes go in and out of focus. I'm not sure of the last time I ate, and I'm very thirsty. Unable to rely on my sight, I switch to auditory mode. Outside the room I am in, the wind is slipping through the trees, some crows are laughing at a private joke, a plane is on its way to some far-off destination. And a man coughs.

In the distance I can hear an engine running. Not a vehicle's engine, no. Another machine of some sort, perhaps a buzz saw, a lawn mower, maybe a wood chipper.

An accidental smile surprises my mouth when I realize, 'Allison, we're not in Brooklyn anymore.'

I stand up and head for the door. Unlike the bunks I stayed in at summer camp, it's the only door in the place. It was unlikely this bunk would pass a safety inspection. *What if there was a fire?* I find myself thinking. With only one exit, who knows what'll happen then.

Then I realize a fire is probably the least of my worries.

Through the screen that serves as a window to the door, I see a lone watchman outside. He's holding his weapon – some sort of rifle – like my dad holds his hunting shotgun: one hand on the barrel, the other cradling the butt, the barrel pointed at the ground. My father would remind me how to hold the gun every time we went out hunting. Someone trained the man watching me well. Maybe his father, or his grandfather. More likely, I think for some reason, his Uncle Sam.

'Safety first, Allison,' my dad would say. 'First, second, and always.'

All of a sudden, I am missing my father, the first man to ever promise to keep me safe forever and ever. *Where is he now?* I wonder. Probably in the barn sharpening tools, maybe mending a fence he's been putting off fixing, or dealing with a cow that's decided she's taking the day off. Maybe putting that World War II Jeep together with parts he finds on the Internet.

I am writing this now only because the men who took me last night are allowing me to do so. They want me to know that. They want you to know that. I am able to post it on our website, again, only because they have given me permission to do so.

The men who took me last night want you to know they are angry; they are scared. And they think you should be, too.

And, for the foreseeable future, these angry and fearful men – they refer to themselves as White Nationalists – who have felt for years their voices have been silenced by politicians and the media, have decided to allow me to make their voices heard.

Allison Rogers for *New York Here and Now*

My first thought was how grateful I was she was still alive. My second was these guys didn't waste any time getting to work. I wondered if they saw the paradox in what they were doing. The countries they railed against, the ones where 'the others' come from, those were the countries with terrorists that kidnapped journalists. Not us; not the good old USA, where we stood on the Constitution, which included freedom of the press. How come these people always skipped the First Amendment on their way to the Second? Was bearing arms so much more crucial than bearing the truth?

This was not the kind of kidnapping where the captors were going to call demanding money or something else of value. They already had what they wanted: Allison Rogers.

From the dark corner of my brain came a rather sick thought: Allison was always thinking about ways to increase circulation, strategies to boost the number of website subscribers. I think she found one. Or, rather, one had found her.

The phone rang again. Detective Royce.

'She's still alive,' I said. 'Did you see the post this morning?'

'Not yet. I'm in the car now heading into work,' he said. I could hear the traffic in the background. 'But the media are gonna be all over this. That can go either way, but I'm hoping it plays in our favor.'

'Yeah,' I agreed. 'I've been instructed to stay away from work starting tomorrow until I hear from my boss. What can I do to help and keep myself sane?'

He thought about that for a bit. I heard some car horns and a large vehicle passing him or him passing it. 'More phone calls,' he said. 'Anybody you can think of. I don't expect you to find any new info, but we do need to rule stuff out. Even the improbable. If you do it, I can put a uniform on something else.' He paused again. 'And don't talk to any reporters. We'll handle all media inquiries on our end. We got folks for that.'

'I wasn't planning on it, Detective.'

'Good. Listen, it's not SOP, but I'm going to check in with you every hour or so, just in case. You don't hear from me, call.'

What was standard operating procedure when your girlfriend has been kidnapped?

'Thanks.'

'Later.'

As much as Royce has busted my balls over the years and threatened me when he felt I was crossing the line, I always sensed the begrudging respect he had for me. And it had nothing to do with the fact that my uncle was basically his big boss. When you put two people in the same space who want to do the same thing – the right thing – they can smell it on each other. That's the way it was with us. I felt that now more than at any other time since I've known him. I was glad he was the one coordinating the search for Allison.

Allison's phone rang again, and again I did not recognize the number. I picked up anyway. 'Hello?'

'Ray,' the voice said. 'Ellen Henry from *The Post*. We met about—'

I hung up. New Rule: If I didn't recognize the number, I wouldn't pick up. Let them leave a voicemail.

Since I was out of bed with no chance of going back, I decided to do at least two things I could control: make coffee and take a shower. I left my phone on the bed. When I came back twenty minutes later, wrapped in a towel and coffee in hand, there were seventeen messages waiting for me. I recognized four of the numbers: my mom, my sister, Uncle Ray, and Edgar. I played back the other thirteen and after a few seconds each – every one a reporter – I erased them. I called my mom first.

'How are you, Raymond?'

'I'm good, Mom. She's seems to be OK for now. She posted on her site this morning.'

'Oh, thank God, Raymond. I prayed all last night for her.' She took a breath. 'And how are you?'

'Still scared and worried, but I'm as good as I can be. Better now that I saw the post. Uncle Ray's got a lot of cops on this and the detective-in-charge is working it hard.'

'When do you want me to come in?'

'Excuse me?'

'When do you want me to come in?'

'To do what?'

'To be there for you.'

'Be there for me on Long Island, Mom. I don't need you here.'

'You don't *want* me there?'

'I didn't say that. I said I don't need you *here*. I'm going to be running around, making phone calls, helping out where I can. I can't do all that with you here.'

'Why not?'

'Because then I'll worry about you.'

'I can take care of myself, Raymond.'

'I know you can, Mom. Just do it from home. I'll call you if I hear anything.'

'You sure? I can be there in two hours.'

'I'm sure. And I love you for asking.'

'OK, but promise you'll call.'

'I already did.'

'OK, Raymond. I'll talk to you later.'

'Yes, you will. Bye, Mom.'

'Bye, now.'

My mother always had to be the last to say goodbye. It was usually 'Bye, now.'

Next. 'I saw Allie's post,' Rachel said. 'Mom's taking credit because she prayed.'

'I know. She wanted to come in and stay with me.'

'What'd you say to that?'

'I told her she could best help from a distance.'

'Ha!' She took a sip of something. 'Listen, Murcer's already spoken to his boss. He's taking the day and wants to help.'

'I don't know, Rache. He's gonna need to call Royce. I'm not sure—'

'He already did, and Royce jumped on it. His captain's only giving him so many officers to work the case. Can't seem to be playing favorites. White, female reporter goes missing and the cops throw everything they got at it is not going to play well in the press no matter who the vic— the missing person is, know what I mean?'

'I do,' I said. 'Thank Murcer for me when you get the chance.'

'Will do,' she said. 'And call when you need to.'

'Thanks, Rache.'

'Love you, Ray.'

Uncle Ray was next. He already knew about Allison's post and the good news that implied. 'We got twenty-one vans on CCTV that vaguely match the description we got from the stoner last night, all heading out of Brooklyn in every possible direction around that time. Highway cops pulled over a few, state cops did the same and both came up with nothing. I don't have to tell you how this goes, Ray.'

'She's been gone for more than ten hours,' I said. 'She can be halfway to Florida, in Maine or Canada, as far away as Michigan. And that's if she's still in the van.'

'We're going with the assumption they're still with the van or whatever vehicle they took her in,' he said. 'Train, bus, or airports would be too risky. My guess, they got her out of the city and into that bunk situation she wrote about in less than two hours. The quicker they get her off the streets, the easier it is to hide her.'

'That doesn't make me feel better, Uncle Ray.'

'No offense, Nephew, but I didn't call to make you feel better. I called to give you an update and a dose of reality. I'm your uncle and a cop. Not a fucking priest.'

And what a loss for the church that was, I thought.

'What does the rest of your day look like?' he asked.

'Yeah. I was kinda hoping I could ride around with you,' I said, completely ignoring what Royce had told me not too long ago.

'It's nice to have hopes. Back in the day, I woulda told you to stay at home in case the kidnappers called, but today, with cell phones, that doesn't make a difference. Why don't you go hang out at The LineUp?'

'It's not even nine o'clock yet.'

He paused. 'What's your point?'

'I'm gonna call Edgar. Maybe I can tag along with him if he's working.'

'Good idea. Keep moving. I'll call ya before noon.'

'Thanks, Uncle Ray.'

'Stay strong, Nephew.'

Before I could say goodbye, call-waiting kicked in. Edgar. 'That's him now,' I said. 'Talk to you later.' I ended that call and pressed the button for Edgar. 'Hey.'

'Ray. How's it going?'

I brought him up to speed on the morning's phone calls. He had already read, seen and heard all the press reports, including Allison's posting on her website.

'I'm still kicking myself in the butt,' he said. 'If I had insisted on putting a more sophisticated tracking device on her laptop, we might have been able to determine the general location of where she posted from. I have that equipment, you know.'

'Edgar,' I said, 'you can't blame yourself. You are not an insistent person and Allison's about as stubborn as they come. Besides, I'm sure she's not using her computer to post the pieces.'

'I guess you're right. But still . . .'

'Anyway, look. What are you doing today?'

'I gotta go over and finish up on that job in Greenpoint, but I gotta be sneaky about it because, like I said, the boss doesn't want the employees to know he put in the second security system and he can't close during the day or they'll know something's up. Why you asking?'

'You want company?'

'Really?' he said.

'I need to get out of here, Edgar. I'm going to go crazy not being able to help with looking for Allison.'

'I'll be right there. And I'll bring bagels.' He hung up without saying goodbye.

THIRTY-TWO

Twenty minutes later the phone rang again.

'There's like a dozen reporters outside your apartment, Ray,' Edgar said.

'Shit,' I said. 'Pick me up on the side street. I'm gonna go out the back, hop the fence, and go through the neighbor's yard. You know the one?'

'The same one?'

'That's it.'

'See ya in less than ten, Ray.'

Years ago when I was looking for Frankie Rivas and was sure my apartment was being watched by other people who were looking for Frankie Rivas, Edgar and I had used this exit strategy so I could leave my building unseen. It worked then and it worked now.

We were in the Greenpoint convenience store in less than fifteen minutes. Edgar had given me a company shirt to slip into and introduced me to the owner as an associate of his. We went into the back where the 'Owner's Office' was, and Edgar put the finishing touches on the surveillance equipment. He then showed the owner how to work everything, and the owner seemed quite satisfied with the work Edgar had done. The owner paid the bill and none of the employees were any the wiser.

'And you're the only one who has a key to this office?' Edgar asked.

'Just me, my wife, and my son and daughter,' the owner said.

'I'll check back in a week. Call me if you have any questions.'

We all shook on it and Edgar and I left the premises.

Back in the car, I said, 'Nicely done, Boss.'

Edgar blushed, started the car, and said, 'Yeah. Wanna go for another ride?'

'Where to?'

'Cab company in the Bronx. Some of their cameras need adjusting. With any luck, I can convince them to upgrade.'

'Lead on,' I said. 'It's cool to watch you work, Edgar.'

'Cut it out, Ray,' he said, but I could tell he was flattered.

By the time we got to the Bronx, Royce, Murcer, and Uncle Ray had all checked in with the same news: there wasn't any. They all promised to call me back soon, no matter what. Edgar and I ended up a few blocks from Yankee Stadium. With today's weather again in the seventies and the Yanks home this afternoon, it would have been a great day to catch a game. Under almost any other circumstances.

We parked in the lot of the cab company, and again, I stayed quiet and watched as Edgar did what he did best. He ended up fixing three cameras as I 'assisted' by handing him tools like a surgical technician, and Edgar then sold the owner three new cameras he had in the trunk of his car. He was very good at this.

By the time we were done, it was well after lunch, so Edgar took me to a pizza place he knew on the Grand Concourse. With Edgar done for the day, we took our time. I got calls from my three favorite cops again – nothing new to report – and ignored any number I didn't recognize. Edgar booked a job for the following week.

I ordered two slices – one with mushrooms, one with pepperoni – because I was hungry and wasn't sure what the rest of the day would bring. The veteran cops taught you that on your first day on the streets: eat when you can. My job at school could be like that, too. The first three months as a dean, I was up and down the stairs so many times and missed so many lunches due to conflicts, crises, and conferences, I lost fifteen pounds. The next time my mother saw me she swore I was sick and not telling her something.

By the time we left the pizza place, the Sunday traffic was so heavy it might have been quicker to walk back to Brooklyn. Royce called again just to check in. When we got back to my block, Edgar asked me if I wanted to go in the back way.

'No,' I said. 'Anybody gets in my way, it's not my fault what happens.'

It turns out we didn't have to worry. Either the reporters had decided I'd skipped out of the city for a few days or they'd all gone to dinner. I said goodbye to Edgar, promised to call if I heard anything, and told him I would talk to him tomorrow. I also thanked him for keeping me busy.

'Any time, Ray. I mean that.'

'I know you do, buddy. Thanks.'

* * *

I spent the next few hours cleaning, channel surfing, staring out at the Manhattan skyline, going through old magazines and catalogs – anything to keep my mind off Allison, but nothing worked. Royce kept to his promise and called just about every hour. I told him I could wait until the next day, unless he had real news for me. He seemed to think that was a good idea. He sounded tired.

I opened up the fridge, but nothing appealed to me. There were a few Brooklyn Unfiltered Pilsners, but I don't like drinking alone at home under stress. I was too tired to hit The LineUp and not tired enough to go to bed. If I were a runner, this would be a good time for a long one. Muscles's gym would be closed by now, but I went into the bedroom and put on a pair of shorts and a T-shirt and my gym sneakers. I went out to the balcony and went through the entire series of stretches I do before a workout. I did it slow and then I did it again.

I remembered Allison had a pair of five-pound weights in the closet that she took out and played with whenever she was feeling 'fat' and didn't feel like jogging. I took them out, and except for the fact that they were pink, they did the job. I did some real slow lifts I remembered from my physical therapy days; that was as close to yoga as I'd ever been. After thirty minutes of that, I actually felt better.

I went back inside and drank two glasses of water and took a long hot shower. I hit the medicine cabinet and without any guilt whatsoever took one of Allison's sleeping pills. I put on a clean pair of shorts and a new T-shirt, grabbed my cell phone and went to bed, where I lay sleepless for at least the next five hours.

THIRTY-THREE

E dgar called at eight thirty-seven. 'Turn on your laptop,' he said.
   'What?'
'Your laptop, Ray. Go to Allison's site.'
I got out of bed, went to the coffee table and went to *New York Here and Now*. And there it was.

ALLISON ROGERS: SPECIAL REPORT FROM THE FIELD

Sometime during the night – I've been unaware of the exact time for a while now – we changed locations. I am no longer at the woodsy camp where I woke up yesterday. The smells of childhood summers are gone, replaced by more suburban sensations: I can hear people moving about on the floor below me, I smell freshly cut grass and coffee, a busy roadway is humming in the distance. And the door to the room I'm in is locked.

When I spoke with one of my captors yesterday – the only one who seemed allowed, or willing, to talk to me – he told me to imagine a bunch of goldfish swimming peacefully in a pond for as many years as any of them can remember. Then one day, some catfish get introduced into the pond. At first it was uncomfortable – catfish look way different than goldfish – but then the goldfish realized the catfish cleaned the bottom of the pond, eating discarded food, kissing moss off the stones, a job none of the goldfish liked to do. So the goldfish tolerated the catfish and allowed them the small fruits of their labor.

Sometime later, more fish were added to the pond. The usefulness of these new fish was not apparent. They didn't clean, they used up oxygen meant for the goldfish, ate food that the goldfish had been the sole consumers of for years – until the catfish arrived – and they took up space. These fish, too, bore little resemblance to the original fish. When the goldfish looked for a meaning to this change, no meaning was to be found.

After many years of new fish moving into the pond, the goldfish realized they were no longer counted as the majority. Each day seemed to bring different-looking fish, less food, less oxygen. One day, the goldfish had a secret meeting and decided that their best – and possibly only – solution was to fight back against the other fish and the powers that put them in the pond.

'We,' this man with the foreign-made automatic weapon and the desire to speak told me, 'are the goldfish.'

'What does that make me?' I asked, and was told that I, too, am a goldfish. 'I don't feel like a goldfish,' I told him. I added that as a white person of Christian background, I'm not afraid of the others. I enjoy living in a diverse city.

'That's why you need people like me,' he explained. 'People like you are blind to the ways of the pond. You like to consider yourselves liberal, progressive, tolerant of others. We were like that, too, once.'

I asked him what had changed. 'Too many others that don't look or pray like us, that's what changed. Our kids go to school and now there are days off for holidays we don't celebrate and never even knew about before the others started sending their kids to our schools.'

When I suggested that diversity was a good thing, that it helps us and our children understand the other people we share the planet with, he scoffed. 'I got nothing against other people,' he said. 'I just don't want them pushing their beliefs on us, taking our jobs, marrying our women.'

If that sounds like White Supremacy, my goldfish will tell you it's not. 'It's White Nationalist,' he explained. 'White Separatist. We're not out there telling people we're better than they are, just different. This nation was born of the White man, the Christian God. When's the last time you heard of thousands of White Christians going to another country and making their homes there, and changing the whole country's way of life? Lessening that country's way of life? You don't because it don't happen.'

I pointed out that history and current events would argue with him.

'Whose history?' he asked. 'Not mine. Not the history I grew up with. The history I grew up with tells me Christopher Columbus came here in 1492 and brought civilization with him. Those that accepted the new ways thrived; those that did not, perished.

'Listen,' he continued, 'I understand not everyone can be white. I took biology. But if these people just accepted the rules of this great White Christian nation, we'd all be better off.'

I asked if he believes all men were created equal like it says in the Declaration of Independence, one of three documents – the others being the Constitution and the Bible – groups like his are known to adhere to.

'Equal's a funny word,' he said. 'What did the founding fathers mean by the word equal? I think they meant equal in your own country. Equal to the people you were born around. Once you choose to pick up and leave your birthplace, I don't believe you have the right to ask for equality. You gave that up when you left your home. If I got up and moved my family to Africa tomorrow, I wouldn't expect to be treated equally.'

Speaking of Africa, I said, what about those who were brought here against their will?

'They're better off here,' he explained. 'You ever see the lives they had before we brought them here? They barely wore clothes, had to hunt for all their food, they didn't own their own homes. I'm not sure they owned anything. They're much better off than they were. We gave them work, steady food and shelter. When slavery ended – and not all Americans believed that it should have, by the way – look what happened to them. Unemployment that we have to pay for; homelessness that we have to pay for; crime rates going up, that we have to pay for. And now, the drug problem is as bad as it's ever been. Who's paying for that? We are.'

When I pointed out that the drug problem recognizes no color or religion or country of origin, he looked me in the eye and said, 'Yeah, it does. It most surely does. It definitely knows all that. And, to make it worse, it knows your status in this world.

'Just like all those other fish we never wanted in the pond,' he concluded, 'it just don't care.'

Allison Rogers for *New York Here and Now*

'They moved her, Ray.'

'I just read that, Edgar. These guys are smart. And organized.'

'And connected.'

That's the part I didn't want to think too much about. Smart, dangerous, and organized are bad enough, but if these guys were part of a bigger network – multi-state, say – we were looking at something that may be even out of my uncle's league. And then, as if reading my mind, David Henderson, FBI, was calling in. 'Let me get back to you, Edgar,' I said. 'I got Henderson on the other line.'

'OK, Ray.'

'David,' I said, 'how'd you get this number?'

'I'm FBI, Ray,' he began. 'I know I shoulda called yesterday, but I was running down some leads on my end as soon as I heard what happened to your girlfriend.'

'Allison Rogers.'

'Yes. Allison.'

'Did you find anything out?' I asked.

'I spent most of my time checking into Mr Biancotto,' he said. 'Our friend from the CCC over in Canarsie.'

'And . . .?'

'From what I could gather, he had no direct involvement in her abduction. But that doesn't rule out any of his known associates. After what I read this morning on your . . . on Allison's website, though, I don't think he hangs with people this organized.'

I was impressed. 'What do you think?'

'I've got a meeting with my Assistant Field Director in about an hour. I'm going to strongly request that, based on Allison's latest posting, the FBI treat her case as a possible interstate kidnapping and a domestic terrorist incident.'

'You think they'll go for that?'

'I think we've got the circumstantial evidence to support the motion and, quite frankly, after Maurice Joseph's murder was solved, I'm back in the good graces of my immediate supervisor.' He paused. 'Thanks again for that, Ray.'

'You can thank me by doing everything you just said you were going to do.'

'I'll do my best.'

'OK. Obviously, call me when you know something and I'll do the same.'

'Roger that,' he said and broke the connection.

I called Edgar back and told him the news.

'Holy Hoover,' he said. Edgar could sometimes sound like Robin from the old Batman TV show. 'That's great news, Ray.'

'Let's hope he can pull it off.'

We were silent for a while and then Edgar asked, 'What are you going to do today? I gotta head out to Forest Hills and give an estimate for a job.'

I gave that some thought and as much as that helped distract me yesterday, I wasn't sure it would do the job today. 'I think,' I said, 'I'm gonna go for a walk to the river. Maybe over the bridge.'

'You sure? We made a pretty good team yesterday.'

'We did, man. I just need to be alone right now. Keep my head clear until something breaks, you know?'

'I guess.' He didn't know and I didn't have the mental energy to explain it all right now.

'I'll call you when I hear something, Edgar. Good luck on the estimate.'

'Thanks, Ray.'

Less than an hour later, I was caffeinated, fed, and dressed for walking. I decided to skip the river and head straight to the Williamsburg Bridge. There were many places in the city I could go to clear my head and paradoxically, the Willy B – as the local kids and hipsters called it – was one of the main ones. This noisy, traffic-filled, smelly monument to the joining of Brooklyn to Manhattan served as my own personal white noise machine. I would walk to the halfway point – where I was now – stop, and look down at the rushing water of the East River as it made its way either north or south depending on the time of day. This particular spot was so personal to me I'd yet to bring Allison here. Now I found myself wishing I had.

There were tourist boats, tugboats, barges, recreational boats and wave runners; any type of water vessel was welcome. I've seen kayaks that go for under two hundred dollars and yachts that go for a few million. Along with the subway system, the rivers of New York City were true Commons.

I was doing a few stretches and realized I hadn't been to Muscles's gym in a while. I was in for a lecture the next time I did go back. I'd have to make sure I went with Allison; he was always easier on me when I was with her.

I looked over to my left, and along with the Hassidic moms pushing strollers, the morning joggers, cyclists, skaters, and folks just taking the bridge to work, I noticed a young man – college-aged? high school? – looking at me. He had blond hair, was dressed pretty much like me in walking clothes, but sported dark sunglasses. Normally, I would have pegged him for a tourist, but they usually travel in packs and have cameras. He was looking at me in a way designed to appear that he was not looking at me. He wasn't very good at it. Maybe he thought he recognized me. Had my picture been in the papers again? I figured I'd give him a few more minutes to figure it out and went back to my stretches.

When I finished up, I looked over and the guy was gone. I guessed I wasn't who he thought I was. I was about to ponder the philosophical nature of that when the phone went off. David Henderson. 'David,' I said.

'Good news and not-so-good news, Ray.'

'Hit me.'

'My AFD went for it – possible interstate kidnapping, possible terrorist action – but she's only giving me five agents at this point. It's a bit too circumstantial right now.'

'Hey,' I said. 'That's five more agents than you had earlier, right?'

'Glad you see it that way. I'm a glass-half-full guy myself.'

'So what happens now?'

He went through a lot of stuff I already knew: how they'd be contacting all the local police precincts with photos of Allison, copies of her postings from the website, and questions about any local White Nationalist groups or activities in their areas. Then he went into some technical stuff about trying to track down where Allison had posted from that was way above my head but would have been right in Edgar's wheelhouse.

'How you holding up?' he added.

'About as well as can be expected.'

He must have heard the noise around me because his next question was, 'Where the hell are you?'

'The Williamsburg Bridge.'

After a brief pause, he said, 'You sure you're OK, Ray?'

I laughed. 'Yeah,' I said. 'This is where I come to clear my head sometimes.'

'Whatever you say, Ray.' I heard a ringing in the background. 'That's my other line. I gotta go. I'll call ya when I hear something.'

'Thanks, David.' He hung up.

I decided to clear my head a little more by walking all the way across the bridge. I found myself navigating between strollers, cyclists, joggers, and roller-bladers. There's a little perch where you can stop before making the commitment of actually stepping onto the island of Manhattan, and I stood there looking down at Grand Street Park.

It was here – down in those tennis courts that were primarily used as skateboard parks now – that my former student, Douglas Lee, had been stabbed to death a few years ago. As tragic an event as that was, and as much as it still hurt, it was the incident that brought Allison Rogers back into my world. She was covering the story when she was still at the paper and wanted a teacher's perspective on the case in hopes of keeping it from fading away like so many other murders of young black men in this city. I helped her with her piece, we started seeing each other, and we fell in love.

Life's like that sometimes.

I grabbed a bottle of water from the hot dog guy and started the slow walk back across the East River. After five minutes or so, I couldn't shake the feeling I was being followed. It was probably just paranoia after what had happened to Allison, but I didn't get strange feelings often, and when I did, I had learned to trust them. I stopped and casually turned around, half-expecting to see that touristy-looking kid who was watching me earlier. He wasn't there. Just more folks on wheels, and joggers and a few walkers who were probably just that – walkers. There were two guys who almost looked out of place only because they were in long pants and long-sleeved shirts and what might have been hiking shoes, but this was New York and it's really hard to look out of place here. One was wearing one of those bright orange knit caps that hunters and hipsters wear. When I stopped, they kept on walking and talking about maybe taking a fishing boat out of Sheepshead Bay.

I took a few more sips of water and the feeling passed. I was home a half-hour later and before going upstairs I went inside the Chinese place and ordered the Shrimp Lo Mein lunch special. I decided to wait the ten minutes for it on the outside bench. When I sat down, my eye caught some movement across the street. There was more traffic going between the two avenues than usual, and when it slowed down, I saw the kid in the blue T-shirt and shorts I'd seen earlier on the bridge. I stood up and he darted away like a track star. Even if my knees had been in shape and there hadn't been traffic in my way, I couldn't have caught up to him. I watched as he took the first right and disappeared.

That was no tourist.

I called Uncle Ray, put my food on the bench, and he was in front of my building in twenty minutes. He officially introduced me to his new 'boy,' who happened to be female. Officer Paulson, the cop who had followed Allison the other day. Long story short, if you were one of 'Chief Donne's Boys,' that meant you were hand-chosen by the man himself to be his driver, Cop Friday, and at his overall beck-and-call twenty-four/seven for six months. It was grueling work, but when the half-year was over, you were given a gold shield and assigned to whatever part of the city was most in need of young and hungry detectives. That's why she had been assigned to watch our place.

Paulson was the second of her family to join the ranks of the NYPD. Turns out my uncle knew her dad and that was one of the factors that led to Paulson's being on the fast track. We shook hands and after I had given her the description of the kid who was following me, she went inside my uncle's official Town Car and called in the info.

'You never saw this squirt before?' Uncle Ray asked.

'Just on the bridge and then now. Before that, nothing.'

'Any ideas who he might be?'

'Been thinking about that and I came up with one possibility.'

After a brief pause, my uncle said, 'Ya mind sharing it with me?'

'Oh, yeah.' I was tired. 'Allison's been doing these pieces on this kid who ran away from his family. A White Nationalist family.'

'Harlan S.,' Uncle Ray said.

'You've read it?'

'Of course I've read it, Ray. You told me about it the other night.'

'Oh, right. Anyway, that's the only idea I have, but I'm not sure why he'd be following me.'

'According to the pieces she's written so far, he's scared and confused.'

'That's the way she described him to me. And that's all she said to me.'

'Scared and confused people don't always make the most rational decisions.'

I let that sit for a bit and came up with, 'If Allison has become the person Harlan trusts the most . . .'

'Then,' my uncle continued for me, 'the person that Allison trusts the most takes her place.' Uncle Ray squeezed his lower lip. 'He's coming to you for protection?'

A loud delivery truck rambled by. 'Makes as much sense as anything else.'

Officer Paulson came out of the car holding a laptop. She went over to my uncle and said, 'I called in the description, Chief.' She handed the laptop to her boss. 'You might want to take a look at this.'

Uncle Ray did and after a few minutes handed the laptop to me. 'Ray,' he said.

I took the laptop and read.

ALLISON ROGERS: SPECIAL REPORT FROM THE FIELD

We are still in the same house as when I woke up. They've let me come downstairs, but I still have no idea where I am. The curtains are all drawn and the house is bare enough to give no clues to its location. No local newspapers, no photos, no phone with an area code. We've just eaten a breakfast of eggs, pancakes, bacon, and really strong coffee.

The men who have taken me – I've counted at least five – are now willing to speak to me and have 'requested' that I just quote them for this entry. No comments from me, just thoughts they wish to share about why they are doing what they are doing. These are their words, unedited by me.

'The Catholic school I went to as a kid,' one man says, 'it just closed last year. My grandfather went to school there. We had to find a new place for our son to attend. Takes two buses to get there now, unless I drive him, and I'm usually gone to work by the time he's ready to go to school.

'Know why it closed? "Lack of enrollment" the diocese told us. Too many Catholics moving out over the last five years, and too many non-Christians moving in. That's not exactly how the diocese put it, but you can tell just by looking around. Lots of dark-skinned people. Not black like the so-called African Americans, another kind of dark. Like from India. Maybe Pakistan. I think they're Muslims or Hindus or something. I know they put a mosque where the McDonald's used to be. Kinda funny. Bunch of people who can't eat the cow 'cause they worship it take the place of Mickey D's.'

'This might surprise you,' another man says to me, 'but I read Voltaire in high school. Not by choice, of course, but because they made us. I still remember some of it. You know what three evils he said work helps us keep at bay?' He counts them off on his fingers. 'Boredom, Vice, and Need. I lost my job because I was told I was being downsized. That's all they told me. "Downsized." My dad never got downsized. He worked for the auto factory in Tarrytown for thirty-five years, never got downsized.

'So, yeah, I'm bored. I'm working part-time at the salvage yard dealing with stuff other people throw away. Buying metal offa guys I'm not allowed to ask where they got it. They just wheel it all in their shopping carts – which they obviously stole – and we buy it. Copper pipes, metal tubing, stuff like that.

'Could I be selling drugs? Damn straight I could. I know lots of white guys who do that. Over half the people I know are on some kind of prescription or another. Can't afford the drugs at the store, they don't have any drug plan, they get on 'em on the streets. Folks don't care where they get their drugs from as long as they make the pain go away. And the irony – I think it's irony – is that the pain was caused by the job they don't have anymore. A lot of them used to do the heavy lifting the machines are now doing. Threw their backs out. Screwed up their knees and shoulders. Something you gotta understand about machines – they don't feel pain and don't have to have a health plan. Just need some power and a little tinkering with now and again.

'That's one of the things I need – a health plan. Insurance. Know where I go when I'm sick? I don't. I can't afford to get sick. One of my kids gets sick we go to Doctor ER. They take care of us, try to bill us, but we don't have the money to pay. The government takes care of that. Used to be my tax dollars went to that. Now, I don't have a job, so I don't pay taxes.

'So, yeah. The guys you see around here? They face Voltaire's three evils every damn day: Boredom, Vice, and Need. Like we need a French guy who's been dead since before we were a country to tell us that.'

One more man chose to speak with me.

'Remember when Obama said when things get real bad that's when folks like us cling to our guns and our Bible. He got that right, at least. Damn near screwed up everything else. We keep hearing the economy's getting stronger and some say Obama started that. I don't buy it. I like this new guy; he may not exactly be one of us, but at least he's from around here and looks like we do. Not African. As far as the economy getting better, look around. These guys look like they got money to invest in the stock market?

'Long as I can remember, we've been hearing about tax breaks for the middle class. Ha! There ain't no middle class anymore. The tax breaks go to the rich and we live with that because we get our Supreme Court judges that we want and get to hold on to our guns. The only "trickle down" we get is when we're getting pissed on by the politicians, the rich guys, and the folks who shouldn't even be around us. Maybe I should be in the Trickle Down Umbrella business, huh? That's kind of funny.'

That's all the talk for now it seems. I'm not sure what the rest of today will bring. Maybe more Boredom, some Vice, and a little Need.

But as they say on TV, 'Watch this space.'

Allison Rogers for *New York Here and Now*

After finishing the piece, I read it again. Maybe I was looking for a clue, a secret message that Allison had placed there only for me, something only I would figure out to let me know where she was. But shit like that only happens in the movies, right?

Anyway, I was able to come up with one positive piece of news. 'They're still in the same place,' I said.

'Maybe,' Uncle Ray corrected me. 'Remember, she only gets to post what they tell her. She could be anywhere, Ray.'

I knew he was right, but I also felt she hadn't been moved since this morning. When they had moved, she mentioned it. Now she mentioned they hadn't moved; she wrote that. Either way, Uncle Ray could have been right: she was writing only what the captors allowed. They had not only taken her, they had taken her voice.

My phone rang. Henderson again. 'What's up, David?'

'Just read the latest post. Sounds like she's doing OK. Considering.'

'I guess. Any news?'

'Negative on that end, I'm sorry to say. We sweated a lot of assholes in the tri-state area over the past twelve hours and have come up empty. Good news is that our profiler says that since the kidnappers are clearly getting what they want out of Allison, the risk is lower at this time of doing her harm.'

'At this time?'

'Yeah.' He paused. 'There's always the chance they get enough from her or that she decides to stop giving it to them. Then the dynamic changes.'

Henderson had a nice way with euphemisms. I told him so and then told him about the kid who'd been following me, and our best guess as to his identity.

'Outstanding,' he said. 'I'll send that out to my people in the field. That's all you got on the kid?'

'Allison made a promise to him to keep his info confidential. And honestly, she didn't know all that much.'

'Gotcha. Later, Ray.'

I put the phone back in my pocket and caught Uncle Ray up on my call with Henderson. 'OK,' he said. 'So we got a little more than we had this morning. Not much, but better than nothing.' He looked around my block. 'I'm gonna put a uniform out here, Ray. Just in case that kid comes back.'

I thought about that. 'If he does come back,' I said, 'a cop's just gonna scare him off again. Wouldn't it be better if we let him make contact?'

He took out a cigar. 'Good point. OK, I'll make it plain clothes. They see anything, they'll observe and only move in if necessary.'

'Sounds fair,' I said. 'Thanks.'

He looked at the bag of food I was holding. 'Go upstairs and eat, Ray. Take a shower, a nap, watch last night's Yankees game. We'll be in touch.'

That was his way of saying that I was back to playing the waiting game again. And he was right. I said goodbye, thanked Office Paulson, and went up to my place.

Allison's and my place.

THIRTY-FOUR

All the stress and excitement of the last few hours had made me hungrier than usual because normally, the Shrimp Lo Mein takes me two sittings to finish. This afternoon it was gone in one. I showered, channel-surfed aimlessly and eventually settled on a nature show about how the coral reefs along the

Australian coast are eroding at a faster rate than scientists originally had thought. I switched to an all-nineties music channel and cleaned up the apartment a little. I even did a mixed load of my laundry with Allison's, although we never normally combined our clothes when washing them.

I fielded phone calls from Royce, Edgar, Henderson, Billy and Uncle Ray. My mom and Rachel also called. It felt kind of like all those years ago when I almost died falling off that fire escape: everyone was checking up on me and asking for new developments. The only thing missing was doctors and nurses coming in every half-hour to make sure I didn't get any sleep. The feeling sucks, by the way.

I poured myself a big plastic cup of water – mostly ice – and went out onto the deck with my cell phone. I grabbed one of the cushioned chairs and stared up at the almost cloudless sky. I watched as one small cloud made its way overhead and slowly broke apart in the upper atmospheric breeze. By the time it had completely vanished my eyes were closed, and I was somewhere between sleep and consciousness, aware of my surroundings yet working them into a semi-dream.

At some point in the dream, I was getting hit by flying insects. Every thirty seconds or so, one would crash into my chest or my lap. A few crashed into the window while others landed on the tile of the porch. Whatever they were, they woke me. Another one came flying in when I realized they were pebbles coming from the back-yard of my apartment. I looked over the edge and there was the last person I expected to see.

The kid who'd been following me.

I was about to yell down but didn't want to draw attention to him. He had come back for a reason, and the last thing I wanted to do before finding out why was to scare him away. I raised my hands palms up and shrugged.

He looked up and mimed opening a door, put his hand to his mouth as if eating, and then pointed to his left. Did he want me to let him in and feed him? I waved him up. He shook his head and went through the motions again: opening a door and eating. Then he pointed to his left again. After he pointed, he scaled the fence and disappeared.

Shit. I had lost him again.

I went through his signs. Opening a door. No, it occurred to me, he was using a key. *Key.* Then he was acting like he was eating. Hungry? Chewing? No. *Food.* And pointing to the left.

Damn this kid was smart. He figured the front of my place was being watched and wanted me to meet him at the grocery store – *Key Food* – on the other side of the avenue. I put my sneakers on, grabbed my reusable tote bag and headed downstairs. When I hit the street, I gave a wave to the unseen undercover cop who was watching my place and headed over to do a little food shopping.

Since it was just around dinnertime, the store was crowded. I looked around for my stalker, but couldn't find him. Confident that he'd find me, I strolled through the aisles making mental notes of things I'd pick up the next time I really went shopping. When I got to the produce section, I felt a tap on my back. I turned.

'Harlan?' I said.

He grinned and took off his sunglasses. 'You can call me that, I guess, sir.'

'So you followed Allison home after one of your interviews, huh?'

'I had to make sure she wasn't a cop,' he said. 'Or one of my dad's people.'

'Smart,' I said. 'What do you want with me, Harlan?'

'I've been reading Ms Rogers' pieces since she was taken.'

'Yeah?'

'I know where they got her, sir. Or at least where they're gonna take her next.'

I took a step toward him. Just one, so I didn't scare him off again. 'And how would you know that?'

He looked down at his feet for a few seconds then back at me. 'Because I offered to trade myself in for her, sir.'

OK. 'Why would you do that?'

'Because I'm the reason she was taken, sir.'

I stayed silent on that point. 'First, lose the whole "sir" thing. Second, how do you know who took her, Harlan?'

He scratched at his blond hair. 'I wasn't sure at first. But I know this one guy who's with my dad a lot, and he's kinda . . . whatcha might call extreme. They keep telling him to tone it down, that if they wanna be taken seriously, he needs to cool it. Out of all the people in the group, he's the only one I could think of who'd do this kinda thing.'

'So you just called him? You had his number?'

'Yeah, we all do,' he said, tapping his temple. 'And I was right. See, when Ms Rogers wrote about that first place they took her, I thought it mighta been the old camp they just bought about two hours north of here, close to the Massachusetts border. That was Chilly's idea. Chilly's the guy who's a bit extreme.'

'Chilly?'

'Guys he used to run with said he's got ice water in his veins, so . . .'

'You and Chilly make a plan for this . . . exchange?' I asked.

'Tonight,' Harlan said. 'Up at the camp.'

'How'd he expect you to get up there?'

'I told him the truth. That you'd help me.'

I paused and said, 'Because I want Allison back as much as anyone else?'

'That was my thinking, sir.'

This was one smart kid. Damn smart. There was one thing gnawing at me, though. A pretty big thing.

'This guy Chilly,' I said. 'Off the rails and ice water in his veins. What makes you think you can trust him?'

'I can't,' Harlan said. 'But he thinks just 'cause I'm a kid, he can trust me. So I think that maybe gives me an edge on him.' He saw my smile and gave me one back. Then he said, 'You can get a car?'

'Oh, yeah. I can get a car.'

He looked at his watch. 'Can you get one in a few minutes? We need to be up there kinda soon.'

'What's kinda soon?' I asked.

'I was told eight-thirty.'

I told Harlan to stay at the store until I picked him up, and then rushed back to my apartment, calling Edgar along the way. I got dressed for a trip upstate and went to the back of my closet to the lockbox where I keep my gun. I've only used it once in the past few years and that was only as a prop to scare some people who needed scaring. I hoped this night would be no different, but I loaded it just the same and put some extra ammo in my vest pocket.

Then I called Billy and David Henderson and told them what was up. They both said they could be at my place in half an hour and I told them there wasn't time for that. I gave them the GPS signal for Allison's phone – Edgar had insisted on installing that – and told them I was on my way to the New York State Thruway. Harlan had a rough idea where the camp was and with GPS he'd figure the rest out. Neither Billy nor Henderson liked the idea, but I really didn't care right then.

Edgar called. He was downstairs.

I was lying to Edgar and he knew it. I told him I had to get the kid back home and needed to do it by myself. Although he didn't buy it for a second, he gave me his car and asked if I'd be at The LineUp later.

'I hope so, man,' I said, patting his shoulder. 'But later than usual.'

We got to the Brooklyn–Queens Expressway, then the Cross Bronx and onto the Thruway in not too much time. I set the cruise control at seventy and started in with the questions.

'How big is this camp?'

'About seventy-five acres,' Harlan said. 'Not including the shared lake.'

'Cabins?'

'A dozen, maybe. Then the main office attached to the staff housing, an indoor all-purpose center, a dining hall, and a maintenance shed.'

'Where are you supposed to meet Chilly?'

'When you turn in there's a long driveway, about a quarter of a mile,' he said. 'There's the main office and staff housing. He said he'd meet me there and then take me to Ms Rogers.'

'When you spoke to him, did you also speak to Ms Rogers?'

'No, I didn't think to ask. Should I have?'

I shook my head. 'Only if you were a cop.'

He nodded. 'Proof of life. I seen that in the movies when they kidnap people.'

'Something like that.' I thought some more. 'Any other ways into the camp besides the driveway? Back roads, anything like that?'

'There's a back road that comes over the hill, but I don't know how to get there.' He thought some more. 'I also saw someone come in once off the lake by canoe. But that means they had to trespass on someone else's property.'

I handed him Allison's phone. 'Do me a favor and text that info to those last two numbers I called. Also ask them where they are.'

He did and then put the phone in the cup holder between us. 'Any idea how much farther?' I asked.

'About another thirty, forty minutes, I think. Your friends are about thirty minutes behind us. We gotta go over the Kingston–Rhinecliff Bridge and then take a left.'

'Text them that, please. It'll make it easier on them.' What would also make it easier was their law enforcement badges. They'd be able to go about ten miles over the speed limit and not worry too much if they got pulled over. It wouldn't be enough to close all the distance, just some. 'You need to pee or anything?'

'I'm good until we cross the Hudson again. Thanks. I'm hungry, though.'

'Check the glove compartment.'

He did and sure enough, there was an energy bar. Edgar usually had one or two around for emergencies. 'You want half?' Harlan asked.

I shook my head. I was too nervous to eat. The sun was almost all the way down now and I realized I needed to put on the headlights. We passed the New Paltz exit and I couldn't help but think how much this area had played into the last week of my life.

After breaking the world record for cating an energy bar, Harlan stuck the wrapper in his jeans pocket, and said, 'I have a confession to make, Raymond.'

'Whatever you've done, kid,' I said, 'you're making up for it now.'

'It's not that.'

'Then what?'

He unbuckled his seat belt and leaned forward. Then he reached behind himself and pulled something out of the back of his shorts. From where I sat, it looked to be a semi-automatic SIG Sauer.

'What the fuck, Harlan?'

'I took it before I left,' he said. 'I was scared and shit.'

'Is it loaded?'

He looked at me like I was a dumbass.

'Put it in the glove compartment,' I said.

'What?'

'The glove compartment. Now!'

He did. And then leaned back.

'Leave it there.' I banged the steering wheel. 'You're a smart kid, Harlan, but that's some stupid shit, you know that?'

'I told you, I was scared.'

'You have that on you when Allison was interviewing you?'

He nodded his head yes.

'Did she know you had it on you?'

He shook his head no.

I slammed the steering wheel again. 'Then you were putting her in danger, damn it! What the hell were you gonna do if someone walked up on you? Shoot it out? With my girlfriend there? Someone who was trying to help you?'

I couldn't see his face real well in the dim light, but I could hear his breathing change. It was breaking up and getting wet. *Shit.* He was just a scared kid protecting himself the only way he knew how. The only way he'd been taught. And here I was making him feel like shit about it.

'All right,' I said after I calmed down. 'Forget about. It's just that you seem so . . . I forgot you're only sixteen. It's OK. No harm was done and you were protecting yourself. It's over.' I reached out and patted his leg. 'Let's focus on tonight. You know there's no way we're trading you for Allison, right?'

'What do mean?' he said. 'That was the deal I made with—'

'Yeah, well, deals get broken all the time. Especially when one of the dealmakers is a kidnapper and the other is sixteen years old.' I looked at my phone as it dinged. 'See who that is.'

He picked up the phone and looked at it. 'Henderson?'

'Put it on speaker.' He did. 'David. Where are you?'

'About twenty minutes behind you,' he said, 'but I got some flashing lights up ahead just short of Exit 18.'

'Must've just missed it.'

'I'm gonna try and badge my way through if it's a problem. Can ya stall?'

I looked at the kid. He shrugged. 'We'll give it a shot.'

'Get right back to me.'

'Call Chilly,' I said to Harlan. 'Tell him we got caught in . . . that thing back there. An accident.'

'He's not gonna believe me.'

'Do it anyway. See what happens.'

He dialed the number. That was another thing about Harlan: how many kids had people's phone numbers memorized these days? Even their own? He waited a while and I could tell the call had gone to voicemail.

'Chilly,' he said, 'it's me. We're on the Thruway but there's some sort of backup. An overturned truck or something. Call me back. Please.' He ended the call and turned to me. 'He's not gonna buy it.'

'Then we keep driving.'

Harlan tried to get Henderson back on the phone, but the signal was too weak. The same thing for Billy. We moved forward anyway.

A few minutes later we took the turn off to Kingston, paid our toll and took the route to the Kingston–Rhinecliff Bridge. It was just after eight now and Harlan had been told to be there as close to eight-thirty as possible. We should make it on time, but I doubted that Billy and Henderson would.

We crossed the bridge and made the first left. 'Now what?' I asked.

'About a mile,' Harlan said, 'there's a car dealership. Make a right.'

I made the right at the dealership and looked over at the kid. 'In a few more minutes,' he said, 'there'll be a real estate office on the right, make that turn.'

How the hell did out-of-town people find their way around here without GPS or teenagers? I would not have seen the real estate place if Harlan had not pointed it out. I made the right and turned onto a road that had no streetlights. I flicked on Edgar's brights. I could see better, but anyone out there could also see me coming from a mile away. Good thing I was expected.

'OK,' Harlan said. 'Here's where it gets tricky. There's a signpost coming up on the left,' he said, 'but there's no sign there, just a pair of chains that used to hold the sign for the old camp.'

'How much farther is this sign that's not there?'

He thought about that. 'About three football fields.'

I slowed down to about maybe one football field a minute. Again, without Harlan pointing and saying, 'There it is,' I would have driven right by it. I could see why Lansing's group would want to buy such a place: the location sucked. I found myself starting to doubt that Billy and Henderson would find it.

I made the left and found myself on a dirt road with tire tracks and a patch of dark grass in the middle. Harlan said, 'This leads right into the main office building. Just go slow, the road hasn't been fixed in years.'

No shit. I would probably owe Edgar for a new suspension when all was said and done. A minute or so later, I could make out the first building. There were no lights on. Probably, it occurred to me, because there was no electricity. I slowed down as we approached and realized I was wrong; there were a few lights on, but they appeared to be the kind you take camping with you that run on gas. There were two in the windows and one around the side. I pulled up in front of the building and parked. I turned the engine off but kept the headlights on, thinking the more light, the better. There was another building to our left with a sign above the door that said 'Dining Hall.'

'Now what?' I said to Harlan.

'We get out and wait.'

'Just like that?'

'That was the de— that's what Chilly told me to do.'

Right. I looked around. Besides the three camping lights and the little bit of the building I could make out, nothing. I considered my options, weighed the odds of Billy and Henderson not only getting here, but getting here unnoticed, and took a deep, yet unsatisfying, breath. I reached into the glove compartment and pulled out the gun Harlan had foolishly brought with him.

'You sure you know how to use this?'

He looked surprised at the question, but said, 'Real sure.'

I handed it to him. 'Put it behind your back. And don't do a thing with it unless I tell you to.'

'I hear you.'

'I know you hear me, Harlan.' Teacher to student. 'But do you understand me?'

He nodded. 'Yes, sir.'

I took my own gun from my ankle holster and put it behind my back. 'Good,' I said. 'Now, we get out.'

Once out of the car, I got a good dose of that camp air Allison had written about. The only sounds were the night-time insects, tree frogs, and the leaves rustling through the trees. The lake was to our right. A few lights were dancing off the water. Like Allison had implied, enjoyable under other circumstances, just not now. Then another sound broke through. A sound I've heard many times before, mostly in the movies but occasionally in real life.

The sound of a rifle being cocked.

THIRTY-FIVE

'How ya doin' there, Harlan?' a voice from the darkness wanted to know.

'I'm here, Chilly,' Harlan said. 'Just like you told me.'

'Yes, you are, son.' A pause. 'Nice to meet you, Raymond.'

'You have Allison with you?' I asked.

Chilly laughed. 'What?' he said. 'No howdy-do? You city folks are rude, you know that?'

'The deal was,' I said, 'I bring you Harlan, you give me Allison. There was nothing said about being polite about it.'

He laughed again and now stepped out from behind a tree into the brightness of my headlights so he could be seen. He was wearing a bright orange knitted hunting cap. 'My mother would disagree with you there, Raymond,' he said. 'She would say that good manners are always expected, and one need not be reminded to be polite.'

He took off his cap so I could see his hairless scalp. Chilly was Charles. And he was one of the guys on the bridge yesterday. He was hoping to use me to get to Harlan. Looked like it worked.

'What would your mother say about kidnapping a woman, *Charles*?' I took the risk of asking. 'That sounds kinda impolite to me.'

He took a few steps closer. 'Ya gotta point there, Raymond. She probably would have something to say about that.' He raised his right arm and made a tight fist. Out of the darkness came three more figures: a man by himself and another with his hand gripping Allison's elbow. The one with Allison was the second guy from the bridge. I did my best not to make any sudden moves and when they got closer, I saw that Allison had duct tape around her mouth and a kind of calm fear in her eyes. She was taking long deep breaths. I had the incredible urge to run up and hug her, but both men were carrying handguns.

Another thing I noticed – a big thing – was that Allison didn't have her bag with her. If she didn't have her bag, this wasn't a trade. It was a trap, set up by persuading a sixteen-year-old who wanted to set things right to convince a grown-up who only wanted his girlfriend back. *Fuck me.*

I looked at the guy holding Allison and said, 'Is the duct tape really necessary? Out here in the woods?'

Chilly answered. 'Probably not. But I don't much care for the sound of women talking all that much.'

I switched my glance to Allison and nodded. My only hope at this point was that Billy or Henderson would come barreling down the dirt road, guns ablazin', giving me enough time to get my own gun out, take down the kidnappers, and rescue Allison.

What I needed was a movie ending.

What I got was the sound of an engine coming through the woods and a pair of high-beam headlights illuminating what I could now see must have been the access road Harlan had told me about. Had Billy or Henderson somehow found that and given me the break I needed?

'The fuck is that?' Chilly yelled.

All three men turned as a red-and-white pickup truck came roaring toward us and skidded to a stop. The men raised their guns and a metallic voice came out of the truck's speaker system.

'Chilly,' the voice said. 'You dumbass motherfucker. Put that thing down before you hurt yourself.' To accent his point, the voice threw on the overhead lamps. Now the place was lit up like a movie set. When Chilly didn't comply, the driver's side door opened and out stepped a very large man dressed in a camouflage jacket, blue jeans, baseball cap, and boots made for shit kicking. I recognized him right away.

Duke Lansing.

Duke was also holding a handgun. What was up with these guys? If you were a White Nationalist, it must have been a fashion faux pas to not carry a firearm.

'The hell you doing, Chilly?' Duke wanted to know.

'This don't concern you, Duke,' Chilly said. 'Not anymore. Me, Tommy, and Louis are on our own now. This is our business. You go on home and let us finish it up.'

I looked over at Tommy and Louis, not knowing which was which, but neither of them looked too happy about Chilly's speaking to Duke Lansing like that. I caught Allison's eye and tried to give her a reassuring look. I'm not sure I succeeded.

'How many times I gotta tell you, Chilly?' Duke said. 'When one of us does something, it reflects on all of us.'

'There ain't no us, Duke! We left.'

'You don't get to leave!' Duke yelled. You could hear his voice echo through the woods and across the lake. 'Not you.' Then he looked at Harlan. 'Not anyone.'

I could see Chilly's rifle start to tap his leg. Duke picked up on it, too. I took that opportunity to reach into the back of my pants and grab my gun. I kept my hands behind me as if standing at attention. I saw Harlan do the same. I shook my head. *No.*

'Don't do anything stupid now, boy,' Duke said. At first I thought he was talking to Harlan or me, but his comment was directed at Chilly, who was tapping his gun a little faster now. 'You've made one dumbass decision this week, let's not make it two.'

Chilly shook his head. 'See,' he said, 'ya can't go around talking to people like that and expect them to follow you.'

'I can if they're dumbasses.' Duke looked at Tommy and Louis. 'You know what I'm saying, right boys?' The boys said nothing. Duke said, 'Tommy, gimme the girl.'

Tommy seemed confused by that command and looked at Chilly. 'Don't you dare, Tommy,' Chilly said. 'We spoke about this. We're making a stand here.'

'Is that what this is about?' Duke laughed. 'Making a stand? Goddamn.' Again, he said, 'Tommy. The girl.'

Tommy took a step toward Duke with Allison. Chilly raised his gun. 'Tommy, you take one more step and I'll put one in your leg.' They looked at each other, each one nervous. 'You know I will.'

Tommy looked at Chilly and said, 'Chilly . . .'

'Bring her over here if you don't know what to do with her,' Chilly said. 'Never were much good with the ladies anyway.'

Oh, boy, I thought. *Why not just call him a pussy?* Tommy looked at Chilly, took a few steps toward him, put his hand behind Allison's back and shoved her. Chilly was able to grab her just before she fell. Tommy then took his gun and flung it Frisbee-style toward the lake. 'I'm done with this shit.' He looked at Chilly and then Duke. 'With both of y'all.'

Duke waved his pistol at Tommy, pointed it at the ground, and said, 'Why'nt you just take a seat right where you are, Tommy.' Tommy again looked confused. 'G'head, right there. Hands on your head. I'll get back to you.' Like a little kid who'd just been taken to task by his father, Tommy did as he was told. Duke looked at Louis. 'Why'nt you go ahead and do the same as Tommy, Louis.'

Louis looked at Duke, then over at Chilly. He made up his mind

right away and said, 'I don't think so, Duke. I'm good right here.'
Then something occurred to him that I'd been thinking about. 'How'd
you find us, anyways?'

Duke laughed and looked at me. 'You that friend of Maurice's,
right?' He pronounced the name 'Moh-reese.'

'I am.'

Duke shook his head and scratched his white beard. 'Boy may
not be too wise in the wife-choosing or baby-making departments,
but he can sure put tracking devices on vehicles. One of the last
things he did before he took that arrow to the back was install them
GPS things on my boys' trucks. Soon as I realized what Chilly here
had done, I just turned them on and voy-lah – found him just like
that.'

'You were spyin' on us?' Chilly asked.

'Imagine that,' Duke said. 'Like I had no reason to. You ungrateful
little shits. You leave, and what's the first dumbass move you make?
Take that little girl there right up to our camp. You're like spoiled
little brats who run away from home and then hide in the
backyard.'

'Goddamn it, Duke,' Louis said. 'You just can't go around . . .'

Louis got so angry he couldn't finish his sentence. He got so
angry he raised his gun a bit. A bit too high, because Duke took a
shot at him and got him in the upper arm, right near the shoulder.
Louis dropped his gun and fell to his knees. In this light, it looked
like someone had spilled chocolate syrup on his shirt. He was going
to lose a lot of blood was my guess, but he'd live.

'You just stay there, Louis,' Duke said. 'Throw that piece of
yours over here.'

Louis struggled through his pain to do what Duke had ordered.
In all the excitement, I didn't notice that Harlan had his gun out
and pointed at Duke. When Duke noticed, he got that grin on his
face again and laughed a little. He lowered his gun and took a step
closer to Harlan.

'What you gonna do with that thing, son?' he said.

Harlan took a big swallow and a deeper breath. 'Whatever I
have to.'

Duke shook his head. 'I ain't no paper target now.' He leaned
forward. 'I shoot back.' He looked over at Louis. 'And I don't miss
much.'

'I just want Chilly to honor his part of the deal and let Ms Rogers and Raymond go back to the city,' he said. 'Then I'll give myself up. I'll come back.'

Duke scratched his head. 'To who?' he asked.

'What?'

'To who?' Duke repeated. 'To Chilly, who you have the deal with or to me, who you ran away from in the first place? You heard what I said about leaving.'

'Boy's coming with me, Duke,' Chilly said.

Enough of this standoff shit. 'Where's her bag, Chilly?' I asked.

'What?'

'Allison doesn't go anywhere without her bag and laptop. Where are they?'

'I don't know. Back at the bunk?'

I turned to Harlan, who still had his gun pointed at Duke. 'This was never a deal, Harlan. Chilly has no intention of letting Allison or me go. I'm not sure what he plans on doing with you. My guess is you're just another Fuck-You to Duke here.'

His gun still on Duke, Harlan looked at Chilly. 'That true, Chilly?'

Chilly smiled. 'Who you gonna believe, boy? Some liberal ass socialist from the city who hangs around with niggers and Jews, or me, a true Christian brother-in-arms?'

You know those moments in your life where you have to make a decision that's going to put you on one path or another? Harlan S. was facing one of them right now.

'So go get her bag, Chilly,' Harlan said.

Good for you, kid.

'Fuck that,' Chilly said. 'I ain't getting shit.'

'Then let her go to Raymond.'

Allison struggled and Chilly tightened his grip. He laughed and shook his head. 'That ain't happening either, boy.'

Duke slowly turned his gun from Harlan to Chilly and said, 'I got a shot from here, son. I can end this right now.'

That got Harlan's attention. 'No, Grandpa! Don't!' he yelled. 'Ms Rogers is right there!'

Grandpa? Holy shit!

'I'm tired of people telling me what to do, boy.'

Harlan swung his gun back toward Duke. Duke did the same.

'Harlan,' I said. 'Don't.'

'You best listen to him, *Harlan.*'

Harlan's breathing started getting heavier again. I could hear him choking on the tears and snot running down his throat. Apparently, so could Duke.

'Aw, now,' Duke said. 'Don't ruin it all now by acting like one of your sisters. You made a man's decision by running away. You were the grown-up who decided to talk to Ms Rogers over here. You got the gun pointed at your own family. Now you gonna pussy out by crying like a little—'

BOOM!

Harlan's gun went off and the upper left part of Duke's shirtsleeve exploded. Duke looked at his arm and the blood like he couldn't believe what had just happened. A small whistling sound came out of Harlan's mouth and then Duke's gun went off. His shot seemed to tear through Harlan's right bicep, forcing him to do two things: drop his gun and fall to his knees.

I looked over to where Chilly was still holding Allison by the elbow. He took in the situation and decided his best move was to run. He turned around, Allison still in his grip and took off around the dining hall. I went over to Duke and grabbed the guns. Then I went over to Harlan and looked at his wound.

'You're gonna be fine,' I said and mostly believed it. I threw the guns away and turned to Louis and Tommy. 'You got any first aid around here?'

Tommy said, 'There's some stuff in the office.'

'Get it and take care of the kid.'

'What about Duke?' Louis asked.

I looked over at the old man. 'I really don't give a shit,' I said, and took off after Chilly and Allison. Behind me, I barely heard Harlan yell, 'He's going for the boat!'

THIRTY-SIX

I ran behind the dining hall and once again found myself in almost complete darkness. I could see I was in a big open field with a baseball backstop to my right and grass that needed a serious cutting. To my left was a stand of trees through which I could make out what must have been the same lights that were bouncing off the lake. I stopped for about two seconds to get my bearings. Something moved in front of me just as it disappeared into the woods next to the lake. I headed off in that direction.

Just before I got there, I heard three sounds in front of me: labored running and breathing, and water running in a small stream. Chilly had me at a few disadvantages here. Not only did he have my girl-friend and a gun, he also had knowledge of the terrain. I entered the woods, mindful of Mother Nature's hidden little tricks.

I crossed a small wooden bridge that went over the stream and almost tripped on a gap between slats. Half a minute later, I passed a campfire site that had recently been used. Judging from the over-turned bucket, the fire had been put out with lake water, but a few embers were still visible and smoking. Without electricity or running water, this was probably where Chilly, his boys, and Allison had eaten today. I kept going.

Up ahead I heard the sound of someone trying to start an engine. I picked up my pace. 'Fuck it,' I heard. Chilly was having trouble. That's what happens when you leave an engine sitting idle for too long. I was reminded of my dad when he got frustrated at the lawnmower for not starting after one or two pulls. I was getting closer now, so I slowed down.

'Stay the hell down,' I heard Chilly say after another unsuccessful pull. They had to be less than twenty feet in front of me. I needed to find a way to sneak up on him without being heard. I figured he'd see me coming in from the trail, so I decided to try the lake. I slipped into the water as quietly as I could, taking a few branches to the face for my efforts. As soon as I felt my feet settle on the bottom, I took my first step and didn't fall. I took a few more until I was up to my waist.

After about twenty sidesteps, I stopped. Now I could make out the boat and Allison sitting in the front with her hands on the side. She couldn't see me, because her view was blocked by some tree limbs and Chilly, who was pulling the cord to start the outboard motor. I took another step and got my foot caught between two rocks. They made a clacking sound and Chilly looked up and raised his weapon. I lowered mine into the water.

'Son of a whore,' he said when he saw me. 'You must love this bitch something fierce, Raymond. You're a regular knight in shining armor.'

I stayed shut because I didn't want him to realize how much pain

I was in. And the more he talked, the more time I had to figure a way out of this. I looked behind him at Allison. She was barely keeping it together.

As if reading my mind, Chilly said, 'Oh, she'll be fine, Raymond. She's more use to me alive at the moment than . . . you know.' He looked over his shoulder at her. 'Just like most women. Once you shut them up, they're OK.' He laughed. 'Kinda like the mud people you work with at the school, right? And the Jews. Why can't they just shut their fucking traps and do what we brought them here for in the first place? We were all much happier then. Least that's what my dad and granddad tell me. I was born into this mess just like you. Except I'm willing to do something about it.

'I'm the one who had the idea to put that fentanyl out on the streets. Make some money, knock off some of the three-fifths. You know what ya call that?' He paused for an answer. 'A good fucking start.' He laughed so hard at that he almost fell out of the boat. Hell, he was laughing so hard he didn't notice Allison come up behind him and slam him in the head with the oar. He tumbled into the water headfirst.

I raised my gun waiting for him to resurface. When he did, he was screaming bloody murder until he realized he didn't know where his gun was. 'Fuck!' he screamed and slapped around at the water in front of him. Then he saw me pointing my piece at him and shut up.

'Do not move,' I said.

'Or what?'

'I'll take it as a threat and shoot you.'

'Why would you do that? I don't have my gun anymore.'

'Because I said so and I'm pointing a gun at you.'

'You ain't gonna do shit.' He pointed at me. 'You're just as bad as those people you spend so much time helping. You're all in this together. The mud people, the Jews, the schools.' He used his thumb to gesture at Allison. 'Fucking media.' He continued to point at me. 'Shoulda killed you as soon as you pulled up. Probably shoulda made you watch as I took a piece of this fine ass behind me first.'

I looked at the unarmed piece of human trash I was pointing my gun at. His words were the words of the determined and the desperate. I almost felt sorry for him.

'Fuck you,' he screamed and the words echoed across the lake and into the woods. He pointed at me and repeated, 'Fuck you.'

The next sound was me putting two in his chest. Those echoes also spread out, taking longer to fade away.

The only sound I could hear now was Allison screaming through the duct tape.

Allison and I took a long, slow walk back to where the cars were parked. Even though I had removed the duct tape from her mouth, we walked in silence. Her hand was shaking and cold. Maybe we were both in shock.

By the time we arrived back at the main office, Billy Morris and David Henderson were there, along with two state troopers. They had Tommy and Louis in handcuffs, but Duke and Harlan were nowhere to be seen. Neither was Duke's truck.

I handed one of the troopers my gun. 'There's a dead guy in the lake,' I said. 'You'll find two slugs matching this gun – my gun – in his chest. You'll find his gun on the lake bottom.' I looked around. 'Where are Duke and the kid?'

Billy shrugged, and Henderson said, 'Duke Lansing? He was here?'

'Yeah. And Harlan, the kid Allie was interviewing.'

'Goddamn it!' Henderson said. 'They must have . . . Fuck!'

Billy said, 'We showed up just in time to catch these two knuckleheads walking up the dirt road.' He looked at Tommy and Louis. 'As you can see, they are exercising their Constitutional right to remain silent.'

Then Allison spoke for the first time that night. 'Can I go home now?'

'I'm going to have to talk with the officers first,' I said. 'Then we'll get your bag and maybe get a hotel in the area.'

'I'd rather go home,' she said, her voice monotone. 'Billy, can you take me?'

'You need to be checked out at a hospital, Allie,' he said.

'Tomorrow. I need sleep and that won't happen in the hospital.'

Billy looked at me. I nodded. 'Sure, Allie. Let's go get your stuff and we'll go.'

'Thanks, Billy,' I said. Billy went over to one of the troopers and explained the situation. He seemed OK with it. I went to kiss Allison and got her cheek. 'I'll see you at home. I might stay up here if it's too late to drive back.'

I'm not sure she heard me. I'm not sure she wanted to.

* * *

It turned out after all the questions and paperwork it was way too late to drive back to the city. Henderson and I grabbed a double room not far from the state troopers' headquarters. I don't think either of us slept. We grabbed a very early breakfast and were back in Brooklyn before nine. When I got up to our apartment, Allison was not there.

Somehow, I expected that.

THIRTY-SEVEN

Tuesday turned out to be an eventful day.

Detective Royce came by my apartment to tell me the ballistics and preliminary autopsy reports had both come back from the upstate lab. With less homicide work, they got stuff done more quickly up there. The bullets – no surprise – had indeed come from my registered handgun, and since I had apparently used it in self-defense, and with a concealed-carry permit, I was in the clear. It was, as they say, 'a good shoot.'

As for the autopsy report, the cause of death was – again, no twist here – excessive arterial bleeding caused by gunshot wounds. Initial investigation revealed that the victim's musculature when shot showed his right arm was indeed raised as if pointing a weapon as per statements of the witness and the shooter.

A good shoot.

'How's Allison holding up?' Royce asked.

'She'll be OK,' I said. 'She's gonna need some more time before going back to work, though.' The truth was I hadn't seen Allison since she'd left the camp last night. She was staying at a friend's.

'Give her my regards,' he said.

'Will do.' We shook hands. 'And, Royce. Thanks again.'

'Yeah. Let's not see each other for a while, OK?'

I laughed. 'I'll see what I can do about that.'

He turned to leave the building and then turned back. 'Hey, Donne,' he said. 'One more thing.'

'Yeah?'

'I never heard of Jessica Fletcher taking down a bad guy like that.'

'Goodbye, Detective.'

I was halfway up the steps when Allison's phone rang. David Henderson, FBI.

'David, what's up?'

'Guess who just showed up at the regional office?'

I hate when grown people do that. 'Jimmy Hoffa.'

'Harlan Fuckin' S.,' he said. 'Along with his mother and two sisters.'

'How the hell—'

'They got dropped off by one of Duke's people. Still can't believe I missed that son of a . . . Looks like they got Harlan – his real name's Tucker, by the way, Tucker Jackson – some real medical care, and he's gonna be fine. We tracked down some family out in Wyoming and they're working out the details now.'

'That's great, David. I'll let Allie know.'

'You do that, Ray. I'll see you soon, OK? Drinks are on me.'

'Then you'll definitely see me.'

I looked at my landline and saw that I had one message. It was from Lisa Joseph.

'Hey, Ray. It's Lisa. Just wanted to let you know I've decided to go back down home and have the baby there. Around family, y'know? It was going to be hard enough up here with Maurice and now . . . anyway call me when you can. I'm not sure how to tell Edgar. Maybe you can help with that. Love to Allison. Thanks.'

I went out for a cup of coffee and a walk. When I came back, Allison was in the bedroom packing her suitcase.

'I'm sorry, Ray,' she said. 'I just can't do this right now.'

'Do what?'

She let out a deep breath. 'Have the talk about how it feels to watch you shoot and kill an unarmed man.'

'He kidnapped you, Allie.'

'He was unarmed, Ray. You shot a defenseless man.'

'That "defenseless man" was going to maybe get ten years in jail for what he did. Ten more years of hanging around people just like him, fostering hate, growing his own, and then getting out in his mid-thirties. Chilly was many things, Allison, but just because he wasn't holding a gun didn't make him less a threat.'

'A threat to whom? You? Me? He didn't have a gun anymore.'

'A threat to society,' I said. 'A threat to non-white Christians. A threat to MoJo's unborn child. We're safer without him. You know that.'

'You're scaring me, Ray. One of the reasons I fell in love with you is your ability to see through the black and white and into the gray. You say that yourself all the time.'

'And then there're people like Chilly.'

'For whom you get to be judge, jury, and executioner.'

'I couldn't fucking protect you, Allison!' I yelled. I could feel my eyes filling up. 'He took you right from our home and I couldn't do a fucking thing about it.'

'Is that what this is about?' she asked. 'You couldn't protect me, so you have to protect all the possible future victims of this guy? I don't need you to protect me, Ray. I just need you to love me.'

'I do,' I said. 'I do love you.'

'I love you, too. But I have to go.'

'Go where?'

'Home for now,' she said. 'I'm going to see my mom and dad.'

'For how long?'

'I don't know. I'll call you when I get there.' Her phone rang. I didn't recognize the number so I handed it to her. She said, 'I'll be right down. Thanks.'

'At least let me take you to the airport,' I tried. 'I'll call Edgar and get—'

'I'm not doing an airport goodbye, Ray. And I'm not going to change my mind on the way to LaGuardia. I just need to go home.'

'I thought this was your home.'

'I did, too. Maybe it is. I need some time to figure that out.' She picked up her bag and kissed me on the lips. 'I'll call you from Missouri.'

I didn't know what to say, so I said nothing.

'Goodbye, Ray.'

I stood there as the door to our home closed and listened to her footsteps going down the stairs. If I were a praying man, I'd have prayed that it wasn't the last time I'd be hearing that sound. Being who I was, I just lay down on the bed and stared at the ceiling.

Maybe if I stared at it long enough, I'd find an answer to a question I didn't know I was asking yet.